Threads
of Silk

Also By Linda Lee Chaikin

Daughter of Silk
Written on Silk

the SILK HOUSE series

Threads of Silk

Book Three

LINDA LEE CHAIKIN

ZONDERVAN®

ZONDERVAN.com/
AUTHORTRACKER
follow your favorite authors

Threads of Silk
Copyright © 2008 by Linda Chaikin

Requests for information should be addressed to:

Zondervan, *Grand Rapids, Michigan* 49530

Library of Congress Cataloging-in-Publication Data

Chaikin, L. L.
      Threads of silk / Linda Lee Chaikin.
         p. cm. — (The silk house; bk. 3)
      ISBN-13: 978-0-310-27310-3
      ISBN-10: 0-310-27310-2
       1. Catherine de Medicis, Queen, consort of Henry II, King of France, 1519 – 1589 — Fiction.
    2. Dressmakers — Fiction. 3. Courts and courtiers — Fiction. I. Title.
    PS3553.H2427T485 2008
    813'.54 — dc22
                                                       2007027367

All Scripture quotations, unless otherwise indicated, are taken from the *King James Version.*

Interior design by Beth Shagene

Printed in the United States of America

07 08 09 10 11 12 13 14 15 16 17 • 27 26 25 24 23 22 21 20 19 18 17 16 15 14 13 12 11 10 9 8 7 6 5 4 3 2 1

Dover

Calais

SPANISH NETHERLANDS

ENGLISH CHANNEL

Dieppe   PICARDY   Guise

Clermont

NORMANDY   *Seine R.*   Paris   *Marne R.*   D. OF LORRAINE   HOLY ROMAN EMPIRE

St.
Germain-
en-Laye   *Seine R.*

BRITTANY   Chatillon   Fontainebleau

Vendome   Orleans

ORLEANS

Nantes   Blois   *Loire R.*   BURGUNDY

Amboise   Chambord

Loire R.   TOURAINE   *Saône R.*   SWITZERLAND

La Rochelle   Geneva

KINGDOM OF FRANCE   Lyon

BAY OF BISCAY

Dordogne R.

Garonne R.   *Rhone R.*

Albret   Nerac

GASCONY   Toulouse   LANGUEDOC

NAVARRE   Pau

MEDITERRANEAN SEA

KINGDOM OF SPAIN

S.J. CHAIKIN

FRANCE IN THE 16TH CENTURY

(showing prominent provinces and cities for this series)

■ Huguenot center

| 0 miles | 50 | 100 | 150 |

| 0 km | 50 | 100 | 150 |

Historical Characters

Duchesse Montpensier — of the House of Bourbon, a Huguenot

M. Jacques Lefévre d'Étaples — translated first Bible into French

M. John Calvin — writer of *Institutes of the Christian Religion* (*Christianae Religionis Institutio*)

Prince Louis de Condé — French general, of the House of Bourbon

Prince Antoine de Bourbon — older brother of Louis. He later became King of Navarre through marriage to Huguenot Queen Jeanne d'Albret of Navarre.

Admiral Gaspard de Coligny — had Normandy and Picardy under his security

Cardinal de Châtillon (Odet Coligny) — brother of Gaspard and d'Andelot Coligny

Mary Stuart (la petite reinette) — married Dauphin Francis Valois who became King Francis II

Charles de Montpensier (Duc de Bourbon) — had rights to the throne that equaled, if not exceeded, those of the Valois

"Capitaine" l'Ollonaise — French pirate

Henry of Anjou — third son of Catherine de Medici and King Henry II (Valois)

Duc Francis de Guise — of the infamous Borgias family from Florence, Italy

Catherine de Medici — Queen and Regent of France over Francis II and Charles II Valois

Princesse Marguerite Valois — daughter of Catherine de Medici and King Henry II (Valois), also called Margo

Monsieur Henry Guise — later a duc, younger son of Duc Francis de Guise.

Anne d'Este — wife of Duc de Guise (Francis)

Charles de Guise (Cardinal de Lorraine) — younger brother of Duc Francis de Guise

Mme. Charlotte de Presney — member of Catherine's escadron volant

Madalenna — Italian serving girl of Catherine de Medici

Prince Henry of Navarre — son of Antoine de Bourbon and Jeanne d'Albret, King and Queen of Navarre

Maître Avenelle — the betrayer of the Huguenots

Princesse Eleonore Condé—a niece of Admiral Gaspard Coligny

Messire de la Renaudie—a leader of the Huguenots, a retainer of Prince Louis de Condé

Ambroise le Pare—physician and surgeon to kings, a Huguenot

Princesse Elisabeth Valois—daughter of Catherine and Henry Valois, married Philip II of Spain

Montmorency family and the Constable of France—Catholics who sided with the Bourbons in the end

Machiavelli—Niccolo Machiavelli, a cunning and cruel man; he was associated with corrupt, totalitarian government because of a small pamplet he wrote called "The Prince" to gain influence with the ruling Medici family in Florence.

Alessandro (the abuser)—a brother of Catherine de Medici

Cosmo and Lorenzo Ruggerio—brothers from Florence, Catherine's astrologers and poison makers

Rene—parfumer, also Catherine's poisoner

Duc of Alva—Spanish general

Marechal de Saint Andre—a marshal of France

Monsieur Theodore Beza—French Reformer, disciple of John Calvin

Cardinal d'Este—from Ferrara, Italy

Poet Tasso—a poet from Italy

Ronsard—a poet who served the Valois Court

Hercule Valois—the fourth and youngest son of Catherine and Henry Valois, little is known of him

Anne du Bourg—a Huguenot man sent to the Bastille by Henry II. He was burned at the stake under the Cardinal de Lorraine when boy-king Francis ruled with Queen Mother Catherine. The Huguenots then felt betrayed and planned the Amboise plot.

Nostradamus—a soothsayer in the Roman Catholic Church

Jacopo Sadeleto—Archbishop of Carpentras

Chantonnay—Thomas Perrenot de Chantonnay, Spanish ambassador to France

Alencome—Monsieur Ronsard d'Alencome, French Ambassador to the English Court and spy for Catherine

Threads of Silk

PART ONE

The Ties That Bind

Refuge

How far behind is the enemy? A day, several hours? Or are they ahead, waiting in ambush?

Mademoiselle Rachelle Macquinet flicked the reins of her horse to surge toward the bridge, listening above the wind for the dread sound of distant hooves pounding in pursuit.

She caught sight of the silhouette of the castle of Vendôme in the distance. *Marquis* Fabien's chief page, Gallaudet, galloped ahead while Fabien rode guard behind her. Here along the rim of the dark woods the forest encroached upon their path, enabling any ambush to avoid detection. Two of Fabien's finest swordsmen rode on either side of the road with an eye toward the dense shadows, one hand near their scabbards.

The cold rain pelted her face beneath her hooded cloak as they neared the castle. The horses trotted over the bridge toward the gate, and the imposing outline of the royal Bourbon estate rose up in the night to meet them with open arms like a biblical city of refuge.

I want to be married here; I want to give birth to his firstborn son here — but with so much in jeopardy, do we even have a chance? Can these sturdy walls offer safety from Madame le Serpent's emissaries?

Rachelle halted her horse outside the gate. The wind clawed at her hood and blustered against her as though snarling a protest over her safe arrival at the first destination in the long, treacherous journey.

She lifted her gaze to the towering wall where an armed guard arrayed in the Bourbon family colors of blue and red appeared, his billowing sleeves flapping.

Fabien maneuvered his horse beside her. "Is that you, Dumas?" he shouted. "Open the gate! It is I, your *seigneur*!"

"*Monseigneur*!" the guard shouted into the wind. "It *is* you!"

"I, and no other, unless on such a night you're expecting the ghost of Vendôme Hall."

Captain Dumas laughed, swung around, and yelled down to the inside of the courtyard, "Make haste, you dullards! It is le marquis, home from sinking Spanish galleons!"

Hearty voices rose and boots scuffled hastily over cobbles. She heard the clanking of bolts and chains, and the massive outer gate shuddered on its hinges and moved slowly open.

Rachelle blinked against flaming torches flickering in the stiff wind as guards drew back, forming a welcoming line and hailing their monseigneur with robust cheers.

She rode beside Fabien into the courtyard of the *palais-château*. Several of the guards closed the gate and replaced bolts and locks.

Horse hooves clattered forward, scabbards clinked, and Toledo steel glinted. The wet cobbles glimmered in the torchlight flowing down from the stone walls encircling the quad.

Wind-driven clouds tumbled across the sky, and from time to time, the pale moon pushed through. She glimpsed Fabien's handsome features, the strong jaw, slashing brows, and wavy hair the color of wheat, but the disarming smile that usually warmed her heart was replaced by a look of gravity beneath his dark, wide-brimmed hat with silver ornamentation.

He dismounted, and coming around beside her horse, lifted her down. She felt the cobbles beneath her thin soles as he escorted her across the courtyard toward a torch-lit alcove. Here, the great wooden entry door was strapped with iron — which encouraged her uneasy emotions.

Rachelle swept through into the grand *salle* of intricate masonry stonework and marble and where a glow from the hearth beckoned with a promise of warmth. Although she was chilled from the rainstorm and her clothing was wet, her attention was arrested by Fabien's sudden preoccupation with some new peril as Gallaudet, fair and lean, stood speaking to him in a low tone.

Rachelle tensed and listened intently, but caught little.

" — doubting his loyalties to you — "

"*Mille diables!* I cannot believe it. Who makes such a charge?"

Gallaudet's answer was indiscernible to her.

Fabien responded with a frown. Rachelle watched him reenter the courtyard where the rain plummeted, Gallaudet following.

Rachelle shivered, but it was not so much from cold as from fear. Mayhap a little excitement.

Pine logs on the grate heated the stones near the embers and released an aromatic fragrance. She stood holding her hands toward the radiant warmth. A drop of rainwater fell from the hem of her cloak and sizzled on the stones. In the light from glowing lamps of burnished brass inlaid with gemstones, she began admiring her surroundings: thick rugs of a design done in crimson, blue, and gold; wood and brocade furnishings; and intricate hanging tapestries.

Would she give Fabien sons and daughters to carry on the Bourbon title? *Not if the Queen Mother has her way!*

Rachelle intertwined her fingers tightly. *Comte Maurice! That scheming fox! I would sooner be dead than married to him as the Queen Mother threatens.*

The wood hissed and snapped. Her taut nerves responded as though the embers spewed forth venom. She could envision the mocking eyes of the Queen Mother watching her from the glowing coals, vowing to defeat their plans.

Why would it matter to the Queen Mother of France whom she, a *couturière*, married? The truth was, it did not. It was Fabien who mattered to her secret schemes.

I am merely the bait she uses to trap him. And what the Queen Mother wishes from him is too dark to contemplate.

From behind her, footsteps echoed and she whipped around as though expecting to confront her nemesis in the familiar black gown and coif.

It was Fabien. She searched his face and found his countenance retained a sober cast. He tossed aside his hat and riding cloak, which were immediately taken up by a serving boy.

He walked up to her. His royal blue tunic with silver threads glinted in the firelight.

Under his gaze, a warmth began to smolder in her heart.

"You are exhausted, *ma chérie.*"

"*Non*, I am well," she insisted, hoping to portray a bravery to match his own. She returned his smile, but his brow lifted in doubt.

"Exhausted — and wet," he said gravely and gently undid the clasp on her cloak. As he did, her honey autumn hair tumbled over her shoulder and across his hand.

She felt herself drawn toward him, even as the coals in the hearth had drawn her only minutes ago. His arm slipped around her, bringing her close. He raised a handful of her hair and looked at it in the firelight. Their lips met and all shadows fled. The rainy night was no longer bleak and dark. They were together in a wondrous place from which she did not want to withdraw, and the Queen Mother's spies seemed to be fleeing. She melted into his embrace.

Her senses immersed with his in the wonderment of their longing. It was incredible how her life had turned about so swiftly by his return to France and his commitment to their future.

"We have until dawn, then we must leave. I could send Gallaudet for a priest or a secret Calvinist *pasteur*. We could be married tonight — though your father is not likely to approve of my taking you without his knowledge. There is risk in whatever direction we take."

"It is you who are most at risk, *mon amour*, because I shall never marry Maurice! I shall go to the Bastille to die first!"

His fingers tightened on her forearms. "You will not die, chérie. I want you alive and safe. The Bastille is out of the question as long as I can wield my sword. The wisest action for both of us is escape to London."

"Then there is little doubt as to whether she may send guards here?"

His gravity returned and he released her. "My sweet, I have not the least doubt of it. She understood from the beginning how I would react when she sent her *lettre* to me in London. It will be to our detriment if we underestimate her vigor now in seizing us." He took a turn before the hearth, a hand at the back of his neck. "Non, we dare not stay here longer than this night. We must ride out by daybreak, chérie."

He saw the platter of roasted fowl and goblets of burgundy and silver cups of coffee. He chose a drumstick from the platter and offered her one. She declined and sank slowly to the stone bench, suddenly aware of her weariness.

She put a palm to her forehead. "So she already knows we are here. That means . . ." She moved her gaze to his.

"*Exactement.* She expected me to return after she threatened to arrange your marriage to that cousin of mine. She would have had spies watching for me in Calais." He tossed the chicken bone aside and reached for another drumstick. "They would have reported to her the moment the *Reprisal* came into port, but I also believe she was notified when I rode into Paris."

She met his even gaze. "Therefore, she will soon know of our escape from Paris; perhaps she already does."

"I've already sent my messenger north to Calais. He takes a risk trying to slip through to *Capitaine* Nappier. The roads are under watch. If my plan succeeds, however, he will inform Nappier to sail the *Reprisal* to Dieppe to wait for us there."

Her stomach tightened. It would be at least a week before the ship arrived at the point of rendezvous in northern France.

She stood, matching his iron calmness, at least outwardly, even while her knees weakened at the thought of the Queen Mother's cold resolve to keep them in France for her purposes.

He drank from the goblet. "Reaching the *Reprisal* will prove difficult. It is a long ride to Dieppe." He studied her. "Can you endure it?"

She arched a brow and placed one hand on her hip. "Did I not keep up from Paris? I thought you would have noticed my riding skills." She cast him a glance and saw his appreciative smile.

"*Ma belle*, I noticed, I assure you—you were wondrous to behold." He lifted the goblet to his lips and eyed her over the rim. "And *charmante* as well."

She felt a flush come to her cheeks and turned back to the fire, holding her palms toward the warmth.

"Do not blame me if I worry for your health," he said. "You are my preeminent concern. I do not wish to see you so weary as you are now. Even so, joining Nappier at Dieppe will present our best opportunity to reach England. If we do not — " He paused, his brows drawn, looking at the goblet.

She pushed her hair away from her shoulder. "But Fabien, as you say, it will take Capitaine Nappier at least a week to reach Dieppe. If the Queen Mother suspects you will marry me before she can thwart us, she will act swiftly."

He set the goblet down and took hold of her gently. His soothing touch reassured her. "I have guards watching the road and horses are ready should we need to leave quickly by way of the woods."

"But if she overtakes us she will insist I marry Maurice. Let us not wait for the dawn. Let us leave at once. Now!"

His eyes, a deep blue with unusual violet hues, held her riveted as his fingers caressed the back of her neck.

"You underestimate my amour for you, ma belle." He clasped her hands tightly to his chest where she could feel his heartbeat, and it thrilled her. "My feelings for you will not endure having you married to Maurice. I will fight to defend you. Do you think I would have returned to France if I were not certain you were the only woman for me? If that were not so, by now I would have been on a voyage to the Americas."

She held him tightly, the thought of losing him forever too much to endure.

She turned her eyes to his. "If you had gone on to Fort Caroline ... I cannot bear to think of what might have happened — "

"The loss, I assure you, would have been mine." He brushed his lips against her forehead, shielding her hands between his. "If I had returned to find I was too late, and lost you to court intrigue, I would have never forgiven myself."

Her heart purred as he stroked her hair and kissed her temple.

He brought her left hand to his lips, kissing her ring finger. "I will not rest content until I place the Bourbon wedding ring on your hand. "You know I love you, Rachelle, chérie, fully and completely. I could wish most profoundly to seal our marriage tonight, but in doing so we face another dilemma, one we cannot ignore. You know, even as I, what it is."

She turned her head aside. Yes ... she knew. Her feelings, so uplifted only moments ago, now collapsed. The Queen Mother was not the only one who could separate them.

"If I claim you in marriage tonight without addressing the matter of my Christian faith to Monsieur Arnaut," he said of her father, "I will surely offend the deep significance of his spiritual belief."

She drew back slightly and then lowered herself to the bench. Feeling cold again, she looked at the red coals but felt no satisfying warmth.

"Oui," she murmured, "I have been thinking of this since we left Paris, and it is a great concern. Père Arnaut will be highly disappointed with me. It is because he does not fully understand you yet, nor does ma mère," she said of her mother, Madame Clair. She turned her head toward him. "But when they know your heart as I do, they will have no such concerns."

"Perhaps. Until then, to Monsieur Arnaut it is an established fact that I've been a practicing Catholic while at court. In my brief meeting with him at Calais, I regret I did nothing to try to bridge our differences."

Rachelle lifted her chin as she thought of the confrontation between her and Fabien over his determination to leave France on a two-year privateering mission against Spain, which had nearly led to the disintegration of their relationship.

"The reason for my reluctance to persuade Monsieur Arnaut in Calais is evident. I'd no idea of the impending circumstance that would lead to my swift return to France to declare myself to you. And now, should I marry his daughter in his absence, he will judge me most arrogant."

Rachelle knew how shocked her parents would be upon discovering their daughter's sudden marriage. Though marriage into the Bourbon family would be considered a great honor, Fabien's perceived loyalty to the Roman Church would distress her parents, ardent supporters of the Reformation in France.

She paraded up and down before the glowing coals, plucking at the damp lace on her sleeves. "Madame Clair was convinced you could never become serious about marriage and wished for me to avoid you. Since you are a royal Bourbon, she thought it likely you would eventually marry a *princesse*." She glanced at him.

"She was correct on the last point, I have found my princesse—it is you."

That thrilled her, but despite his fervor, a tiny fear gnawed at her. "Yet, your Bourbon family, the princes of the blood—" she tossed up her hands in a helpless gesture—"they are not likely to be pleased with your choice."

"I have considered them," he said briefly. "But I decided years ago that I would not marry a woman merely to gain possessions or influence. I have come forward to commit myself to you in Christian marriage. Even so, we know, do we not, it is your parents' reaction that will be important should we marry tonight without seeking their permission. Their faith in the Scriptures is strong, as it should be. That I am Catholic—or was—will worry them. Assuredly, I will be accused of taking unfair advantage of their daughter in their absence. This is likely to breed resentment. It is no light thing, chérie, for a Catholic marquis to marry a Huguenot when France totters on the edge of religious civil war."

She moved away, restless, clenching the folds of her skirt between her fingers. "Oh, if only they were here to speak with you, to see your faith as genuine. Instead," she said, "they are in London. We could journey to Lyon, otherwise, to the Château de Silk, and meet with them. Mère speaks of the admonition from Scripture to not be unequally yoked together with unbelievers."

"We are not unequally yoked in belief. Pasteur Bertrand, for one, could bear witness of that."

She recalled the unusual circumstance of her father's cousin, Bertrand Macquinet, a Geneva trained pastor, who sailed with Fabien on his last voyage to aid Holland against Spain.

"He could convince your parents. Unfortunately, we would have to contact him by lettre. We can be in London sooner ourselves by voyaging from Dieppe on the *Reprisal*."

If only Cousin Bertrand were here! She had always been close to Bertrand; he'd become a second father to her. He could not only convince Père Arnaut and Mère Clair of Fabien's faith in Christ alone for salvation, but he could perform the marriage ceremony. But Bertrand was in England leading a Huguenot church in the Spitalfields district outside London, where many French Protestants had fled from the fiery stake in France.

Her hope for marriage before reaching London was disintegrating, which meant she remained at risk of falling into the will of the Queen Mother—and Maurice.

"If I brought you to Geneva and held audience with Monsieur Calvin, our marriage could be performed in the heart of the Reformation by Calvinists. This would satisfy your family. We could reach Geneva in less than two weeks."

She lifted a brow. "You would meet with Monsieur Calvin?"

"Assuredly. I have wanted to meet him for years."

Surprised, she watched as he tapped his chin, mentally debating the options. *Geneva?*

"There is also the possibility of the Huguenot kingdom of Navarre," she said.

"To my kinswoman Queen Jeanne ... yes. She would do everything she could to protect you. She is a bonne woman, intelligent, and of rare spirit. I am most fond of her."

Navarre, Geneva, London — at present it mattered little to her as long as their destination secured them from the reach of the treacheries that lurked.

"Oh, this is madness, mon amour. If only my parents understood my fate if we did *not* marry! They should thank God we married in time to thwart the Queen Mother's plans with Maurice."

"I vow, chérie, if there is no way out of this, we will marry without Monsieur Arnaut's blessing."

She threw herself into his embrace and rested her cheek against his chest, taking solace in his determination, his masculinity.

A measure of peace and confidence had returned in the passionate silence as they held to one another, hearing the crackle of pine in the hearth. He spoke to her tenderly, calming her fears.

"Ma belle, you have endured a long and tense day. Come, let me escort you to your chamber. I regret we have no maid to attend you. There are some wives of my men-at-arms, but they are all retired by now. Perhaps I could rouse one of them."

She shook her head and offered a brief smile. "It is not necessary. Let them sleep." The mention of maids brought to mind her own Nenette, whom she had to leave behind at the Louvre in Paris while making her unexpected flight with Fabien two days ago. Was Nenette safe?

Fabien walked her toward the great stairway carpeted in burgundy, where elevated wall lamps and candles cast a glimmer of golden light.

They ascended together in silence through the grandeur of the Bourbon *palais* to the carved door of the majestic bedchamber. It was the same she had occupied for a short time almost two years ago when fleeing the beheadings of the Huguenots at Amboise castle. How long ago that seemed!

He caught her hand to his lips, turned it over, and kissed her palm, his gaze speaking words so filled with amour, they set her heart racing.

"Adieu, mon belle amour."

After he had left the corridor, she closed the door quietly and tried to collect her thoughts. So much had happened so swiftly, her mind was whirling. For every blessing there seemed a thorn — but also a promise from God's Word for every need.

I must keep my courage. I must keep my faith in God's purposes.

Such was essential to nourish thanksgiving in her heart, and to keep from growing weary in times of spiritual struggle.

AT FONTAINEBLEAU, THE ROYAL HUNTING CHÂTEAU, Andelot Dangeau lit the large candles in his cramped chamber and stooped to the side of his narrow bed. Prayer objects lay on the bedcover as a precautionary safeguard for sudden intrusion. He lifted the edge of the straw mattress and glanced over his shoulder toward the open doorway that led into the larger book-filled study chamber used as a classroom by his tutor.

He hesitated, hand on the edge of the mattress. Had he heard a squeak of leather shoes on the carpet? He listened. Perhaps it was some crackling in the hearth.

Outside the windows, the wind shook the forest trees. With caution, he removed the French Bible. He held it and sighed as a hungry man eyeing roast meat. He ran his fingers across the worn leather binding. He'd had to stay up nights to read it by candlelight to avoid getting caught. Even so, he had not read it nearly enough to know the words and make them his own. Now that his new tutor had arrived from Paris University to occupy the chamber across from his own, reading would be even more precarious. Not that he knew the mind of the renowned scholar Thauvet, or what he might think about the Bible translated into French, since there was little freedom to debate such matters. Should a scholar endorse the forbidden translation, or if a copy was discovered to be in his possession, it would mean death, unless one recanted.

He could speak only for himself, and he'd discovered that to read the words in French warmed his soul as no religious ritual ever could.

He ran his fingers through his thick, wavy brown hair and drew his brows together. Even so, he must return the Bible to its owner as he had promised his *oncle*, Comte Sebastien. Sebastien was due back here at Fontainebleau tomorrow from Paris, so Andelot had come to the decision that he must bring the Bible late tonight to the fallen tree where the old Huguenot pasteur had hidden it from the Dominican in the Fontainebleau Forest. *At least I have memorized many passages. No one can take my memory from me. I have the freedom to think about these words as oft as I wish, even in the presence of the cardinal —*

He was startled at overhearing a familiar voice.

"Ah, Monsieur Thauvet! I anticipated that you had retired by this hour so I did not knock . . . I hope I am not disturbing you? I have a message from the cardinal. Is your pupil Monsieur Andelot yet awake?"

Thauvet's low voice answered Père Jaymin, who was a secretary on the cardinal's staff.

Andelot swiftly thrust the Bible back under the mattress. He was smoothing the bedcovers in place when Jaymin loomed in the doorway. Standing in the shadow with the lamplight behind him, he appeared taller and thinner than usual in his religious finery adorned with the colors of scarlet and white, identifying him with the cardinal.

Andelot believed him a kindly man, though he held no sympathy for those considered heretics.

Jaymin's spaniel-brown eyes dropped to the bed. Andelot felt a twinge. *I almost believe he can see through the mattress.*

"Am I intruding upon your prayers?"

Andelot smoothed the bedcover again, giving it an extra pat. "Non, Père Jaymin, a fair evening to you." He picked up the sanctified prayer objects and returned them to their niche along a wooden shelf on the wall. From the corner of his eye, he saw Jaymin's gaze encircling the small chamber in much the same way, reminding Andelot of a hawk circling in search of prey.

Andelot gently cleared his throat. "You wish for my duty in some matter, Père Jaymin?"

"Ah, non, non." His mouth spread in a benign smile, almost apologetic. "It is late of hour. It is the bon cardinal who summons you to his chamber." He clicked his tongue. The smile gave way to a sigh. "I warn you afore. Expect hard questioning concerning your guardian, Comte Sebastien. You best go posthaste. I will say no more. The cardinal shall speak."

About Oncle Sebastien!

⁂

ANDELOT, GARBED IN HIS NEW SCHOLAR'S ROBE with fur collar, adjusted the golden chain about his neck so the large cross was in the center of his chest with his robe open at either end. He waited in the front of the cardinal's *appartement* that was one of the finest at Fontainebleau. He slid his gaze up and down the crimson draperies fringed with golden tassels and marveled at the marble statuette by Michelangelo on the pedestal near a wooden door carved with intertwining orange blossoms. He discovered that while he admired the beauty of all that he beheld, he no longer desired them to enhance his personal esteem as he had when he'd first come to court. He'd read in the French Bible that he was a member of "the household of God," which made him valuable and secure.

I shall admire these treasures from afar, and honor those whom God has gifted with skills to create such marvels, but I do not need to possess such luxury.

What he desired now was to go to Geneva to hear Monsieur John Calvin, to perhaps attend the great theological school there.

He gazed toward the archway where a door opened and a rustle of silky material alerted him. The fire flickered in a hearth, and a lamp was burning. There appeared to be someone else in the cardinal's *salle de séjour*, but the figure slipped out of view before Andelot could fully see. He saw the handsome young Charles de Guise, the Cardinal de Lorraine, the most powerful religious messire in all France. Andelot caught a whiff of fragrance that he had come to associate with him.

He was tall and slim with large, languid almond-shaped eyes. His mouth was sensuous, his long graceful hands adorned with gold and ruby rings. His lips were too often curved with what Andelot thought was amused cynicism. A woman in the other chamber quickly vanished through drapes. Andelot blinked, thinking he might have imagined her. No longer was he the gullible boy who had first come to Amboise to meet his Guise kinsmen. The first time Marquis Fabien had told him that the Cardinal de Lorraine kept mistresses, Andelot had been offended, thinking the marquis was being irreverent toward the cardinal. How gullible he had been to think that high church titles and religious ceremonies would make the man holy without the indwelling Spirit of God.

If I must depend upon this manner of religious messire to stand between my soul and God, I should despair!

Jesus, our great high priest, is holy, harmless, undefiled, and separate from sinners. He ever lives to make intercession for us. Our great high priest is moved with tender compassion for each of His own.

Andelot suddenly smiled, joy dancing in his soul. "Bon jour, Monseigneur." He hastened a small bow.

The cardinal's brow shot up. "You are full of *joie de vivre* I see, Andelot. Am I to take your deportment as happiness that your guardian oncle has fled Paris for England?"

Andelot stared. *What! It could not be true! Comte Sebastien, gone?*

"Monseigneur? Fled Paris?"

"Like a rat fleeing a burning ship. Your shock indicates surprise. You were unaware, is that it, Andelot? I wonder if I can permit my sounder judgment to believe you?"

"Monseigneur Cardinal, I vow this news astounds me."

"As it does us all." He walked into the salle and sat upon an ornate chair, gesturing Andelot to do the same.

"Sebastien has betrayed King Francis by this dastardly action. Not to mention inviting the rage of the Queen Mother, who trusted him as a member of the Privy Council. Without a word, he has taken his wife and child and his wife's sister and abandoned his duty to the throne of France. And this betrayal, mind you, after the kindnesses bestowed upon him. We should have left him to his just imprisonment in the Bastille for his part in the Huguenot rebellion at Amboise against the king."

Overcome by this development, Andelot remained silent.

"Then you are willing to swear you knew naught of this vile treachery, Andelot?"

Whether Sebastien's actions were treacherous, Andelot would not judge, but he could vow that he had not been privy to the plans.

"This is the first I have learned of it, Monseigneur. He did not speak of it to me, and I knew not that he was planning an escape."

He must have fled to Spitalfields to be with Pasteur Bertrand and the Huguenot church there.

A feeling of loss rolled over him. He would miss the shrewd but kindly and protective Sebastien, who claimed in some complicated manner to be his oncle, even as the powerful cleric who sat watching him with measuring eyes was also said to be a kinsman. The facts had never been explained to Andelot's satisfaction, and perhaps they never would be. The idea that he might be a Guise no longer straightened his shoulders and fed his desire for advancement at court.

Why did Sebastien not tell me he was fleeing France? I might have chosen to flee with him.

His loss waned with the growing realization that Sebastien, unhappy at court and at serious risk in his faith, had outmanipulated the Queen Mother. Relief roused in his heart and almost sang from his lips until he became aware of the languid eyes staring at him so keenly.

"May I ask when Comte Sebastien left the Paris Louvre, Monseigneur?"

"If we knew that, he might have been captured and arrested posthaste," the cardinal said wryly. "We thought you might be able to tell us."

"I knew nothing of this, Monseigneur."

"So you have said. The road out of Paris to Calais is under watch on orders from the Queen Mother. He will be captured, you can be sure."

The cardinal's confidence threw a dagger of fear into his belly. If Sebastien and his family were caught, it would mean their imprisonment, or worse.

Lord God, protect them and send angels to help them.

"You are not looking well, mon petit," came the cardinal's mocking voice. "You would not have in mind the fate of your secret amour?"

Dulled by the senseless question, Andelot wondered what to say.

"Monseigneur, I do not understand what you are suggesting."

The cardinal produced a lettre, a cynical smile on his lips. "Does the name of Mademoiselle Idelette Macquinet awaken your understanding at all?"

Andelot remained mute, wondering if Idelette had gone with her sister and Sebastien. The cardinal offered him the lettre.

"This was found in Sebastien's appartement at the Louvre by a maid of the Macquinet family. She arrived here with a peasant boy of about twelve. They came from Paris to find Duchesse Dushane. The guards intercepted the *demoiselle* and discovered this lettre written to you. Will you still swear to me that you knew nothing of Sebastien's well-planned escape to England?"

Andelot recognized the handwriting as belonging to Idelette, for she had corresponded with him on occasion in the past. He took the letter, and, uneasy under the cardinal's gaze, read Idelette's message.

"We anticipate the day when Macquinet-Dushane silk cloth is shipped to the Spitalfields district where we will open a business with the Hudson family and employ many of the French, Belgian, and Dutch Protestant immigrants. There is another reason why I have chosen to leave France and take up residence in London, but I cannot bring myself to explain to you now. I will write you again, *cher* Andelot, after we have arrived safely by God's grace."

Andelot's sudden alarm surprised even him. There could be but one reason that would motivate the cool-headed and unemotional Mademoiselle Idelette to leave her beloved home in Lyon, the Château de Silk, and risk the journey to England with Sebastien and his family: that was Idelette's respect and affection for a man who shared her interest in silk and design. And the only monsieur that he could think of was Sir James Hudson, the English couturier that both Idelette and her sister Rachelle had written about to him in the past.

Andelot's spirits slumped. The obvious "other reason" for going to England was that Sir James Hudson had not as yet asked for her hand in marriage.

"Ah," the cardinal said, "so you do have a secret amour. The look on your face informs me you are disappointed by the news of mademoiselle's departure."

"Yes, Monseigneur, it is all so unexpected."

"Even so, your behavior of late is most unsatisfactory, Andelot. I can only hope your studies under Scholar Thauvet will vindicate your pledge to me that you wish above all things to pursue your education."

Andelot bowed. "I assure you, Monseigneur, that it is so."

"We shall see. It is fortunate that the mademoiselle has removed herself from becoming your distraction."

How many distractions did the cardinal have?

The cardinal stood, signifying an end to the meeting.

"I shall consider your vow that you are not involved in this treasonous behavior against the king."

Andelot bowed again. He was on his way toward the door when the cardinal's voice halted him.

"You were wise to end your friendship with the Marquis de Vendôme as I instructed you."

Andelot arranged a blank expression before he looked back at him.

"Monseigneur?"

The cardinal's long mouth turned upward. "I have word from elite spies that the Queen Mother has lured the Marquis Vendôme back to France."

Andelot tensed.

"The marquis waits to be ensnared in the net she has laid for him. It is well you are not deemed his ally when he is brought before the *Duc* of Alva. The duc is most displeased over the sinking of his galleon off the coast of Holland."

Andelot concealed his apprehension. The infamous Spanish Duc of Alva! Marquis Fabien was walking into a trap. The Duc of Alva was here at Fontainebleau at this very moment.

Andelot felt a rush of horror as he imagined Marquis Fabien and Comte Sebastien both being brought to Madrid in chains.

How might he warn the marquis? Was he at Calais? Paris?

Is the cardinal testing my response?

"As you say, Monseigneur," he replied, keeping emotion from his voice and manner. "I have not seen the Marquis de Vendôme in months. Is he coming here to Fontainebleau?"

The cardinal gave no answer and turned away to show Andelot he was dismissed. Andelot narrowed his gaze at the cleric's back and went out, his palms sweating.

Trouble and woe. His soul could hear the cackles riding the autumn winds outside the diamonded windows. Clouds hurtled their way across the sky above Fontainebleau Forest.

Idelette . . .

Marquis Fabien . . .

Andelot walked slowly down the corridor toward the other section of the palais, toward Scholar Thauvet's chambers and his own antechamber.

What could he do? He must do something! He must think, plan, and act.

Laying the Trap

WITHIN HER ROYAL CHAMBERS AT FONTAINEBLEAU, THE QUEEN MOTHER of France composed her secret lettre, sealed it with the royal Valois seal, and placed it out of sight.

At one of the windows, she gazed off toward the darkening Fontainebleau Forest. The crooning wind moved through long, swaying branches. The messenger she expected could arrive at any moment now.

Catherine left her royal chamber and made her way by a circuitous route to an antechamber. Once inside she lit a candle and carried it to the other side through a narrow door. She peered down the secret steps. She turned her ear toward the hollow, listening, waiting. Then a small gleam from a candle appeared below. The messenger's footsteps sounded, and a moment later a shadowy form emerged, shrouded in a hooded cloak like a traveling monk, and climbed upward. He had served her since her days in Florence, and he now bowed in obeisance.

Catherine extended her hand for the coveted parcel. Her heart beat faster as her fingers clasped hold. "It is all here then?"

"Yes, Your Majesty, it is from *him*, the master of mysterious sayings, delivered to me by his servant as arranged."

"Very well. Madalenna will see to your needs in the forest. Let no one see you."

"No, Madame. No one will see me."

Catherine returned to her royal chamber and forbade her servants to disturb her. She entered her writing closet and shut the door.

Her stiff black skirt rustled as she sat at her desk, swiftly opened the package, and removed a rolled parchment. She drew the candles closer and spread the roll across the desk. Ah! Here it was! The future prognostications created for her and her royal Valois family from the diviner, Nostradamus.

She pored over the strange allusions of muted rhymes and meditated on the divination charts alleged to forecast the triumph or doom of her sons based upon the signs of the zodiac.

She smiled at the favor bestowed by the planetary system upon her favorite little son Anjou, drummed her fingers and scowled over Mad Charles, and narrowed her gaze thoughtfully over the present young king, Francis II. Soon, however, she set this portion aside, for it was the secret disclosure on one messire in particular, her enemy, that she had desired and negotiated to gain. And here it was! The dark forecast held her breathless and engrossed.

Ah yes, yes ... I see it. Blood and darkness ahead ... now is the time to act. Ah yes, I must not step back in timidity. Here at last is the death sign — she tapped her finger on the drawing — *his bright star is dimming, it is falling, it is going out. If this knowledge is acted upon, he will die, the readings tell his fall. That noisome plague, Duc de Guise, is going to die!*

She considered the plans stirring in her mind and the personal consequences to her and Anjou. King Philip of Spain, her opponent, could prove to be a danger. If Spain should come to believe she had a personal hand in the duc's death, Philip could invade France, and with a quiet nod from the pope, remove her and her sons from the throne and put a Guise in their place. She must save the throne of France for her sons, especially her Anjou.

If only I could use poison.

But not on this occasion. She dare not bring suspicion to her door. Not with a monsieur as beloved in Spain and Rome as Duc de Guise. The Spanish ambassador had already sent lettres to his master Philip accusing her of using poison against her personal foes at court. If the duc died by poison, they would turn on her like starving wolves. As for his popularity, all Paris cheered when the duc rode his horse down the street, calling out, "A Guise for a king!" Those same citizens, however, whispered their dislike and distrust of that "Italian woman."

There must not be even a hint of suspicion suggesting her involvement. Both the pope and King Philip had accused her of protecting the heretics and were looking for reasons to remove her from power, though the Huguenots would mock any claim of her protection. Daily across France, the religious burnings continued unabated upon orders from the cardinal, another Guise.

Someone other than herself must be used to remove the duc. It was essential she remain shielded from the murky details. She rolled up the parchment, convinced this was the most favorable time to arrange for her plan to be carried out. Using a key on her wrist, she unlocked a large drawer concealed in the wall and placed the parchment inside. She left her closet and entered her main chamber.

Spies had already sent word that Marquis Fabien had taken the Macquinet couturière from Paris and escaped with her to the Bourbon castle at Vendôme. She retrieved her sealed lettre from the desk and struck her gong.

Her servant girl, Madalenna, appeared and bowed.

"Yes, Madame?"

"Take this to the dwarves to deliver at once."

<hr>

At Vendôme, Marquis Fabien left Rachelle in her chamber and went back down the stairs to the grand salle. He frowned, caught up his hat and coat, and went through the archway into the courtyard.

The rain had temporarily ceased, while the sky was awash with wind-tossed clouds. Lightning flashed over the forest and the trees bent before the irate wind. It was a night for trouble.

Gallaudet was waiting for him in the shadows as planned and came quietly to him.

"We will handle this ourselves," Fabien said. "Where is he now?"

"He is in his bungalow."

"Under whose watch?"

"Julot is near at hand."

Fabien would trust Julot with his life. "Come."

During his absence at sea, Fabien had left the security of the Bourbon estate under the command of the captain of the castle guard. Only those unmarried *chevaliers* who were skilled swordsmen and anxious for adventure, had accompanied him on the privateering mission against Spain. The others, the married and those content to remain at their positions here in Vendôme, had stayed behind. Even so, there was not a monsieur among any of his loyals, whether men-at-arms or castle guards and lackeys, that Fabien had not chosen with care.

The bungalow was ahead, a small light glowing in the main window. Fabien's gaze searched the area—nothing stirred. Gallaudet returned with Julot.

"No one has come, Monseigneur. Captain Dumas's wife came out and returned, but that is all," Julot said in a low voice.

Fabien disliked the thought of barging into the bungalow with the man's wife there.

"Knock and tell him I wish to see him at the castle," he told Gallaudet. "If what you have heard is true, he is likely to slip out the back."

He motioned for Julot to move to one side of the bungalow. Fabien made for the shadows and came around the other side to watch the window. Gallaudet had gone to the front door and was speaking with Dumas's wife. Fabien waited in the shrubs unseen. All was still, then came a rustle of movement. The man had climbed out the low window with a satchel on his shoulder.

The man held a sword, but his face was in shadow. Fabien felt a moment of grief. This was the captain of his home guard, a monsieur Fabien had trusted above many others. That his character had a price of betrayal was a stinging disappointment; he would never have thought it of him. Dumas's hearty cheer tonight was naught but hypocrisy. *Honneur* in a man was as priceless in Fabien's estimation as virtue in a great woman.

Disappointment over Dumas's betrayal turned swiftly to anger. Fabien lifted the point of his sword. Within the bungalow, another lamp was lit and the glow came through the window and fell across the escaping man's face. It was not Captain Dumas!

Fabien stepped forward, sword lifted. "So, you join my traitorous captain. Where is he?"

A lean, dark young man whom Fabien knew as Sully turned sharply at the sound of his voice.

"Monseigneur, I—I am no traitor to you, I had naught to do with it."

"Where is Dumas?"

"Dumas?"

Fabien's sword leapt to life and pricked dangerously close to his jugular.

"I am in no fair mood for games, Sully."

The guard fell to one knee, his sword clattering to the stone walkway.

"Monseigneur, I confess all! His wife told me he left soon after your arrival when he saw the boy seek out Gallaudet. The boy did not know much, only that his Oncle Dumas had met with the Comte Maurice Beauvilliers."

Maurice! That pariah! He'd managed to bribe the captain of the guard! How much had he paid Dumas?

"Go on. Be quick."

"I heard Gallaudet knew of the captain's treachery, so I came here to find him, but he'd already fled."

Gallaudet appeared in the open window and leaned out. "Monseigneur, we have the captain's wife. Do you wish to speak with her?"

Fabien stepped back from Sully and pointed him toward the front of the bungalow with his sword.

"Inside," he said roughly. "We shall see if your testimony bears with hers."

Madame Dumas was in tears, sitting hunched in a chair when Fabien entered with the guard Sully. Her bent figure, the rough worn hands that clasped and unclasped in her lap, softened his mood. Fabien gestured to Julot to remove Sully's weapons.

"Captain Dumas has already escaped, Monseigneur," Gallaudet said. "Would you that I run this other traitor through with my blade?" He cast Sully a cold look.

"One's enemies are always best dead," Julot said, eyeing Sully with scorn as beads of sweat formed on his forehead. "Let me have him, Monseigneur, and spare you the trouble."

Fabien saw the anxiety on the poor woman's face, for her husband was a worse traitor than Sully. Her eyelids were red and puffed from crying. He vaguely remembered hearing from Dumas how their child caught a sickness and died a year ago. Before that, there had been a baby born dead.

"Enough," he said to Julot and Gallaudet, and turned to the woman, ignoring Sully, who crouched in a corner under the stare of Julot.

"Where is your husband, Madame?" he asked quietly.

She looked at him, then away quickly, lowering her face with evident shame.

"He fled away, Monsieur Marquis. Where, I do not know, and that is the truth. All I know is he told me he'd be coming into twelve gold pieces."

"Twelve pieces of gold? Who would give him such a reward, and why?"

"I swear he never told me."

She pointed a finger toward Sully, no sign of geniality in her prematurely lined features. "I do not know what Sully told you, Monsieur Marquis, but he knows what it was about. Sully was to get some of the gold pieces."

"And the plan?" Fabien asked. "Were any other of my guards involved?"

She shook her head. "Ah, Monsieur Marquis, I know nothing more of it, I swear it. I have been busy working the castle gardens with the other women. My husband told me none of the details. He thinks little of a woman's tongue."

He believed her.

She pointed at Sully, and resentment flickered in her eyes as though she blamed him for her husband going astray. "He knows. He came here for supper, too lazy to make his own, always talking in whispers with my husband."

"You lie," Sully said. "I sometimes brought things to pay for my supper. More times I brought you a fat duck."

"Likely stolen from the marquis as not."

"I stole nothing from the marquis! I got the ducks honest, and I will swear to it."

"Enough," Fabien said.

"Ask him, Monsieur Marquis, about the gold pieces."

Sully's mouth twitched. He shot her an ugly look.

"Take him outside," Fabien told Julot. "I want the truth from him."

Julot grasped his arm. "On your feet, traitor."

In the trees, some distance from the castle Fabien stood by, affecting indifference to Julot and Gallaudet's pretense of savagery as they tied Sully to a tree. They began arguing about the best way to kill him.

"The new methods I learned from the Dutch pirate are certain to loosen the tongue," Julot said. "The Dutchman learned them from his Spanish captors."

Sully looked wildly from one to the other, as if assured his old comrades-in-arms had degenerated into masters of Spanish cruelty since sailing with pirates.

"Now, if you want my opinion, there's no reason for such unpleasantness," Gallaudet said. "Traitors that don't speak the truth are best just dead and buried, or even better — alive and buried."

Fabien turned away to start back for the castle. "Let me know when it is over."

"Monseigneur," Sully screeched. "Do not go, Monsieur! I will tell all I know."

Fabien turned to look at him. "Very well, say on."

Sully swallowed and licked his lips. "Comte Maurice Beauvilliers promised Captain Dumas a dozen gold pieces if he would play the spy for him here at the castle. He was to inform the comte of all that went on here. He was to send word as soon as you returned and — and send someone to open the gate when he and his men-at-arms arrived."

"And who might that be?" Julot snarled in his face.

"Tonight when the captain saw the mademoiselle with you, he rushed away to tell the comte. True, he was affrighted the boy would tell and put his spying to an end, but the captain knew the arrival of the mademoiselle was the grand news the comte needed to give Dumas his gold pieces. He was to deliver the news to the comte, then sneak back here. It was my duty to let him in through the western postern gate. He would get his wife, and we would be ready to leave as soon as the gate was opened for the comte. We would be gone before anyone missed us in the battle. I was to get two gold pieces, and the captain would keep the rest."

Fabien watched him evenly, hands on hips, and Gallaudet turned his back.

"Who planned this?" Fabien asked.

"Comte Maurice. He first sent a messenger to the captain. Then matters were arranged between them. Comte Maurice is rash, Monseigneur. He will act soon when he learns you are here. He will come with his men-at-arms."

"No doubt. He will wish to duel for mademoiselle. And if so, I would not wish to disappoint him."

"His belief, Monseigneur, is that the mademoiselle is promised to him in marriage by decree of the Queen Mother herself. He believes he has just cause."

Fabien's temper flared when he thought of the lettre the Queen Mother had sent to him in London. Her intention was clear: if Fabien wished to stop the marriage, he must return and yield his service to the Queen Mother's dark intrigues. She cared nothing for Maurice's interest in Rachelle; he was merely an expendable pawn.

"That jackanapes," Fabien said harshly. "He will guess at once my plan to take Mademoiselle Macquinet out of France to her family."

"Then we are too late, Monseigneur," Gallaudet said. "Captain Dumas will soon contact Comte Maurice."

Yes, the news that Rachelle was here with him at the castle would provoke Maurice to action. Fabien had no doubt of Maurice's temper and abilities.

"It will take Captain Dumas the rest of this night to reach Fontaine-bleau, and half the morning for him to return with the comte and his men," Gallaudet said. "Should we not be gone by then, Marquis?"

"The comte is not at Fontainebleau," Sully said. "He is near at hand. Captain Dumas rode there tonight."

"Where then?" Fabien demanded.

"I do not know, Monseigneur."

Fabien took a step toward him.

Sully cried, "I swear I speak the truth. Comte Maurice's whereabouts were never told me."

"Did you not take Dumas's messages to the comte?"

"I did, Monseigneur, but it was the comte's own messenger I met on the road. Only Captain Dumas knew of the comte's whereabouts."

"What road?"

"Why, the road from Amboise, Monseigneur."

Amboise! Could Maurice be at the fortress of Amboise?

Fabien's royal kinsman, the Bourbon Prince Louis de Condé, was being held there in the dungeon on charges of treason. Why was Maurice there?

Fabien frowned, pacing before the tree where Sully remained tied. Intermittent raindrops were falling, and the sound of the drops on the leaves broke the silence.

Perhaps the king's court was moving to the Amboise castle from Fontainebleau? If so, it placed his enemies closer to Vendôme. It was now imperative to leave at dawn for Dieppe to take Rachelle to safety.

He turned to walk back to the castle, when Sully's plaintive cry halted him.

"Monseigneur, I beg of you, leave me not in the hands of these men. They will surely see me dangle from the highest branch."

Julot's voice mocked. "That branch above your head will do. What think you, Gallaudet? Is it strong enough to support a traitorous jackal?"

"Let us not hang him, Julot; let us drown him in the water below the bridge."

"Let him live with his conscience," Fabien said over his shoulder. "But send him away from the castle. I'll not have such a fellow among men-at-arms of honneur."

"Monseigneur, give me another chance, if you please. I will serve you faithfully."

"Non. Go and serve my cousin the Comte Maurice."

Julot took out his knife and cut Sully loose. "You live because the marquis is a better monsieur than the likes of you and your fellows. If it were my decision, you would dangle."

"Be gone," Gallaudet said. "You have caused us all great harm."

They turned their backs on him and strode away.

Rachelle, though weary from travel, found herself unable to sleep after Fabien escorted her upstairs to her chamber.

With a pang of regret, she realized that while she was soon to become Marquise de Vendôme, she was not to live here and bear the family that would carry on his title and rule. They must leave France, and while she did not think their departure would last forever, it might be the rest of her lifetime. And what of her Macquinet-Dushane family roots at the Lyon Château de Silk?

Alas! Her place of refuge here at Vendôme, away from the snares and schemes of royal intrigue, was not to endure. Even if they were to avoid the long shadow of the Queen Mother, the flames of religious persecution crackled across the kingdom. If one was not loyal to the Roman Church, one was branded a heretic for the slaughter. And while the light of the Scriptures was shining across parts of Europe and England, the pope was determined to crush "the new opinions" wherever they took root by declaring them satanic heresy.

Rachelle tried to avoid dwelling upon her fears. She went to the small hearth with glowing wood coals, removed her wet clothing, and draped it over the backs of chairs to dry. She donned her wrapper over her chemise and enjoyed the luxury of thick carpet beneath her bare feet. Outside the windows, she heard the wind tossing the shrubs. The rain started up again, sending large splats against the panes.

Dawn would come quickly. She must rest, yet the more she concentrated on the need for sleep, the less sleepy she became. She began brushing her hair.

If only there were someone in the family to consent to her marriage to Fabien in Père Arnaut's absence, someone with authority . . .

She set her hairbrush down with a clatter. She must be mad to have forgotten the one person in all France who had such authority! *For did not Père Arnaut and Madame Clair leave me under her care when they went to London? Of course!*

The duchesse! They could marry at once without waiting until London, which would foil Maurice.

This could be the answer to their dilemma at last! She must go down and tell Fabien. Her heart felt light for the first time in days, and she threw off her wrapper and dressed hurriedly in one of the two other dresses she'd brought, this one a comfortable apple green linen. She slipped on dry stockings and her still-damp shoes, and fled from her chamber through the corridor, down the many stairs, lifting the folds of her gown from her ankles as she ran to the man she loved.

She saw him coming in from the courtyard and stopped short, grasping the banister with one hand, confronted by his formidable mood. Fabien was drenched with rain, his handsome features grim. She could imagine he'd just returned from a skirmish of sorts. Still, nothing short of a bearish growl could have altered her joie de vivre, and she started down the stairs toward him.

"Fabien, mon amour, I have the answer to our dilemma."

He looked up at her, showing faint surprise at her presence, then his gaze softened. An amused half-smile appeared.

He obviously did not take her seriously. She hurried down past the stairs. He came to meet her, taking her hands and drawing her to him. His smile deepened. "It is late. The wolves are baying at the moon hidden behind dark, sinister clouds, and you, my sweet, are looking as fresh as a fairy in a garden. It is your ability to go without sleep that surprises me."

She smiled. "I am in a state of bemusement, if you wish to know, but pay no heed to that. I've the answer that will permit us to marry at once, or at least as soon as we have her response. I am most sure she will say yes. So you see, I have every cause to appear most cheerful — despite the wolves baying at the moon."

His brow arched. "Well, I too am bemused. Who is this she?"

"Duchesse Dushane," she breathed jubilantly.

His gaze sharpened. "Ah! Madame wholly slipped my mind."

"As she did mine. I must have been too distraught to think of her at once. I had been left under Madame's supervision, but I never gave her a thought until I remembered we had sent my maid, Nenette, and also the boy Philippe to Duchesse Dushane at Fontainebleau."

His fingers tightened around her waist. "Your father left you in her supervision?"

"Yes, and she is at Fontainebleau."

"Then there is cause for the gleam in your eyes. When she understands the danger you are in, she will agree."

"She must."

"She knows me well. If she does not agree to the request, I will hound her until she does. I can have a man at Fontainebleau by morning." He took her face into his warm hands and tilted her lips to meet his.

"If I did not have concerns about leaving you here alone, even under the protection of Gallaudet and Julot, I would ride there myself this night, but—"

She clung to him. "No, I shall not permit us to be separated until the final ceremony is finished."

"I will not leave you. One of the men I trusted here at the estate, my captain of the guard, was bribed by Maurice to gain access to the castle. He escaped but an hour ago to take word to Maurice that we are here. Maurice is not at Fontainebleau. He is near at hand, and he is reckless enough to come here."

That Maurice would bribe one of Fabien's guards infuriated her.

"If he is not at Fontainebleau, then he could be here in Vendôme," she said uneasily. "He and his men-at-arms could be concealed among the peasants."

"I would have denied such an idea earlier this evening, believing in my serfs' loyalty, but I've already lost my captain of the guard to a few gold pieces. There may be more among the citizenry willing to conceal Maurice. I've sent some of my loyals into the villages to ask questions among the serfs, but I rather think he is at Amboise. If I knew where he was camped, I would call him out at once and be done with it."

She read the familiar resolute glint sparking in his eyes. "Maurice, too, will have men-at-arms, and he is as cold-blooded as a snake. He is very proud of his skills with his rapier."

"I know. He has long desired to best me with the blade."

"He is arrogant," she said, and hid a shiver at the thought that Maurice might be near at hand, much nearer than they had anticipated, and likely under cover. How dare Maurice cast his shadow over her marriage here at Vendôme to the one and only *galant* she would ever desire?

Fabien gazed at her with tenderness and stroked the side of her face.

"Have no care, ma belle. I have said I would not see us parted now, and I meant my words." His jaw hardened. "If Maurice comes, he will regret it. Come, I will write Madame. We will both sign our names. If she agrees, by tomorrow evening there will be no need to delay the wedding ceremony. I will make you mine before the journey to Dieppe."

And her heart's desire would come to pass. She would marry Marquis Fabien at Vendôme in the Bourbon castle where princes of the blood were married, and their sons and daughters born — and perhaps one day, even a king of France!

Her joy prompted feelings of courage, and she smiled her confidence at the man before her who would bring it to pass. Together they went to write the lettre that would forever change their lives.

Later that night, after the lettre was entrusted to Julot, Rachelle returned to her chamber. She took several steps to the side of the grand bed and knelt in earnest prayer, petitioning God for the sufficiency of His grace to uphold Fabien in what must surely be an ordeal to come.

Deliver us from the wicked traps set for us, O Lord, and bring us safely, in Your will and with Your blessing, to London.

❄

DUCHESSE DUSHANE HELD THE LETTRE from Marquis Fabien. Matters were most grave. If a trap had been set for him as he suggested, then Catherine would be aware that his ship had docked at Calais. Could she even know he had sent this lettre?

She tightened her fingers around the jeweled handle of her walking stick.

Is she making fools of us? She was watching me yesterday with that unblinking gaze of hers. Perhaps she realizes I have known of Sebastien's plan to escape with his family to London for weeks. And if she believes I have betrayed her —

The duchesse walked with slow, weakened gait to a tapestried chair and lowered herself, her breathing tight. She would have to be wise about the use of new herbal remedies. *Surely it is only suspicion on my part that convinces me I have become unnaturally tired recently.*

She remembered her recent meeting with Catherine and Cardinal de Lorraine. The muscles along her back tightened. They had turned against her with new vigor.

She was no weakling. If she were, she could not have remained alone at court these years while under scrutiny by the cardinal and the King of Spain's spy, Spanish ambassador Chantonnay. They had guessed her to be a secret Huguenot, but did not move against her. The blooded nobility escaped outright death by burning because of their titles; if death came early, however, it came mysteriously or by secret assassin. It was the middle class and serfs that were tortured openly and burned by the thousands. And so it was the duty of Huguenot nobles to try to defend them by appealing to the king for edicts of toleration. Even so, the cardinal set the edicts aside while the pope and the armies of Spain stood behind him.

She looked down at the marquis' lettre. What should she do about his request to marry Rachelle? She understood his quandary; she shared it.

"Maurice! That scoundrel." She banged the end of her ebony stick on the carpeted floor.

She must warn Marquis Fabien of the grave danger awaiting him, for the infamous Spanish war genius, the Duc of Alva, was coming to hold the Queen Mother's hands to the fires of Spain's wrath. Even Catherine, with all of her Machiavellian maneuverings, was not relentless enough in her warfare against the heretics to satisfy Spain. The Duc of Alva liked to bury Protestants alive in Holland, the women and children together for an added touch of tenderness. The duchesse relaxed her fingers. She'd been gripping her walking stick so tightly that pale impressions showed on her palm.

The Lord knows about poor, brave little Holland. I must remain calm and pray for the steadfast courage of the saints. What dedication to go to their deaths rather than deny the teaching of Scripture. What love they showed for Christ!

She pushed herself up from the chair and moved across the chamber to the window, still holding Marquis Fabien's lettre. She must think.

Below in the garden, two people were strolling. Her muscles tightened. Who could miss the white and scarlet cleric's garments and the stiff black gown and coif of the woman beside him? There they were, enemies at heart, with their heads together planning and plotting, perhaps discussing the impending arrival of the Duc of Alva.

She must contact the marquis and warn him. She would be taking a grave risk to send a message to him about the Duc of Alva. Who then, should deliver it?

Few, very few could be trusted.

The duchesse stepped away from the window. From behind her, the fire hissed in the hearth.

A footfall, or was it? The wind was boisterous this late afternoon. The duchesse turned her head in the direction of the alcove. Had one of her ladies returned?

"Who is it?" she called abruptly.

She walked in that direction but saw no one in the shadowy alcove. *My imagination is all.* Her gaze moved to the cabinet where her remedies were kept.

Yes, watch your medicine. Remember your cousine, Dame Joan Dushane, known as grandmère to her family. Remember how she was poisoned with gloves?

She walked back to the chair and sat down, rubbing her forehead. Perhaps she should leave Fontainebleau and take refuge at one of her estates near Saint-Germain-en-Laye.

Her gaze dropped back to the marquis' lettre. Sebastien Dangeau's neveu, Andelot, impressed her with his growing character and insight. Andelot . . . oui, he could be trusted. He had matured from the naive boy that Sebastien had called to court to meet his unanticipated kinsmen, the Guises. He was now a comely young man with wavy brown hair, winsome dark eyes, and an increasingly masculine appearance. He'd also become a scholar in training with knowledge of how politics and religion worked together, ofttimes in unholy union.

She went to her desk, lit the lamp, and wrote to Fabien of the danger confronting him and Rachelle, giving him a brief account of the troubling events at court since his voyage, knowing he would receive a fuller report through Andelot.

Perhaps ten minutes passed. She was ready to sign her name, but paused. She drummed her fingers on the desk. She must decide whether to give her consent to the marriage in the absence of Monsieur Arnaut. She hesitated, stood from the chair, and leaving the lettre on the desk, rang the bell for her chief page, Romier.

The young page, an *ami* of Andelot and about the same age, came at once.

"You called, Madame?"

"Find Andelot. Do not let anyone know you are seeking him or why. I need to speak alone with him. Tell him it is about Marquis Fabien and his oncle Comte Sebastien Dangeau. You have heard about Comte Sebastien and his family?"

"Oui, Madame. Everyone at court has been wondering how it was possible. He must have been most clever, they say."

"Desperate, perhaps. Go at once, Romier, and be exceedingly cautious."

"None shall see me, Madame."

The duchesse nodded her approval and watched him withdraw.

A CRITICAL TASK NOW compelled him. Andelot went to the window and peered below. The courtyard was bleak and mostly dark with only a few torches weaving in the chilly gusts. He turned away, lifting his olive green velvet beret from the footstool and arranging it to one side of his brown hair in customary style.

He opened the door of his bedchamber a crack to look into the large adjoining study-chamber. Scholar Thauvet always took his evening dinner at this time with friendly colleagues, and the chamber stood empty as Andelot expected. More than one lamp burned, and the manuscripts Thauvet was using were not yet stored away for the night, indicating he intended to return and work a few hours longer. Thauvet was in the long and tedious process of transcribing an ancient manuscript that would go to the library of Notre Dame when completed, and Andelot was assisting.

He turned back to his own chamber, shut the door softly, and lifted the mattress to remove the French Bible. He must be wary. He could not prove that he was under Père Jaymin's surveillance, but on more than one occasion he'd come within a breadth of getting caught with the forbidden Bible in his possession. Several times Andelot had noticed Jaymin's inquisitive eyes probing about the chamber.

He wrapped the treasured Bible in his cloak and carried it into the study-chamber where he removed several narrower volumes from a bookshelf at the far end. Placing the Bible at the back of the shelf, he replaced the books in front of it. They protruded slightly from the shelf edge but not enough to be noticeable. This concealment would do for now —

"I have caught you at last!"

He turned sharply at the footstep behind him.

A young monsieur stood there with jaw-length hair the color of amber, smoothly waved and turned under at the ends. His nose came to a peak and his chin was angular. He wore green satin with silver fripperies, but he'd had the wits to pocket his tinkling silver bells before sneaking up on him.

Andelot formed fists to keep from grasping Romier by the collar of his silver and green satin uniform and shaking him.

"*Saintes!* I should thump you until you rattle!"

"Still your tongue. Will you that someone hear us?" He looked toward the door to the outer corridor.

"At the moment? I do not care!"

"Tut, tut."

Though at first glance Romier appeared foppish, the duchesse kept him as her chief page because he was a swordsman, a marksman with a dagger, and he took pride in serving her.

"Madame wishes to speak to you in her chambers." Romier looked over to the bookshelf, hand on his sword hilt. "So, ami, you yet have it! You are certain it will go undiscovered?"

Andelot remained irritated. His heart was still pounding in his chest. He'd been convinced the voice was Jaymin's. He glared and snatched the olive green cloak he'd wrapped the Bible in.

"I shall return it — perhaps tonight."

"You should have disposed of it weeks ago as Comte Sebastien warned."

Andelot was well aware, but he had not wanted to part with it. "Never mind about that. If Madame wishes to see me I will go now. Most of the courtiers are at dinner."

"It is about the marquis and the comte — did you know Sebastien had made plans to escape?"

"Non, and there is no certainty he will make it to London. He is in danger at this very minute."

"So true. He took Mademoiselle Idelette with his family."

Romier threw him a questioning glance, but Andelot refused to catch it. He had never mentioned holding a muted interest in Mademoiselle Idelette to anyone, not even to himself until recently. There was a reason for his reluctance; at times she intimidated him with her maturity. She was theologically knowledgeable as well, and he was but a learner. Her superiority in these matters kept him at a distance. Secretly, he'd been attracted to her golden fairness and her calm, reserved demeanor.

Andelot opened the door to the outer corridor and glanced out. It was deserted. He stepped out, and Romier followed with the pompoms on his slippers bobbing — and one practiced hand on his sword hilt.

***

Père Jaymin stood in the shadows at the other end of the corridor watching Andelot Dangeau leave the scholar's chambers with Duchesse Dushane's page. Andelot was a young monsieur of bon character, but Jaymin did not trust his loyalties to the Church. He was most sure that Andelot wavered on the cliff's edge of heresy.

When Andelot was out of sight, Jaymin left the shadows and walked in long, soundless strides to Thauvet's chamber, opened the door, and stepped in.

He crossed the study and entered Andelot's chamber, going straight to the bed. He turned his mouth grimly. He bent down and lifted the straw mattress, holding a candle to look underneath. Nothing.

He must have hidden the forbidden book, the one I'm sure he was reading that night when Sebastien intervened, snatching the book away and asking questions about Erasmus. Andelot speaks ideas that sound like a Calvinist. He must have a heretical French Bible — not a true Latin translation. Ah, the devil was ubiquitous.

Jaymin dropped the mattress into place. He straightened, frowning.

Perhaps he has hidden it elsewhere. He may know I am suspicious.

I shall find it. If not tonight, then sometime when he is lulled into over-confidence. Andelot must be saved from himself. Like Sebastien, he must come to see the dangers of playing with heresy. In the end, the cleansing fire will burn away the dross of false beliefs and save him from Satan's stronghold, from that wicked city, Geneva, and its antichrist, John Calvin.

Jaymin took another look around, finding nothing to confirm his suspicions. He knew that Andelot attended all the religious ceremonies daily, as required, and behaved as piously as the rest—perhaps even more so.

Still, he makes me uncomfortable as only heretics do. It is as though I can smell them out.

Jaymin slipped out the door into the corridor and walked away in silence. *I will keep watching him. Eventually, he will give proof of his heresy.*

✦

ANDELOT WAS USHERED into the duchesse's chamber by Page Romier. She gestured with her jeweled walking stick toward a small chamber. Romier led them across the floral rug. Inside, there were brocade chairs in her colors of green and silver and some white stone tables. Andelot entered behind the duchesse, and Romier departed, drawing heavy emerald draperies closed.

The duchesse sat and motioned for him to sit opposite her. She held a lettre in hand. He noticed pronounced lines of concern around her eyes. Andelot felt a flash of anger. The cardinal and Queen Mother had upset and wearied her with their badgering questions about Sebastien's escape.

"I have unsettling news, Andelot."

"Yes, Madame. Cardinal de Lorraine has already spoken to me about Comte Sebastien."

There was a flicker of sympathy in her eyes. "I am aware that Sebastien's departure must sadden you."

"Indeed, Madame. Even so, I am not altogether disappointed after his suffering in the Bastille."

She nodded understanding. "And as a member of the Queen Mother's inner council, Sebastien was subject to her daily scrutiny. Now I am concerned because the roads are under watch, and traveling with two young women and a *bébé* makes him vulnerable."

"Unless they are in disguise."

"Even so, Andelot, if they went to Calais to catch a ship, spies will be abundant." She looked at him with thoughtful concern and lifted a lettre. "Marquis Fabien has returned to France and docked his ship in Calais."

Andelot felt a surge of enthusiasm. "Marquis Fabien in France?"

"He is. At Vendôme. And Mademoiselle Rachelle is with him."

Confused, he glanced at the lettre. "But I had been told, Madame, that from England he'd voyage on to Fort Caroline in Florida. He was most adamant in pursuing his plans to strike a blow to Spain."

"I had more in mind than Sebastien when I mentioned unsettling news. I am concerned about Marquis Fabien. The Duc of Alva is soon to arrive. It was his galleon, I believe, that the marquis sank. My own spies at court report that the Queen Mother has lured the marquis back to France with a plan involving Rachelle."

Andelot's dismay grew as the duchesse explained the Queen Mother's threat to marry Rachelle to Comte Maurice.

So that was why Fabien had not sailed to Florida. "But surely it will do the Queen Mother little good to turn the marquis over to Spain."

"She has another plan in mind. But while the Queen Mother may have had no wish in the beginning to relinquish him to Spain, the Duc of Alva will have other ideas. The marquis must be warned of this new danger."

"By all means, Madame! And the marquis and the mademoiselle are even now at his estate in Vendôme?"

"Yes. I received this a short time ago."

He took the lettre she handed to him and read.

Madame, with the Queen Mother's threat to marry Rachelle to my cousin Comte Maurice, it is wise that Rachelle find refuge in England. I have made plans to take her there, but the roads to Calais will be watched because of Sebastien's escape. Also, by now I have no doubt Catherine knows I am here at Vendôme with Rachelle. Our time is limited and any delays place Rachelle's future, and mine, in danger of ruin. Therefore, Madame, we have decided our love for one another is great enough to risk all in marriage. This is an urgent necessity to safeguard her from royal plots and to foil the comte in his selfish endeavors. Can you agree to this, and will you send your permission by lettre tout de suite?

Au revoir,

Marquis Jean-Louis Fabien de Vendôme of the house of Bourbon

It took Andelot a minute to look up from the correspondence to meet her gaze.

"It was always the marquis," he said. "I knew that. Mademoiselle Rachelle looked upon me as an ami, a cousin, Madame."

She nodded in silence.

"I have naught but respect for Marquis Fabien," she said. "But I should have more peace in this matter of marriage if Pasteur Bertrand were here. He knows the marquis, as you do, Andelot. What is your opinion of his faith in the crucial doctrines of Christianity?"

Andelot hesitated, realizing his answer could influence the outcome of Fabien's marriage.

"Madame, I met Marquis Fabien for the first time at the Louvre when he was sixteen. He came to my aid then and always has. As you know, it is he who privately arranged for my schooling with Scholar Thauvet. I owe him my loyalty — "

"Ah, yes, of course, it is unfair of me to ask such a question now."

"But, Madame, what I will say now is based not on loyalty, nor even my affection for him, but the truth as I see it. My perception is, and always has been, that he is a secret Huguenot."

She drew back, her brows lifting. "A Huguenot? The marquis?"

"I have no doubts about his honor, or his belief in Christ. Even at Amboise, before I ever read the Bible, Marquis Fabien spoke in depth about the doctrines that prompted the Reformation. My perception was that he had a good understanding of them and of the need for revival in the church and a debate over doctrines accepted as divine, which are not in the Scriptures. He fully supports the need for the upcoming colloquy between Catholics and Protestants at Poissy."

"Monsieur Arnaut and Madame Clair have serious concerns about his faith, but I am pleased you feel otherwise, Andelot. You know Marquis Fabien better than any of us. I too feel confident he is a firm Christian, as I have known him at court since he was a young boy attending school with the royal children."

She frowned thoughtfully, drumming her fingers on her knee. "In these circumstances I am granting my permission for their marriage in the absence of Monsieur Arnaut and Madame Clair."

"That is well, Madame." *And even if you did not give your permission, Fabien would marry her anyway.* He held back a wry smile.

It was late when Duchesse Dushane sat at her table to write a message to Scholar Thauvet, explaining how she must borrow Andelot for a few days and requesting that he make an excuse to Père Jaymin for Andelot's absence. Andelot was impressed that she had confidence in Thauvet, which added weight to his belief that he could be a secret reformer.

"I told him I will explain all when he comes to have dinner with me tomorrow," she said. There was another lettre on the desk, and she drew it toward her and signed her name. "And this one is to be delivered to Marquis Fabien."

The duchesse pushed her chair back and stood. "Can you slip away without being noticed?"

"I shall manage, Madame. I must go back to my chamber first. There is something I need to return on my way to Marquis Fabien."

"How seasoned a horseman are you?"

"I count myself better than most. I—er, won a race on Marquis Fabien's golden bay."

"Then my confidence is well placed."

She handed Andelot the sealed envelope for delivery to Fabien and the folded message for Scholar Thauvet.

"I need not tell you to let no one know what you are about, Andelot."

"God willing, Madame, I shall accomplish this task."

"Bon. Here are your instructions. Follow them and you will come to a certain cottage, deliver this message to the elder monsieur who lives there."

Andelot took the message from her hand, along with the lettre to Marquis Fabien, and put them inside his tunic.

"One thing more, Madame, if I may. Mademoiselle Rachelle's sister also went with Comte Sebastien to England . . ."

"Mademoiselle Idelette? Yes, she went with them."

"I cannot imagine any reason that would prompt her to give up her life's work in silk at Lyon to live in Spitalfields," Andelot said. "She gave me her reasons in a lettre, but I admit they did not satisfy me. I thought you, Madame, might know."

She heaved a burdened sigh. "So Idelette wrote you, did she?"

"We had begun to exchange lettres a few months ago when she was at the Château de Silk."

"I see . . . I was not aware. Ah, then, that adds to the present tragedy."

Andelot looked at her, wondering. "Tragedy?"

"The tragedy surrounding Mademoiselle Idelette has prompted her decision to risk going to England. Even I did not know about the situation. I wish she had confided in me. I might have sent her to Queen Jeanne of Navarre who has open arms for young women disowned by their families for becoming Calvinists, and though Idelette's situation is very different, Queen Jeanne could have assisted her."

Andelot grew tenser by the moment. So much was happening of which he'd not been informed. "What has happened to Mademoiselle Idelette? You speak of a tragedy?"

"It is well that you know. I realize now that you have strong feelings for both Rachelle and Idelette. The incident took place during the church burning in Lyon. Avril Macquinet, their petite sister, as you know, was killed, but what we did not know, was that Idelette — well, I shall be blunt — was violated. She is expecting a child."

Andelot stood in stunned silence. What! Idelette? The lovely, pious Idelette, whom he secretly felt was far above him on a pedestal, was now expecting a child. That she should endure such a thing kindled his rage. "Madame, if I knew who committed this outrage against her, I myself would hunt him down."

"Mon cher, sit down," she said gently. "That you are outraged at the dishonor done to her pleases me, and I know it would please her if she knew, but the soldier who did this is most likely dead."

He looked at her in doubt, thinking she was appeasing him. "A soldier in Duc de Guise's men-at-arms?"

"Yes. There was an incident soon after the church burning that took place at an inn near the Château de Silk, in which the marquis and his chief page encountered two soldiers boasting of the church burning. I do not know the details, but the lettre from Rachelle tells me a swordfight ensued and the soldier was killed."

Expecting a child . . . Idelette. How alone she must feel in this, angry, afraid, helpless —

He came aware that the duchesse watched him curiously. He pulled his emotions together and bowed.

"Adieu, Madame."

"Yes, and godspeed, Andelot."

A SHORT TIME LATER, Andelot slipped back into the study-chamber, shutting the heavy wooden door in silence. He went straight to his sleeping chamber and stood still for a minute while mixed emotions filled his mind. That she would love the marquis and marry him was inevitable. *I knew it would happen.* He had not lost Rachelle. She was never his to lose, he told himself again firmly.

And Idelette . . . He shook his head with anger and grief and sat down on his bunk, head lowered for some time thinking and praying for her. What would happen to Idelette?

Some minutes later, after praying about his troubles and disappointments, he got up and went into the study-chamber again, glancing about for Scholar Thauvet. He was still out.

Andelot looked around the chamber until his gaze moved to the wall of books. He froze as he saw the volumes that protruded a little, hinting at his hiding place. He should have been more careful!

He swiftly removed the volumes and reached behind to retrieve the

Bible. His fingers closed about the leather binding. He drew it down, stuffing it under his tunic.

He peered over his shoulder. The fire had burned low, with glowing embers on the grate projecting moving forms on the far walls where large comfortable reading chairs were grouped.

Was he mistaken? Andelot squinted to see if he could make out Thauvet's form, seated with graying beard, a book on his lap.

He called out in the dimness, "*Maître* Thauvet? Is that you?"

There was no answer.

It must be these shadows — weaved by sinister forces. And Romier and his antics!

He stepped back and went quickly to his sleeping chamber and packed his satchel. He took one last look about. He left the chamber as he had anticipated, unseen by probing eyes.

❄

It MUST HAVE BEEN after midnight when Andelot departed from Fontainebleau with assistance from one of the duchesse's friends in the royal guards and Page Romier.

"So you will not have me come with you?" Romier whispered, scowling beneath his pointed hat, the tassel swinging in the breeze.

"Non, mon ami, but I will have much to tell you when I return."

Romier's scowl deepened. "And I, your loyal ami. Why do I not come with you? Madame will gladly release me if you request I ride with you."

"I must go alone. Madame needs you here. She too is at risk."

Romier did not look entirely appeased, but he nodded at the mention of caring for the duchesse. They walked with the guard through the dark courtyard to one of the tributary postern gates.

"Farewell." Andelot lifted a hand and slipped through the gate into the dark night. The golden bay had been quietly brought from the stables and was tied in the trees, waiting.

Andelot mounted Marquis Fabien's horse and rode off into the night, alert to avoid notice by guards and soldiers on patrol.

ANDELOT RODE THE GOLDEN BAY beneath the canopy of silvery light from the full moon that sat like a pearl gracing the dark sky. He rode deeper into the woods around Fontainebleau, following the duchesse's instructions. After a short time he came upon a small log cottage. There, he dismounted and went to the door and knocked with the rapping code the duchesse had given him.

A moment later the door opened, and he was ushered in by a dignified gray-haired man wearing dark, somber clothing. Andelot handed him the lettre from the duchesse. The elderly monsieur read it in silence before his hearth. Andelot recognized a look of pleasure, and even amusement, as the man's mouth turned up at the corners and he raised his eyes to look more keenly at Andelot. He nodded to himself and beckoned Andelot to follow him into the small cooking room.

He was given food to last him the journey and a change of clothes. Andelot put on the rough peasant's clothing, and the student of the famous Thauvet became Andelot the serf. The elder smiled at him. "I am the pasteur you rescued that day when the Dominican caught us in the woods near here. Duchesse Dushane tells me you have embraced the redemptive work of Jesus Christ, the Son of God."

Andelot, surprised, remained speechless for a moment, then broke into a smile. "Monsieur, it is you! And to think I expected to leave here and replace the Bible where you hid it under the old log. The Lord has many pleasant surprises for us. Ah, Pasteur, I owe you much — for being able to read the Scriptures in my native French."

"And I owe you much, Andelot. Your courage that day with the angry cleric has spared my earthly life that I may continue to serve God. I assure you, young messire, that whenever you wish to come to read this Book you will be most welcome. There is much we can discuss concerning the Word of God. We must, as the apostle Paul has written, "rightly divide the Word of truth.""

"*Merci*, mon pasteur. I will surely call upon you when I return. But I ask how you knew about me?"

"Duchesse Dushane spoke of you in this lettre. She has sent messages before. I always burn them, for one never knows if the messenger has been followed."

"Indeed, Pasteur."

Followed . . . Andelot glanced uneasily toward the cottage door. The wind rattled the windows. He could imagine the broad face of Père Jaymin suddenly appearing.

"I know Madame well, though from afar," the pasteur said. "She is a firm Huguenot, even as we. She has granted us much assistance and also sends warnings when we may be in more than usual danger."

Andelot nodded. "The duchesse, oui—but how did she know I had your Bible? I told no one except mon oncle, and I would not have told him except he came upon me reading it." Andelot told him of the time when he'd nearly been caught reading the Bible and how Sebastien had come to his aid at the precise moment to save him from discovery.

"Madame mentioned that Comte Sebastien had told her of your experience with the Bible. He was concerned for your safety, you see. She mentions that he has escaped with his family. May the Lord grant them a successful voyage to England."

After they had discussed Sebastien's escape for a few minutes, Andelot went on to tell him about the upcoming religious colloquy to be held at the Monastery of Poissy, near Saint-Germain-en-Laye.

"Perhaps I can slip away and come here to give you the news of what is occurring," said Andelot.

"The debates over Scripture and the decisions made there will be of utmost concern, I assure you. Any news you can bring and share will be received gladly. I am told Monsieur Beza himself will speak for the way of grace alone, proving it from the Word."

Theodore Beza was the primary Huguenot theologian for France and was a close associate of Monsieur John Calvin.

"Yes, and Monsieur Calvin will also send twelve theologians from the school in Geneva. They will bring many writings from the early church fathers and copies of the originals to debate doctrine."

"We will surely pray that the minds and hearts of those in authority will be opened by the Spirit to receive God's unchanging truth. How wondrous it would be if our beloved France were shaken to its foundations with the light of God's timeless Word. Oh, to cast aside the mere outward display of religion that leaves our hearts unchanged!"

Andelot set aside his reservation and threw an arm of brotherly affection around the older man.

"My prayers will follow you wherever you go," the pasteur said.

The pasteur then bowed his head, speaking Andelot's name in prayer, and committed him to Christ. The experience of hearing a pasteur pray for him personally in an audible voice was altogether new, and his heart was stirred.

A few minutes later, with the pasteur accompanying him, he walked back to his horse and mounted in silence. *I will come back for a longer visit.* He lifted his hand in salute, and rode on toward Vendôme.

❊

IN A BUNGALOW NEAR VENDÔME, Comte Maurice Beauvilliers fixed a withering stare on his page.

"You are most certain of this news?"

"Monseigneur, the spy discovered it from one of the duchesse's own servants. He has ridden through the night to arrive ahead of Andelot Dangeau."

"Send me this spy. I would hear it from him."

"He is unconscious, my lord Comte, deep in sleep—"

Maurice set his goblet down with a snap. "Tell me the news again."

"Andelot was summoned to visit Duchesse Dushane. What was discussed could not be overheard, but it was about your oncle, Comte Sebastien, and Marquis Fabien. Andelot was sent with a lettre from Madame for the marquis."

Maurice raised a lean, tanned hand and smoothed his ebony mustache; the long folds of crème lace at his wrist fell leisurely over the burgundy sleeve.

"No doubt the titled fox has protested my engagement to Rachelle. I'll wager she has sent a reply saying she knows nothing of our upcoming marriage."

"It would seem so, my lord Comte."

Maurice's heart began to pound like a battle drum. "Andelot must not deliver that lettre."

"Men are stationed along the road to watch for him."

I must have that lettre. In the hands of the Queen Mother it will become a millstone around Fabien's neck. And Andelot! That serf that deigns to call me cousin. The intolerable impudence — and after spilling wine on my silk doublet in Oncle Sebastien's appartement! I warned Andelot I would not forget, and I keep my word. Now he will pay for my insulted honor and ruined silk shirt.

"Saddle the horses. We will ride forth to meet him. I will deal with Andelot myself."

"By now he should be nearing Vendôme. As soon as he is in sight, word will be sent."

"I will be waiting."

News from a Far Country

M ARQUIS F ABIEN , RESTIVE , MOVED ABOUT THE LARGE SALLE THAT con- nected to his sleeping chamber. He stepped onto the balustrade and swept a glance about the courtyard. A lavender haze settled gently across the horizon of the forest, and evening shadows lengthened.

He looked toward the tower turret. One of his watchmen stood gaz- ing toward the road and bridge. Farther down the road, settled out of sight within the thick forest trees, he knew there would be another sentry keeping vigil, followed by more guards on patrol ready to send their sig- nal back to the castle should enemies approach.

Mille diables, but matters are progressing slowly!

He drummed his fingers on the rail and narrowed his gaze, looking toward the ominous road to Fontainebleau. Shadows crept forward. The trees rustled. With each passing hour spent waiting for the lettre from Madame, more opportunity was granted his opponents.

His ventures as a privateer for England would pursue his steps, but the danger stewing in the political and religious cauldron of France was due to far more than his escapades for Holland. Persecution of the Huguenot middle class would result in their seigneurs calling for war to protect them. *Noblesse oblige!* He too had an obligation to the citizens of Vendôme. Leaving France for England when a civil war was about to break did not rest easy on his conscience, but he could not relinquish Rachelle.

Below, he saw Gallaudet coming across the courtyard from the direction of the gate. Earlier, Fabien had sent him to check on the men-at-arms watching the road. He was waiting for the report when Gallaudet arrived, solemn-faced.

"You have news?"

"Dark news, Marquis. Until an hour ago only serfs and a few monks had traversed the road."

"And now? Is there sight of that jackal, Maurice?"

"Non, but the dwarves of the Queen Mother are coming."

❦

Outside in the passage, Rachelle knocked on the door to Fabien's chambers.

She heard footsteps. A moment later Gallaudet opened, as fair of countenance and hair as the paintings of angels she remembered from the Louvre. "Mademoiselle," he acknowledged with a small bow, opening the door wider. "One moment, *sil vous plaît*." Gallaudet turned his head and spoke. "Mademoiselle Macquinet wishes to see you, Marquis."

Fabien came to the doorway, his violet-blue gaze taking her in with his disarming smile. She had not seen him since last evening's dinner, and his expression at seeing her brought her happiness. He wore a white Holland shirt open at the neck and dark breeches.

"Come inside, ma chère. Your presence invigorates my chamber like the fragrance of a jasmine garden on a warm day."

Gallaudet cleared his throat as though the marquis had forgotten he was there, but Fabien seemed to enjoy his reaction.

She smiled and brushed inside with a rustle of green skirt and found herself in his private sitting chamber. It was handsomely furnished in masculine shades of earthy browns and forest greens. A calm mood pervaded the chamber, but even so she gathered that he and all his men were aware of the increasing peril of delay.

He took her hand and pressed a warm kiss on her wrist. "What do you think, Gallaudet? Will she not make the most belle marquise?"

"Assuredly, Monseigneur, though Maurice is convinced she will be the most belle *comtesse*."

"Maurice will feel the thrust of my rapier through his gizzard if he tries."

A horn sounded in the distance, and Rachelle turned swiftly and faced Fabien.

"No cause to be alarmed yet, ma chère. That is the caution signal. Visitors approach with the knowledge of the guards," he said calmly. "If it were a contingent of soldiers, they would have sounded a warning."

Fabien turned to shoulder, into a splendid jacket that matched the color of his eyes as Gallaudet held it for him. The hounds were barking below in the courtyard. Rachelle rushed to the balustrade and looked below, but saw nothing of visitors, only lackeys and guards running toward the gate. Another horn sounded. She glanced at Fabien over her shoulder to see his reaction. She caught an exchange of glances between him and his page that did not bring her comfort. A galloping horse on the short ascent from the road was soon heard approaching the inner yard.

Fabien moved quickly onto the balustrade beside her, Gallaudet with him.

"There are two visitors," Rachelle said. Her heart pounded when she caught sight of them. One black horse with two riders as small as children. "The Queen Mother's dwarves," she whispered. The sight sent a shudder along her nerves.

The twosome left the horse with the hostlers and marched resolutely in quick, short steps toward the court entrance, with their black capes over crimson waistcoats fluttering like bat wings in the wind.

"Romulus and Remus, the twins," Fabien said wearily.

The dwarves raised their heads in unison and looked up toward the balustrade.

"Go down to meet them. Find out what treachery they bring," Fabien said to Gallaudet.

When he'd gone, Rachelle flung her hand to her forehead and paced.

Fabien snatched up his scabbard. "I should never have remained here waiting for the lettre from Madame. I knew I should have ridden out this morning! Even my men-at-arms are restless. I am playing right into her trap."

Rachelle rushed to him, gripping him desperately. "Non, you did the honorable thing to write to Madame." Even so, she felt a dart of guilt.

She was the cause of their delay. Had it not been for her, they would be on their way to Dieppe to rendezvous with Capitaine Nappier.

His arms tightened around her. "Honorable? Perhaps, but she's had time to arrange her traps. If nothing more, I should have sent you ahead with Gallaudet until I knew what the duchesse would say."

"Non, I would not go without you."

He smiled, but there was a flash of steel in the blue gaze. "You will, and must, do what I tell you."

"Perhaps I should return with the dwarves. I will face her and convince her that I cannot marry Maurice. You go on to Dieppe with your men. Perhaps I will soon be able to slip away."

His mouth tipped with a cynically amused smile. "That would be nearly impossible, ma belle. I would kill if need be before allowing you to be taken captive."

She stared at him. The hard glitter in his intense gaze convinced her. "Fabien, mon amour, do not even say it."

"Rachelle, you do not understand. The Duc of Alva is at Fontainebleau, his blood boiling to take me in chains to Spain for sinking his galleon. The Queen Mother has her plans, and Maurice his. And my plans oppose all three of them."

"You should not have come for me," she cried. "Your life is in danger now because of me!"

His eyes narrowed. "I came for what I wanted, and I expect to have you in marriage." He loosened his hold on her. "The dwarves have seen you, so we will bluff them with our boldness and portray cooperation. It will confuse them, and give us more time."

"They turn me cold. I am sure one of them entered Grandmère Dushane's bedchamber when she lay dying and removed the poisonous gloves."

"Yes, the gloves ... another of Catherine's distinctive ploys."

"Then you, at least, believe as I, that she did it?"

"I know what her royal ambition is capable of, and that sort of poisoning is typical of her past tactics."

"After Grandmère's death I sought for the gloves in the Louvre appartement and could not find them, yet the ladies-in-waiting said she'd left them on her bureau after returning from shopping. Only later did one of them tell me she saw "a small ghost" coming out of Grandmère's bedchamber late one night after her illness deepened. It must have been one of the dwarves; she described him perfectly."

"I am not surprised, chérie. The Queen Mother must have instructed one of them to remove the evidence. They rival only Madalenna in doing her bidding. The motive for your grandmère's death remains a mystery, but I suspect the Queen Mother discovered that you had entered her private chamber, taken the key to the listening closet, and passed it to me. While she spies on others, she cannot endure the thought of someone spying on her. I think your grandmère and Madeleine were simply part of her long, vengeful reach."

"And yet the red gift box she gave me was the only one that did not contain poisoned gloves."

"So Andelot told me. It held a pearl pendant. You wore it several times and it did not affect you. You may have received a straightforward gift because some different plan formed in her mind, convincing her that she would have need of you. Now that I've guessed her desire to use me to rid her of Duc de Guise, I think we may settle upon why she wanted you alive. Why she at this moment continues to take an interest in you."

She clutched at his sleeve. "This is my opportunity to ask the dwarves about the gloves."

"It is not wise. Nor will it serve your purpose. They will report every word you speak back to the Queen Mother. It is enough Madalenna saw you follow Catherine to the Ruggerio Brothers' shop on the quay."

"But surely the Queen Mother must already suspect I know about Grandmère."

"*Précisément.* And if she suspects your motive for following her to the quay, questioning her dwarves about the gloves will reinforce her resentment. For your own sake it is best you say nothing."

"Why doesn't she realize I have no power to harm her, while she can do anything she wishes?"

"Catherine cannot do anything she wishes, chérie. You must understand. It is true that she sits as Queen Mother and you cannot harm her. She has power, but she is no longer the queen of France. Her son Francis is king, but Duc de Guise has great influence over Francis, and is also more powerful than she."

"Duc de Guise!"

"Yes, the house of Guise. The duc has Rome and Spain behind him, as well as an army of mercenaries should he need to fight a religious civil war. The silver and gold Spain takes from the Americas on her treasure galleons pays for Spain's armies. Both the pope and King Philip would like to have Catherine put aside entirely in order to place a Guise on the throne. A Guise could then move against the heretics once and for all."

"But she is no amie of the Huguenots! Remember Amboise? Two thousand men and nobles beheaded at her order—"

"And the Cardinal de Lorraine's order. She did so because *she* was threatened. The Huguenots wished to place her under palais arrest along with the Guises, and make my kinsman the prince become regent of young King Francis. Of course she is no amie of the Huguenots or the house of Bourbon. Catherine is on the side of the strongest force in France who will support her while avoiding civil war. Presently she needs the Huguenot nobles to oppose the house of Guise and keep some power. But she is one faux pas away from slipping—and she knows it, so she maintains a grasp on power through secret manipulations, schemes, and murder."

Rachelle shivered. "You seem to know her well."

"I have watched her at court for years. I was there when the dauphin died, some say of poison, allowing her husband, Henry, to come to the throne. From what I remember of her while growing up, she tries to spin her webs in the shadows, unnoticed. She trusts few and is wary of anyone disclosing her Machiavellian schemes. She lives for the day when her precious Anjou becomes king, yet she knows she is disliked by the people of France. The Guises control her son King Francis, and that likely keeps her awake at night, worrying and planning as she fears losing power. That is why she wants Guise dead. He is the one leader in France who could rally the people against her. She also fears that if word begins to circulate that she has used poison again and the Ruggerio brothers are named as accomplices, they could go to the Bastille, and under torture, they would implicate her."

"You mean no one knows about the Ruggerio brothers?"

"Very few. Why do you think she masquerades when she visits them on the quay, and uses secret stairways and listening closets? She does not want the Guises to talk about her use of poison in their appeals to the King of Spain. You do not want to become a goad to Catherine, chérie. It is as dangerous as cornering a viper."

She remembered that Père Arnaut had given her much the same advice in Paris.

She leaned her cheek against his chest and held him tightly. In the moment of silence he stroked her hair and held her close. Then he lifted her face toward his and kissed her.

"We must go down now," he said quietly, his voice offering confidence. "Are you ready?"

She gave a nod. A few moments later, with dignity, Rachelle went down the steps at Fabien's side and entered the receiving salle. The two Florentine dwarves donned in costly garb with diamonds on their doublets bowed low to Fabien. They straightened, their black curls bouncing, their ebony eyes bright and cunning beneath heavy brows.

Rachelle found it difficult to tell the twins apart, except that Romulus always smiled, though his eyes held no humor.

Fabien left her on the landing and stepped forward. Romulus bowed again, then approached. In full height, he came just above Fabien's knees.

"Bonjour Monseigneur de Vendôme," came his tenor voice. "We have traveled from Fontainebleau with a message for you from Her Majesty, the Queen Mother. Do you wonder how we knew you were here?"

Rachelle tightened her hand on the banister. She glanced at Fabien and saw that his manner was reserved.

"We have bonne amity with the crows," Remus said.

Rachelle could see he was serious. She felt a chill, remembering the credence paid to the occult and astrology charts made for the Queen Mother.

"Yes, as soon as I was outside of Paris, I did notice the crows kept pace with me," Fabien said.

Only those who knew Fabien as well as she could have read the sarcasm in his response.

"Did you come alone — except for the crows?" he asked.

"We came alone, Monseigneur. Your men-at-arms on the road will tell you so. On the other hand, you did not come here alone."

Rachelle kept her dignity.

Fabien gave him a stern look. "What message do you bring me from the Queen Mother?"

Romulus extended an envelope sealed impressively with the royal fleur-de-lis.

"Her Majesty wishes an answer be returned by our hand, and so we will wait for it, if Monseigneur permits."

Fabien walked away and used a jeweled knife to open the sealed envelope, turning to watch them as he did. He would not be rushed into a response, this Rachelle knew.

She remained where she was, her palms perspiring. She noted the dwarves wore ceremonial swords the size a young page boy would carry and guessed they were poor swordsmen but probably deadly marksman with daggers. She did not think the Queen Mother wanted Fabien dead, however — at least not yet.

Fabien walked over to Rachelle and with lazy grace, leaned against the banister and read the Queen Mother's lettre aloud to her.

"I have received news from my daughter Elizabeth, Queen of Spain, that His most Catholic Majesty, King Philip II, is aggrieved by certain actions taken off the coast of the Spanish Netherlands by certain French pirates united in purpose and religion with the Dutch. You in particular, Marquis de Vendôme, have been implicated as one of those adventurous sea wolves. I am most certain this outrageous charge laid against you by the esteemed Duc de Alva, who is here to see the king, will prove to be in error. We need to discuss this grave matter firsthand. It therefore becomes imperative that we meet at Fontainebleau, which will likewise afford you the opportunity to clarify your reasons for having taken the belle couturière, Mademoiselle Rachelle Macquinet, from her duties in Paris. I assure you, my lord Marquis, that both of you will be treated as family upon your return to court. Fear not; bring mademoiselle and brighten our lives with your appearances. I am certain this misunderstanding with the Comte Beauvilliers can be settled in peace. Also, Princesse Marguerite longs for her favorite lady and for newly crafted gowns to meet your friend Prince Henry of Navarre at the Poissy Colloquy this coming summer.

"Understand that this summons is for you and the mademoiselle to appear before me. Your presence is most assuredly required."

Fabien lowered the lettre and slowly folded it, meeting her gaze. She read the meaning of the hard glitter in his eyes. The Queen Mother's ruse did not deceive him. He looked across the salle at the dwarves.

It was just as Fabien had warned her. The Duc of Alva was at Fontainebleau and the Guises would like nothing better than to turn Fabien over to Spain. But would the Queen Mother agree to this if she needed him?

The chilling answer was no — on the condition he did as she demanded.

"You may tell Her Majesty that as her most loyal servant — " Fabien bowed — "I await with anticipation the meeting to be held with her at her discretion."

"Then you will come to the private château near Fontainebleau, and bring Mademoiselle Macquinet, Monseigneur?"

"Would I disregard a summons by Her Majesty?"

Rachelle recognized Fabien's evasive question, though it appeared the messengers did not.

"Surely not, Monseigneur de Vendôme," their tenor voices echoed.

"Surely not," he said in a scolding tone. "Therefore, monsieurs, until the day and hour proffered by Her Majesty, I bid you adieu."

The dwarves bowed to Fabien. "Merci, Monseigneur. We will wait, however, to deliver your lettre of response to Her Majesty."

"Ah yes, *bien sûr* ... I shall have my response written and delivered to you in the morning."

They exchanged glances. "In the morning, Monseigneur?"

A delay, Rachelle thought.

"I would not think of sending you back tonight," Fabien told them. "Your ride was very long, you are most assuredly tired and hungry. Your fine horse must rest and eat its fill of oats. And I should word my response to Her Majesty with utmost care and respect."

Gallaudet had entered the receiving salle and eyed the dwarves warily. Fabien turned toward him. "See that the Queen Mother's messengers are given refreshment and rest before they ride back to Fontainebleau in the morning."

"Just so, Monseigneur." Gallaudet spread a hand toward the outer passage. "This way, sil vous plaît."

Rachelle narrowed her gaze as she watched them marching toward the outer passage with Gallaudet. As she looked at the determined set of Fabien's handsome features, she took solace in knowing he would do all that was possible. Her admiration grew. She was blessed to possess the love and devotion of such a man.

When the dwarves had gone with Gallaudet, Fabien turned to her.

"It is as I expected. We will carry through with the plan to reach Dieppe. My response to the Queen Mother by lettre will give us another day to hear from the duchesse."

She pondered the not-so-subtle statements in the Queen Mother's summons and felt the muscles at the back of her neck tighten into knots.

Put to the Test

THE MOON WAS SETTING BEYOND THE HILLS OF THE FONTAINEBLEAU FOREST, and Andelot was well on his way southwest toward Vendôme.

After long hours of riding, he felt the need for rest and refreshment for himself and the golden bay. He drew the horse to a slower trot until he came to what he could make out as a hollow. He drew the reins, bringing the horse to a full stop, and listened above the soughing wind.

Below in the hollow, he could hear water cascading, which should mean a stream and tall tender grasses for his horse. The golden bay snorted restlessly in that direction. Andelot patted the horse's neck.

"You smell your supper? Come, let us make use of the Lord's provisions."

He edged the horse forward off the road onto a narrow path and rode toward the hollow. The song of the stream and the wind in the trees mingled in a duet that grew in intensity. After a minute the water was in view, a dark opal in the starlight. The large stand of trees he took for fir. He swung to the ground and stretched, then walked the horse to the streambed and prepared a long tether where the grasses and water were easily reached. He loosened the saddle and took time to rub him down with some dry grasses.

The golden bay snorted and rolled an eye at him.

"By tomorrow afternoon, ami, we shall be taking our rest with your true master. You will have your fair oats, and I shall have my hot bread and maybe a leg or two of fat goose. And if you behave, I will have some apples sent out to you in secret."

The horse stomped and shook its lustrous mane.

Andelot removed his cup from the saddlebag and went to the lively stream. He stooped to dip and drink, then spread a blanket under a tree. As he stretched out, hands interlocked behind his head, he shut his weary eyes and wondered if Marquis Fabien knew the Duc of Alva was at Fontainebleau. He must. There were many worrisome happenings to warn the marquis of when he saw him tomorrow.

Soon, lulled by the sighing wind and sound of water splashing over stones, his concerns ebbed as his tired mind gave way to sleep.

The uneasy whinny of the horse dragged him from slumber. He squinted toward the sun, now climbing in the sky. He looked toward the horse. Was it pulling at its tether? It was pawing the turf with one of its hooves.

Andelot scrambled to his feet and shook out his blanket. There was no time to waste. He must set off at once. The crunch of footsteps caused him to turn swiftly.

A half-circle of men-at-arms wearing the colors of the Comte Maurice Beauvilliers surrounded him. Andelot recognized the leering, hawkish faces of the comte's lead men. Then he saw Maurice.

"Cousin Maurice!" he said in genuine surprise.

"How many times have I told you not to call me cousin?"

Andelot offered a stiff nod of his head. "As you wish, Comte Beauvilliers."

"I tell you, Andelot, you will pay for your treachery to me."

"Treachery!" Andelot pushed his hair back from his forehead.

"Where is the lettre from the duchesse that you carry to the marquis? Hand it over and I will spare your life at least. For I have no longing to see you dead and buried."

He knew. How? "A lettre from Madame?"

"Do not play the game with me. It is the will of the king that Rachelle become my comtesse. He will not fault me for confronting the marquis for abducting her."

"It is you, Comte, who has connived to abduct the mademoiselle and force an unwanted marriage."

"So you persistently defend him. So be it. A sword!" he called to his men. He looked toward Andelot. "Do you suppose I have forgotten how you deliberately spilled wine on my white silk shirt in Oncle Sebastien's appartement? I told you then to learn the blade, did I not? I gave you ample warning. And now! You will cross swords with me, I demand it on behalf of my honneur."

"Your pride, Comte, exceeds the famed peacock, I vow it."

One of Maurice's men whipped out his rapier and offered it to Andelot with a mocking bow.

"If you know how to hold it."

Andelot glared. "I know how to hold it. And I do not need your sword. I have one of my own."

Ignoring hoots of laughter, he went to his baggage and took up his scabbard and buckled it on.

"When Marquis Fabien hears of this, you will pay profoundly, mon Comte."

"He will have his own woes, I assure you."

"If you kill me, he will see that you pay with your own life, of that I am certain."

Maurice whipped out his rapier and held it menacingly.

"The lettre from Duchesse Dushane, where is it? Hand it over, Andelot."

"You will not have it."

Maurice lunged, and before Andelot could bring up his blade, Maurice's rapier had darted off his hat. The move startled Andelot, and Maurice smiled.

"Come, mon petit. I shall teach you a few things about fighting with the blade."

Andelot attempted to parry and thrust as Maurice came after him on light, dancing feet. He moved about Andelot flicking his shirt, his sleeve, his belt, toying with him as a cat with a captured mouse.

Andelot, humiliated, became more clumsy amid laughter from the men-at-arms. In a quick parry of whiplike blades, Maurice struck Andelot's wrist with a sting that slackened his grip and sent Andelot's sword tumbling to the ground.

"Come, come," Maurice taunted with a wearied tone. "Can you not do better than this? A bon ami of Marquis de Vendôme? I would think such a famed corsair able to sink the Duc of Alva's galleon would at least have taught you how to hold your blade."

Andelot angrily snatched up his sword again and swung it. Maurice paused for an opening as Andelot's blade passed, and he was on Andelot in a flash, the point of his rapier at the page's jugular.

"I have you, Andelot."

Andelot's throat felt the threatening point. Sweat dribbled down his neck and his heart thudded painfully.

A poignant silence held them all; a gust of wind rustled the leaves in the branches above them.

"The lettre!"

Andelot gritted his teeth, but kept silent.

"Search him." Maurice lifted his rapier, stepping back. "And his baggage."

As two men laid hold of him, Andelot fought to free himself, landing a few good punches in his favor until a blow from a big fellow with a curling beard jarred his teeth and sent him reeling backward. Then the bearded giant held him down while two others searched him.

"Ho, you gargoyles! What need to destroy my garments — "

One of them was using a long knife to rip through his tunic. In a moment he'd found the sealed lettre.

"I've got it, my lord Comte."

"What shall we do with him now?" the other fellow asked.

"Look, there is a tree limb strong enough to hang him, Comte," one of the men said.

Maurice sheathed his blade. "He is fit for naught but books and running errands for the marquis. I will spare him to go to his master, but he should be shorn of his locks and breeches. Cut off his hose, well above his knees."

Andelot smarted under their laughter. He fought, but it was hopeless against so many. When they had finished with their sport, he was left with scant to cover his legs, and his brown locks were scattered on the ground around his bare feet.

"This, Andelot, is your reward for the wine on my silk shirt." And with the sealed lettre in hand, Maurice turned his back, swaggered over to his horse, and mounted.

With grins on their faces, his men went to their horses, and with the comte's colors fluttering boastfully in the wind, they rode off in triumph.

Andelot sat on the ground for several minutes before he pulled himself to his feet and limped over to the golden bay. He rummaged bitterly through his bag and saw that they had thrown his things about with contempt. His search grew more desperate. Those dogs! They had deliberately taken his extra pair of breeches and left him with nothing else to wear!

He formed fists, then snatched up his sword and looked at it grimly. *I shall learn to use this until I can best them all! And when I do —*

Eventually, his emotions spent, he threw the sword down and sank onto the blanket. Neither self-pity nor anger would aid him now. He must be practical. He must ride on to Vendôme regardless of the humiliation of arriving in such fare. He ran his stiff and bloodied fingers across his scalp, feeling the nicks and uneven condition of what once had been a fine head of hair.

I must look a pitiable creature.

He dug around for what scraps of food were left from the bread and cheese provided by the pasteur and nursed his downcast spirit. He took account of his situation with a cooler mind and decided that while he was physically bruised and battered, he was otherwise intact. It was his pride that was injured.

How can I show myself like this to Marquis Fabien and Mademoiselle Rachelle? And the lettre! Gone. What now? Regardless, I must go on to Vendôme to warn the marquis.

He picked up the sword again. His fingers closed about the hilt tightly. His burning rage demanded the satisfaction of revenge. *I will let my studies wait. I will think of nothing except learning to be the best swordsman in France. I will have my satisfaction.*

He gritted his teeth.

This time I will not forgive.

The Broken Lock

MARQUIS FABIEN SUSPECTED THINGS WERE NOT AS THEY APPEARED. The Queen Mother's dwarves had departed soon after sunrise, carrying his lettre to the Queen Mother. It was afternoon when he called for Gallaudet.

"We should have heard from the duchesse by now. With or without her permission, I'm taking mademoiselle in marriage tonight. We leave tonight for Dieppe to await the ship."

Gallaudet went to the wardrobe, setting out a handsome attire of rich black-and-silver Genoa velvets for the marquis to wear.

Fabien heard the blast of a horn announcing a horseman's arrival and he hailed his page to see who it was. The sound of a trotting horse followed by the uproar of hounds barking in the courtyard, came with a foreboding remembrance of the arrival of the dwarves the day before.

Gallaudet went to the balustrade. "A lone horseman, Monseigneur — a stranger. He looks injured — but he is riding the golden bay! But it is not Andelot — Sainte Barbe! It *is* Andelot!"

Fabien strode onto the balustrade. It was Andelot, but he looked a pathetic sight as he dismounted and limped on bare feet into the courtyard. Fabien's gaze took him in from head to toe. An ugly suspicion rose in his heart.

Andelot looked up toward them and saluted with a short bow.

Fabien scowled. He leaned over the balustrade. "Bonjour, mon ami. Surely trouble brings you here."

"Oui, trouble aplenty. Duchesse Dushane has sent me with her lettre. Alas, Marquis, it was stolen from me."

"You look as though you were set upon by a pack of humorless wolves."

"I would have preferred wolves, Marquis. Maurice came upon me."

Fabien's anger flashed. "Maurice did this to you?"

"He insisted I duel him and had great sport with me as you can see." He ran his hand through his shorn hair. "He and his men."

Fabien turned to Gallaudet. Anger had tightened his fair features. "Go down and see that he has garments," Fabien said in a quiet but strained voice. "Take care of his bruises, then see that he's brought to me."

As Gallaudet departed the balustrade, Fabien called down: "Andelot, come round to the kitchen. Gallaudet will see to your needs and bring you up. You are in time for roast pheasant."

Andelot grinned ruefully. "Merci, Marquis. That will help at least satisfy my appetite if not my injured pride."

Looking down into the courtyard, Fabien saw Gallaudet check the golden bay, then turn him over to a hostler to take to the stables. He then brought Andelot around to the back of the palais.

Fabien entered his chamber from the balustrade. He stood hands on hips, eyes narrowed. His anger turned cold and silent.

***

HUMMING TO HERSELF, her heart full of purpose and excitement, Rachelle shook out the gown of finest burgundy velvet with black ecru lace falling softly around the wrists. She wrinkled her nose. This was not her ideal choice for a wedding gown! She thought of the ivory lace and satin gown at the Château de Silk handed down from the Dushane family. True, it was becoming limp with age and yellowing a bit here and there, and yet there was so much to be said for its tradition.

"Well, this will have to satisfy me for a less-than-perfect wedding," she murmured. After all, her family would be absent, and without Mère and Grandmère — better not think of her beloved grandmère now. She also realized that Fabien's family would not be present, and while vows were being exchanged and the pasteur pronounced blessings from the Word of God, they would still be watching over their shoulders for signs of soldiers. Non, not the wedding she had longed for. Even so, she knew that not having her choice of wedding gown would pale in comparison with having the man she had dreamed of. *I must not be overcome with details, but with the knowledge that I will soon be married to Fabien!*

She ran her palms across the skirt, trying to smooth out the wrinkles gathered on the journey. It was a mistake to have used it as padding to expand her girth when she'd left the Louvre in disguise, but it had enabled her to bring several of her gowns without carrying a trunk, which would have alerted the guards.

Now she wondered if the disguise had done them much good. She imagined the shrewd dark eyes of the twin dwarves watching her knowingly when she had stood near the stairway addressing Fabien. They knew well enough she had bought the animosity of the Queen Mother.

Fabien's resistance to the will of the throne by ignoring the royal summons and then taking her in marriage would place him in a state of rebellion which would cast its shadow upon their long journey by horseback to the coast of Normandy.

Would he ever be able to return to his marquisat? Perhaps during the reign of a new king who would forget the present intrigues. Fabien's commitment, no matter the cost, deepened her love, while the thought of his thrilled her to the core. She was humbled and thankful to God. She thought of the women, honorable and dishonorable, who had attempted to win him and failed.

She looked down at her left hand. As yet there was no ring. But surely he had not forgotten. He was merely occupied, worried about bringing her to safety.

Another commotion led her toward the open window. Had the Queen Mother's dwarves brought more trouble? She left the gown and went to the window.

Her spirits sparkled with relief and she turned her lips into a smile as she recognized Andelot—but *ça alors! What had befallen him?* He was limping on bare feet and his finest asset, his thick wavy brown hair, was unevenly chopped off, showing bare spots. His breeches were also shorn!

She drew her brows together. Someone had set out to torment and humiliate him. Her temper flared. What loathsome person would do such an awful thing—and why? Andelot had been at Fontainebleau with Scholar Thauvet. What was he doing here?

Rachelle hurried from her chamber into the passage. She was descending the stairway, feeling indignant about injustice, just as Fabien rounded the curving banister. He halted, thrilling her senses with his beau appearance in handsome black and silver finery.

She rushed to him. "It is Andelot. He is hurt."

The cool sobriety in his eyes confirmed her suspicion of turmoil.

"He was set upon by Maurice and his guards. Madame sent her lettre, but Maurice has it in his arsenal. If he chooses to show it to the Queen Mother, Madame will be in danger."

"Where is Andelot? I wish to see him."

"Not yet, ma chère. He needs some time alone to be made presentable."

"Oh, but it's just mon ami Andelot. I do not care about his appearance."

"But he does," Fabien said gently, wrapping a curl of her hair around his finger. "It would add to his shame if you barged in to see him now."

"Barge!"

He smiled. "But there is some bonne news, ma amour. He tells me Madame gave family consent for marriage."

Rachelle's emotions burned with excitement. She was held captive by his intense gaze.

"What do you prefer, my darling?" he asked softly, brushing her temple with his lips. "Do we slip away now and marry on the way to Dieppe, or do you wish a ceremony here?"

She turned her lips to his and they met and lingered.

"Here, mon amour. Who can say whether we shall return to your ancestral home. I wish to be able to tell our children that I married you here, at least."

He made no comment on their future as Bourbons in France.

"Fabien," she said gravely, "I know you have said so, but are you certain you wish to risk so much? Your lands, title, the future of your offspring—even your very life?"

His mouth turned. His kiss was firm and long, taking her breath away. He held her away from him.

"Rachelle, Rachelle … As for giving up the Bourbon inheritance, I do not anticipate surrendering anything that is mine by right of birth. However, you are wise in saying time will need to pass before any king welcomes us or our sons to court." He raised her hand and kissed her ring finger.

"And daughters!"

"And daughters!" He grinned. "Come, I desire to present you with an appropriate ring." He took hold of her arm and led her back up the stairs. She smiled and could have danced along beside him.

"There are several kept in a treasure box. You can try them on."

"Whose were they, or am I not supposed to ask?"

Again he laughed, as though he had all the time in the world. "Why shouldn't you ask?"

"Well—"

"You wouldn't suspect I 'borrowed' them when boarding a Spanish vessel perchance?"

She laughed. "That's absurd. I merely wondered if the wedding rings belong to the Bourbon family and to whom?"

"Most are definitely Bourbon. Some from a marquise, a duchesse, a princesse—though most of the jewels are not in my authority now. What I do have came from my immediate parents, Jean-Louis and Marie-Louise. There are also some pieces from my grandparents on both sides, and more distant relatives."

Rachelle found herself back in the outer salle of his private chambers, waiting while he opened a door into a small antechamber. He returned with an intricately carved mahogany chest inlaid with silver and mother of pearl.

"There is something I want to show you besides choosing your wedding ring. It is the Bible belonging to Duchesse Marie-Louise de Bourbon, my mother."

Rachelle was thrilled to learn more about his personal matters at last. She sat on the velvet footstool he brought up for her.

"That your mother owned a forbidden book both surprises and excites me. Was she a supporter of the German Reformer, Luther?"

"I would not go that far, though she was considered a Reformed thinker. The 'new opinions' was the way they spoke of it then. I remember that she gave asylum to the French translator, Lefèvre d'Étaples. Jean-Louis was most irate that she would protect a heretic daring to translate Latin and Greek into French."

Everything about Fabien's life interested her. "Then Duc Jean-Louis was a devout Catholic?"

"He and Duc de Guise shared the same fervid dedication to all things Roman."

She noticed a hardening come to his jaw at the mention of Guise.

"The two were close amis — back then."

That surprised her. She asked with gentle caution, "Do you still believe Guise arranged the assassination of your father?"

"Yes. I admit there are seasons when I would most gladly cooperate in Guise's assassination. Does that shock you?"

A dart of fear struck her heart. The Queen Mother would tempt him to do so, if the opportunity to confront him with an ultimatum were given her.

"I am not shocked. When Avril was murdered at the church burning and Idelette was violated, I knew burning rage. I still cannot think of the details without being tempted to give in to feelings of the utmost hatred. It was Madame Clair and her faith in the wisdom and goodness of God, despite the tears on her face, that spoke to me of leaving the unsolvable to Him."

Fabien's fingers massaged the back of her neck. He kissed her forehead. "When you speak words of discernment, chérie, I realize why I was impressed with you from the first."

She lowered her eyes. "Your words please and honor me, though I did not say it for that reason."

"I know. The Bible Marie-Louise received was one of the first Lefèvre d'Étaples translated."

"How did she come by it since your father stood against it?"

"The king's sister smuggled it to her sickbed. My mother read it secretly for the two years she was ill. She taught me as a boy, secretly, and my father did not know."

Something awakened in her memory and yet remained undistinguished in the fog. *Was there not something about this family Bible she should recall?*

"While a valiant monsieur who loved her, he held no liking for the Reformers. He connected the religion of Rome with the kingdom of France. To leave certain traditions was seen as betrayal of the country, the king, and the Bourbon family."

"Then Jean-Louis never learned about the Bible, or knew she taught you?"

"Précisément. He would have been affronted to have it in the château."

"You sided with Marie-Louise." She found his actions in shielding his mother a matter of commendation.

"I was interested in the words she read me, so I kept her secret from him. Before she died of her illness, she called me to her and left the Bible to my care."

She remembered that his father married again. "Then your father married Sebastien's eldest sister?"

"Making the insufferable Maurice my cousin by marriage." He stood, hands on hips.

She clasped her hands together, intertwining her fingers, resting them on the lap of billowing green skirt. She smiled up at him.

"And the French Bible?"

"I hid it here at the castle for years. That was when my kinsman Prince Louis was made my protector and took me to court. There I joined a group of children raised and schooled with Francis, Mary Stuart, and others. I was then a bon Catholic. It suited my purposes." Fabien met her gaze. "Even so, I never forgot what Marie-Louise taught me. When coming to Vendôme, as opportunity permitted, I would retrieve the Bible and read. Naturally some of it was difficult, but later, when I procured copies of the works of Calvin — I shall not say how — the Bible became more understandable."

"You never told me. Not even that night in Lyon at the Château de Silk when the religious differences between us seemed to hold us apart."

"I suppose I have not elaborated as fully as I might have. Though I possessed the Bible, I cannot say it truly possessed me. For personal reasons I did not desire to portray myself as a Huguenot. Remaining a Catholic allowed me the freedom at court to do as I pleased, to watch Guise — and avoid committing to you before I was prepared to do so.

But then I realized I could lose you to James Hudson, an English Protestant and a couturier, surely an excellent match for your silk family."

"James Hudson? You thought I was in love with him?"

"Non. I knew you loved me."

She lifted a brow rather haughtily, and he offered a light bow. "But time was working against me since I knew that Monsieur Arnaut would wish you to marry Hudson."

"Mère did wish me to marry Monsieur Hudson ... and for Idelette to marry Andelot. That was before—" Before Idelette was *enceinte*. She hesitated before going on, then smiled. "So you thought I would marry James Hudson?"

"You are pleased I can see. Yes, I saw him at the court in London. He presented the queen with a gown that she and her ladies nearly swooned over."

Rachelle laughed with joy. "Oh, if I could have been there to see it presented to Her Majesty."

"Hudson presided over a grand display, I assure you," he said dryly. "He boasted that you were coming to London to stay with his family and open a drapery for gowns and such. So you see, I was debating my return to Paris even before the Queen Mother's *lettre* arrived. I decided it was time to declare my faith if I were to convince Monsieur Arnaut I should have his daughter. I intend to take Communion with you publicly when the Huguenot pasteur comes to marry us."

She stood and went eagerly into his arms. "Mon chéri, oh, I am over-joyed. If only Bertrand were here, he would be jubilant."

"He does know of my decision. Do not forget he went on that infamous voyage with me to sink Spanish galleons! We had many long discourses debating theology. An odd place to discuss such matters, but then again, perhaps not. He knew from my answers that I hold no faith in religious works and rituals for acceptance with God, but in Christ's blood and sufficiency alone."

She laid her cheek contentedly against his chest, feeling the velvet against her skin.

"Show me the wedding ring. I long for you to place it on my hand."

He stooped to the chest and produced the key to the lock. A slight intake of his breath drew her attention.

She sank on her knees beside him. *The lock had slid open without the key.*

She looked at him. "Perhaps you failed to lock it last time you looked in the chest?" Her optimistic suggestion sounded implausible even to her.

"Non, it has been forced."

He lifted the heavy lid and she watched as he searched through items of Bourbon family import and sentiment. He lifted a gold box and opened it. She drew in a breath as her eyes feasted on jewelry that sparkled and flashed.

"Most interesting. Nothing of monetary value has been taken. The Bible, however, is missing."

"The Bible?" she whispered, tensing.

"The lock has been pried open, and not so long ago. See the marks in the brass?"

"A servant perhaps?"

Fabien shook his head, scowling. "Those who have access to this chamber I would trust with my life. I wouldn't have thought anyone would dare enter my palais and private bedchamber and break into a family chest. There are guards stationed about the lands. The serving men and women are multigenerational serfs. They accept me as their liege, and they grant me their affection and loyalty. Except Dumas."

"Dumas?"

"The captain of my home guard, or he was. He went over to the side of Maurice. I cannot see how it could be Dumas when the jewels were left undisturbed and the Bible taken."

An ominous shadow fell across her memory.

"Someone wanted to confiscate the forbidden translation."

"The question is, who would dare enter my chamber, who had the opportunity, and how did this worm know to look in the chest for the Bible?"

Fear tightened about her like grasping fingers. *Now she remembered what disturbed her earlier. She knew who it was.*

Fabien continued, "A common thief, if he could have gotten in here, which I doubt, would have searched the chamber for precious objects. When the chest was found and broken into, would a thief suddenly covet

God's Word instead of worldly wealth? Not likely. He must have known where the Bible was hidden."

His eyes were coolly observant. "What is the most nefarious reason for wanting it?"

"To use it as evidence against you. But he would need to prove it was yours."

"Duchesse Marie-Louise signed the Bible over to me upon her death bed. I have written my own name in it as well."

Fabien glowered down at the chest.

"Maurice," he said, "who else?"

"Yes." She bit her lip, recalling the incident. She turned to Fabien. "I remember now. He came to the Château de Silk to take me to Fontainebleau. It was then he allowed some words to slip from his tongue. He said you were a Huguenot, that you had a heretic Bible in your chamber. I asked how he knew what was in your private chamber. He made some vague excuses." She laid a trembling hand on his arm. "He is avaricious enough to bring his evidence of heresy to the Cardinal de Lorraine. Maurice will become furious when he learns we have married."

"It isn't the cardinal that troubles me as much as Maurice. He sorely tempts me to want to rid him of his front teeth. He has blundered into my life, stomping all over things most dear to me. You, Andelot, and now the Lefèvre d'Étaples Bible."

He stood, helping her to her feet. "I must make certain, however. Though all evidence crowns him the thief, I will speak to my chamberlain. It will be interesting to see what he can say about this."

Fabien sent for him, and the chamberlain appeared, looking distraught over the breach to his master's private chest.

"What do you know of this, Raymond?"

His eyes widened with fear. "Monseigneur, nothing, I vow! No one has entered your private bedchamber during your absence at sea. I permitted the chief serving man entry to dust and clean only on the night of your arrival."

"The chief serving man?"

"Henri has served you for years, Monseigneur. He would—"

"Call him."

"At once!"

The chief serving man returned to face his seigneur with twitching hands, his eyes fixated on the chest as though he expected a cobra to slowly raise its head.

The chamberlain spoke for them both. "The two of us will lay our necks to the chopping block, Monseigneur, if I thought for even one moment that either of us failed in our duty to guard the inner palais château during your courageous absence."

"I do not doubt the loyalty of either of you, so there is no need to carry on about chopping blocks. Just tell me when someone might have had undue access to my chambers. Mademoiselle believes there may have been a singular time when the Comte Beauvilliers entered. Do either of you recall this?"

The chamberlain was adamant in his denial, but the serving man looked at Rachelle then at Fabien, smoothing the front of his tunic with uneasy movements.

"Mademoiselle is correct, Monseigneur de Vendôme. She came here to take refuge for a few days after the Amboise rebellion, and Comte Beauvilliers was with her."

"Yes! So it was," she said quickly, remembering.

"Did either of you allow Beauvilliers to enter my chamber?"

The chamberlain exchanged a frown with the serving man.

"I saw him come out of this chamber, Monseigneur," the serving man said, moistening his lips.

The chamberlain drew in a breath. "What! And you failed to tell me so?"

The serving man shot him a glance then focused on Fabien.

"When I asked le comte what he was doing in the Marquis de Vendôme's chambers, he called me a prowling dog. He had merely entered the wrong chamber, he told me."

"He had the key?" Fabien asked, arms folded, looking pointedly at the chamberlain, who was in charge.

The chamberlain blotted his forehead with a kerchief, looking at the chest. "He received no key from me, Monseigneur. Is — are there family jewels missing?"

"And I have no key, my lord Marquis," the serving man hastened to say, looking pointedly at the chamberlain. He continued, "When I began to press Comte Beauvilliers on how he entered, he insisted the door was unlocked."

"Did you notice if he carried anything, a book perhaps, a cloak?"

"No, my lord Marquis. Whereupon he insisted I bring one of your best wines to his guest chamber. I fear the event slipped away from me once the dark news of the slaughter of the Huguenots at Amboise castle came to us here."

The chamberlain's mouth tightened as he looked at the chief serving man. Fabien dismissed the two men, telling them the fault was not theirs. Even so, Rachelle saw that Fabien could not easily put the matter from his mind.

"Here is one more grievance against Maurice," he said when they were alone. He scowled to himself, walking about, then after a moment, as the silence grew, he looked at her.

"My apology, belle amie." He came swiftly to her and offered a smile, but she could see he fought inner anger over Maurice.

"This has not been the romantic atmosphere I had in mind when I brought you here to choose your wedding ring."

He brought out the box of jewels. She sat down at a low table where a gilded lamp burned. He opened the box.

She drew in an audible breath. "Fabien, I have never seen such beauty."

Her fingers caressed rubies, diamonds, emeralds, sapphires, topaz, pearls — all set in gold rings — as well as pendants and bracelets.

"So many to choose from!" she murmured, putting a hand to her forehead.

"There are more — but not here. Which one suits you for the ceremony?"

She laughed. "Which one? All! All are stunning." She glanced at him. "You must give me your opinion — which means the most to you?"

He did not hesitate to lift out a small gold box and open it. A ruby and diamond ring set in gold flashed its beauteous glory.

"This was the wedding ring of Marie-Louise de Bourbon, passed on for several generations. Let us see if it fits. That is always the difficulty."

He took her left hand and slipped the ring on her finger.

Rachelle gazed at the ring with a sigh. She blinked to refuse entry of a tear. "Exquisite."

"It was meant for you, belle amie. You see? It fits well."

She gazed enthralled, moving her hand under the lamplight so that the glitter of the blood red rubies and flashing diamonds shimmered in unity.

She looked up at him. The momentous decision intertwined them in silence. He took her hands and drew her up. The flame in the depths of his eyes caught up her emotions and filled her heart.

"I am honoré, Rachelle, to take you as my bride. It must be here, tonight."

This moment made up for her heartbreak at the Château de Silk when she had unwisely fought to keep him from leaving for England. Then, in devastation, she believed her lack of wisdom and fairness in understanding him had lost him forever.

Now it was his own heart that had brought him back to her. The wedding cup would taste far sweeter in knowing their passion was shared, their love and need of one another equally desired.

She looked at her hand. "I will wear this ring proudly." Slowly she began to remove the wedding band from her finger. "But you keep it until the ceremony," she said, but he enclosed her hand in his.

"Do not remove it until we stand before the minister." He directed her attention back to the jewelry. "Take something else. Then I must conceal the chest somewhere until I am certain our lives will be secure in France."

She sighed over each piece of jewelry, undecided.

He gave an affectionate flip to one of her stray auburn curls. "Come, *mignon*, you are as indecisive as all women. What about this brooch? And the bracelet?"

"Oui! Oh, I adore them! The sapphires gleam like brilliant blue stars." She swept over to a gilded mirror and held the brooch to her gown and the bracelet against her wrist, striking a pose.

He smiled. "Belle des belles, chérie. I will send Gallaudet for the minister."

"Oh, I must change! And my hair, I must do it with more flair. I wish

Nenette were here; I wonder if Andelot may know of her safe arrival at Fontainebleau with Philippe."

"We will ask him. While you ready yourself, I shall seal the jewels and gold to be buried on our way. There is no guarantee the palais château will not be searched and even burned."

She turned, aghast. "Burned!"

"The son of a duc and duchesse who rebels against the throne is treated as a rebel and an enemy."

She looked about her at the wondrous furnishing and tapestries, sickened. "Burned ..."

He cupped her chin. "Maybe the order will not be given. But I will take no chances. I shall meet you at the foot of the stairs in five minutes."

"Five minutes?"

"Very well, then — ten minutes."

She looked at him, stunned. Ten minutes to dress for her wedding to the Marquis de Vendôme? Oh, come, most surely he jested?

"I will need an hour at least!" *Oh, if ma mère were only here.*

"An hour! You are charmante as you are."

"Very well, half an hour. And Fabien, what if Andelot is wrong? What if he misunderstood Madame's mind on the matter?"

He appeared to consider, his smile tilting. "I trust him, but if he is wrong, I shall ever be indebted to him. Our marriage will soon be a fait accompli, ma chérie. Let us agree that the duchesse has given us her bountiful blessing."

She smiled and hurried from the salle down the passage to her chamber. Half an hour!

To Bury a Treasure

FABIEN GATHERED THE MOST CHERISHED FAMILY TREASURES AND STRODE off to find Gallaudet. After sending him to locate a Huguenot minister, Fabien went to meet with Andelot in the bedchamber where the chamberlain had taken him.

Andelot was scrubbing himself in a round tub of hot water when he entered. The chamberlain had brought in handsome articles of clothing and displayed them upon the wide bed.

"Merci, a thousand thanks, Marquis."

"How do you manage to ride into these situations, mon ami?" Fabien said in a light tone. "I begin to think you hunger for battle." He came up and inspected Andelot's shorn head, asking the chamberlain to find some ointment to rub on the nicks and grazes Maurice's men had made as they hastily removed his hair.

"On the contrary, Maurice finds *me*. I am an offense because I'm privileged to be your ami."

"It is I who am privileged to have such a loyal ami, Andelot. Maurice will pay for this treatment, I assure you. Was it he who did this to you?"

"Well, one of his bodyguards. A giant of a fellow of an otherwise mellow mood. At one time, I had rather liked him. Now I should like to put a sword in his portly belly."

"It is not for you to talk like that."

"I find no dishonor in following your steps, Marquis."

Fabien frowned. The notion unsettled him. Though he believed he acted in honor and valor, he did not wish for someone like Andelot, whom he saw as sensitive and gentle, to mold his life after his own.

"My steps do not always lead wisely. Follow Pasteur Bertrand or Calvin. I could wish for you to go to Geneva for the rest of your learning, even though you are a Roman Catholic."

An abashed expression came over Andelot's face and Fabien wondered why. What had he said that brought Andelot such a look of guilt?

"I have something to say about my Christian faith, Marquis, but not yet." He touched his cropped head. "I shall be well enough. It will grow out again soon."

"You are being most courageous," Fabien said dryly. He looked about at the items of clothing the chamberlain had brought up. "Let's see, what can we do until your hair fills in? Ah!" He turned to the chamberlain. "Hats and scarves — or a large kerchief — made of cotton. You will find a few in the trunk I brought back from the *Reprisal*."

The chamberlain left and returned with some cotton kerchiefs and several hats.

Fabien went through them, rejecting most, as Andelot looked on, curious but smiling. "There has never been an ami like you, Marquis."

"This one will work." Fabien took a black beret style hat and a dark forest green scarf. "Until your hair grows, or you get hold of a periwig, you will cast the shadow of being a buccaneer. You will look most dashing. This is how the pirates do it: take the scarf like so — " he folded it and placed it around Andelot's head — "and tie it in back with a seaman's knot — there! The beret goes on like this, tipped to the side, and — *voilà*! Capitaine Andelot Dangeau!"

Andelot looked at himself in the mirror and grinned. He thrust out his chest. "Bon!" he rubbed his hands together and cocked his head, turning about and looking at himself. "Ah, Marquis, I like it much! Oui! Now — my scabbard and sword — "

Fabien laughed. "Wearing a sword will tempt brigands to have a go at you," he said quickly. "Wiser to stay to your studies, I beg of you."

Andelot frowned at himself in the mirror and sighed. "At this moment I would give much, Marquis, to be Capitaine Nappier! If only I knew the sword as well as you. I'd hunt Maurice down and see him humbled."

Fabien kept his anger toward Maurice masked, lest it heighten Andelot's.

"Maybe, Marquis, you could teach me. You started to do so once, but all of the trouble that has come upon us since Amboise has intervened."

"What I wish for you, cousin, is an education par excellence. That is the path for you, among books and monsieurs of greater learning. You are too fine for violence and intrigue."

"Me?" Andelot questioned in mock self-deprecation.

"You."

Andelot appeared to reconsider as he rearranged his beret a trifle more to the left eyebrow. "Geneva would be most interesting, I admit. I have my Latin down and wish to learn even more Greek. As for the Reformers, I have something to tell you of utmost importance." He cleared his throat. "It all began when I came across some Huguenots in the woods around Fontainebleau. The old pasteur hid a — "

Fabien hastened to speak. "I will look forward to hearing all about it, but we have not the time now. Come with me. I must conceal some Bourbon treasures and I want you, at least, to know where I bury them. Who knows, Andelot? Anything might happen. It is a long way from my family estate to my ship at Dieppe."

Andelot showed surprise. "You are leaving, Marquis? But — "

"I must." He had delayed telling Andelot, knowing it would sadden him. They had, in the last two years, grown as close as brothers. "Leaving France is my only option. Rachelle must be brought to safety and I will remain with her." He glanced at Andelot to see how he was taking the idea of their marriage. Andelot showed no ill feelings, and Fabien was relieved. "How long our stay in England will last, I cannot say. My possessions here in Vendôme may be confiscated by the throne. Some generations ago, all this region of France was Bourbon.

"My ancestor, Duc Charles de Bourbon was perhaps only a step from the throne, but Francis I decided all of France should become one kingdom with himself at the head. He began incorporating territories that belonged to the ducs. The Bourbon duchy was one of the most powerful, and Francis seized it. The Bourbons fought, but in the end my kinsman had to flee — to Spain of all places! He joined them and fought against France. As you can imagine, it took his ancestors some bon effort to make peace with Francis. We have ruled over smaller territories to this day. It may be, Andelot, that I too will not return to rule even my marquisat."

"Do not even say it!"

Fabien threw an arm around his shoulder. "We shall always be bon amis. Now come, there is no time to lose."

The sun had just set behind the forest trees and the horizon blazed vermillion. They walked from the palais toward a distant copse to a stone court surrounded by hickory trees.

Fabien discussed the darkening political news of Europe and the events in the Spanish Netherlands, and wondered if Capitaine Nappier and the crew of the *Reprisal* would be able to sail safely to Dieppe.

Andelot offered what information he had gleaned from the duchesse, who evidently knew much of what was transpiring across Europe. He mentioned the surprising news of how their Oncle Sebastien had taken his wife Madeleine, bébé Joan, and Rachelle's sister Idelette, and escaped the court.

"I had no inkling he was planning to flee," Andelot went on.

Fabien noted a faint disappointment in Andelot's voice. "He was wise not to inform you for your own sake. You did not want to go with him?"

Andelot shrugged. "My emotions remain divided. I would not mind England — and yet ..."

Was he considering Idelette's dilemma? Fabien doubted Rachelle's belief that Andelot was in love with Idelette. If he were, would he not go to her now in her time of despair? Perhaps he was unsure of his reception.

"You have heard what happened to Mademoiselle Idelette in Lyon?"

"Madame told me. That dog is one I should like to put to the sword."

"You need not concern yourself about him. He and I crossed blades, and he is now deep down below."

The silence lasted only a moment. "You are certain he was the one?"

"Assuredly. I have yet to make it clear to Rachelle, but I will. She may tell her sister as she pleases, or no."

Andelot nodded. They came to the copse as the vermillion sky was deepening to pewter. After a moment Andelot went on. "About Oncle Sebastien, I did notice his recent interest in maps, including one of England. I might have guessed then, but I thought it was due to Monsieur Macquinet's wish to start a silk plantation there."

Fabien left unsaid what worried him most about Sebastien's escape—the road to Calais was usually well traveled by the king's soldiers. His kinsmen, the two Bourbon princes, were another concern that would have consumed his waking hours if it had not been for the dangers surrounding Rachelle. Louis was held in the Amboise dungeons, and Antoine was under palais arrest at Fontainebleau.

"Was there any suggestion from the duchesse that Prince Louis might be released from the dungeon?"

Andelot winced. "Then you have not heard—ah, Marquis, he is to be executed for treason in early December."

Fabien gritted his rage and clasped the hilt of his sword. *If only . . .*

"A curious factor, Marquis, is that the Queen Mother leaves Fontainebleau often to visit him."

Fabien turned his head sharply. "Catherine speaks with him in the Amboise dungeon?"

"They say her visits to his cell are frequent and secretive. At best, her motives are conspiratorial, so the duchesse believes."

If only I did not need to depart at once—

"The bonne news, if any, is that the duchesse and Admiral Coligny are working feverishly with other respected nobles of Huguenot and Catholic persuasion to convince the king to stay the prince's execution."

Fabien quickened his step on the pathway. He shook his head. "My hands are in chains, Andelot. There is naught I can do to save my kinsmen if I wish to save Rachelle. We marry and leave tonight." He clamped his jaw. "It is settled."

Andelot nodded in grim silence. "Once she is safe in England with Madame Clair . . . Perhaps then?" He glanced at the marquis, but Fabien behaved as if he'd not heard the tempting suggestion to return.

They walked on and came to a courtyard where there stood a white stone pavilion with Corinthian pillars.

Inside, Fabien lit a lantern and carried it past stone benches and statuary.

Andelot followed him to the back of the pavilion. "Here," Fabien said. "Under these squares." He lifted two heavy marble floor tiles, unveiling steps leading to a small cellar lined with stone. Fabien placed the family treasure chest at the bottom of the short flight of stairs. He replaced the marble tiles.

"Will the box last in there, Marquis?"

"It should stay dry, so it will last a long time if this pavilion remains. We Bourbons have a penchant for garden pavilions and Grecian statuary, and there is no reason for anyone to tear it down. Besides, ami, precious jewels do not rust and decay, and no moth can destroy them."

"Most interesting you would say that now."

"Why so?"

"I was reading about laying up treasure in heaven. Our works will be tested by fire. Did you know that? Gold, silver, and precious stones will endure the searing flames of the Lord's searching gaze; but works done for purposes that do not glorify Him will burn like wood, hay, and stubble. I suppose, Marquis, many of us will have big bonfires."

"Assuredly so. How did you come to read these words?"

Andelot smiled and Fabien noticed a difference in his countenance. "That is the tale I wish to explain when there is time."

Fabien looked toward the entrance. "We have time until Gallaudet returns with the Geneva minister."

Darkness was now creeping up the steps into the pavilion. The breeze had come up with the first sign of the moon, sending dried hickory leaves tumbling across the floor.

"I am interested. Say on. This may be our last opportunity for camaraderie for who knows how long." Fabien leaned against a statue and Andelot sat on the stone bench.

"It all began when the duchesse's page, Romier, wagered me he would win a race in the woods against the golden bay."

"Folly. The horse rides like the wind."

"Exactement."

"By the way, Andelot, I want you to keep him. I know you will favor him well."

"Merci, Marquis! He is a great gift. I have grown most attached to him."

Fabien smiled, amused. "And so I have no doubt you won the race."

"It was not even close, Marquis. As I entered the woods of Fontainebleau, I came upon a Huguenot meeting with a Dominican attempting to arrest them for heresy. I noticed the elder pasteur hide something under a felled log. It was a Bible—in the French tongue. I kept it and read it. I only just returned it to the pasteur on my way here to Vendôme."

Fabien listened as Andelot went on to tell how he'd almost been caught by Père Jaymin.

"I now believe as the other Huguenots do, though I continue to attend Mass with Maître Thauvet."

Fabien was pleased but urged caution. "At least complete your studies with Thauvet. Afterward, consider journeying to Geneva for more training, or even England. A lettre of recommendation will open a door for you to meet personally with Calvin."

"I will take to heart your interest in Geneva, Marquis. Thauvet has mentioned his concern of a religious civil war in France between Catholics and Huguenots. If it comes to that, it would be a wise time to visit Geneva for myself."

"I tell you, Andelot, as long as the Guises have authority from Rome and soldiers and gold from Spain, the Huguenots will never have the freedom of worship in France. At best, the fragile peace holding the two camps together now hangs by a spider's web."

"Admiral Coligny is convinced the upcoming colloquy will bring about change."

As Fabien knew, the colloquy would bring Monsieur Calvin together with Cardinal de Lorraine and other bishops and clerics for a debate of Christian doctrines that separated Catholics and Protestants. This was to become the supreme effort to capture France for the Reformation, or at least to gain toleration to establish a national Protestant church.

"I understand Admiral Coligny's hopes for peace and reconciliation," Fabien said. "Even though I remain a skeptic where the colloquy is concerned. Although the king signs edicts of toleration, neither the duc nor the cardinal will abide by any law but those favoring destruction. The Queen Mother knows this as well."

"One wonders, Marquis, why she risks the anger of the Guises to have the colloquy?"

It was only Fabien's understanding of her Machiavellian philosophy that convinced him her reasons had nothing to do with religious convictions. She could abide either a Catholic or a Protestant France as long as it supported her.

"Why does she risk it? Because after the Huguenot plot at Amboise to overthrow her and the Guises, she fears a national civil war between Huguenots and Catholics. The admiral has quietly warned her and the king that if the serfs under Huguenot nobles continue to be persecuted, tortured in prisons, and burned at the stake, the uprising that took place at Amboise was only the beginning."

"You mean the Huguenot nobles like the Admiral will lead a rebellion?"

"Exactement. The Queen Mother must find herself in a quandary between the two religious factions. She so fears a civil war that she will risk angering the Guises by allowing the Huguenots their colloquy. No doubt she hopes the two sides will come to a meeting of the mind, if not the soul."

Andelot's smile showed his hope. "Maybe you are pessimistic, Marquis. Why, even Queen Jeanne of Navarre will come to hear Monsieur Calvin," he said of Prince Antoine's wife.

Fabien worried about Jeanne and her devout Huguenot convictions. She was secure if she remained in her small kingdom to the south of France. Otherwise, who knew? He hoped she would not risk coming to the colloquy.

"Well, Marquis, if you are right, then there does not seem to be much hope."

"I see very little of that," Fabien said with brutal frankness. "I remember Pasteur Bertrand aboard ship saying in that dry wit of his that the only way for unity is to agree to unify around nothing."

"He must have spoken in jest."

"Bertrand? Non! As he said, 'How can two walk together except they be agreed?'"

Andelot wrinkled his brow thoughtfully. "That verse, where was it? I remember reading it somewhere in the Bible."

"The pathway is crucial lest the church wander off with a false teacher into the wilderness."

"Who would wish for Christianity to tolerate error in the name of unity?"

"Those who yield truth for tolerance's sake."

"A church such as this would no longer represent biblical Christianity."

"Précisément—a lukewarm church going into apostasy."

Andelot tightened his mouth. "What Christian would ever wish to belong to such a church?"

"Many. They believe they are rich spiritually and have need of nothing. While Christ is on the outside knocking to enter for fellowship."

Andelot gave him a doubtful once-over. "How and why do you know such truths?"

Fabien smiled. "Perhaps I am repeating only what I recently heard from Pasteur Bertrand aboard the *Reprisal*. Remember," he said with a lifted brow, "I was with him in close quarters for *many* long weeks."

Andelot grinned. "I think it is the reason he went aboard. He wished to win you for the cause. It appears as though he may have accomplished his purpose."

They lapsed into silence. Fabien stared at the lamp. The glow from the candlelight wavered in the contrary wind. *I am grateful for that accomplishment.*

Andelot remained silent. The chill wind rushed through the treetops and a few sprinkles of rain wet their faces as they walked back toward the palais château.

Once inside the courtyard near the front entrance they came upon a small tumult of activity. Gallaudet saw Fabien and rushed forward, saluting him.

"The pasteur has arrived, Monseigneur. He has come in masquerade to foil notice by his enemies. He awaits now."

Rachelle would soon be his!

With This Ring

RACHELLE WAITED UPON THE STAIRWAY, GLANCING BELOW THE SLEEK banister into the wide salle where the activity commenced. The wedding vows were soon to be spoken before God, followed by a reading from Scripture, prayer, and the taking of Communion. Then they would be off for the journey to Dieppe to await the ship that would take them to England. Oh, this was quite unlike any wedding she'd ever heard about! She smiled and smoothed her bright burgundy velvet gown. Once again she touched her elaborately done hair — Fabien described it as the color of chestnuts with autumn lights — and wished that her petite maid Nenette was with her.

A hundred thoughts whirled in Rachelle's mind. In one moment she wished for the smiling presence of her family, in the next she worried over their response when she arrived a married woman. Would they accept the consent she had received from the duchesse to marry?

She awoke to the precious moment as below, in the grand salle, the pasteur appeared, a Bible in hand. Next came Fabien flanked by his highest ranking men-at-arms, all dressed to precision in handsome clothes with Bourbon colors. Andelot too was there, and several of the male and female servants. He looked none the worse for having been bullied by Maurice and his bodyguard. Her gaze, however, could not be held by any of them for long and moved swiftly to lock on her beloved. Fabien was watching her, which made her heart sing. *My bridegroom comes at last!*

The marquis came forward now, most dashing in black and silver. He came midway up the staircase where she waited, and he bowed to her.

She dipped a low curtsy. He took her arm, tucking it under his, and, walking slowly with her down the staircase, led her to where the pasteur waited. The men-at-arms stood at attention, guarding the salle in a half circle.

The pasteur opened the Bible —

Several blasts from a horn ripped through the silence, followed by shouts and raucous voices outside in the courtyard. Stunned, Rachelle looked at Fabien. He whipped out his sword. He shot a warning glance at Gallaudet.

Rachelle's heart leapt into her throat.

Fabien's fingers tightened on her arm and he propelled her backward toward the staircase calling, "Pasteur! Up here, quickly!"

Gallaudet and the guards turned toward the door, swords ready. Andelot shouted: "Marquis! It is that cur, Maurice! He has one of your men, wounded."

"Who was guarding the gate?" Fabien demanded.

No man had the answer, but they all looked as foul of countenance as did Fabien.

"Treachery, Monseigneur!" Gallaudet warned, his eyes narrowing as he looked in turn at each of the inner guards.

"By the saintes!" the lead captain called up to Fabien. "We would die first, Monseigneur! It was none of us, we vow it! Surely you know our fealty is yours!"

"They must have been surprised or tricked at the gate!" Julot called.

"Or bribed!" Gallaudet lifted the point of his blade, still glancing about at the others.

"If one of the guards is wounded, he must have put up a valiant fight," Fabien called down to his men from the stairs, still holding onto Rachelle's arm. "We shall do no less."

Rachelle forced a calm demeanor, lifting her chin as she stood beside him, and looked at each of his men-at-arms below. Inside, she was trembling at the outcome. *Men will die.* She would not worsen matters by crumbling to pieces now, adding to Fabien's concerns.

A group of bloodied court guards now burst in through another entrance, let inside by Julot. They grasped swords in hand and bowed toward Fabien, fists at heart.

"What happened?" he demanded.

"A traitor, Monseigneur, another ally of Captain Dumas, arranged to open the gate. We were deceived, then overwhelmed—the Comte Beauvilliers is not alone—some soldiers from Duc de Guise are with him."

Duc de Guise. A rush of darkened memory came to Rachelle, bringing back another warning from the boy Philippe at the Château de Silk. *"Soldiers are coming . . . run! It is the Duc de Guise—"*

In a horrifying instant of relived terror she could see the barn church smoking and in flames. She heard the echo of voices crying out. She saw again the body of her petite sister Avril lying dead in the field, trampled by horse hooves.

Rachelle's fingers tightened on Fabien's arm. Her gaze caught his face, but his gaze was fixed on his men below the stairs.

"How many?" Fabien demanded; his voice was iron calm.

"I saw nearly a hundred—and with Beauvilliers, maybe forty—they are fighting their way into the courtyard from the road—your loyalists are fighting well, Monseigneur. Julot lifted his head. "But one of the men is a prisoner and is bleeding badly—le comte threatens to kill him unless you surrender in the name of the King of France."

"There will be no surrender! Bolt the door," Fabien ordered.

Rachelle sucked in her breath. No surrender!

As his men rushed to take positions to guard the stairway, she heard the shouting and fighting getting closer and louder, the clash of steel against steel.

Fabien gestured to Andelot.

"Marquis?" he asked quietly.

"We will do what is needed to hold them off as long as possible. You will take Rachelle to Dieppe."

"I will do my utmost."

Fabien touched Andelot's shoulder, then turned to Rachelle. He drew her toward him. "You and Andelot will escape. I will send Gallaudet with you. He is the finest swordsman in my service."

"I will not leave you!"

"Chérie, you must flee. But not without becoming my wife!" he said fiercely. He turned his head, still holding Rachelle. "The pasteur—Andelot, where is he?"

"Here, Marquis," the pasteur stepped forward from the corridor to the stairs.

Fabien snatched the wedding ring from his pocket and glanced below in the salle. A slow periodic bang of a ramming pole on the door made Rachelle's blood run cold. "We will hold them back, whatever the cost!" He turned back to Gallaudet. "Leave by the back passage, ami, you know where it is."

"As you wish, Monseigneur."

But it was clearly written on Gallaudet's face that he wished to stay with the marquis and fight.

Rachelle was trembling. She gritted, clutching Fabien's arm.

Fabien drew the pasteur forward on the stair landing. "Pasteur! Marry us!"

"Yes, yes . . ." He opened the Bible and began to read quickly.

"Do you, Monseigneur Fabien Jean-Louis de Bourbon take this woman, Mademoiselle—" He looked at her blankly.

"Rachelle Dushane Macquinet!" She glanced over her shoulder at the door.

"Yes, yes—do you take this woman, Mademoiselle Rachelle Dushane Macquinet, to be your wife?"

"Yes, I do."

"And do you, Mademoiselle Rachelle Dushane Macquinet, take Marquis Fabien Jean-Louis de Bourbon to be your husband? To love and obey—"

"Yes! I do!"

"The ring—"

Rachelle thrust her hand into Fabien's, and she felt the ring slide on.

"I now pronounce you man and wife. The God of grace, mercy, and forgiveness through Jesus Christ our Lord and Savior guard and bless you always. Amen."

With a little cry, she fell into Fabien's crushing embrace and met his burning kiss, her arms going about him tightly. A moment later his violet-blue eyes answered her questioning gaze with a promise.

"I will find you again in Dieppe aboard my ship—or, if all else fails, in England—as soon as I can. Au revoir, my beloved bride."

He kissed her again, then handed her over to Gallaudet and Andelot. "Go, mes amis."

Andelot clasped her hand. Gallaudet saluted him, then led the way down the corridor, his sword in hand.

Below, she could hear the clash of blades. It sounded as though the door was finally cracking. In only minutes now, the enemy would be inside.

Andelot pulled her along. They ran toward the back of the palais to a secret exit. Just before they rounded a corner in the corridor, she looked back for a last glimpse. She saw the pasteur wisely duck into another chamber out of sight. Fabien remained on the stairway but now faced the front door. She heard a loud crack as the door split, allowing the enemy into the salle.

God be with you, mon amour.

❧

MAURICE, SWORD IN HAND, appeared in the doorway. Fabien unsheathed his blade as he faced him.

"I have been waiting for you to arrive for three days; what took you so long, mon cousin?" Fabien mocked.

Maurice's gray eyes, usually languid, sparked anger. "I will keep you waiting no longer."

"Bon! I grow impatient to thrust you through."

For a moment Maurice looked uncertain. "Who said anything about a duel?"

"I did."

I must gain time for Gallaudet and Andelot to take Rachelle safely away.

Fabien stood, one hand on hip in an arrogant manner, knowing it infuriated Maurice. "There are other matters between us besides the mademoiselle. The matter of my bon ami Andelot must be answered. Ah, yes. *That* incident cannot be forgotten. Then there is your clumsy thievery. Ah, yes. *Thievery.* You entered my sanctuary, broke into my private chest, and removed a family possession deemed precious, having belonged to Duchesse Marie-Louise de Bourbon. For that insult alone, Maurice, I have been waiting for you. I insist on an *affaire d'honneur*."

"By the saints, you shall have it, marquis."

"Bon. And now — you have offended my honor. First, you may begin by bowing to your Bourbon liege." Fabien smiled. "Come now, Maurice, come forward and bow. If not, your defeat by my expertise shall be slow and humiliating."

Maurice turned ruddy of face. A small glint of unease showed in his eyes, as though he had not expected this willingness to be put to the sword.

"It is *you* who have offended your superior, Cousin Fabien."

"Do not call *me* 'cousin,' " Fabien said disdainfully, mocking Maurice. "Do you not always throw those same words into Andelot's face? You are but a Beauvilliers. I am a royal Bourbon." Fabien stood on the stairway, looking down at him. "And who might this superior be that I have offended? You? A comte by marriage?"

Maurice's nostrils flared. "You, Marquis de Vendôme, are under arrest in the name of the king. Ha! What think you of that? Where is *my* fiancée by the will of His Majesty?"

"Such dreadful manners you have, Maurice. You break down my door, barge into my palais, join an attack against my men-at-arms, and then dare to call Rachelle your fiancée? You even make boast of the king as your sponsor in this outrageous behavior. I tell you, such haughtiness is beyond reason."

Maurice took a step forward. "I have come to claim what is mine, Marquis de Vendôme."

Fabien leaned against the rail as though bored. *Had Gallaudet and Andelot gotten Rachelle into the forest yet?*

"Do you dare fault His Majesty the King of France for granting Rachelle to be my wife?" Maurice shook out the perfumed lace at his cuff.

"I do, undoubtedly. It will be most ignominious, I assure you."

Maurice dropped a hand on his narrow hip. "Need I warn you that when such words reach the throne they will be considered traitorous, Marquis?"

"Have you a missive signed and sealed by King Francis de Valois?" Fabien asked silkily. *It would not be surprising if Maurice did have such a lettre.*

Maurice glanced about the salle at Fabien's grim-faced men-at-arms facing him with drawn blades. Behind him, just outside the entrance-way, there stood at least a dozen. Fabien knew there were more soldiers in the courtyard awaiting instructions, but from whom would they take orders? Guise was not here, and Fabien could not conceive of the duc's proud guard leader surrendering his command to Maurice.

"A royal missive? Aha! You shall soon find out just what King Francis thinks of you now, Marquis. There will soon be issued a lettre for your arrest on charges of piracy against Spain."

"Soon? You mean you do not have it with you while daring to thrust your uninvited company into my castle? I ought to string you up on the highest rafter for your uncivilized manners."

Maurice was taking all of the bait Fabien was tossing him, arguing back and using up time, time so precious for Gallaudet.

"Your ami, the king, will do nothing to protect you this time, Marquis; not with the Duc of Alva at his side and Duc de Guise and Cardinal de Lorraine supporting Spain's call for your arrest."

"Should I be surprised to hear that the Guises are loyal to Spain? They are nothing but King Philip's legates. The charge of piracy must be proven before I can be considered guilty. If I fought Spain under legal letters of marque from Holland or England, I am not a pirate but an honorable privateer."

Maurice waved his hand. "I have naught to say of that. However, I shall make you a bargain. Relinquish Mademoiselle Rachelle to me now, and I will tell my men to step aside. You can spare your own life and your chevaliers' lives and ride out free."

Fabien smiled. "And ride into a trap that you and Guise's men have deceitfully agreed upon? You would then have mademoiselle without even a duel. And Guise would have the satisfaction of presenting me to the Duc of Alva. *Ah ça non!* You must take me for a fool, Maurice. Non, now that you are here, there are grave matters that must be settled between us. But as for la belle des belles, you have been foiled. She is now Marquise Rachelle de Vendôme. We were married before you arrived."

Maurice stared. Color came into his cheeks and he let out a furious cry.

A horn blasted from outside. The boom of a drumbeat signaled the drawing of weapons in preparation for battle. Guise's soldiers began moving to take the castle.

Maurice waved his sword with a vicious flourish and bounded toward Fabien, who threw aside his cumbersome scabbard and baldric to meet Maurice's lunge. Fabien took his footing to meet the onslaught and parried as their blades clashed and ground together, the two swordsmen testing and feeling each other's skills. Soldiers followed, bursting through the open door into the salle as Fabien's swordsmen threw themselves into the fray. The salle erupted into warfare, the clash and ring of steel upon steel.

Maurice advanced, then leapt aside, testing Fabien's guard at each engagement with catlike movements as he circled.

Fabien's confidence and precise moves caused Maurice to attack with fury. Fabien deflected a thrust and parried with a swift unexpected counterthrust that drove Maurice back from his stance. Maurice recovered and moved in more cautiously.

They fought, thrusting, circling, parrying. Their blades clashed, disengaged, then met again, testing each other. Around them, Fabien's men-at-arms were in clashes of their own, steel ringing against steel as they held off Maurice's loyals and the Guise guards. Tables were hurled, chairs crashed, shouts and insults bounced from wall to wall.

Fabien found an opening and thrust, feeling his point tear cloth. Maurice flinched; a spot of blood seeped through his sleeve. He came at Fabien, feinted and lunged, springing away. Fabien moved in again swiftly. They circled, their swords flashing, seeking, caressing. Fabien feigned a disengagement only to swipe Maurice's peacock feather from his red velvet hat.

Maurice glared and wiped the sweat from his forehead, realizing he had taken on a swordsman who was testing his skills beyond any he had fought at the armory.

From the corner of his eye, Fabien saw Captain Dumas, the traitor, in a battle for his life with one of Fabien's men. In one swift thrust of his sword, the guard rammed Dumas through his chest.

Maurice advanced again and again, sweating profusely. Fabien's blade consistently met his, turning it aside. Maurice thrust high. Fabien parried lightly with the forte of his blade and countered promptly, but Maurice swept the blade aside and lunged for the shoulder. "Aha! Blood for blood!" Maurice cried with pomp.

Angered, Fabien attacked with cold deliberation. When Maurice was momentarily unguarded, Fabien's blade nicked his cheek.

"As you boasted," Fabien said.

Maurice looked shaken but leapt away. Fabien whirled and thrust. Maurice parried late, and Fabien's point, driving straight at Maurice's breast, was barely deflected by an upward swing.

After several such engagements, Fabien didn't follow up Maurice's backward leap, so Maurice could pause for breath.

"What ails you, my dashing comte? And now, may you taste the humiliation that you forced upon young Andelot, a far better man than you. You are but a messire who hounds pups that you may imagine yourself master of the pack."

Fabien could see anguish creeping over Maurice's face as he anticipated approaching defeat.

Fabien's sword point leapt past and again flicked him, this time in the neck. Maurice's face was pale with the heat of flush, smeared with sweat and blood.

Fabien gave no more pauses but kept up the vigorous attack, forcing Maurice to concentrate on defense. Maurice continued to fall back. Fabien pursued relentlessly, avoiding a death thrust but punishing the comte, forcing Maurice to taste humiliation and futility.

Finally, he stepped back. "Did you truly fancy yourself the chief swordsman at court? You are indeed a wonder, Maurice."

Thus goaded, Maurice bounded forward, wasting his energy. Fabien sidestepped to avoid a thrust, but as they disengaged Fabien missed his footing.

"Ho!" Maurice breathed jubilantly. "I am not finished yet!"

"You will be!"

Fabien came in close; Maurice would not be put off. Following a parried thrust, he found the opening he sought. Fabien made a thrust at Maurice's throat, but despite his anger with him, he did not wish to press it home. As Maurice swept Fabien's blade aside, his neck was cut again. Maurice dropped low and crouched in an Italian lunge, intending an upward thrust into Fabien's chest.

Fabien sidestepped Maurice's low lunge, and Maurice lost his footing. Fabien, with his left hand, landed a sharp blow to the back of Maurice's neck, and he went down. A push in the right spot with his boot sent Maurice over on his face, his sword clattering on the floor.

Standing over Maurice as he lay prone, Fabien placed his point at the back of Maurice's neck.

"It is over, Maurice. You have been sorely defeated."

He withdrew his blade, and Maurice pushed himself up to his knees, catching his breath. They locked gazes for a long moment, then Maurice threw up his hands in a gesture of surrender.

"Well played!" Maurice admitted with a sigh. "Your triumph, Marquis."

Fabien stepped aside, catching his breath and wiping the sweat from his brow with the sleeve of his Holland shirt. "If I had the time I would shave your conceited mustache and send you to Fontainebleau with your breeches cut off at the thigh."

Maurice groaned.

Fabien was weary of him and glanced around the salle as confusion reigned. There were injured and dying men everywhere. Furniture was overturned, and irreplaceable statues and vases broken. He saw one of his men swing from a chandelier, then connect with a Guise captain, knocking him down to the floor before finishing him with a short blade.

Fabien caught a movement from the corner of his eye. He turned to see Maurice lunge toward him, sword in hand. Fabien moved out of his path, avoiding the full force of Maurice's thrust into his side. But Maurice did nick him. He went down.

Maurice stomped on Fabien's hand and kicked his blade across the corridor out of reach. Maurice grasped his sword hilt with both hands and was about to plunge it through Fabien's chest when a heavy brass urn from farther down the corridor smashed into his head, sending him reeling. Maurice collapsed, unconscious.

Fabien turned onto his side, looked down at his bloodied clothing, and tried to raise himself. The bloody floor made his hand slip, and he went down again. A moment later he opened his eyes to a pair of small red leather boots with gold spangles. Through blurred vision he looked up at one of the Queen Mother's twin dwarves. So they had returned with Guise's soldiers.

Fabien looked past the dwarf. Four soldiers faced him with drawn swords.

The dwarf shook his bountiful black ringlets.

"Ta, ta, Monseigneur. You should be duly ashamed of your trusting spirit. You turned your back on the serpentine comte, believing him a true brother at heart." He bent over Fabien and wagged a finger at him. "You should have thrust him through when you had your point on his neck. But—alas! Her Majesty wishes to see you, as I said several days ago. We cannot have you delivered to Fontainebleau a corpse now, can we? Therefore my aim with the brass urn was excellent, was it not?" He straightened to his full height. "I could have sent my dagger through the comte's heart, but he is still needed by Her Majesty." He looked over at Maurice, whose chin slumped upon his chest, his arms extended outward from his sides. The dwarf shook his head again.

"The comte may have headaches for the next few days. I shall send him one of my herbal teas to help." He chuckled, then turned and spoke to someone—no, to several. Guise's soldiers had invaded the corridor, obviously having overcome his own men-at-arms. The dwarf gave an order: "Stop the rambunctious Marquis de Vendôme's bleeding. Then hold him in the name of the king."

"What about the mademoiselle?" an insolent voice demanded. "I was told to bring her as well."

"Search every chamber. She is here. I saw her loveliness but yesterday. The Queen Mother wants her most unaltered. Put the marquis in chains. We will ride out tonight."

Foes

Marquis Fabien de Vendôme, weakened from the wound in his side, felt heavy chains binding his wrists behind him as he walked between armed guards across a familiar stone arcade that in his memory was both hallowed and nefarious. He thought it ironic that he should end up in the very Amboise castle courtyard where two thousand Huguenots were murdered by axmen at the behest of the Queen Mother and the Guises nearly two years ago. It was here that he had vowed to strike against Spain's wars of inquisition, and it was here that he would answer for sinking the Duc of Alva's galleon and several smaller vessels bringing soldiers and weapons to reinforce their massacre of Protestants in Holland.

He looked toward the royal stand with fringed canopy, the Queen Mother in her usual black gown with severe coif to the right of King Francis, and the Cardinal de Lorraine and Duc de Guise just behind and to the left of him. Francis looked unusually tired and pale, his young shoulders slumping. *Reinette* Mary was not present. Beside the Duc de Guise stood the infamous Duc of Alva, Spain's chief war general for the inquisition and spokesman for King Philip of Spain. He was here to protest France's failure in the eyes of Rome and Spain to rid the land of its Huguenots. This was the man Fabien was sure would rejoice to have his head on a platter to carry back to Spain.

"What better gift for the Duc of Alva than my capture?" Fabien murmured to the guards. "I am in bonne company—where is the dungeon with Prince Louis de Condé?"

The guards looked uncomfortable but kept silent.

Fabien stared at the royal assemblage. His staunch gaze crossed with Duc de Guise, who glowered self-righteously, then with the Duc of Alva, who looked victoriously smug. His black eyes raked Fabien.

A pity you were not aboard your fancy galleon when we sent it to the bottom!

❋

RACHELLE'S HEART SLAMMED AGAINST HER RIBCAGE. *Where is he?* her thoughts screamed. *Where is Fabien? What have they done with him? Did they surrender her beloved to the infamous Duc of Alva? Please, Lord, anything but that! I cannot live and endure the thought that Fabien is a galley slave on Alva's ship!*

Royal guardsmen and soldiers serving Duc de Guise appeared in number in the courtyard at Amboise castle. Beneath a canopied platform, the Queen Mother sat still. The breeze ruffled her coif and the black hem of her skirt. She reminded Rachelle of a winged black carrion crow ready to swoop down upon her prize.

Beside the Queen Mother, the young king, thin, pale, and looking ill, slumped in his throne, vulnerable between the two dominating figures standing beside him, the militaristic Duc de Guise and his brother, the Cardinal de Lorraine. They were *smiling*!

Rachelle clamped her hands into fists until her nails dug into her palms, fully aware of the guards at her elbows. She stood a short distance from the royal platform, a prisoner with Andelot and Gallaudet. While escaping the Bourbon palais château they had been overtaken in the woods by a band of Guise's soldiers and brought here to Amboise, where they'd been told Fabien was being held a prisoner of the king.

They were amused! The duc and cardinal were laughing and exchanging what appeared to be glib remarks with a dark-haired Spaniard with hawkish features and a short pointed beard. This must be the notorious Duc of Alva, the terror of the Dutch Protestants. Her heart throbbed as she read their victorious smiles. The cardinal, in spotless white and crimson, turned his head and spoke to Alva. He was here to collect the prize who had sunk his galleon and to haul Fabien away in cruel chains as a gift to King Philip of Spain.

Again Rachelle scanned the courtyard with anxiety eating at her heart. *Where was Fabien?*

⁂

SEATED ON THE PLATFORM over the courtyard, the Queen Mother tightened her fingers around the armrests of her royal chair and fixed her gaze below, where soon the marquis would be brought before the king for judgment.

The marquis had showed boldness and resolve in marrying the Macquinet belle couturière, but now, along with piracy against Spain, he must pay for his rash actions.

If only my weak son possessed some of the marquis' stubborn determination. Then I would not need to worry about the Guises manipulating the throne of France.

Duc de Guise, standing at the elbow of her son, fumed, for as Catherine knew, he wanted no delays where the marquis was concerned. Guise would be pleased to see the marquis dead — *just as he had seen the marquis' father dead at Calais?* She heard him muttering into his ginger-colored beard and beginning to pace about the platform at the delay. She would have liked to make some barbed retort to him, for she despised his rigid self-righteousness, but dared not. They were too powerful for her to openly oppose. She must move behind the scenes on shoeless feet, keeping her feelings toward him and the cardinal a smiling mask, just the way she had kept herself seemingly humble and unknowing when her husband had openly scorned her in public while honoring his mistress.

Just thinking of these humiliations made her angry. She forced herself to put them from her mind and fixed her gaze on Cardinal de Lorraine standing behind the king. The cardinal wore his familiar scornful little smile, as though bored by an inconsequential fuss. The Duc of Alva, all in black, stood in austere silence, the essence of Spanish pride. His hands dripped with Protestant blood. Since his severe master wanted this infamous "corsair" marquis brought to Spain, there would be no relenting of Alva's purpose unless she thought quickly to counteract his plans. If Alva had his way, the marquis would soon be a galley slave on his way to Madrid.

Duc de Guise leaned down toward Francis and spoke in a low urgent voice that Catherine could just barely hear.

"Do you not see, sire, that to be rid of such a dangerous messire in France is to your benefit?"

This constant chipping away at the ailing young Francis was wearing him down.

"I do not see that Marquis de Vendôme has done me harm." Francis's voice rose in its usual soft nasal twang caused by a breathing problem from which he had long suffered.

"Sire," came Cardinal de Lorraine's scornful tone, "sinking Spanish galleons is both a harm and an affront to all France."

"If the marquis did sink the Duc of Alva's galleon ..." Francis ventured.

"There is no question of that, sire. The marquis boasts of it," Duc de Guise said in an impatient voice.

Francis and the marquis had been friends since they were boys, and Catherine was aware of the king's reluctance to move against him. She was not supposed to know, but even her daughter, Princesse Marguerite, had sent a secret message to Francis asking that he not turn the marquis over to the Duc of Alva. Marguerite had once thought to begin one of her many flirtations with the marquis, but he had been wiser than most.

While the duc and cardinal were speaking to the Duc of Alva, Catherine leaned her head toward Francis.

"Remember, my son: with the Bourbon Prince Louis in the dungeon, and his brother Prince Antoine under palais arrest, sending the marquis to Spain might be the final stroke that provokes a religious civil war from their Huguenot serfs. Remember also who it is that becomes stronger if the Bourbons become weaker in France."

"If I do not do as the duc and cardinal advise, Madame Mother, there may be war with Spain. I do not see how I can prevent turning the marquis over to Alva," Francis whispered.

❈

BELOW THE PLATFORM, NOT far from where Rachelle stood under guard, a disturbance erupted among the soldiers coming from the castle. Her tormented gaze sought Fabien.

Just then, she heard a racket, followed by a bellow from a horn. Maurice, garbed in a crimson and black tunic, was followed by five guards roughly escorting a prisoner to a place just below the platform.

Rachelle stood a mere twenty feet to the side so that her full gaze fell upon the prisoner. She sucked in a tormented breath. *Fabien!*

The king's guardsmen were on either side and behind him, and there was blood on his face and on the side and front of his ripped tunic. A stab wound from Maurice's treacherous rapier?

Rachelle could see that he'd opposed his enemy in a laudable battle. He wore that resolute expression she knew so well and had come to respect and love. Viewing the garment he had worn as her bridegroom torn and bloodied was almost more than her heart could endure.

She fought back tears. Despite his rugged stance and unbowed head, she could see that he was suffering. He appeared to lose his balance for a moment, and she cried out in alarm. At once her voice arrested his attention, and his head swerved in her direction. For an agonizing moment their eyes met and held.

Rachelle snatched her arm from the guard, breaking free. She bolted toward Fabien.

Grabbed by a guard, she was pulled back.

"Let me go to my husband. Let go of me! Let go — "

There was a commotion. She saw Fabien had broken free of his guards. He caught hold of Maurice's shoulder, spun him round, and a solid fist thudded into his jaw. Maurice was knocked off his feet and landed hard backward on the court.

One of the guards struck Fabien, and Rachelle screamed her rage, but Fabien did not go down. Another guard struck him from behind, and finally the others wrestled him down.

The Queen Mother stood.

"Cease, you fools! You will reopen the Bourbon's wound!" Her voice carried loudly where her son's did not, and everyone looked up at the platform, startled and uncertain.

In the tumult of the brawl, Rachelle's guard was distracted. She ran forward and knelt before the Queen Mother.

"I beg of you to intervene, Madame."

A look of pleasure flashed across Catherine's face. She threw a victorious glance in Fabien's direction, as though desiring him to see his wife pleading for his life to be spared. At the traumatic moment Rachelle did not care. She would do most anything to free him if she could.

"The Marquis de Vendôme is loyal to France and a friend of His Majesty the King. The marquis has done nothing to receive such treatment as has befallen him." Rachelle flung a hand toward Maurice who was being aided to his feet, his hand held against his jaw. "The Comte Beauvilliers is small of spirit and jealous of the marquis who is a messire of honor."

The Queen Mother's face was immobile. Francis leaned forward. "You are now the *Marquise* de Vendôme?"

"Yes, Your Majesty. We married two days ago at the Bourbon palais château. But this monsieur — " She pointed again to Maurice.

"Sire," Duc de Guise said, fretting with his beard. "This distraction has nothing to do with the crime of high treason on the seas in which the Marquis de Vendôme and his crew of corsairs attacked, looted, and sank several ships of the King of Spain, destroying the lives of hundreds of soldiers who went down off the Spanish Netherlands!"

"He is innocent, Monseigneur. The corsairs you speak of were English corsairs!" Rachelle called to Duc de Guise. "The marquis is a lawful privateer sailing under a marque from Queen Elizabeth."

"Ah?" came the cold response of the Spanish Duc of Alva.

"Rachelle . . ." Fabien's weakened voice came with great effort from some distance behind her. "Be still . . ."

She turned, alarmed that she may have spoken unwittingly.

Maurice pushed his way forward to stand beside her. His face was bruised, and he dabbed at his cut mouth with a bloodied kerchief. Rage made his gray eyes glow. "Your Majesty, there are no witnesses to the 'innocence' of the marquis as the mademoiselle unwisely claims out of her duress. The marquis' ship, the *Reprisal*, is not an English vessel but a French man-of-war, with 'French' corsairs — like that one!" He turned and pointed, lifting his lace-encrusted wrist, now stained with blood, toward Gallaudet.

"And at this moment, Your Majesty, that buccaneering vessel, in the absence of its true capitaine — " he now pointed at Fabien — "Capitaine

Fabien de Bourbon, is commanded by one who is just as nefarious—Capitaine Nappier."

Fabien was now being held by several rugged guards who held his arms behind him, but his head was lowered against his chest as though he struggled with consciousness.

"It is the same Nappier, Your Majesty, who abandoned his post at the Royal Armory in Paris over a year ago to sail the vessel for the marquis. I now have information from one of his guards that the marquis was about to flee to Dieppe with my fiancée to meet that same Nappier and board his ship for Plymouth, England. Whereupon they would make even more attacks on Spanish galleons under the secret approval of England's heretic Queen Elizabeth."

Another commotion broke out as Maurice's detailed betrayal of their plans was being unmasked before all. Gallaudet wrested free of his guard and threw himself at Maurice. "You dawcock, you have no honor—" He was brought down by guards who were now thoroughly alert.

Gallaudet was already bloodied and bruised from the valiant fight he had put up to keep Rachelle from being taken in the woods. Andelot had a bruise on his cheekbone, and his arm was wrapped in a blood-stained cloth, evidence of the same fight. *Such loyalty is not easily come by*, Rachelle reflected, her throat dry and cramping from her emotions.

"Your Majesty, having defeated Marquis de Vendôme in a duel, I ask that he be turned over to me as my prisoner," Maurice said. "I shall have him guarded at the Beauvilliers estate in Clermont."

"*Your* prisoner?" the Duke of Alva's nostrils flared. He turned sharply toward the Duc de Guise. "Unheard of! Your king surely errs if he does not appease my King Philip. I am expected to return with the brigand marquis to Madrid."

Rachelle whirled toward the Queen Mother with outstretched hand.

Catherine leaned forward from her chair with a stern frown toward Maurice, as though angry that his boast of taking Fabien a prisoner had riled an even stronger opponent than the Duc de Guise—the Duc of Alva. She struck a hand toward the guards to silence Maurice.

Maurice stepped swiftly aside and bowed low, as though he realized he'd gone too far and was in danger of royal displeasure. Rachelle glared at him, but his eyes were on Alva, who looked with disdain upon all that he had witnessed.

The Queen Mother turned to Francis, who was looking more ill by the moment. Rachelle could rise above her own dilemma to feel a pang of sympathy for him. She heard the Queen Mother say, "This matter must be delved into, my son. We must not make the grave error of sending a messire of such blooded nobility to face the wrath of Spain. Remember, your grandfather was a king, and was held a prisoner of Spain, and was shamed for it. If there are witnesses of the marquis' innocence of piracy, as the mademoiselle says, then we must hear them before deciding such a serious matter."

Did the Queen Mother believe Fabien innocent, or was this a delaying tactic to thwart the Duc of Alva? Whatever the cause, Rachelle held her breath, hoping Francis would use the opportunity his mother had presented in his ear.

Francis stirred as if forcing himself awake to think. "Yes, we must have all the facts, Monseigneur Alva," Francis said quickly. He added gravely, lifting a hand to Catherine, "I trust you, Madame, to see that we come to the truth in this matter."

The Cardinal de Lorraine, his crimson robes rustling, the silver cross on his chest glimmering with rubies and diamonds, moved closer to the Spanish duc. His voice came snidely for all to hear: "As you see, my lord Duc, France embraces the bravest of sovereigns."

Rachelle's hopes crashed again.

"And do not forget France also embraces the most saintly of cardinals," came Catherine's smooth retort.

The cardinal smiled coolly at her.

The Queen Mother turned to the captain of the king's guard. "At the king's command, take Marquis de Vendôme to the dungeons."

Rachelle bowed. "Madame, I beg of you to allow me to stay at Amboise near — "

The Queen Mother did not favor her with a glance. She stood, her black gown rustling in the breeze, and flicked a hand of dismissal toward the guards, indicating that she wished no more pleadings, then turned her back toward the courtyard.

Rachelle jerked her head toward Maurice, who hovered nearby as if to make sure Fabien was indeed bolted into a dungeon. "You!" she said with contempt. "You betrayed your cousin Fabien — and Andelot. You are selfish to the core of your heart, Maurice."

Maurice's mouth curved with a cool smile. His limpid eyes ran over her.

"Your so-called marriage, mademoiselle, will not stand the test of the church or of time. That, I promise you. You will see me again. And when you do, you will cooperate or be sorry you did not."

She jerked her head away, hoping to discourage him from the idea that he cared for her.

The guards propelled her away from the courtyard toward the Amboise castle.

Weary and heartsick, she looked back over her shoulder, trying for one last glimpse of Fabien, to speak her love in a glance, but he was no longer in sight. *If I held no faith in God's purposes, I should utterly despair.*

❦

INSIDE THE AMBOISE CASTLE with its cold stone walls and footsteps echoing in the imposing corridors, the Queen Mother bit back her anger. Threats! *Always threats from Spain.* She faced the sullen Duc of Alva and the angry Duc de Guise.

"Madame, you have caused the young king to err in this needless delay," Guise stated.

"Ah, my restless and impatient ducs," she cajoled with a meaningless smile at both men. "I assure you, the king will make the final decision after he has rested himself this afternoon in his chamber. He is not well, as you have seen. The docteur insists that my son rest himself. Meanwhile — " she turned with a sober nod toward her enemy, Alva — "the duc can also rest assured that his concerns for His Majesty King Philip will be given the utmost consideration. The marquis will be confined as securely in his dungeon as his Bourbon kinsman, Prince Louis, is in his."

The semblance of a smile showed on Alva's sharp features, tanned by his months on the fields of battle. He nodded his head.

"Let us hope so, Madame, for the sake of your son the king and for your sake as well. Be assured that we have much to talk over. I bring many words from my master, His Most Christian Majesty, Philip." He bowed deeply with false congeniality and walked away, his black polished boots clicking on the marble floor.

Reptile, she thought, maintaining her own misleading smile.

The captain of the guard bowed to the cardinal, who'd been listening to her exchange with Alva.

"Monseigneur, what does my lord wish me to do with this student of Scholar Thauvet?" He pointed toward Andelot Dangeau, who stood alone some feet away.

Catherine too paused. Andelot was looking after the marquis, who was being taken by six armed guards toward the Amboise dungeons beneath the fortress castle.

"I request with all humility, Monseigneur," Andelot called, hastening a deep bow, "to accompany Marquis Fabien to his dungeon that I may attend him. He is in a fevered condition and I — "

"Andelot, keep silent," the cardinal broke in with a voice to bring a shudder. "You trouble yourself far too much with this traitorous marquis. I have said so before. You have paid too little heed to your superiors and kinsman. And it is I who shall deal with you, my nephew, a wayward scholar-in-training."

Catherine resented the cardinal's bold interjection. Not that she cared about the young monsieur called Andelot. She had hardly been aware of him, though she knew of him at court. She took a hard look at him.

Duc de Guise interrupted her thoughts, speaking to the cardinal. "Andelot remains a boy to be trained." He waved an indifferent hand. "Let him return to Thauvet."

"A boy!" scoffed the cardinal. "Come, come, my brother."

"He remains our responsibility. Now more than ever," the duc said with impatience.

Catherine looked from the cardinal to the duc. She wondered at what appeared to be an insignificant exchange between the brothers. But was it?

The duc is not known for a spirit of lenience toward one whom he thinks has wronged him. Andelot Dangeau's favorable interest in the mar-

quis should annoy him. Why then, is he coming to the young man's aid? Did he entertain plans to use Andelot for some future purpose? Most likely. Andelot too would bear watching.

She turned her unblinking gaze upon Duc de Guise, studying him. There was nothing about him she liked, from the scar on his cheek and eyelid taken in a battle for France, to his small, mean mouth and self-righteous eyes. The duc and cardinal had shown some interest in the young monsieur whom they laconically received as a kinsman. Was not Duchesse Dushane sponsoring him as a student of the respected Thauvet? There was something odd here.

Even so, she did not wish for Andelot to be providing the marquis' encouragement in the Amboise dungeon. She wanted the marquis in a weakened condition of mind and spirit when she called upon him in a few weeks — worried about Rachelle and in confusion over what would befall her and Gallaudet. She wanted the marquis without hope.

✳

LIKE A RAT IN A TRAP!

Marquis Fabien's first response to his captivity and the treacherous triumph of Maurice and the Queen Mother was rage. He came alert again as the guards hauled him across the courtyard toward the dungeons. He fought his captors every inch of the way as they struggled to haul him into the stone cell beneath the Amboise castle. He managed to break free of their grasp. His fist smashed the first jaw that came within reach. They jumped on him, wrestling him to the floor.

"Where is Maurice! I will tear him limb from limb!"

Someone ran up shouting orders. "I am his docteur! Careful, he is bleeding."

"Docteur, the marquis is going mad!"

Fabien felt some strong vapors held by the docteur over his nose and mouth, and after a short struggle he sank into a strange oblivion.

When he opened his eyes, he was in a dim cell with one small high window with bars. A candle flickered on a small table. He was lying on a low mattress feeling hot — then damp and chilled. He clamped his jaw to keep his teeth silent. Rage surged through him again with the memory of Rachelle.

Fevered, with a persistent and sickening pain in his side, he tried to get to his feet, but his head throbbed and the cell began to sway as though he were aboard a vessel in a storm.

He spied the docteur, a gaunt figure with high cheekbones, mixing something in a cup. In Fabien's fevered condition, he saw him as the offender responsible for his woes. He glared and fumbled a hand for his sword.

The docteur's grim gaze measured him. "Messire, if you are expecting to find your rapier, you are more feverish than I anticipated." He walked over, looked down at Fabien, and extended a cup. "Here, drink this. You will need it. I intend to clean debris from your wound. Infection has already begun. You are fortunate, nonetheless. The blade missed your vital organs. Next time, messire, if there is a next time, do not turn your back on Comte Beauvilliers."

"Next time I will kill him."

The docteur held the cup to his lips. Thinking it wine, Fabien gulped willingly, then gagged and knocked the cup away.

"Slime!" He spat out the last gulp angrily and again tried to get to his feet.

The docteur raised himself up with grave dignity. "Marquis, it is a valuable herbal medicine that I discovered during my travels to Istanbul."

"Istanbul—mille diables!" Fabien said with scorn, trying to get up.

"Do not be a spoiled patient." The docteur motioned calmly to the guards to subdue Fabien. "This will be painful, messire."

"Spoiled! I am not afraid of pain. It is not the pain that riles me. I want to know what they did with the marquise!"

"Messire?" The docteur looked down at him as though he thought Fabien were delirious.

"What did they do with my wife?"

"Do you not mean *Mademoiselle* Macquinet?"

"I mean *my wife*, Marquise Rachelle de Vendôme! We were married at my palais. If anything happens to her, I will get free and kill them!"

"Ah. She was taken under guard with Andelot Dangeau to Fontainebleau. Your belligerent page—I believe his name is Gallaudet—has also been subdued at last with something to make him sleep, such as I will give you. He is below you—" he pointed to the floor—"in the dungeon. I will be treating his injuries after I have finished with you."

Fabien's anger calmed. So, then Rachelle was with Andelot. He felt a little assuaged. They would both be held at Fontainebleau. Gallaudet was alive. He would be taken care of. Fabien slowly laid his head back down and stared evenly up at the docteur.

"When will I see the Queen Mother?"

The docteur shook his head. "Of that, Messire, I have no such knowledge. I hardly know of Her Majesty."

Fabien gave a hard laugh. "You will."

"I am new at court, having ended my long medical travels in the East. I was recommended at court by the royal surgeon, Ambroise le Pare, the king's personal physician. And now, I will need to treat this infection or you shall surely succumb to it."

Fabien gave a nod of assent.

Weary, his mind growing lazy from the effects of whatever he had swallowed, he was now noticing how sick and exhausted he was. He closed his eyes, and his thoughts drifted into a listless fog.

SCORNED

November found the leaves on the deciduous trees about Fontainebleau preparing for an autumn of crimson and gold. Rachelle kept track of the days since her arrival at Fontainebleau. Three weeks had passed. The chill that had settled over her heart made it seem as though it was already winter. She was locked in her chamber with none permitted to call upon her except Madame Trudeau, the older maid sent by the Queen Mother.

Rachelle spent her long days and nights of isolation wondering about Fabien. She touched her wedding ring, remembering those final moments on the stairway in Vendôme. She feared the ring would be taken from her. She'd seen the humorless Madame Trudeau looking at it with no favor in her bleak eyes. Rachelle stood from the gilt brocade chair where she'd been praying. She heard footsteps in the outer corridor, then the familiar rattle of the key in the lock. The heavy ornate door opened boldly and her keeper entered in her usual heedless manner. This time she was not alone. A young girl tottered behind her, carrying the evening tray.

"Your dinner, Mademoiselle—"

"Merely set it on the table, Thérèse. No need to prattle on in this fashion." Madame Trudeau folded her hands in front of her long black skirts.

"Oui, Madame."

"I am sure Mademoiselle Macquinet does not wish to be interrupted in her meditation."

Rachelle ignored the impertinence. Madame Trudeau was a distant relation to the Comtesse Françoise Dangeau-Beauvilliers, Maurice's mère. As such, she would be loyal to her kinswoman and in sympathy with her unhappiness over Maurice's discontented spirit.

Rachelle had tried to get Madame Trudeau to talk whenever she came to her, eager for news about Fabien as well as Andelot and Gallaudet, but the older woman retained a distant demeanor. No doubt this was why she'd been chosen to be her keeper. This afternoon, however, the woman seemed to linger. When the maid had accomplished her duties and departed, Madame Trudeau stood near the closed door. Whatever little appetite Rachelle had was spoiled by the woman's presence. Her face was angular and white, her eyes perfectly round and dark, like two polished wood buttons.

"Did Comtesse Beauvilliers send for you to come to court recently, Madame?" said Rachelle.

"Mademoiselle, I have been my kinswoman's most trusted lady since before you were born. I have also seen you about on many occasions and was at Chambord when you and your Grandmère were couturières for Princesse Marguerite and Reinette Mary Stuart. I was also at Amboise during the treasonous act of the Huguenots and saw them justly beheaded. That you have not seen me heretofore may speak more of your giddy behavior than of my absence."

"Madame, I have never been giddy, as you suggest. Had I been so,

Her Majesty would not have chosen me to become Princesse Marguerite's maid-of-honor."

"A noble position, Mademoiselle, which you disgraced by fleeing to Lyon without leave of Her Majesty or the princesse."

She could not easily deny it, at least the part about fleeing to her home, the Château de Silk in Lyon. She might have told her that she now had a far greater blight upon her, that of having Madalenna catch her spying upon the Queen Mother at the quay in Paris. Madame Trudeau, evidently, had not learned of this. Rachelle was waiting for the Sword of Damocles to fall on her, but as yet she had not even been called before the Queen Mother. Rachelle's lingering anticipation made it all the more stressful — that, and worrying and wondering about Fabien.

"You seem to know a good deal about me," Rachelle said.

She glanced at Rachelle. "Comte Maurice speaks incessantly of you."

Rachelle ignored that. "You do not like me. Surely it isn't because I fled the blood orgy at Amboise. Princesse Marguerite, too, was sickened by it, and if the truth were known, so too, the Comtesse Françoise."

"That is beside the fact," she said stubbornly.

"And it was Françoise's son, Maurice, who brought me from Amboise to Vendôme."

"So now it comes out that he saved you. Yet it is widely known you reward Maurice with open contempt."

Rachelle answered abruptly. "*I* treat Maurice with contempt! He who was defeated honorably in a duel by the marquis, then stabbed him when his back was turned — after the marquis spared Maurice's life."

"Lies, Mademoiselle. Who told you such?"

Why was Madame Trudeau so defensive of him?

"The Queen Mother's trusted dwarves spoke to us of what happened after I fled. Following my wedding vows, I had to save myself from this same Maurice whom you defend as honorable!"

Madame Trudeau's lips rounded in a patronizing smile. "Comte Maurice has quite another story, Mademoiselle. You are his fiancée and he had a gallant right to do as he did. I am sure the marquis' pride had much to do with the story of backstabbing."

"I am not now, nor have ever I been, Maurice's fiancée. I have promised him nothing of my heart or my loyalties, ever. And I am now married to Marquis de Vendôme. Nothing Maurice says will change that."

"Do not be so certain, Mademoiselle." With a secretive smile, she turned toward the door. "That Bourbon ring on your finger will not secure your future if the king wishes it differently."

Alarmed and indignant from her words, Rachelle followed her to the door.

"What do you mean by that? I am married. That cannot be changed."

Madame Trudeau shrugged her narrow shoulders. "I have already spoken too much. It is best I say nothing more."

"I wish to see my kinswoman, Duchesse Dushane."

"It is the order of the Queen Mother that you see no one except me, Mademoiselle."

"Then do take her a lettre from me, I beg of you."

"I am not under Her Majesty's leave to carry messages."

"At least tell me about my *husband*." She said the word proudly. "Is Marquis de Vendôme still being held at Amboise? Has he recovered from his injury?"

Her eyes hardened. "Mademoiselle, it has not yet been decided whether you have a husband or not."

Rachelle clenched her fists. "I am a married woman. I am Marquise de Vendôme!"

"A lofty title, Mademoiselle, if it is true, but I have not yet been told by the Queen Mother to address you as thus. My orders remain the same. Adieu."

She departed without a backward glance. Rachelle heard the sound of metal on metal in the sturdy lock.

❋

FAITH LIGHTS A CANDLE

Andelot could not sleep. He paced in his small, stuffy chamber. What to do about Marquis Fabien? He had done all within his power, which was feeble at best. His main hope came from his daily prayers for Fabien's deliverance and Rachelle's continued safety. Even Madame Duchesse was weak of hand. Andelot had spoken to her when he returned to Fontainebleau weeks ago and she had become most distressed. She had gone to meet with the Queen Mother to appeal for the marquis' release, but she'd not been received.

Andelot ran his fingers through his shorn hair, which was beginning to grow out again, and stared, frowning down at Philippe as though he no longer saw him but instead imagined Marquis Fabien on the floor in chains in the dark, rat-infested dungeons of Amboise. Weeks and no word of how he progressed or what would befall him. Nor had the Duc of Alva as yet returned to Spain, so confident was he of returning with the Bourbon prize for the Spanish king.

If only there were a way to help the marquis escape. The Queen Mother boasted that she had put much effort into strengthening the prison at Amboise and improving its security.

Andelot rubbed the tired muscles in the back of his neck.

Madame Duchesse had written to Pasteur Bertrand Macquinet at Spitalfields in London and informed him of the situation. Much prayer would ascend to God once Bertrand knew of the present situation. Andelot wrote Oncle Sebastien — and Mademoiselle Idelette, owing much to Scholar Thauvet for smuggling his lettres out of the chamber. They would go to Cambridge with other mailings Thauvet was making to friends in London. Someone would deliver Andelot's letters to the Macquinets, but as yet there was no certain news on whether they had arrived in England. His nights were long and plagued with forebodings. All those he cared about the most were far from his reach and confronting danger. How was he expected to give his mind to studies?

There was no hope of seeing Rachelle in her chamber. The duchesse had tried to send Nenette, but the guards were adamant. Until the Queen Mother altered their orders, Rachelle would receive no company except Madame Trudeau.

Andelot scowled to himself. There was something about Madame Trudeau that was vaguely familiar. What could it be?

It was late, and Thauvet had retired over an hour ago.

Andelot extinguished all but one candle and moved in silence to his bed.

Outside, the chilly headwind moaned around his window eaves. He was anxious about Marquis Fabien, Gallaudet, and Julot, and grieved over what had happened at Vendôme to the honorable men-at-arms.

Andelot prayed for their families. He tried to repeat some of the wondrous Bible words that he'd memorized before returning the Bible to the Huguenot pasteur in the Fontainebleau woods.

Although the night was dark and the struggle in the battle for truth just beginning, the path was sure, as was his faith in the King of kings.

Your Word is the light for my path. I believe, Lord, that You may yet have purposes for us. May You therefore secure the way forward, and strengthen us within.

<hr>

ALONE WITH GOD

Even after all these weeks, Rachelle had received no word about Fabien, nor had the Queen Mother called for her, which kept her anxious and troubled.

If only I might get a message to Princesse Marguerite, perhaps then I could learn about his health.

Marguerite had long been Fabien's amie. She would surely have heard the news about his arrest and confinement at Amboise and would soon contact her. Marguerite was not as politically minded as the Queen Mother, but she did have her ladies scampering about in important places, and she would have heard about the duel with Maurice and the ungallant treachery against the marquis. The princesse and her ladies would despise Maurice for such dishonor.

Marguerite, I am sure, is here at Fontainebleau, as is Duc de Guise's son, Henry, whom Marguerite loved as well as she could love. If I have not heard from her, it may be that even she dare not risk contacting me.

Rachelle knew the cold taunt of being utterly alone and without any present hope of changing her circumstances. *I am not alone — like King David*, she encouraged herself. *My soul, why are you cast down? Hope in God.*

She paced the carpet in her stocking feet, whispering to herself, her peignoir of blue lace floating behind her. Her chamber was by now so familiar there was no need for a candle in the dead of night when sleep evaded her tired mind.

If only Fabien and I had left an hour sooner. If only we had slipped away, just the two of us, to find the pasteur and marry in his cottage — we could have escaped the arrival of Maurice and Duc de Guise's soldiers.

If only.

Rachelle stopped at the window and looked below into the dark courtyard, seeing the familiar flaming torches, the uniformed guards on duty, looking like small toy soldiers from where she stood on an upper floor. The duchesse would be trying to contact me. And Andelot. She knew he was at liberty, for Madame Trudeau had let that escape her cloistered tongue. Perhaps even Marguerite had tried to send word to her. With so many failing to breach the walls that kept her enclosed in the splendor of her prison, what did it say for the power of the Queen Mother? Not even a note could be slipped beneath her door or smuggled in on a tray of food or with her laundry.

And her beloved at Amboise? Amboise, with its cold, gray stone walls, impregnable dungeons, and equally gray River Loire that not so very long ago was clogged with the headless corpses of Huguenots. Fabien was in its dank dungeon, thinking of her as she thought of him, both pained in heart, wondering if they would at last meet in an embrace.

Rachelle longed for him. She shivered, rubbing her arms and staring at the torch flames along the walls of the courtyard and at the gates. She tormented herself with the thought: What if Fabien were dead?

Non, do not even think it. If he were dead, I would be useless to Catherine. She would send me away at once or perhaps even put me in the dungeons for having followed her to the quay.

Was it possible Madalenna had kept silent about having seen her?

She remembered what Fabien had said about that. *Why then does the Queen Mother not call for me? Why no threats, no ranting?* Rachelle narrowed her eyes as she stared out into the darkness. *Because she has some diabolical plan in mind. What could it be except to convince him to carry out her wish to eliminate the duc? To torment Fabien with threats against my safety until he agrees to do her evil bidding. Yes, she has a scheme, and Fabien and I are caught in her sticky web.*

She turned from the window in restless anxiety.

God is our hope.

Her heart lifted heavenward.

"O Lord—Father God!"

Again, she sank to her knees beside a chair, resting her head. *I won't weep. I won't!*

She prayed, wrestling her doubts into submission to truth. She thought of the promises she had memorized in Lyon at the family Château de Silk. She recalled the meaning of Christ's mercy, His gracious dealings with those who called upon Him.

"He is here with me through His Spirit whether I feel His nearness or not. He promised to be with me always, even to the end of the age. In times of fear, loneliness, confusion, or doubt, and even danger and death."

I wait, and am alone, like a sparrow upon the housetop.

Tenez ferme. *Stand firm.*

And if deliverance does not come?

Peter was released from prison by an angel; but James was killed by Herod.

Esther became a queen and was used to deliver her people, but Joseph was sold into slavery and endured years of imprisonment before being elevated to deliver his family. God has no favorites, only different purposes.

Across her mind marched a company of spiritual heroes and heroines who had been delivered: Daniel in the lion's den, Peter in prison, Moses, Joshua, Gideon, Deborah, Sarah, Rahab!

But others, whose names were known only to God, did not receive spectacular deliverance. They were mocked and tortured, imprisoned and killed; yet these others were as victorious in their faith.

Rachelle rubbed her temples as Psalm 37 came to her: *Commit thy way unto the Lord ... Rest in the Lord, and wait patiently for him: fret not thyself.* She smiled as the words became steps that led her heart upward: *commit* your way ... *rest* in the Lord ... *wait* patiently, and finally, *fret not.*

"Stand firm," she whispered again to her soul.

Why did I not think of using this possibility of getting a message out before?

Rachelle moved about her chamber awaiting the arrival of Madame Trudeau, who rarely missed her schedule. Did not Princesse Marguerite expect gowns to wear to Spain?

Was not this the singular reason for which she'd been called to Paris from the Château de Silk, to create such dresses for Marguerite? And a gown for the Queen Mother as well!

A shiver ran along the back of her neck. There was no avoiding that uncomfortable possibility. Well, then. A Macquinet couturière must first decide the colors of the silks and velvets, the manner of lace and threads to present to the princesse so that she might choose. Therefore, it was necessary to see Marguerite. And once she was in her presence Marguerite would surely come to her to aid and help smuggle a message to Fabien at Amboise.

Rachelle's sewing equipment remained at the Louvre, including her special Macquinet hand case with her initials embossed in gold. Unless, hope of hopes, Nenette brought it with her when she and Philippe came here to Fontainebleau. At least Rachelle assumed her *grisette* had safely arrived by now.

If only that tight-lipped Madame Trudeau would tell me more!

She heard footsteps approaching from the outer corridor followed by low voices.

The key rattled in the lock.

Intruder

RACHELLE STEPPED AWAY FROM THE DOOR AND FEIGNED A MOOD OF composure. Her affectation nearly crumbled when Madame Trudeau stood back and Comte Maurice walked in with a look of triumph on his saturnine face.

"Mademoiselle." He bowed, removing his hat. He was garbed in purple and black satin with a white plume in his Spanish hat.

"It is *madame*. For I am married to le Marquis Fabien."

"Not for long, *Mademoiselle*, I assure you. This mockery of a marriage is to be dissolved by the cardinal."

Dissolved? She tried to hide the fear his words evoked. Was it possible? What of the Huguenot weddings of Admiral Coligny, Prince Louis de Bourbon, and many of the Huguenot nobles? Their marriages were legal throughout France, as was her own parents' marriage and that of Comte Sebastien and her sister Madeleine. Rome did not bless or accept them, but they were accounted as legal. But she put nothing past the Queen Mother, the cardinal, and Maurice's machinations.

She put on a calm face to deflect his attack. "I am married before God to Fabien and nothing will change that. I shall never submit to a false marriage to you, Maurice. You might as well understand that I love Fabien with all of my soul. And even if I were not married, after the shameful way you treated him and Andelot, I would never consent to becoming your wife." She held out her left hand and the Bourbon family ring belonging to Fabien's mère, the duchesse, glimmered like fire.

His mouth twitched as he looked at her hand, then his gaze shot back up to hers.

"A ring does not make a marriage."

"Nor does an undesired arrangement by a queen."

"You insult my honneur. I have fairly bested the marquis, a famed swordsman, with superior swordsmanship of my own."

"You have not defeated Fabien."

"He is in the dungeon, and I am not—a fact that should overcome your objections."

"It merely shows that he was wrong to trust you with his back turned."

"Gibes, mademoiselle, lies."

"There are witnesses to your treachery, mon comte."

"And such witnesses! *Par exemple?*"

"The dwarves of the Queen Mother. Would you dare call them liars? Do so, I beg of you, before Catherine and see where it leads you."

Maurice flung an arm upward in a gesture of dismay. "These tiring words prove nothing. There is naught else to be said. The marquis abducted you from Paris and has proven himself inferior to my tact and honor. He is where he belongs due to his rebellion against His Majesty by sinking Spanish galleons."

"I left with Fabien most willingly from Paris, I assure you. You may deceive yourself on these matters, but you will not deceive me. If Comte Sebastien were here, he would assuredly be ashamed of your act of treachery against both Fabien and me."

"After Fabien abducted my fiancée, an affaire d'honneur is not to be called treachery."

"I was never your fiancée. Do you not see that the Queen Mother used you to lure Fabien back to France so she could arrest him? You fell into her ploy like a bird in a snare and helped to bring us all to harm. Sebastien thought better of you."

A startled look flickered across his face, as for a moment he hesitated in consideration. But the look disappeared as swiftly as it came and impatience contorted his face.

"By Saint Louis, the guardian of our race, do you take me for a fool?"

"I take you for a traitor. Sebastien is likely to feel much the same when he hears of your actions. And I cannot even imagine his rage over your treatment of Andelot. Do not forget that Andelot, too, is his neveu, even if you prefer to treat him as a serf."

He flung a hand in dismissal and walked away. "I would have thought it more honorable of mon oncle Sebastien had he cared to at least inform me of his departure from France," he said defensively, showing resentment.

"Could he trust you?" she asked smoothly.

His head turned sharply. The gray eyes were frosty pools. "As I trusted him! I suspected all along, but did I speak of it? My mother, his sister, mourns for his loss. And I miss the evenings spent over a glass of wine in his presence. Now mère is also denied seeing her petite niece bébé Joan grow up in France."

Rachelle turned her shoulder to him, ignoring Madame Trudeau, who hovered behind the back of a tall chair in the corner. "Far better petite Joan grows to womanhood in England."

"Tut! England," he said. "Nor did anyone in the family inform me of Mademoiselle Idelette's dilemma."

"My sister is not likely to go about sounding the trumpet, Monsieur."

"Had I known what happened I would have hunted this derelict down to the grave. As for *your* ill treatment of me, Mademoiselle, I can only confess my shock, having thought better of your fairness and virtue."

"I have done you no harm. Au contraire, after your boorish treatment of Andelot, do you speak of fairness? I should think you would apologize to him and begin to make amends."

He walked around the chair restlessly, went to the window, and returned to face her.

"What he received for working against me was nothing more than sport. Why, the pages receive far more teasing when they first enter the *Corps des Pages*."

She moved away from him, staying out of his grasp, giving him no occasion to reach for her. She glanced toward the door; Madame Trudeau's fingers plucked at her high collar.

"I shall not be content ma belle chérie, not until this matter with Fabien is over and we are rightfully married by the cardinal."

In one quick move he was in front of her, cutting off her escape. His lean fingers grabbed hold of her arms, pulling her against him. He bent over her, his kiss urgent and demanding.

She wrestled to remove herself from his stubborn grasp, biting his shoulder.

He flung her loose, infuriated, the back of his hand flying to his mouth. He glared and reached for her again. Her hand shot out, connecting her palm to the side of his face.

"Messire! Command yourself!"

Madame Trudeau rushed forward to tug at his arm. "Oh Messire, you must not!"

He jerked his arm free from Madame Trudeau and narrowed his gaze upon Rachelle.

"This spurious marriage to Fabien will be declared void; the cardinal himself said so. And the Queen Mother promised you will be given to me. And when you are — "

"The cardinal would say anything. And you are foolish to trust the Queen Mother's baiting promises."

"Take caution when you speak so of the mighty ecclesiastic and the Queen Mother. The church will not recognize your marriage to the marquis by an unknown monsieur, a mere Huguenot," he said, scoffing, "one who deigns to call himself a true and established minister of God."

"A minister of God is more than an elevated religious official with a crimson robe. It is the doctrine and the fruit that declare a monsieur to be truly of God."

"Enough." He flicked his hand as if at a gnat. "I do not wish to speak of religion."

"But you will speak of Christianity when you wish to profane it for your unjust cause. That, monsieur, is the vilest hypocrisy. You scorned what is honorable just now and forced me to your unwanted attentions."

"That is not all I shall expect of you!"

"Out!" She turned in a rage to Madame Trudeau, whose hands were at her mouth, her eyes wide. Rachelle walked toward her. "And you. You had no authority to bring him into my chamber. Go, both of you! I demand to see Princesse Marguerite!"

She raised her voice louder so that a guard appeared unexpectedly in the doorway, looking from her to Maurice and then to Madame Trudeau.

Rachelle rushed toward him with exaggerated relief. "Make this bane of my existence leave me!" She pointed to Maurice, dramatizing her emotion by placing a weak hand to her forehead. "He is forcing his unwanted attentions upon me. Look at the lace on my sleeve — he tore it just now, grabbing me."

The guard frowned. "Messire Comte, is this true what Madame says?"

"Do you think I shall answer to you? I am a comte!"

"You are, Messire," came the sober voice and even stare. "And a prince of the royal blood is in the dungeon. So too is the Marquis de Vendôme. One might ask if a comte will fare better with the Queen Mother? It was she who sent me here to guard Marquise de Vendôme. You must leave, Messire."

Maurice's cheeks flamed a ruddy color. He stammered and whirled toward Rachelle. "Again you besmirch my honneur."

"Then hate me and find another amour, Comte, one who adores you, I beg of you."

"I meant you no harm and you know it, Mademoiselle."

"I know nothing of the sort, Messire," she said loftily, and stepped closer to the royal elite guardsman, lifting her chin.

Maurice's gray eyes snapped. "This is not over, Rachelle." He walked over toward the doorway, pausing to throw a cold glance at the guard before looking back at her. "I shall win when the marquis is dead." He passed on out the door.

Rachelle turned away, folding her arms, her back straight so as not to show weakness. She was afraid she would encourage him to more threats and bullying if he knew his threat frightened her. Even so, the word *dead* pierced her heart like a fiery dart. *What could he mean? What a ghastly encounter.*

The guard stepped back into the corridor and closed the door.

She turned toward Madame Trudeau. "This was your doing. You should never have let Maurice in here."

"I had no idea he would behave this way, Mademoiselle."

"Yet you claim to know him so well?"

"I have never seen him like this, I assure you." She dabbed at her eyes with her handkerchief.

"Maurice has always been very temperamental," Rachelle said. "Comtesse Beauvilliers has spoiled him all his life."

"That was only after his younger sister died. Athenais — "

"Now he believes his desires should be granted and satisfied at any cost, even murder."

"Murder!" Madame Trudeau's hand crept up to her throat.

"What do you call it? He tried to kill Marquis Fabien."

"I cannot believe it of him, Mademoiselle. Comte Maurice is emotional, oui, and he can be reckless, but he is not deliberately evil. He does not coldly connive. He reacts in bursts of energy when provoked — puff!" She opened her arms wide and looked at the ceiling.

Rachelle lifted a tired hand. "Say it as you will, Madame, but see that you do not allow him in my chamber again. I shall attempt to appeal to the Queen Mother if you disregard my wishes."

She bowed her head, looking genuinely contrite. "It will not happen again."

Rachelle believed she truly was shocked by what she had witnessed and heard and wished now that she had not been so rash to favor the son of the Comtesse Beauvilliers.

"And Princesse Marguerite?" Rachelle asked, taking advantage of the moment of the woman's meekness. "Will you see that she has my message? I speak the truth when I say I was summoned from Lyon by the Queen Mother to serve as her daughter's couturière. If the journey to Spain draws near, then I must begin work on her wardrobe."

"There will be no journey to Spain this spring. The journey was again delayed."

Rachelle felt the sting of disappointment.

"Delayed?" She sank onto the settee. "Are you certain of this?"

"Comtesse Beauvilliers learned of it only this morning. The Queen Mother and the Duc of Alva came to an agreement of cooperation on certain matters, but not marriage for the princesse. No new date has yet been set for a journey to Spain."

"The hoped-for marriage between the princesse and Don Carlos is delayed?"

"It may not happen at all. As for Princesse Marguerite's reaction, she is busy with Messire Guise, the duc's son." Her mouth tightened sourly.

"The only talk of marriage has again turned toward the Huguenot, the young Prince Henry of Navarre."

With Antoine, the King of Navarre, his père, here at Fontainebleau under palais arrest?

Rachelle's tortured thoughts once again turned back to her amour Fabien in the Amboise dungeon. Her emotions were raw with a hundred horrible thoughts of what they might do to him, but did they dare? He was of royal Bourbon blood! Had not the Queen Mother sent a guard to ensure her own security? How much more then would she take measures to guard Fabien, whom she intended to use for her nefarious work against Duc de Guise?

Perhaps I should worry and pray far more about what she will expect from Fabien in return for his freedom and mine.

A knock on the outer door sent Madame Trudeau hurrying to answer. Rachelle waited tensely, hearing a soft muttering of voices.

A moment passed before Madame came back. Her hands were clasped together at her bosom, fingers intertwined.

"The Queen Mother has called you to her chambers. You are to go there at once. Madalenna is waiting in the corridor now."

Madalenna! Rachelle stood transfixed.

THE SILK WEB

A short time later, Rachelle, wearing a gown of blue satin embroidered with silver and carrying a pink feather fan was momentarily to enter the serpent's den. Her heart thudded. Just a few feet ahead was an alcove to the side of the corridor —

Swiftly she caught hold of Madalenna's arm and pulled the thin girl into the wall recess, half expecting her to scream her protest, but she did not. Rachelle held her firmly against the wall.

"Quiet, do not cry out. Tell me, does the Queen Mother know about the quay? Speak! I want the truth."

Madalenna's eyes were like silent, deep pools staring up at her.

"Answer me. You saw me there. Did you tell Her Majesty?"

"Yes, she knows. I was not going to tell—but I had to."

"Why has she not called for me before now?"

"She needs the Marquis de Vendôme. She needs you for a time. But later—later, watch out."

"Oh Madalenna, why did you tell her?"

"Because she already guessed I was holding back from her. She always guesses. I cannot keep anything from her. She owns me. I have no choice."

"You do have a will of your own. You are her slave, but she cannot own your mind and soul unless you surrender them."

Madalenna's shoulders slumped beneath Rachelle's hands. "There is no hope for me."

"There is hope as long as you are alive. There is hope with your true Master, Christ. Turn to Him, call upon Him, and He can make a way for the freedom of your soul."

Madalenna dropped her eyes and said nothing. At last Rachelle gently released her.

"I know you told her because you fear her. I hold nothing against you. I want you to know that. And I hope you will consider what I told you about Jesus. Attend the prêches when they begin in June. Seek to talk with Minister Beza when he comes. God will open a door of forgiveness for your soul."

Madalenna's lips remained tightly closed, but a lone teardrop oozed from the corner of her eye and trickled down her sallow cheek.

Rachelle swallowed. "We had better go to the Queen Mother's chamber now. She will wonder why we tarry."

The girl turned and entered the corridor, and Rachelle followed, feeling a mixture of anger at Catherine and a new compassion for Madalenna. Until now, she had been but a sinister shadow creeping about; but now, she had a heart, a soul, and teardrops.

What excuse could she possibly use to justify following the Queen Mother to the quay?

They neared the royal chambers with the imposing guards posted on either side of the door. Was this to be her end? But Madalenna said the Queen Mother still needed her. She needed Fabien, and Rachelle was the hostage to compel him to do as the Queen Mother wished.

Besides fear, Rachelle felt her anger reawaken. Though her mind had been filled with her own difficulties, she had not forgotten her suspicion that this woman may have brought about the death of her grandmère.

She forced herself to remember what Pasteur Bertrand had said to the family about obligation to the throne.

"The Spirit of God admonishes us through the apostle Paul in Romans to honor the king. If we say that is impossible, then let us remember who it was that sat upon the throne of the Roman Empire when this admonition was written, the insane Roman emperor, Nero."

Rachelle's heart began to calm. She looked ahead. Madalenna stood passively waiting in the doorway to the Queen Mother's chambers. Two Italian-looking royal guards stood at either side.

The Lord would handle all disagreements in His own time. Even the kings and queens of France would bow before Jesus Christ one day as the King of all kings. *I should show my trust now by waiting for Him to judge wisely. If I know the injustice done to grandmère will be taken care of one day by the Lord, whether in this life or in the next, then I can leave my anxieties and frustrations in His hands.*

"Avenge not yourselves, but rather give place unto wrath."

With a prayer in her heart, her palms sweating, she was granted entry into the imposing sanctuary of the Queen Mother.

The *élégante* chamber waited in silence. The Italian frescoes and rose accents in cushions, floral rugs, and draperies lent an atmosphere of Renaissance grandeur and authority that left Rachelle with a tight throat.

With head lowered, Rachelle curtsied. "Your Majesty," she said, her voice calm and unstrained, through much practice.

Out of the corner of her eye, she saw Catherine de Medici dressed in black. *Like a spider in a fresh web.*

She waited to hear sharp words, like the crack of doom.

Catherine stood tall and erect, her hands at the sides of her stiff skirt. Since the death of her husband, King Henry II, in a friendly jousting match, in celebration of the marriage of their daughter Elizabeth to the austere and morbid King Philip II of Spain, Catherine de Medici almost always wore mourning black. But she had wanted a new gown. Was this true, or an excuse?

Rachelle, even in her anxious state, could not help noticing her wardrobe. Her gown was of exceptional texture, suggesting that the Queen Mother might take some interest in fashion.

As a Florentine, one might have expected the Queen Mother to have black hair and dark flashing eyes, but such was not the case. Catherine's mother had been French — in fact, a Bourbon. And her eyes were light colored, her hair thick and curly. Rachelle might describe the color as blonde, yet not a golden blonde like her sister Idelette's, but an almost yellow-brown.

Her hair was parted in the center, drawn back beneath her typical cap, or coif.

Rachelle tried not to notice Catherine's prominent teeth that gave her a rather robust look.

If Catherine had intended to rebuke her it was not obvious now. She wore a smile. Rachelle knew better than to trust the false smiling face of the Queen Mother.

"Ah, then, we have our charmante couturière back with us, do we?" The Queen Mother motioned for Rachelle to rise. "But are you our couturière Mademoiselle Macquinet, or is it Marquise de Vendôme?"

"It is true, Madame, that Marquis de Vendôme has taken me for his wife. We were married at Vendôme."

The Queen Mother leaned forward, her hands gripping the armrests. "We cannot always keep what we desire, is that not true, *Mademoiselle Macquinet?*"

Rachelle read the warning in her cold gaze, and it chilled her to the bone.

"As loyal servants to France we must walk the path of duty," the Queen Mother continued. "The Marquis de Vendôme has agreed with me."

What had Fabien agreed with her about? Not that their marriage could be annulled? Non, she would never believe that he would agree to that.

Catherine stood and moved about slowly. "The Cardinal de Lorraine insists marriage outside the sanction of the Roman Church is no true marriage at all."

What was she implying? Rachelle's tension grew. This meeting was not what she had expected. There was no dreaded mention of the incident on the quay.

"Madame, before God I am married to the marquis."

Catherine snapped her fingers, her eyes glinting. "Silence."

Rachelle bowed her head.

Catherine strode up to her, shoulders back, looking down through heavy lids.

Rachelle held her breath, waiting.

The moments crept onward. She could hear the Queen Mother's breathing.

"Marriage is a duty performed for the good of one's king, of his kingdom. As daughters of France, we show our dignity and accept what we must."

Rachelle's heart began to beat with the quickening drumbeat that sounded the portent of danger.

Catherine began her pacing again. Back and forth . . . back and—

"You will oblige the throne," Catherine said. "It is your duty. And if not, I could send you to the Bastille."

Rachelle tried not to tremble. She sensed the Queen Mother did not appreciate weakness.

"Mademoiselle, I would remind you that your family's future also depends upon your cooperation. Do you wish for the Château de Silk, so long in the fair hands of its couturières, to continue as it has in past generations?"

Rachelle met her eyes at once. "Madame, with all my heart."

Catherine gave a brief nod. "You are wise. Then you will do what is required of you. Of this I remind you, but with sorrow. Ah, it brings me sadness to speak of such matters, but when necessary, speak of them I shall. Believe me, Mademoiselle, so much is at stake."

The spell of terror was eased as Catherine turned away— deliberately?—and sat down upon her ornate royal chair, gazing across her chamber. Rachelle, however, understood the message conveyed.

Catherine reached for several correspondences from a white marble stand veined with gold that stood beside her armrest.

"I have a few matters to discuss with you. I will begin with the lettre I received from your kinswoman, Duchesse Dushane, regarding the marquis. Most naturally she begs for his deliverance from the grip of King Philip."

Rachelle tried to glean a ray of hope from her statement, but caution challenged.

"The duchesse promises to work tirelessly in the hope of granting pardon on his behalf." Catherine shook her head as though weary. "Ah, Mademoiselle, this most unfortunate situation was of the marquis' own doing. Even so, you may have a reason for hope. It is my intent to help those who serve my plans. There are, of course, certain conditions."

Rachelle's gaze flew to Catherine's, searching, and found both promises and warnings. Rachelle was already aware of what those conditions were. She remembered seeing the Spanish ambassador pacing up and down the outer salle with open disdain written across his swarthy face.

"Madame, dare I hope you are suggesting the Marquis de Vendôme can be spared from the clutches of Spain and released from the Amboise dungeon?"

Catherine tossed the lettre from the Spanish envoy on the ivory stand. "You are the first one to whom I speak this. Yes, there is a rare wind of fortune blowing, that could perhaps return him to my son the king's favor."

As if King Francis were so fiercely against Fabien!

There was little doubt that once the Queen Mother's purpose was accomplished, she would cast them aside without qualm to the dogs.

Duc de Guise must be assassinated, that is what the Queen Mother meant, and she would expect Fabien to end the Duc's life. And if Fabien refuses? She will have him turned over to the Spanish envoy to be put on a galleon for Madrid.

Rachelle's aching heart thudded in her chest. "Madame, if the release of my husband, the marquis, could be attained, then I should be a most grateful servant, Madame."

Catherine leaned back into her ornate chair and smiled.

"Ah, most pleasing, Mademoiselle. I am sure you will be most anxious to see your bridegroom. You are favored, for many have sought him here at court. Your family will be pleased when they learn the news, I am sure. You now enjoy a title. Your family will attend the colloquy this summer?"

Rachelle tried to keep her composure. "Oui, Madame. They must return from London to attend to the silk business at Château de Silk. It is now under an overseer, but cannot remain so much longer without suffering from lack of Monsieur Macquinet's knowledge."

"I am sure Monsieur Macquinet is concerned for the good of his silk estate."

Abruptly she stood, changing the mood again. "Did you know of the plans of Comte Sebastien to sneak away from his duties to the king and flee to London?"

Rachelle's hands were damp. "Non, Madame. The day also took me by surprise."

"I am most sure it did." Her teeth showed in a mocking smile. She came down from her elevated chair and moved closer to Rachelle. The smile vanished. "You were busy elsewhere on the morning Sebastien and your sister Madeleine left the Louvre," came her low voice. "Were you not?"

Rachelle's heart sounded in her ears. Now it was coming — the trap was ready to snap shut.

"They must have departed in the night, Madame."

"In the morning when you first arose, you did not see them?"

"I believe they must have already departed."

"Where did you go when you arose so early, Mademoiselle?"

Rachelle stared into the heavy lidded eyes that confronted her without blinking.

"Go, Madame?"

"Yes, where did you go when you left the Louvre? To the quay?"

There it was. If she could somehow admit she had gone, but avoid alerting her ...

"The quay? Madame, I did go for a morning walk, but it was a chilly morning. It was very foggy, and I found that I did not enjoy the stroll and returned."

"Madalenna saw you on the quay. She followed you. Just as you, Mademoiselle, followed me."

Rachelle's mouth went dry. There was no way out.

Catherine's strong fingers clamped around her arm, pulling her closer. "To whom have you mentioned this?"

"No one."

Catherine's eyes turned into slits and her fingers tightened until Rachelle gritted her teeth to keep from wincing.

"The truth, Mademoiselle."

"To no one except the marquis."

"The marquis!" She flung Rachelle's arm away and stepped back. "You fool."

"I did not think it was important."

"You lie. But I shall speak the truth to you. If your tongue slips this information to anyone at court, I will see that the marquis becomes a galley slave on a Spanish galleon. You will never see him again. He will die a slow, painful death. You will remain alive in a dungeon to worry for years to come. Understood?"

Rachelle dropped her head into her sweating palms. "Yes, I understand," she choked out in a cracked whisper.

Silence enveloped the chamber, then Catherine stepped back. Rachelle, her head still in her hands, heard the movement of stiff skirts.

"Sit down on that stool before I have a fainting damsel on my hands," she said shortly.

Rachelle raised her face. She was not about to faint. She would stand against this woman's evil schemes no matter the terror inflicted. Catherine was also seated again and the old demeanor was back. Rachelle sank onto the velvet stool. Her knees trembled, but she met the even gaze without faltering.

"So your sisters Madeleine and Idelette told you nothing of their planned escape?"

"Nothing, Madame."

"Ah, Madeleine … She is doing well in London, she and the bébé, and recovering from her sickness?"

Rachelle's skin tingled with fear, even while anger seared her heart. She wanted to veer her gaze from those prominent, watchful eyes, but it might unmask her.

The Queen Mother knew of her suspicion, knew why she had followed her to the quay. Rachelle had heard her ask for poison that could not be traced.

"Madeleine is growing stronger day by day, Madame, as is her infant daughter, Joan."

Catherine smiled. "That is bonne news. Sebastien's release from the Bastille was life to Madeleine's heart, I am sure."

With every beat of her own heart, she disliked this woman who bullied, threatened, and boasted that her personal actions were for *la gloire de la France*.

How long would this game of diversion go on? What was she trying to learn? What did she want? Merely to intimidate, to assure cooperation and silence?

"May I ask, Madame, what it is I may do to bring about Marquis Fabien's release from Amboise?"

The Queen Mother rose swiftly, her arms dangling at her sides, and looked down at her. "You will know quite soon, I assure you. Tomorrow morning you will go with me on a small journey to speak with him."

Startled, Rachelle did not reply.

"To make certain of your discerning cooperation with my plans, it is necessary we convince the dashing marquis to join us in our bond of cooperation."

Rachelle scarcely breathed, wondering, waiting for what trap came next.

The Queen Mother widened her eyes in mock surprise. "Surely you wish to speak with the marquis?"

Speak with him? But of course she did, with all her heart, and the Queen Mother knew it, so what was behind this unexpected event? Something sinister, of course, something intimidating, or she would not arrange the brief meeting with Fabien. Rachelle had wished to see him in his dungeon at Amboise immediately after his arrest, and at that time the Queen Mother swept aside her plea.

Wary, Rachelle hesitated.

"Madame, is the marquis here at Fontainebleau?"

"He remains at Amboise, as does his worthy kinsman Prince Louis. I will journey secretly by coach to speak with both messieurs in the morning. You, Mademoiselle, will accompany me. I am certain the marquis will be entirely pleased to see you, are you not?" She broadened her smile, then walked to her desk and sat down, drawing her lamp closer.

"You may return to your chamber now. Madalenna will come for you in the morning. I shall leave quite early, so be ready." She dipped a gold quill into a jeweled inkwell and began to write, and the scratching sound across the surface of the paper clawed along the back of Rachelle's nerves.

Catherine looked at her with raised brow, and Rachelle managed to dip a curtsy. She turned and moved toward the door.

Trapped. We have taken the place of Sebastien and Madeleine. No, we are in more danger.

The Ultimatum

WHY DOES THE WOMAN NOT COME TO ME WITH her venomous bribes? Why does she delay? Has she changed her mind about assassinating Guise?

The boring days and nights in the dungeon plagued him. Fabien moved to and fro across the stone cell, a tormented panther in a small cage. As soon as he'd grown strong enough to convince the prison captain that he would recover from his wound, guards were sent to take him to the filthy dungeons below Amboise castle. There he had remained for the last few weeks.

"I suggested to the Queen Mother they keep you in your first cell," the docteur said on his last visit before returning to Fontainebleau, "but she overruled me."

So she was behind his move to this dark and stinking dungeon. He might have guessed it.

"She is here at Amboise?"

"She comes often to speak with your kinsman, Prince Louis. They engage in quiet discussions on the state of matters in France. Civil war, I believe, is their topic. I am surprised she has not yet called for you, for her interest is avid. She desires to know the details of your health and spirits. Well, Messire, bon luck to you."

A guard outside the dungeon walked by, glancing in. Fabien lowered his voice to the docteur. "Do not forget."

The docteur glanced toward the guard and gave a slight nod. His answer was barely audible. "I shall do my best."

He would try to deliver Fabien's message to Andelot, who in turn would pass news on to Rachelle and Duchesse Dushane.

The docteur had already been taking verbal messages back and forth between Fabien and Gallaudet, and the news that his page had recovered from his wounds had lightened Fabien's concerns. This communication would cease with the docteur's departure.

Fabien would receive little information now that the docteur was leaving, since the Queen Mother's elitist guards were ordered not to communicate with him. They kept their eyes averted when passing his dungeon and bringing his food and drink. He tried to maneuver them into talking, but they resisted.

"When I am freed from this place, I will remember your miserable silence," he goaded, hoping to crack through their apparent indifference or fear of retribution. Finally, there was a day when the youngest of the guards was on duty alone, and Fabien spoke these words to him. The guard responded by looking over his shoulder uneasily. Fabien seized the advantage.

"It has been over two weeks since the docteur went to Fontainebleau. And over six weeks since I was arrested. I understand the Queen Mother is here. Send word I wish to see her."

The guard again glanced over his shoulder to make sure they were alone. He took longer delivering his bread and boiled grains. He sized Fabien up as if deciding whether to break his silence.

"She is busy with your Bourbon kinsman, Prince Condé," he finally whispered. "She meets with him in his cell for long discourses."

"Is the execution still planned?"

"It is."

"What of the Duc of Alva? He has left for the Netherlands?"

"He remains at Fontainebleau in company with Duc de Guise. They are hoping to have you turned over to a Spanish galleon soon."

"He is lacking a few galleons' worth of soldiers," Fabien said with deliberate cheerfulness. "That is my consolation."

If Alva remained in France, then Catherine must be intervening with King Francis to keep him out of the hands of Spain. She still needed him. Nothing had changed. She must come . . . soon.

The sound of footsteps and clinking chains echoed through the dungeon, signaling the approach of another guard. The younger guard would say no more and quickly went out.

There was nothing to do except wait. Matters were made worse by the condition of his cell. It was encrusted with the filth of years, dank from seepage from the Loire River, which ran through sections of the underground dungeons, and stench ridden with the rotting smells of death.

What a wretched situation! Still, there was no remedy for it but to sprawl upon the fetid hay and submit—something every inch of his body and mind found repulsive.

For one who enjoyed cleanliness, the filth was intolerable. He scratched his usually pristine head of golden brown hair—lice. He moved his fingers slowly and nabbed a flea under his arm. He lifted it and looked at it in the feeble light coming in through the tiny barred window, squishing it between thumb and finger. Large roaches and at least one family of water rats kept him company at night. He'd not had a change of clothing or a bath since the docteur left.

Nothing she ordered for his torments would shatter his resolve, he decided, except ... Rachelle.

The Queen Mother also knew that. Denying him information on Rachelle's condition was deliberate.

He thought of the Huguenots tortured for their faith in these very dungeons and beheaded in the courtyard. Their memory brought him renewed respect. He looked up at the stone ceiling that dripped with moisture. Above was the castle with its burgundy carpets, its velvet hangings, and brocade tapestries fringed in gold. Above were rich foods and wine and fragrant air. He'd taken it for granted while Christians were tortured here below, their screams muffled by the rock walls. Throughout France, men and women and their children continued to suffer agonies at the perverted hands and minds of their captors.

He thought of the upcoming colloquy to be held in the summer. Was it possible that good could come from the doctrinal debates between Calvin and the cardinal and bishops? Many nobles like Admiral Coligny and Queen Jeanne of Navarre held expectations for its enlightening outcome. Fabien remained doubtful.

Another week inched by. Had he been wrong about the Queen's purposes?

He was lying on the hay when a key rattled and the small door to his cell creaked open. He turned his head, his arm still resting across his forehead, and squinted. Even the feeble lamplight seemed to glare in the dismal dungeon. After all these weeks he knew the guards by their faces, and felt his first spark of interest when the captain of the guard himself appeared.

"On your feet, Messire. You are to have a bath and a change of raiment."

"The Queen Mother is here?"

"She is. Up with you, Messire."

An hour later, Fabien was escorted to the salle de garde. When he entered, the Queen Mother stood inside, arms folded beneath her long, full cloak, and her coif giving the impression of an apparition.

"Marquis de Vendôme," she said in a low voice.

He offered an élégant bow stained with mockery. "Your esteemed Majesty."

She gestured to the guard. "Leave us."

With a grave, sympathetic face that he would have found amusing had he been in a more conducive mood, she gazed at him.

"Marquis, I want you to know that your circumstance brings me no pleasure."

"I am most confident, Madame, that your every word can be trusted."

"Do not be impudent with me, my young tiger, or you shall indeed go to Spain." With a swish of her stiff skirts, she walked up to him, holding a rolled parchment. She tapped it against his chest, which was covered with a clean but ragged tunic dug up by the guard.

"I have here, Marquis, among many such correspondences from Spain, a most bitter indictment from King Philip. His emissary, the Duc of Alva, also bedevils me to my sickbed with his daily rantings. The Spanish authorities charge you with piracy, the sinking of several galleons bringing soldiers and arms to Holland, and of the theft of many ingots of gold, silver, and emeralds. 'Booty,' I think it is called, that you and other corsairs gifted to the English heretic queen. This charge, as you can well imagine, is most severe."

"Indeed, Madame. One can hardly fathom that I could accomplish so much."

"Then, there is always the axe. And do remember that you are at Amboise."

"What then, Madame? Have you come to relinquish me to Duc of Alva or the axe?"

"The Spanish envoy awaits, most impatiently," Catherine continued, moving about, holding the rolled parchment. "It will delight him to see you handed over to him in shackles."

"I am well aware, Madame, from the last meeting in the courtyard, of Alva's salivation at the prospects."

"What will it be, Marquis, the dungeons of Spain to face the Inquisitors who doubt your allegiance to the pope, or perhaps it would be poetic justice to send you back out to sea as a galley slave, chained at the oars of the Duc of Alva's new ship?" She scanned him. "You are a strong young seigneur, well able to work. You will not die easily. And now he awaits an audience with me at Fontainebleau on my return. I can hold him off no longer. My poor son Francis has been badgered nearly to death by the duc and the Guises. Alva will once more demand that the king put forth a communiqué for your deliverance to his soldiers."

She stepped back with an even stare. "Then, again, my lord Marquis, you and I may come to some mutual agreement of our own. I can release to you your heart's treasure, your belle des belles, Marquise Rachelle de Vendôme."

That she used the title inherited through the marriage was not lost on him. She would accept the marriage. If—

"And what, Madame, if I am permitted to ask, would be the reason for this suggested bonne fortune and reprieve?"

She moved about, restless as always. He leaned a shoulder against the stone wall and watched her in the light of the oil lamps. Her strong features were immobile, but her eyes were bright and alert to his response. She must know her deadly game had won her the prize she had schemed for.

"Your protection from the clutches of Spain is possible, but it will require your cooperation in exchange. Your usefulness to me is in aiding my plans for the good of France and the house of Valois. Shall we spare ourselves from subtlety and come to the bold facts as they are?"

"Your Majesty, I have wasted too much time as it is. The bold facts, as you say."

"You shall have them."

She looked triumphant as she went to the door and opened it. Fabien heard her clear voice: "Bring in the prisoner."

He straightened from the stone wall. Prisoner?

A strong guard roughly propelled Fabien's beloved into the chamber while another guard came in behind with a drawn blade. He raised the tip as Fabien made a gesture toward the guard who held Rachelle roughly by her arm.

"Make no move, Messire," the guard said, holding the blade. "I am under orders to thwart you at any cost."

Rachelle turned her head away, but Fabien saw the slight wince as the guard tightened his burly grip. If Fabien could have gotten to him he would gladly have broken his fingers. He jerked his head toward the Queen Mother, who stood back in the doorway.

"If you do not release her at once from this dawcock, you will never get from me what you want. I promise you that."

"On the contrary, if you do not cooperate fully, Rachelle goes to the Bastille where a hundred such soldiers wait."

She turned abruptly to the guard. "Leave her here. We will give the little lovebirds a few minutes before they are forever separated. Fabien to the oars of the Alva's galleon—and the belle mademoiselle to her unpleasant fate."

She swept out the door, the guard following, while the swordsman backed out after them, his eyes as hard as the rocky dungeon. The door clanged shut.

"Rachelle!"

They came together. He held her so tightly he heard her slight gasp, and loosened his hold. His lips sought hers, sweet and tender and warm. "You are in my dreams," he whispered. "I can think of nothing but having you in my arms ..." Her anxious kiss turned his heart into a thudding hammer. Her hair, fragrant and soft, was like silken threads in his fingers, her throat fragrant.

"Stop..." she whispered weakly, turning her face away and burying it against his chest.

"Have they hurt you?" he whispered.

She shook her head. "Oh, are you all right, mon amour? You are recovering? You are not sick?"

He turned his mouth. "No, just half-starved. She was a devil to bring you here to torment me. She means what she says, Rachelle. I know her too well. She will send you to the Bastille. There is no alternative but to agree to her wishes."

"And then what? How can you do such a deed as she wishes done?"

"I will find a way to delay until we can escape as we planned."

"She is cunning. She will never let me out of her sight."

"We will play her game for as long as it takes."

She looked at him, and he read the anxious fear. "And in return?"

He tightened his hold on her waist. "In return we will be together."

"Then it will be worth the struggle."

"In the end, we will outwit her. I'll not rest until you are on the *Reprisal* sailing to England."

"Until we are on the ship, mon amour."

"As you say ..." He kissed her softly this time, restraining his passions. He would not tell her that his first ambition was to see her to safety, whatever the cost to himself.

The door opened, and the Queen Mother stood there, the two guards on either side with glum faces.

"It is time to bid adieu," she said.

Fabien released Rachelle, whose gaze adhered to his. He squeezed her hand encouragingly and brought her wedding finger to his lips.

He watched her leave the guard chamber, this time free of the soldier's grasp. In another moment he was alone again with the Queen Mother.

"If anything happens to her ..."

"Nothing will befall her as long as you serve me loyally. You know what I want, what I must have for the good of the house of Valois, for France. Naturally, this must be done without so much as a hint of suspicion coming back upon my sons, or upon me. You must understand this perfectly."

"Perfectly indeed."

"Then do you agree?"

"What about Alva? That parchment you brought bears the heart of Spain. They will never be content to see me free."

"Never mind that. I will deliver you from the grip of Spain, but know that it will be at a cost to me. The Duc of Alva will depart for his royal master with my words in his ears and a message in hand that I shall surely deal with you and all the enemies of the true religion in my own time and way."

Now what could she mean by that? Had she intended to let those words slip off her tongue so easily? Her own time and her own way? The enemies of Rome? What might she be planning down the road for the Huguenots?

"And the Duc of Alva, Madame, will he accept your promising words?"

"Marquis de Vendôme, you are clever enough to know he would not relinquish his claim upon you easily. I must convince him. And I shall. One does not turn down the mighty seigneurs of Spain and bask in their condescending favor. In sparing you from Spain I have lost, for the present, the opportunity of discussing marriage between Philip's son, Don Carlos, and my daughter Marguerite. I have been told that there will be no consideration of marriage as long as heretics roam France at liberty. I will resume negotiations for the princesse's marriage to Henry of Navarre."

Her words were plain enough, yet he sensed she was toying with him and others, including Margo. He perceived that something important must fill in the empty spaces between her comments, but what? Perhaps even she did not know what it may be as yet. Some move against the Huguenot leaders perhaps? His apprehension alerted him.

"I have spared your bodyguard, Gallaudet, the student-scholar, Andelot Dangeau, and more importantly your amour, Rachelle."

He wanted to gain as much information as he could in her own words so that later she might not say he had misunderstood her intentions.

"Cardinal de Lorraine would annul your marriage if he could."

"Cardinal de Lorraine has no jurisdiction over my marriage."

"Mademoiselle Rachelle dangles over the flames by a spider's thread."

He pushed the stakes higher. "In return I want my freedom to come and go as I wish. What you ask of me demands careful planning."

"You will have certain freedoms to move about, but Mademoiselle will remain under palais arrest. I will have no more ventures such as that accomplished by Comte Sebastien and Madame Madeleine. Eventually, however, full freedom for both of you will be restored to what it was in the days of your father, Duc Jean-Louis, whom my husband the king oft called to service at his court."

So, then he was called to a life at court with Rachelle amid luxury, intrigue, and murder … until he managed to escape.

She must have understood some of what his feelings were, for she smiled her empty smile.

"Ah, Marquis, once the deed of your service to France is done all will be well. Until then, you must remain available at court. You will be given the appartement so unexpectedly vacated by my loyal counselor, Comte Sebastien," came her words thick with mockery. "You will take his place. You shall attend the council meetings in full view of our grand Duc de Guise."

He retained his studied composure, his feelings held down with an iron grip.

"I wish to send the marquise to her mother in London."

"What?" she mocked cheerfully. "So soon, Messire? And such a belle mademoiselle too."

He bowed smoothly. "With regret, Your Majesty, I assure you. I cannot accomplish this deed of which we both desire in one day. It may take months to plan. I must have a free hand, and a free mind where the gracious marquise is concerned."

"We both need our gracious Marquise Rachelle. Moreover, you will surely keep your promise to me with Rachelle my palais prisoner. Do you not see my position? Of course you do. Marguerite is to renew her friendship with Henry of Navarre at the colloquy. A marriage with Navarre will be in the making. Your delightful marquise will design and make the princesse gowns to wear. And truly, her skills with the silk and lace go beyond anything the best couturières at court can offer."

Her cunning was evident.

"Well, Marquis?"

He bowed. "I will see that your wish, and mine, is fulfilled, Madame."

"Ah. Then there is nothing more to discuss at this time. I shall return to Fontainebleau with Mademoiselle."

"What about my release, Madame?"

"I will see to the matter on my return. It will take a few weeks. You must be patient. I shall see you are moved to a more comfortable cell."

She gave a nod of her head. To the Queen Mother, the matter was settled.

She swept toward the door.

"And Rachelle?"

"She will be waiting for you at Fontainebleau."

"What of my kinsman, Prince Louis?"

Her face sobered. "That, Messire, I cannot promise. The king has ordered his death."

He bowed to her ultimatum, struggling to keep hatred from crushing his soul.

❄

Upon Fabien's release from the Amboise dungeon two weeks later, he reclaimed his sword and Gallaudet sent a message ahead to Rachelle that he would arrive at Fontainebleau as soon as possible after making a brief call at Vendôme. He hoped to visit with Louis but was hindered by the guards.

"It is by order of the king, Marquis. It will mean our heads if we favor you to speak with your kinsman, the prince."

He left Amboise with Gallaudet, and they rode toward the Bourbon palais.

❄

TRIBUTE

Fabien arrived at Vendôme in secret. He could imagine the disarray inside his palais after the battle that had been fought. To his satisfaction, the bandits living in the woods had not ransacked the estate in the absence of his guards, and his loyal domestic attendants had remained, but scars from the battle were in evidence. Pieces of broken furniture had been stored away with the Viennese chandelier which had come crashing down in the salle de jour. His servants greeted him with surprised delight; the older women, who had known him as a boy, wiped tears from their eyes.

Later, he had his chamberlain go on a sober walk with him to where members of his men-at-arms were buried in shallow graves. There were no markers, and Fabien ordered them identified with honors and crosses for each.

"Did any of the wounded escape?"

"Oui, Monseigneur, several. There is no word if they are yet alive, or of their whereabouts. It has been ghostly quiet here. Shall I seek to learn of them?"

"Do so with all speed, and in secrecy. Gallaudet will distribute to the families of the dead and injured. They are to be well provided for."

Later that day Gallaudet was seated behind a desk with a mound of gold coins, carefully counting them as he read from a list of names. He was still pale from his injuries and imprisonment and had lost weight. Fabien scowled to himself. He had a strong desire to reap vengeance on Maurice. Had he kept to his own affairs at Fontainebleau, there would not be such losses among his men.

Fabien hardened his mouth as he went upstairs toward his chambers. What would Maurice's response be to the news of his release and his return to Fontainebleau to live with his beloved bride?

He paused on the landing, looking at a broken section of railing and a dark stain on the carpet where he had lain. He recalled Maurice's shout of triumph when the dwarves had the Queen Mother's soldiers carry Fabien to a wagon to take him to Amboise. Maurice's words to his men-at-arms had haunted him on the long, bumpy ride to the dungeon: "We shall overtake Mademoiselle on the road to Dieppe!"

And so they had. Fabien stood soberly, looking below to the salle where most of the fighting had occurred. How could he replace the loyalty and camaraderie of those who had been killed? They had gone with him to London and to the waters off the coast of Holland. They had cheered together, fighting side by side with Capitaine Nappier and the privateers when the Duc of Alva's war galleon caught fire during the cannon exchange. They were with him when they boarded another Spanish vessel on the way to Holland to carry out Alva's inquisitional orders. The new men-at-arms he planned to secure would in time generate their own record of brave deeds. He was sure that danger would hound his steps at court in the months to come.

He frowned, thinking again of the Queen Mother's statements during the interview at the dungeon. She reminded him of a sleeping viper. With the Duc de Guise's assassination settled, who would become her next target? The Huguenot chieftains? And yet, she was reaching out to them, even risking angering Spain and Rome. Had he misunderstood her?

He set aside his concerns for the present and thought longingly of Rachelle. Soon he would be with her again.

He relished a bath, and soon his barber arrived, sharpening his instruments.

After donning fresh clothing, Fabien enjoyed a sumptuous supper of pheasant. The absence of many of his old comrades cast a cloud, but his stirring memory of Rachelle diverted his thoughts as it had so often aboard the *Reprisal* on lonely evenings at sea. He thought of her waterfall of thick brown-auburn hair, lively brown eyes, and the dimple at the corner of her so kissable lips when she smiled. How longingly he had thought of her in the foul dungeon!

He drummed his fingers on the table, staring moodily at the flickering candles at either end.

Gallaudet said smoothly, "It is too late, Monseigneur, to begin our journey to Fontainebleau tonight."

Fabien laughed. Gallaudet had too easily sensed that Fabien's thoughts had drifted back to Rachelle.

"You are right, mon ami. It is wise we get a good rest before starting the journey. I shall discipline myself and leave tomorrow morning, just as I wrote her." He raised his goblet, and Gallaudet did the same.

"Our work is far from over, Gallaudet. We return to court as in the past, but our dangers and troubles are doubled. Let us toast the Huguenot chiefs and Admiral Coligny. May his presence there bring light where there is shadow."

"To the Admiral! To the colloquy!"

At Fontainebleau, Rachelle heard the door to her chamber unlock. Madame Trudeau entered much the same as she had done twice a day for the past six weeks. Rachelle, however, could see that a matter of consequence was at hand. Madame Trudeau's voice was humbled, and she dropped in a curtsy. Her wary eyes looked toward Rachelle, then faltered.

"Bonjour, Marquise de Vendôme."

Marquise . . . What was this?

"The Queen Mother has instructed Comtesse Beauvilliers that my oversight of you is over, Madame. I am to escort you to the suite of chambers granted to you and Marquis de Vendôme while at Fontainebleau."

To you and the marquis! Rachelle stared at her.

"Are you saying that Marquis de Vendôme is to be set at liberty?"

She smiled lamely. "Oui, Marquise, he has been released."

Rachelle's joy exploded. Forgetting the sour old woman who had worsened the past weeks, she dashed across the floor and threw her arms around her rigid shoulders as though she were responsible for freeing Fabien. Madame Trudeau looked as surprised as Rachelle. They looked at each other, then Madame Trudeau broke into a smile, and Rachelle laughed.

"Oh, Marquise, I do feel ashamed for my manner in treating you these weeks. I hope you will think it a gracious thing to forgive me and count me among those who wish you and the marquis happiness and a full life."

"The past is over. Let us remember it no more. I am pleased to have gained a supporter in place of an enemy. I hope you will promise me one thing."

"Oh certainly so, Madame. Anything."

"That you will not bring Comte Maurice to our appartement," she said. "Especially now with my husband Marquis Fabien there."

Madame Trudeau looked appalled, then she saw Rachelle's half smile.

"Oh, Marquise, you may be assured I shall never again be so bold as

that. I confess, my only knowledge of you was what I had heard from —
well, others. Now I have had my own dealings with you and know what
manner of honorable young mademoiselle you are."

Rachelle smiled. "Merci. And now, take me to this suite of chambers
that has been granted to the marquis and me by the Queen Mother."

Rachelle was so delighted and relieved by the sudden turn of events
that she refused to allow concerns of what lay ahead for her and Fabien
to ruin her happiness. The weeks ahead would have time enough to face
whatever may come. Now, the gate to a garden was open and flowers
of May were in fragrant bloom, enticing her desire to dream. It was a
time for amour, for expectations of a long and happy life with Fabien
as her husband, and she would guard the rare time together alone with
sacred jealousy. Enough of the fomenting evils of court intrigue between
the Guises, Valoises, and Bourbons. Not even the awkward fact that
the appartement was once occupied by her sister Madeleine and Comte
Sebastien detracted from her joie de vivre! She already had plans to hang
new velvet curtains, and of course, all the bedding was new, for Nenette
was returned to her, and Rachelle would have time at her leisure to think
about choosing her own ladies and pages.

How good it was to see Nenette again. They greeted as long-separated
sisters rather than as mistress and grisette and maid. After Nenette shed
her tears of joyful reunion, vowing she'd never given up on daily prayers
for Rachelle's safety and that of the beau marquis, she told Rachelle how
she had arrived at Fontainebleau with Philippe, and through a series of
twists and turns, had finally been taken in by the duchesse.

"There is talk Philippe may go live with a certain pasteur of the religion. Andelot knows of him. He has said he would find Philippe useful
company."

Rachelle was pleased to hear the news. "There is news Marguerite is
to marry Henry of Navarre. We will have her wedding trousseau to make
in the future. I can see myself needing Philippe for some of the work, but
we will wait to see. No date yet is set for the marriage."

"They have long talked about such a marriage," Nenette said doubt-
fully. "I cannot see it happening myself." She lowered her voice. "They
say she meets often at night with young Henry de Guise."

Rachelle already knew this. "I prefer not to join the other talkers in gossip. This is a time for my own joy, Nenette. And you have not even congratulated me. I am Marquise Rachelle Dushane-Macquinet-Bourbon! Think of that."

"Oh, Mademoiselle Rachelle, it is most *merveilleux*. I have thought about it ever since I heard of your marriage. Oh, that I had been there to see you and the dashing marquis! Life is unfair. I should have been there to help you dress in a most belle gown and to help the other maids to carry your train. And instead—"

She clasped her hands together in agony.

"And instead," Rachelle told her dryly, "I had to keep telling the minister to hurry up and marry us. And my gown was the burgundy one with the black lace—black, Nenette, black!"

"Non!"

"And then Comte Maurice arrived with at least thirty swordsmen, and there was a horrendous swordfight and a personal duel between the marquis and the comte. And you know of the treachery Maurice turned on the marquis. Ah, I tell you, it was a shameful deed. And that, Nenette, was my wedding day."

"And then you were separated from him. And you have been married over six weeks!"

"But my bridegroom is coming," Rachelle said, sweeping about from chamber to chamber with fanfare of ecstasy. "He will come, and I must get ready for him, Nenette. I want flowers in the appartement and all manner of fresh fruits and delectables. I want my gowns ready too and the most belle wedding chemise ever—all lace and—"

"Ooh!" Nenette cried, dancing about. "And sprigs of blossoms from the garden. Oh, Mademoiselle! How I envy you. How I wish I could find my own amour and get married."

"Nenette, you are too young. A few more years must pass. And then we shall find you someone special. I will ask Fabien to find a dashing beau for you among his pages or men-at-arms—" She stopped.

The sober reality slapped her. Men-at-arms. Most of Fabien's galants were dead or maimed. Gallaudet was alive, and Julot Cazalet, but the others? He would find new chevaliers to swear fealty to him, but it was tragic that the other brave monsieurs were dead.

Nenette was still sighing as she danced about, her red curls bouncing, lost in romantic reverie. Rachelle smiled as she watched her. If Idelette were here, it would seem like old times at the Château de Silk again.

Idelette. How was her sister faring in England? There was no chance she would be able to come to the colloquy with Madame Clair and Père Arnaut in September. By now the baby would be growing with all bonne speed in her womb. Would it be a boy or a girl? And what would its future hold? Would the baby grow up to return to France?

May God preserve you both, she prayed.

"Marquis Vendôme is arriving now, Mademoiselle Rachelle," Nenette called from the window. "Ooh, Chevalier Gallaudet is with him — and others — these monsieurs I have not seen before ... they are all most beau. One cannot guess le marquis to have been in a dungeon, nor Gallaudet!"

Rachelle's heart beat faster. She applied the finishing touches to her hair, arranging the autumn brown waves over her shoulder. She smoothed the lace of finest point de Venise at neckline and wrists. The cloth of her gown was a rubbed satiny rose with slashings of golden tissue in the ballooned sleeves. The gown had been given to her by Princesse Marguerite de Valois and sent over with the words written on a perfumed parchment: *I envy you. Margo.* Applying some tucks here and there and lowering the hem, for Rachelle was taller than Marguerite, she and Nenette had spent the afternoon fixing the belle gown to a perfect fit, so that Rachelle herself could not have guessed that she'd played seamstress.

Duchesse Dushane had visited the appartement, bringing greetings over Rachelle's and Fabien's release. Beneath the older woman's smile and show of warmth, there'd been a worried look in her eyes, as if she had wished to speak of some matter that troubled her but refrained from doing so because of the pleasant purpose of her visit. Thereupon she had presented Rachelle with a wedding gift of Dushane family diamonds: sparkling earrings, a bracelet, and a necklace.

Rachelle wore them now as a customary family tradition for the continuation of the Macquinet-Dushane silk house. "Now we have the added blessing of the royal Bourbon family," the duchesse had said. "A most astonishing feat on your part, ma petite."

A grand catch, to be sure.

Rachelle left the bedchamber mirror and waited while the page announced Fabien's arrival. Nenette, looking flushed and excited over this wondrous moment, swiftly departed the appartement to join the duchesse's ladies.

Rachelle stood in the midst of the salle de jour waiting for him. Fabien entered alone and saw her. Drawn by the flame in his eyes, she went toward him.

He tossed aside his plumed hat and velvet cloak and moved to claim her. They came together, embracing tightly.

Her eyes closed with relief and joy, as for the moment they clung together as though some unseen menace threatened to again rob them of this moment. Her heart thundered in her ears as his kiss became one with hers.

He smiled, his warm fingers caressing the side of her face, then her throat.

He bent to kiss her again. "At last."

Serpent in the Garden

AT FONTAINEBLEAU THE EXTENSIVE FOREST ABOUNDED WITH GAME FOR the king's table, granting the royal guests opportunity to indulge in one of their favorite activities, the hunt. That morning, after partaking of breakfast with the king, the party of nobles and mademoiselles entered the courtyard where the grooms and attendants waited with the horses.

In the grand salle, the Queen Mother, known for being bold in the chase, was on her way to the courtyard to join them when the sound of quick footsteps detained her. She turned toward the archway that led into the outer corridor.

Duc de Guise, hard and lean, stood in the archway, the scar across his cheek and eyelid pronounced in the streak of light that came through the diamond-shaped window panes. He wore a short green coat with threads of gold, and his powerful hand rested on his scabbard.

Catherine lifted her head to her full height. For one insolent moment the duc's bold presence confronted her with wordless authority, then, and only then, did he bow his head. She found herself both intimidated and angry. *How dare he!*

"Madame," he said stiffly.

"My lord Duc."

He approached boldly, for he was fully aware, as was she, that he was the favorite of King Philip of Spain.

The duc basks in his own strength and popularity throughout Paris. But his days will soon come to an end.

Catherine held out her hand to receive a royal missive that the duc handed to her. As she suspected, it was from the King of Spain.

"More veiled threats, my lord Duc?"

"Madame, it is said that all Spain and the Vatican is astounded by your boldness. You have unwisely promised the Huguenot leaders the freedom to bring Geneva ministers here to teach their heretical viewpoints."

"Duc, the colloquy is a debate of the differences between Catholics and Huguenots. Surely you will agree that such a debate, if it can humor the Huguenots to actions of peace, is worth giving them a few days to speak at Poissy."

"A few days, Madame? Is it not rather months? Why should heretics speak at all? There are those who question your loyalty to Rome in the lettres they send."

"I am loyal to the Pope. Who has deigned to stain my reputation in false lettres to Rome and Spain? Could it be King Philip's ambassador to the court, Chantonnay? Has he nothing better to do than to spy on the Queen Mother of France?"

Duc de Guise's face did not relinquish its severe cast.

"Madame, it is said that a host of heretics will be permitted to gather freely to debate a gathering of bishops and the cardinal of France. This, Madame, is unthinkable, when your son the king has denied to me ever authorizing such a meeting."

The self-righteous chill in his eyes angered her. She had few friends at court except her own spies and secret poisoners, and it was the cause behind her effort to reach out to the Huguenot Admiral Coligny and promise the colloquy he wanted. She must work her craft in the shadows to bring her plans to pass. Guise was a formidable opponent, but after today, if all went as expected, she would not need to concern herself with the duc.

She forced a smile. "My lord Duc, I can assure you that both you and the King of Spain misunderstand my intentions toward the Huguenots. I have no more patience for these troublesome heretics than you or the Vatican."

His stare rejected her declaration. She stepped closer and bent her head toward his, laying a hand on his arm. She lowered her voice, still smiling. "If there is to be a religious colloquy, mind you, it will become a trap for them."

His left eye with its scar across the lid watered incessantly. He blinked. "If your words can be relied upon, Madame, why did you intervene with the king to permit the enemy of Spain to remain at court? The Marquis de Vendôme should be in the dungeon with his Bourbon kinsman Prince Louis Condé. Both should be executed. Do you think the King of Spain will forget that you have sent his emissary the Duc of Alva away with his chains empty of their prey?"

She lifted her head. "Patience, Monsieur Duc. Spain's enemies are also France's enemies. They will be dealt with, but in subtle fashion."

His thin mouth twisted. "Let us hope such delays as you suggest do not bring the wrath of Spain's armies down upon us, Madame. Surely King Francis will hear again from me of the folly of permitting this swarm of heretics from Geneva to teach and debate their lies at Poissy."

He bowed stiffly and strode away, his short cape floating behind, his sword clinking in its scabbard as a reminder that he was head of the French army.

Catherine was left in the quiet salle with an empty smile that faded. She walked swiftly to the archway and looked into the outer corridor. The duc *must* go on the hunt. Where was he going now — to turn Francis against the colloquy? And if the young king refused the colloquy, there would be a civil war in France.

In the corridor her gaze fell upon the Spanish Ambassador Chantonnay. It appeared as though he'd been waiting for the duc.

"Madame, the King of Spain will not permit heretics to overwhelm this court."

"I assure you, Monsieur Chantonnay, that heretics will never take over the throne of France, which belongs to my son."

He bowed his head briefly, turned, and then looked at her again, his eyes reflecting dislike.

"The Duc de Guise is a messire loved throughout France. Madame, consider well before you make an enemy of his family." He went after the duc.

Spy! And yet fear latched hold of her. Of what was he hinting? Was it possible he knew of her secret plans?

In the courtyard the nobles were gathering for the hunt, but some minutes later, when the king did not appear with the duc, Catherine worried as she mulled over the ambassador's words. Her position of power was slipping from her grasp. Each day that Francis grew older, he grew closer to the young queen, Mary Stuart, and Mary was devoted to her Guise oncles.

Uneasy, Catherine decided to not go on the hunt. If her plans succeeded today through the marquis, it would be wiser to have remained at the château. She wished to be far removed from any scene where the duc met with an accident.

Catherine left the château unseen and entered a section of the shadowy arbor along one side of the courtyard. She was out of sight, yet she retained full view of the hunting party. She would not be content until she witnessed Duc de Guise riding out with them.

The minutes crept by. Neither Francis nor the duc appeared. Her tension climbed. She realized her fingers clawed her stiff black sleeve, and she forced her hands to be still. She watched through the lattice, but neither the duc nor the king emerged from the palais château. Her gaze switched to Marquis Fabien. He held the stirrup for Rachelle to mount her horse. Rachelle's loathing of the hunt showed on her face. She sat straight in the saddle with her chin lifted, tugging on the wrists of her riding gloves. The marquis, dashing in a plumed hat, mounted his horse beside her. He said something to her that caused her to laugh. He appeared to enjoy the adventure, but was it a false face? His head turned and he glanced about the court. Did he also notice the Guises were unexpectedly absent? Was he also suspicious that Guise had been warned?

Catherine did not entertain much doubt that the marquis would fulfill his mission now that Rachelle was under palais arrest. Then again, he had little choice. His love for his bride placed him where she wanted him: in a vulnerable position. Yes, the marquis was accepting his dilemma well enough.

He's grown up in the court in the midst of the little foxes, so he knows what to expect.

Was he too knowledgeable for her to manipulate? He was sharp-witted. That, too, could pose a danger. But as long as she held the safety of his amour in her palm, he would behave. Ah, yes, Rachelle was most needful.

Dangerous pets that might turn on you were all the more rewarding when their strengths were harnessed.

Amid much fanfare, the château door opened and her son the king appeared with petite Mary.

Where is the duc? Why is he not with him?

Could Ambassador Chantonnay have somehow overheard her brief conversation with the marquis last night after the royal dinner? She had whispered her veiled suggestion to Marquis Fabien, knowing he would understand. She'd been careful to see that no one heard, but with Chantonnay one could never be certain.

Chantonnay was her equal in intrigue and spying. Incriminating reports were often sent to Rome and Spain on her every encounter with the Huguenot leaders. She would have liked to encourage her son to cast him out of court, but the Guises held the upper hand and would never send their chief ally away. France was in financial debt, and Duc de Guise controlled the army, which was dependent on assistance from Spanish soldiers and Spanish gold from the New World.

The royal hunting party rode out the gate toward the forest without the duc, foiling her plans for an accident. She must be even more wary now that the first attempt had failed.

There is something afoot with the ambassador.

Earlier at breakfast, the duc and also the cardinal mentioned going on the hunt. Where were they? Rare indeed was the hour when the Guises did not form a possessive flank around her weak son Francis, prohibiting anyone except themselves from influencing him. Why were they allowing him to ride out with only the nobles and guards in attendance?

A movement near the château steps drew her attention. Her earlier suspicions that the Spanish ambassador was plotting something were vindicated. He disengaged himself from the morning shadows and began walking swiftly in the direction of the garden. She pressed her kerchief to her mouth in frustration.

Madalenna, that sloth. Where is she when needed?

Catherine allowed him to walk ahead, and after a minute she left the arbor and followed.

The morning breeze was chilling and sent the dry autumn leaves rattling in the trees along the garden way. She quickened her steps.

Ahead, she saw him near the fountain where he was joined by the messieurs, the duc and the cardinal. She stopped and stepped aside.

Ah, the three cozy reptiles sunning in the garden.

Keeping behind the trees, her black gown affording helpful concealment, she strained to hear what was said between them and fumed over her powerlessness. If she drew closer, her stiff skirts would rustle.

They began walking ahead into an open area of the court, away from trees and bushes, showing their practice in guarding their words from being overheard.

Unable to proceed, she backed away, just as her daughter, Princesse Marguerite, emerged from some secret path, glancing over her shoulder.

Look at her! Even now slinking off to meet young Guise, the duc's son, in the forest!

Marguerite ran toward another section of the palais grounds to keep her tryst.

No doubt she assumed Catherine had ridden out on the hunt as she so often did.

Catherine narrowed her gaze. Her fury rose like a tempest.

I should have her whipped again!

Catherine did not believe the duc when he claimed he was not encouraging his son to marry Princesse Marguerite. What better way to take the throne of France than to become the king's brother-in-law?

Another reason why the duc must die — or his son.

There was no time to confront her wayward daughter now. Catherine returned to the château in dark musings.

As the days went by at Fontainebleau, Catherine cautiously weaved new plans and began putting them into action, fearing that if she hesitated, the Guises and Chantonnay would surprise her with some unexpected coup d'état. First, she began to reach out to Prince Antoine de Bourbon. Although under arrest like his younger brother Prince Louis for the Huguenot rebellion at Amboise, Prince Antoine was merely under palais constraint and therefore at liberty to move about comfortably. He could also have visitors, mainly his own kinsmen at court, including Marquis Fabien.

One afternoon when the Queen Mother knew the Guises were elsewhere with the king, she sent Madalenna to call for Antoine to stroll with her under the arbor within the garden court.

"Ah, Monsieur Prince, when I met with tragic news this morning I asked myself with whom should I speak of such heartbreak? And my thoughts turned to you, my brother, a monsieur with many troubles, and through no fault of your own, I assure you," she lied. "And so it is grievous news I choose to share with you today. I hope I do not impose upon you, but I am just a poor woman alone and need a strong messire to hold in confidence."

He looked flattered that she had turned to him, as she had intended, but mention of her ploy of grief and tragedy brought tension to his face, a handsome Bourbon face, though his was weak of jaw.

"Grief? Ah, say it is not Louis, Madame," he breathed, hand flashing with jewels laid at his heart.

"Ah, no, my prince, it is not your galant brother. It is my son, the king. I have spoken with Docteur d'Fontaine this morning after his visit with my son. The docteur tells me what I have longed feared—but it is too soon, yes, much too soon. My poor Francis will not live long."

"Madame, a poignant grief, surely. Then is there nothing to be done? What of the great Docteur Ambroise Pare?"

"I fear his words will be the same. It is a matter of time ... but this woeful news we must keep secret for the sake of those nearest him who love him."

"I understand perfectly, Madame, for the sake of his beloved wife, Reinette Mary."

"Not that this should come as a total surprise. Far from it, I assure you."

"So true, Madame. We have all known that the king suffers from the blood disorder. You have my sympathy and my prayers, as does His young Majesty. Perhaps, who knows? Docteurs are sometimes in error, Madame. King Francis may have more years left than we know. He may yet live and come of age to reign—with Mary as well."

The fool. He thinks he is encouraging me.

Antoine went on in a comforting tone, "Soon, in just a few more years, Mary Stuart will become Queen of Scotland as well."

Catherine paused and turned to see if there could possibly be mockery in his eyes. *No, the undiscerning royal peacock is actually trying to cheer me with the very words that turn my heart to ice. Mary, becoming the Queen of France, reaching the full reign of authority and power. Mary, who did everything her Guise oncles wished, anxiously seeking what she should do to please them.*

As if I could ever abide having Mary Stuart as Queen of France ruling under the duc and cardinal.

"Alas! My brother, that bonne fortune would indeed come to pass — but," she said with a sigh, "most unfortunately, I fear you are too hopeful."

"Truly, Madame? Say it is not so."

"The docteur tells me that Francis will not live long enough to see Mary come into her own."

"The king seemed most promising in strength since I have come from Navarre."

"Have you not noticed these last several days how his illness strikes suddenly — " she snapped her fingers — "and takes hold of him? How he tires more easily and looks pale of cheek?" She patted her own cheek.

Antoine nodded his dark head, his gold earrings set with diamonds sparkling.

"Now that you mention it, Madame, yes, I have seen a change — recently."

"But, my brother, woeful as this news may be to my heart, the good of France must go on, and my son would not have it otherwise. So you see, I must make plans for the future."

"Well said, Madame."

She brought her lace kerchief to her eyes. "I must also say this, my brother. You should not think it was I who planned your arrest, and that of Prince Louis. It was the house of Guise, the enemy of my house and yours, Monsieur Prince, who had the trap waiting when you both arrived. King Francis was furious with Louis for his part in the Amboise plot, and so insisted that Louis would die for his betrayal," she lied.

"Madame, it is as I have heard even in Navarre before we ventured here. My wife Jeanne, the queen, warned us both of that danger. But who can resist the summons of our king? Even so, perhaps we should have listened to Jeanne."

Catherine stopped on the garden path. The mention of her enemy, Queen Jeanne of Navarre, another devout Huguenot, alerted her. *So Jeanne had seen through the Guise plot. She would, for she was shrewd and open in her dealings. Had Jeanne also suspected that Catherine had been privy to the plot to arrest her husband and brother-in-law? Yes, Jeanne would have guessed.* Catherine had cooperated with the Guises and King Francis so as not to risk losing what authority she had.

Catherine put her mouth next to Antoine's ear. "If my son, the king, as sick as he is, dies — then Prince Louis will be spared execution. You also, my brother, will be free again to pursue plans worthy of your royal rights."

Antoine looked startled, then swallowed.

"Why should you not think of the consequences, Monsieur Prince? My son's departure even in its gravest moments to me, brings good to the Bourbons."

"Meaning Madame, that —?"

From the corner of her eye, some feet away, she saw the bushes move. She stiffened. "Come to my state chamber tomorrow. I will send Madalenna. We will resume our discussion then." She walked abruptly away, leaving Antoine to gaze after her in wonderment, no doubt believing that she was upset over discussion of Francis.

Who had been watching them? Had her voice carried?

She was more determined than ever to be free of her enemies.

The next day Antoine arrived at her chambers, where Catherine sat waiting for him. Here it was safe to talk.

Antoine bowed. Catherine stared down at him. He looked nervous over what might be awaiting him, and this pleased her. She deliberately addressed him from her elevated chair.

"I shall speak most plainly, my brother Antoine. If my son Francis dies — then my next son Charles will be king. He is too young to bear such a heavy yoke as you are well aware. So France must have a regency." She paused to see if he followed where her words were intended to lead.

"Yes, Madame, I am aware."

"You, my brother, are the first prince of the Bourbon blood royal, and I am aware of your rights to hold the regency according to the law. Should my son Francis die — you will be expected to play a large role in the kingdom." She leaned toward him, her voice hushed. "Is that not what the Amboise plot was truly about? So the Huguenot Admiral Coligny has told me! The Huguenots wish to be rid of the Guises who dictate their will through their adoring niece, Mary. And my poor sick Francis, so enamored with his little reinette that he does all she wishes? Or rather, as the duc and cardinal wish?"

Antoine swallowed. Rather than taking her words as an encouragement as she meant them, he seemed to grow more cautious.

"Madame, I had nothing to do with the Amboise rising. I was in Navarre with my wife, ruling our shared kingdom."

She had never believed Antoine to be involved with Prince Louis and his retainers and waved his words aside.

"Ah, but my son Charles is not Francis. The Guises could not rule Charles through Mary, or the cardinal. Only I can handle my son in his bouts of frenzy. You understand?"

There were beads of sweat on Antoine's forehead.

"I see you *do* understand." She shook her head sadly. "Charles, too, is sometimes sick. Sick—here—" she tapped her temple. "But I, his loving maman, can curtail this madness when it strikes him. I can handle him. I know what to do. But you must realize that I am the only one who can handle Charles."

She saw that he watched her uneasily yet with growing excitement.

"Yes, Madame, I believe I understand your intentions."

She smiled at him, then leaned back into her gilded chair. She fixed her eyes upon him, lowering her lids, and her smile ended so that there would be no misunderstanding.

"I must be awarded the regency in your place, my brother. You comprehend? If not, your brother Prince Louis will die—and so will you. But if I become regent I will make you my general in place of Duc de Guise. You will have the second highest position in France. All edicts will be signed in our names."

Antoine licked his lips.

"But the Guises must not know of our plans for the regency, not if you value your life. They will lose a great power through their niece Mary should my poor son Francis die soon."

Antoine cleared his throat as though it constricted on him. A faint color painted his cheekbones.

"Madame, I fully understand the danger and will do as you wish."

Catherine smiled and put a finger to her lips. She leaned forward. "The regency is our secret, my brother," she whispered.

Antoine bowed stiffly, his mouth taut. His eyes shifted about uneasily.

"As you say, our secret, Madame."

Satisfied, she watched him leave. He was afraid, as well he should be. She would not have taken no for an answer. The regency belonged to her.

RACHELLE'S FINGERS CURLED INTO FISTS at the sides of her velvet gown. She walked quietly across the blue-and-gold carpet in the appartement salle de sejour toward the door to the outer corridor. *Almost there.* She glanced back toward the archway that opened into the small salle containing a large desk and a wall of leather books with gold embossing. Fabien was in there now, and she could just see him standing by the window beside the desk reading a lettre from Capitaine Nappier delivered by Julot Cazalet through Andelot. At any other time she would have wanted to know what was in the lettre, but her mind was in a turmoil. She must leave without alerting Fabien. Quietly, she slipped out and closed the door behind her.

FABIEN TURNED AND LOOKED toward the door inching closed behind Rachelle. He lifted his brow. He was aware of some unusual behavior this morning. It began when her little Nenette arrived to do her hair. He had already been up and about his business, but could not help hear them in the bedchamber, Nenette with her fluttery emotions, and Rachelle with abrupt questions, which alerted him to a problem of some sort or other. He had expected that Rachelle would confide in him when she came to join him for petit noir.

With intrigue surrounding them, he was more observant to possible danger than he might otherwise have been and decided he could not ignore her uncharacteristic behavior. He was amazed at his awakened capacity to love her as much as he did.

"Nenette!" he called.

The mademoiselle appeared as softly as a kitten in the archway, her eyes wide and her hands hidden beneath her white sewing apron.

"Monseigneur?"

He fixed her with a level gaze. "Where did your mistress go?"

She swallowed. "Go, Monsieur Fabien?"

"Yes, go. Where? Do not lie to me or keep back the truth."

She withdrew her hands from her apron and intertwined her fingers.

"Oh, Monsieur, to meet Comte Maurice Beauvilliers."

He was astounded. At first he could not believe it. He walked over to her, taking her arm and looking into her eyes. "You jest."

"Non, Monsieur Fabien, I would not do such a thing when the matter is most dangerous."

"What! And you did not tell me?"

"She commanded me to say nothing—"

"Where did she go to meet him? Quickly! Out with it!"

"To the garden."

He brushed past into the bedchamber closet, grabbed his scabbard, and strapped it on. "This time, Nenette, there will be no turning of my back."

"Oh, Monsieur!"

Fabien strode out, snatching up his hat as he went.

❧

ANDELOT, GARBED IN BLACK scholar's cloak with fur collar, walked down the corridor with his Latin book under his arm to join Scholar Thauvet for the morning's lesson. He looked up to see a severe figure, also in black, striding toward him.

Andelot paused. Was it too late to slip into an antechamber?

"Monsieur Andelot," Père Jaymin called.

Andelot sighed.

In his dark robe and sandals, Jaymin looked taller than usual with his large, shiny scalp rimmed with thick curling black hair. The large silver cross on his chest flashed in the sunlight coming in through the row of windows that overlooked the front courtyard of Fontainebleau.

"Bonjour, Père Jaymin."

"You are on your way to Monsieur Thauvet? It must be delayed. You are summoned. Cardinal de Lorraine is waiting in His Majesty's chambers. Go at once."

"Surely you do not mean the king's chambers?" The thought amazed him. He had been in the august company of royalty before now, of course, but the thought of meeting the cardinal there was most curious. "Is Marquis de Vendôme there as well?"

"Non, I saw him rushing toward the garden. It appears he is in an ill-tempered mood this day, for he would not answer my mellow greeting."

If Fabien were not with the king and cardinal, then Andelot found his call to the royal chamber even more unusual. What could the summons be about?

"Then I had best go to His Majesty," Andelot said. Père Jaymin detained him.

"Andelot, one moment ... Have you any notion why your cousin, Comte Maurice Beauvilliers, is holding secret meetings with the Spanish Ambassador Chantonnay?"

Surprised, Andelot turned back. He met the doleful eyes and saw curiosity swimming in the brown pools. "I have not heard of these meetings, Monseigneur. I have not spoken to the comte since my return to Fontainebleau." He could have added that it was not surprising since Maurice deemed him an enemy and that the feeling was not far from mutual. "Is there something more, Monseigneur?"

"I shall say this as a spiritual instructor, Andelot, and you would be wise to pay heed. If you have one of the forbidden Bibles of the heretics, you should burn it at once and seek pardon at Mass today. The times grow dangerous, even here among the nobles. There are secret heretics among us, and the cardinal is urging King Francis to ferret them and their forbidden literature out into the light."

Andelot was surprised by his bluntness. He had guessed that Jaymin suspected him of owning a French Bible, but he had expected him to go directly to the cardinal with his suspicion, without so much as a warning.

"Merci, Père Jaymin, but I have not the Scriptures in the French language."

Jaymin looked doubtful but said no more, and after bidding him adieu, departed on his way.

For a moment Andelot considered the circumstances hedging him in, but he was even more concerned about Marquis Fabien and Rachelle. He knew about the Bible belonging to Fabien's mother Duchesse Marie-Louise and how it was stolen from a chest of heirlooms at Vendôme. Maurice was suspected, but as yet there was no further news about the troubling incident.

Andelot quickened his stride down the corridor. Marquis Fabien had also told him what had taken place at the Amboise dungeon when the Queen Mother met with him. Andelot frowned over the matter, just as he had been doing ever since he learned of it. The very mention of Duc de Guise now made him anxious. That Fabien was at liberty here at court was due only to his agreement to fulfill the Queen Mother's secret plans. Fabien was as much in danger as the duc.

Andelot wrestled in his mind, wondering how the dark and sinister matter could possibly end well for any of them.

❦

ANDELOT ENTERED THE ROYAL CHAMBER with its grand canopied bed and fleur-de-lys in gold. He had heard the king was resting after having expended himself on a hunt. Mary did not look at Andelot when he entered, but her eyes were fixed on the tired face of Francis in his regal chair. He was smiling at her as if receiving strength from her nearness. Andelot felt a surge of sympathy as he saw the king's wearied condition.

Duc de Guise was moving about restlessly as usual, and the cardinal, in crimson and white, looked down on Francis with a bored expression.

Andelot quietly entered, approached the royal chair where the king sat, and then bowed.

"Your Majesty," he said quietly.

Francis smiled briefly and gestured toward Mary. Andelot stepped toward the reinette and bowed.

Cardinal de Lorraine extended his pale, slim hand with his clerical ring full of jewels. Andelot bent his head over the hand in obedience, telling himself that to refrain would not be worth the consequence. *If I must die for my faith, then let it be over the deity of Christ and His blood atonement. Nodding to Cardinal de Lorraine's gold ring means naught to me.*

The cardinal put an arm around Andelot's shoulders. Andelot breathed a whiff of parfume.

"Well, Andelot, I have heard bon things about you from Thauvet. He tells me you have an exceptional thirst for knowledge. I am pleased you are keeping yourself from joining the raucous behavior of the young rapscallions in the Corps des Pages."

Why would he even care, with his own reputation stained as it was?

"They are a trouble to the towns," the cardinal was lamenting. "They are mostly scions of the best French nobility, so even I cannot do much to rein them in."

Andelot doubted that, but as the saying went, *He who keeps his tongue keeps his life.* The cardinal went so far as to say that, on hearing how Andelot was showing such propensity in his studies, he was going to grant him two hundred extra francs a year just so that he might keep himself in finery.

Andelot was bewildered by this unexpected generosity. It worried him.

"Your thirst for learning has impressed Thauvet, who has said he has seldom taught such a studiously inclined young messire — and so prepared for advanced learning too."

"I am most grateful, Monseigneur."

Why is he saying all this now? Thauvet had made these statements weeks ago.

Andelot glanced at King Francis. He was quiet, still looking at Mary in her belle gown of rose and gray damask.

Duc de Guise ceased his pacing. He came up beside his brother the cardinal and stood with hands behind his back. "We have an important announcement, Andelot," the duc said, nodding to the cardinal for agreement.

"Indeed so," the cardinal said, his cleric garments of silk and satin rustling.

Andelot looked from one monsieur to the other, feeling most uncomfortable.

The duc gave his curdled smile. "Yes, the past is buried. Amboise and the Huguenot rebellion is all but forgotten."

Was it? Andelot doubted that.

"So is your unwise action with Prince Charles when you hid to watch the mass beheadings of the Huguenots," the duc said.

Andelot tensed. He had not deliberately hidden in the court to watch the revolting spectacle, but he would not permit his mind to go back too far.

"You have grown up, to be sure." Duc de Guise looked at the cardinal for affirmation.

The cardinal nodded, giving Andelot's shoulder a small friendly shake. "A bon young man, you are, Andelot. A fine nephew."

Andelot continued to doubt his blood connection to the cardinal and duc. Was he a Guise?

"We have a most important announcement where you are concerned," the cardinal said.

"Do not keep him guessing, " Duc de Guise said with a note of feigned cheer.

"You will be sent to the Guise family château in the Duchy of Lorraine in the fall. You will be privileged to live in Lorraine, our own province, and come to know our mother, the Duchesse of Guise, and the rest of our family. Afterward, come next year, we intend to see you admitted to the same theology university I trained at in Paris, the College de Navarre. One day, Andelot, my son, you will follow my steps to become the Cardinal of France."

Andelot stared at him. *Son?* But that term was merely one of common usage, he hastened to insist to himself. *Cardinal!* They watched him with expressions that told him he should be most proud of the announcement. If he had heard these words before Amboise, before the death of

Grandmère, before the arrest of Prince de Condé — then he would have been thrilled at the prospects. But now ...

"Monseigneur — I find myself speechless." That, at least, was truthful.

They smiled, obviously satisfied.

The Duchy of Lorraine to the northeast of France. Did he want this far-reaching change?

He had no doubt they offered him a vast honor, but why? Why such an honor when until recently they had forgotten him. And had he not been found guilty of trying to aid Marquis de Vendôme with his plan to leave France with Rachelle? He had been warned on several occasions to end his friendship with Marquis Fabien. Why then this great honor of being accepted into the Guise family?

"He is too overwhelmed to speak now," the cardinal said.

Duc de Guise watched him with a benign smile. "That is as expected."

"And now — " The cardinal exchanged a look with his brother.

The duc, still wearing a fixed smile, motioned Andelot to sit on a chair. It was unusual to sit when in the presence of the king, and Andelot turned to Francis to see his response. It did seem as though the Guises had all but forgotten he was there. The power of these two men over the throne was amazing.

Andelot felt compassion for Francis. He might have wished to exert his own authority over his oncles by marriage, but he looked cowed, especially by the sneering, dominating cardinal. What was it that made the cardinal resent Francis so much? Mary stood up, as if on cue, and after whispering to him, left the chamber through a crimson-and-gold drapery.

Uneasy, Andelot sat down. The Guises continued standing, looking down at him, now unsmiling.

"Andelot, it is time you knew and understood how the house of Bourbon is a threat to the house of Guise, of which you are now a member," the cardinal said. "The duc believes that you, too, as a cousin to his son Henry, should feel as strongly as he that our family house should prevail at court. Noblesse oblige, Andelot. We possess the right, now let us fulfill the obligation to prepare to deliver the throne from the dread possibility of rule by that inept Antoine de Bourbon."

What was he expected to say to such false profundity? How could they speak so plainly of rights to the throne of France and the possibility of Antoine's rule, when King Francis sat there listening? Francis might be of frail health, but he was not on his deathbed. Why, he and Mary might easily have a son, perhaps more than one. And yet, when Andelot glanced toward Francis, feeling embarrassed for him, he was surprised to see that he appeared amenable to the discussion.

Why was he included in this meeting? Apart from some vague connection to the Guise lineage, which remained limpid and undefined, what did he have to do with either the house of Guise or the house of Bourbon?

"Andelot, for the good of France, we must act while we have time," Duc de Guise said. He strode around the gilded chamber, deep in thought.

Andelot glanced over at King Francis. He merely watched, sometimes closing his eyes as though he were too tired to concentrate on what they were saying — or perhaps did not want to.

"Antoine de Bourbon is a threat. He seeks to weaken, then overthrow the king."

Antoine? So weak and vacillating? He'd been much in the company of the Queen Mother recently, but overthrow the king? Andelot could not see the threat they made so much of.

Duc de Guise lowered his voice. "The Bourbon, Prince Louis, will be executed soon. So too Antoine must be removed. We have a plan involving the king and you, Andelot. For the good of France, you will assist him."

Andelot's throat turned dry.

The cardinal leaned over, his arm around Andelot's shoulder again, and said with a pleasant tone as he sought to win him over, "Remember, the king is privy to our plan and agrees to everything we are about to tell you in the strictest secrecy."

Andelot shot a glance toward Francis. His face was pale, his mouth formed a thin line.

The duc and the cardinal turned toward Francis. "Is that not so, sire?" suggested the cardinal. "You also are privy to this all-important decision?"

"Yes," Francis said. "It must be, as you and mon oncle the duc have said."

The cardinal's steadfast gaze pinned itself to Andelot.

"We are all in agreement. And you also will surely agree and help your king."

"This is our plan," the duc said. "You have the honor to serve your king."

The king's young face remained pale and tense.

The cardinal said, "Sire, you have said this action is a most necessary decision, have you not?"

Francis nodded. "Yes, it must be. Antoine and Louis rebelled against my rule at Amboise. I cannot trust them. They encouraged the rising of the Huguenots against me. Now, if they live, they will seek to usurp the throne."

The cardinal looked down at Andelot. "Our spies, and those of the Spanish ambassador, have unearthed a plot by the house of Bourbon to overthrow the king. This must be stopped. We are all in agreement, as you see."

The smile, the settled tone of voice, all bespoke the fact that Andelot would indeed assist his king in stopping what was said to be a Bourbon plot, but assist him in what way? Marquis Fabien was also a Bourbon. What would this mean for him?

Andelot tried not to grip the arms of the chair as he was hearing both the cardinal and duc plotting the actual murder of Antoine de Bourbon, to be followed by the swift state execution of Prince Louis. There was no mention of the marquis, but could he trust the silence to mean he was to escape the plot of death?

Once the Bourbons were dead, the way would then be left open for a Guise to rule France *should* King Francis die of his blood disease. Andelot saw the truth now. If there was a plot to overthrow the king, it did not come from the Bourbons but the Guises. It was the Guises who insisted that Louis and Antoine must die because the Queen Mother had gained their loyalty. Antoine was seen too much in her presence, weaving plans that the Guises insisted took away their rightful authority.

They had convinced King Francis through Mary as well, that Antoine was a grave threat to his life. It was necessary to kill Antoine and Louis, or they would overthrow, even assassinate, the king.

❊

RACHELLE MOVED UNEASILY THROUGH the royal gardens at Fontainebleau until she came to the fountain where Maurice's message told her he would be waiting. The trees and flowering shrubs stood against the backdrop of the blue sky, and robins trilled in the branches. All this, she thought despondently, while the Guises and the Queen Mother connive and plot to overthrow one another at any cost, even to the shedding of blood. Power, ambition, and glory set the hearts of opponents on a race to the cliff's edge. Even the church was represented as a mustard plant that had become overgrown into a tree that nested the birds of the air. It was fear of losing power over kings and nations that kept the midnight lamps burning in Rome.

And now Maurice's selfish ambitions and jealousy had turned him, a once friendly opponent of Fabien, into a relentless enemy, willing to see Fabien delivered yet again to the authorities, this time to the Bastille.

She emerged through the trees and heard the fountain splashing. Yes, Maurice was there, waiting, moving across the court with animal-like restlessness.

He looked up and saw her. He removed his hat and bowed. Her eyes dropped to his scabbard. Yes, he wore it, his hand rested there as though the sword were the remedy to whatever stood in his way to gaining his desires.

Rachelle walked toward him. He came to meet her, a defensive gleam in his gray eyes.

"Where is the Bourbon Bible?" she demanded.

"Not so quickly as all that, Madame."

"The Bible belongs to Duchesse Marie-Louise de Bourbon and you stole it from Vendôme, from the private chamber of the marquis. What you have done is outrageous!"

"Ah, yes, I have the forbidden Bible. And I will take it to Cardinal de Lorraine."

She sucked in her breath and stepped toward him. "Maurice, you would not be so vile!"

"Ah?" He scanned her. "Maybe not."

"He is quite capable of contemptible behavior," interrupted Fabien's cold voice.

She whirled.

Fabien came from the trees. There was a calm about him that alarmed her. He walked toward Maurice.

Maurice stepped as warily as a cat, moving away from the fountain in a half circle until they faced each other.

"I suspected it was you who broke into my chest. You cannot imagine my satisfaction at hearing you admit you are a thief. That you did not also cart off the Bourbon family jewels is a surprise. It gives me pleasure to take back what you stole. Where is the Bourbon Bible?"

Rachelle's heart thudded. She looked at Maurice's hand tightening around his sword handle. She rushed forward, standing between them.

"Maurice," she hissed, "do not play the fool. Your pride will be your end. I know him better than you. If you have any wisdom at all, you will call this ridiculous warfare to an end. You are a young man. Everything you think you have lost can await you in the future. Return the Bourbon possession and walk away."

"Step aside, Madame. If he wishes a rematch, so be it."

"Rachelle, you have warned him, now go back," Fabien said. "Maurice, I have not forgotten the deaths of my men-at-arms. It need not have happened except for your selfish folly. Men better than you are buried at Vendôme, their families grieve, there are young widows, one with a child. All because you were not willing to accept losing something you merely wanted. You can either leave Fontainebleau now for the Beauvilliers estate, or you can draw your blade and die."

Rachelle held her breath. Her hands were cold and damp.

Maurice stared at him. There must have been something in Fabien's calm, low voice and fixed expression that slapped him into his old sensibilities, for he spoke not a word in reply and stood still, looking at Fabien. The haughty demeanor, the flare of the nostrils, and the curl of the lip were gone.

Rachelle stood with her skirts rustling in the breeze. The robins ceased to trill.

Running footsteps sounded over the courtyard, but neither Fabien nor Maurice moved. Rachelle turned her head. Madame Trudeau rushed breathlessly forward, her dark dress and coif trailing in the breeze. She brushed past Rachelle and made for Fabien, falling to her knees in a gasping cry, holding a Bible to her bosom.

"Monseigneur, I beg of you, forgive my son his folly. He is impulsive in many ways, but perhaps it is not all his blame but mine. You see, he was my child, but I—I was unmarried and could not keep him—and Comtesse Francoise Beauvilliers had no son and we agreed to—to keep the secret from everyone except Comte Sebastien, who knew—yet he kept his silence to the end, even when he was disappointed in Maurice. Oh, Monseigneur, here is Duchesse Marie-Louise de Bourbon's—Book. Take it, I beg of you, and be content to let this folly go. I vow that Maurice will be no more trouble to you or to Marquise Rachelle. The comtesse will send him to Beauvilliers's estate, and I will go with him."

They stood bound in silence. No one moved. The wind rustled the leaves. Maurice gaped at the woman on her knees before Fabien.

Maurice seemed to be trembling, his eyes wide as he stared down at Madame Trudeau.

"You? You—are—my—mother? *You!*"

Tears streaked her thin face and her mouth trembled. "Yes, Maurice. I speak the truth at last, I swear it, though I wished you not to know."

He walked slowly, clumsily toward her, now apparently forgetting Fabien and Rachelle.

"Who is my father? *Who?*"

Madame Trudeau dropped her face into her palms. Rachelle believed that Maurice hoped it would still be Comte Beauvilliers, even if Madame Trudeau had not been married to him.

Madame Trudeau kept her face in her palms. Her voice was muffled. "Your father is dead."

"Who was he?" Maurice demanded in a shaking voice.

Madame Trudeau shook her head as though the words were too painful to speak. At last her voice came, tremulous.

"He was a soldier under Duc Jean-Louis de Bourbon."

"W-what rank?"

"Ensign."

Maurice groaned, as if this were the final humiliating blow. His hands dropped listlessly to his sides. Even the cocky ostrich plume in his red velvet hat appeared to dampen. He lowered himself upon a large rock in a bed of periwinkles and removed his hat, setting it on his knees. The plume ruffled in the wind. His shoulders stooped.

"His name was Ensign Maurice Fontaine," Madame Trudeau said in a muffled voice.

Rachelle felt inclined to walk over and comfort Madame Trudeau, who obviously had not wished to share her shame in the open. Not knowing whether her action would worsen matters, she refrained. Fabien, too, looked startled by the disclosure. He turned and walked a short distance away, his back toward them.

Rachelle had the uncomfortable notion that if it had not been for the presence of Madame Trudeau, Fabien's laughter would have filled the garden. *Maurice, the illegitimate son of a common foot soldier; Maurice who flaunted his title as comte, who scornfully refused to call Andelot his cousin! A serf of Fabien's father.* Rachelle bit her lip and cast a furtive glance down to the bed of periwinkles.

Maurice sat, head in hands, so still he might have been a marble statue.

A few moments later Fabien walked up, took the Bourbon Bible that Madame Trudeau had laid down on the stone court, said something in a kindly voice to her, and then turned to Maurice. Fabien's mouth turned up at the corners. He picked up Maurice's plumed hat and straightened the feather.

"Well, Maurice, let me assure you that your father fought under a most excellent Bourbon duc." With exaggerated attention, Fabien placed the hat on Maurice's head with a final but gentle pat.

Maurice stared glumly at his boots, all the bluster and revenge emptied from him, his ego dwarfed.

Fabien walked over to Rachelle, and after taking her hand and kissing her fingers, took her arm with a glint of amusement in his violet-blue eyes, and walked her back toward the château. The robins, she noted, were trilling again.

Andelot paced his chamber floor that night. The wind found ways to invade through the stairways and corridors of Fontainebleau, chilling him, despite the fire in the hearth.

I must do something to stop the murder of Antoine.

He ran his tense fingers through his hair. He had already sought wisdom from God.

Who might he warn of this diabolical plan?

But then he remembered how murder oft was committed behind the scenes in the dark cloisters of court politics. What about Mademoiselle Rachelle's Grandmère Dushane, that silver-haired grande dame of the Château de Silk? Was she not poisoned with gloves by the Queen Mother? There was no certain proof, and yet he was sure of it; so were Rachelle and Marquis Fabien.

He could warn Prince Antoine himself, but it would be most difficult to get an audience with him, for he was under close watch. Even if he could, would that solve the dilemma? What could Prince Antoine do except try to escape from Fontainebleau? If he managed this, he could not get far before guards alerted Duc de Guise. The attempt would grant the duc the excuse that Antoine's death occurred while attempting to flee to Navarre.

Marquis Fabien must be warned of this evil plan against his kinsman! There was little time to waste. He caught up his cloak and turned toward the door.

Outside, the courtyard was bleak and mostly dark with only a few flaring torches. Now and then the moon showed itself but was soon covered with racing clouds.

He hurried to Oncle Sebastien's old appartement.

Murder?

NEAR THE CRACKLING HEARTH IN THE APPARTEMENT, RACHELLE WAS LYING on the chaise beside Fabien.

"Are you sure the Queen Mother does not have a listening tube in Sebastien's appartement?" she whispered sleepily.

"Must you mention her just before we go to sleep? She incites you to nightmares, chérie. You shall awaken as you did last night with a high-pitched scream and startle me into a frenzy. I actually had the rapier in hand before I realized you were hallucinating. Unless it truly was our cardinal you envisioned," he jested wryly. "He may have crawled through the window with a pitchfork."

"Hush." She looked around at the walls with priceless tapestries and gilded ornamentation. "He might hear you mocking him."

"It is ironic that the Queen Mother would put us here in Sebastien's old appartement, but it is like her. In her vindictive mind, I have replaced Sebastien as one of her counselors on state matters."

"You are wise enough, and you know state affairs well."

"It is a trap. One I hope to avoid. Like a prisoner occupying the cell of a previous victim."

"Now it is you who are giving me nightmares." She looked around again at the figures in the various weavings, imagining the Queen Mother peering at her through the faces in the tapestries.

"I have plans for our escape," he said quietly. "I am working on one now with Gallaudet. Julot and Nappier are also involved. But it will take time. It may not be arranged until the colloquy when so many will be coming and going out of Geneva."

"I could write Père Arnaut and Madame Clair not to come to Poissy, but I fear nothing would change their plans. Père and Cousin Bertrand are coming in cooperation with Geneva."

"I doubt that anything is likely to keep them in London except a civil war between Catholics and Huguenots."

She turned her head to see his expression and found it calm.

"Do you still think there will be a war?"

"If the colloquy fails as the Guises wish it to and the persecution continues, yes."

She lapsed into silence. Would a religious civil war convince him to remain in France? Fabien's main reason for wishing to depart for England was centered in concern for her safety. So far there had been no further response from the Queen Mother. If she were safe, would Fabien then feel an obligation to fight in a war on the side of the Huguenots? He held great feelings of responsibility for his serfs in Vendôme. She was pleased when she learned his delay in coming to her after being released from the dungeon was because of his concern for the families of his men-at-arms. The idea of a religious civil war and what it would mean for the Huguenots was so weighty that she pushed the possibility from her. There was so much to be concerned about now that she did not wish to consider the outcome.

She laughed suddenly.

"What amuses you now?"

"Did my scream last night truly frighten you?"

"Oh no, I am quite used to being awakened from a sound sleep by a high-pitched shriek."

She snuggled against him. "I thought I saw a dark figure rushing toward the bed. It was very tall with a long black gown."

"Most certainly the cardinal in his finest night robe."

"Or Père Jaymin."

"Another comforting figure. With such monsieurs as these, no wonder the chapel is empty."

"Let us not talk of them."

"Agreed." He turned her face toward his and kissed her. "This is much more interesting—" he kissed her again—"and more fun."

There came a tap on the door. A quiet voice ventured: "Monsieur le Marquis? Madame?"

Rachelle freed herself from his embrace and stood, smoothing her loose hair into place.

"Yes, Nenette? What is it?"

Nenette entered, casting a glance toward Fabien, who remained lounging on the chaise by the fire. He lifted his goblet.

"Go ahead, Nenette," Rachelle said.

"It is Monsieur Andelot. He says it is most urgent he speak with the marquis."

Fabien set the goblet down. "Andelot? Send him in at once." He stood and reached over to turn up the lamplight.

Rachelle rushed into the bedchamber to put on a high-collared chemise and pin her hair up from her back. Now why would Andelot come at this hour?

Rachelle heard Fabien and Andelot's voices as she slipped into a pair of satin shoes. She joined them by the fire in the salle as Fabien gestured Andelot to the table of various refreshments, fruits, and cheeses.

Rachelle noted Andelot's tension, and her light mood of a short while ago fled. Something was wrong. What was it this time?

Andelot stood by the fire, so preoccupied with whatever he had come to see Fabien about that he had forgotten to remove his wide-rimmed hat. She went over and plucked it from his curly dark head. He grinned suddenly.

"Merci, Madame Rachelle, I had forgotten."

"Do cease calling me madame," she scolded affectionately. "It has always been Rachelle, your amie, and so it is now."

"Oui, madame — " he cleared his throat — "I mean Rachelle."

"Sit down, mon ami," Fabien said gently, a faint look of sympathy in his gaze. Could Fabien still think Andelot cared for her? But that was silly. A lettre had arrived for him recently from her sister Idelette, safely arrived at London with Madeleine, bébé Joan, and Sebastien.

"What ails you?" Fabien asked Andelot. He drew Rachelle into a white-and-gold chair, then seated himself, studying Andelot. Fabien wore a sober expression now, as though he knew Andelot well enough to realize when trouble threatened.

Andelot drew a hand across his brow in a restless movement. Rachelle saw him glance at her, then back to Fabien. From the corner of her eye she saw Fabien give a slight nod. Rachelle sat a little straighter. Fabien's inclusion of her in whatever trouble was at hand made her feel mature and trusted.

"Did anyone see you come here?" Fabien asked.

"I was most wary, Marquis."

Fabien gave a slight nod. "Then?"

"I am here, Marquis, to prevent a murder, and only you can help me."

The mood plunged into icy silence. Fabien stood, hands on hips, frowning down at him. "Who is the intended victim this time?"

Andelot plunged his fingers through his curly brown hair, which again covered his head. He moved to the hearth, then turned around quickly, scowling. "Your kinsman, Prince Antoine de Bourbon."

Rachelle drew in a sharp breath. She darted a glance from Andelot to Fabien. Now both of his Bourbon kinsmen were in danger of losing their lives.

"But why Antoine?" she whispered.

Andelot cast a cautious glance toward the tapestries as though they had ears. "They planned the death of Prince Louis — and now Prince Antoine, and both are of royal blood. I fear you too, Marquis, could be in danger."

Rachelle stood, heart thudding. "Fabien!"

"Who are *they*?" Fabien's voice was hard. "You mean the Guises, do you not?"

"You speak the truth. Duc de Guise, Cardinal de Lorraine, and another monsieur I have not met before who is often at court, the Maréchal de Saint Andre. It is he who will be close at hand."

"Then the diabolical plans are already made?"

"I heard them spoken, Marquis. There was no shame in stating their plans. I was called into the very chamber of the king where the duc and cardinal waited for me."

Fabien scowled. "Are you saying Francis knows of this murderous plot?"

"He does. They have convinced him that Prince Antoine means him ill and is waiting to usurp the throne for the Bourbons. The king is to call Antoine to his chamber as though to ask him something in particular, but it is a ploy. Francis is to then provoke Antoine by calling him a traitor and most vehemently insulting him so that Antoine becomes angry. Antoine will think they are alone and is expected to lash out at the young king. Then Francis is to slash at him with his dagger and call out for help. The duc, cardinal, and Maréchal de Saint Andre will be just out of view behind a curtain and will rush in. All three will then plunge their daggers into Antoine at the same time, as though they were protecting the king. No single monsieur will be to blame for Antoine's death. They will say Antoine was furious over his detention, over the looming execution of his brother Louis, and that he lost his senses, stole into the king's chamber, and tried to put a dagger in his heart."

Rachelle sat down weakly.

"I knew they would stop at nothing to keep control of the throne, but outright murder by their own hands surprises me," Fabien said. "What role did they so graciously assign you in all this?"

"That of witness, Marquis. I was to say that Prince Antoine lost his senses and jumped on King Francis to kill him."

"I have got to warn Antoine," Fabien mused, pacing. "This could be the incident Catherine has arranged against Guise, an opportunity for the duc's death, and yet ..." He frowned. "I do not think she is privy to this."

Rachelle looked at him, doubting. "Why do you think so? I put nothing beyond her."

"True, and I happen to know she carries a secret dagger for her personal protection. But when it comes to her enemies? She prefers a more 'quiet' departure." He turned to Andelot, who warmed himself at the fire, looking glum. "What do you think? Is the Queen Mother involved with them in this treachery?"

"Non, Marquis, I think not."

"And if I had to guess, I would wager she does not want Louis executed either. It will only strengthen the grip of the Guises on the throne. She has been most friendly with Antoine recently ..." He tapped his chin. "One wonders if she might not be secretly working with him to secure the regency."

Rachelle was frightened. What if some suggestion had reached the duc that the Queen Mother hoped to use Fabien to assassinate him? Even if Fabien had no intention of fulfilling her plans, the duc would believe him capable, knowing that Fabien blamed him for the death of his father.

"Andelot is right to be concerned about you. If two Bourbons can be murdered, why not a third?" She went to Fabien. "We must stop them, but how?"

"When it comes to weaving intrigue, Catherine is equal to the Guises," Fabien said. "I will seek an occasion to speak with her."

"But you are at risk even now. What if the Guises learn you were the one who informed the Queen Mother? And what about Andelot—they will know he told you."

"They will not know, Mademoiselle," Andelot said hastily.

"Catherine is too subtle for open confrontation with the Guises," Fabien said dryly. "Of one thing you may be sure. She will keep her true face behind a masque." He turned to Andelot. "Did the Guises offer you anything?"

Andelot frowned and ran a hand through his hair. "Well, yes."

Rachelle frowned upon hearing how he would be sent to the university the cardinal himself had attended.

Andelot smiled uneasily. "He said it was in the realm of possibility for me to take his position one day as the greatest cardinal in France."

"He was generous with his words," Fabien said with sarcasm. "Sending you to the Guise château at Lorraine is all but legal adoption."

"They hope to ensnare you with grandiose promises," Rachelle said. "Do not do it, Andelot."

Fabien put a hand on her back and gently tugged at a curl behind her neck. "Andelot is wiser than that, chérie."

"I would rather be an orphan and without family than be embraced by such bloody men.

"The wisdom of the Proverbs is a light unto my path to warn me. 'These six things doth the Lord hate: yea, seven are an abomination unto him: A proud look, a lying tongue, and hands that shed innocent blood, an heart that deviseth wicked imaginations, feet that be swift in running to mischief, a false witness that speaketh lies, and he that soweth discord among brethren.' "

"Well said. You should study at Geneva to be a pasteur. The calling, mon ami, is in your heart."

❦

GARBED IN BLACK VELVET AND SILVER, Fabien entered the royal chambers of the Queen Mother and removed his hat with a bow.

She sat in pitiless silence while he gave account of what the Guises planned against his kinsman.

"You have proved an asset at court, Monsieur Marquis, if what you say is true. And I in no way doubt you, or the cunning schemes of the house of Guise. If the hunting accident had occurred ..."

He remained silent.

She took this as assent. "What else have you planned?"

He expected this and was prepared, speaking with strong passion. "When Duc de Guise may be aware? Madame, it is folly. If I blunder in haste, the King of Spain will suspect *you*. The Spanish ambassador will be the first to write him. You have kept me from his chains for the very purpose of eliminating Guise, he will say. The King of Spain is looking for an excuse to turn on you, Madame. You know this well. My hasty move against the duc could provoke the king to order the Duc of Alva to withdraw some of his soldiers from the Netherlands and invade Calais, or they could cross the border through the duchy of Lorraine, at the cardinal's secret order."

He saw the flicker of alarm in her amber eyes. She gave a brief nod but paced restlessly, watching the burgundy rug beneath her.

"Yes ... caution. Always caution." She snapped her fingers. "Then there is no choice for me except to move to protect Antoine."

"If, Madame, you were to find a way to also save Louis, you would have a strong soldier on your side. So also Admiral Coligny would rally to you," he suggested silkily.

She focused her unblinking stare upon him. For a moment he expected her to accuse him of deliberately baiting her.

She did not respond, however, and merely said, "I believe I can guess why Duc de Guise wishes the swift demise of Antoine upon the execution of Louis. I have discussed the worsening health of Francis with

Antoine. Young Prince Charles is next in line for the crown. If Charles comes to the throne, there will be a regent for some years, and only I can control Charles."

So then it was the regency that propelled her forward in her actions. He became more convinced than ever of her secret plan to align herself with the Bourbon-Huguenot alliance against the house of Guise.

"And my kinsman Antoine?"

She smiled. "Antoine will become general of France in place of Duc de Guise."

The position was one of great power. Catherine and Antoine would rule France in coregency. The Guises, of course, would lose as much power as the Bourbons gained.

"You understand the reason why the duc and cardinal wish for Antoine's demise? My spies tell me they discovered my meeting with Antoine several weeks ago on this subject. And now they see the danger to their house."

No wonder the Guises were afraid and planning desperate measures.

"Go to Antoine and warn him," she said. "Under no circumstance should he enter the king's chamber if he is called."

Fabien bowed over her hand and left the chamber.

Did Rome encourage the assassination of the Bourbon princes because of their Huguenot leaning? Or did Spain?

He walked along the corridor and through a salle in the direction of Antoine's chamber.

❧

CATHERINE LEFT HER CHAMBER and entered the royal chamber of her son, King Francis, but she did not go alone. She made certain her excuse for being there would go undetected by the Guises and Mary, for Mary would be certain to be there, keeping Francis under watch, no doubt as the cardinal had told her.

Catherine stood at the foot of the grand bed, her arms folded across the front of her black gown. She looked sympathetically at her son Francis.

Francis was resting as the docteur attended him, asking about his condition.

I must get Mary out of the chamber so I can speak to Francis alone.

When the docteur turned to leave, Catherine asked him to speak with Mary of the young king's condition.

"While I bid my son adieu, you understand. Just a small mother and son talk. Ah, how I worry about my ailing son, my petit Francis, my young and brilliant king ..." And she brought a lace kerchief up to her mouth and bent her head. "I worry so."

"Of course, Madame," the docteur said gently. "I shall speak to the queen in the next chamber."

From the corner of her eye, she saw Mary watching her. She appeared about to protest when the docteur took her aside, but at last she went with him into the other chamber, leaving the door between ajar.

The spy!

Catherine sat down on the bed beside Francis, laying her palm on his forehead. She felt his body tense under the satin cover.

"Ah, my poor sick Francis, how tired and worried you look. Is there more that disturbs you than physical weariness?"

"Madame Mother, do not worry. I — I am well."

She leaned toward him and whispered urgently, "Tell me, my son, keep nothing back from me. What have Duc de Guise and the cardinal planned for the poor little Bourbon prince, Antoine?"

His eyes swerved to hers, and she saw fear in their depths.

"Is there a diabolical plot to involve you in the murder of a prince of the royal blood?" she whispered. "Oh my son, do not do this deed. Do you not know that none can strike a prince of the blood and not suffer a curse?"

Francis bit his lip, and his thin, nervous hands plucked at the cover.

"Yes, I know. I do not want to do such a thing, but the Bourbons wish to destroy our house, Mother. We must fight back for the sake of the Valois heirs."

"Is that what they told you? And you believed them! It is only for the power of the house of Guise that they will murder Antoine — and Louis! And what of your ami since childhood, the Bourbon Marquis Fabien?"

"They do not trust him either. A word was given to the duc to be alert. His life may be in danger."

Fear grabbed hold of her. It was true, then. The Spanish ambassador had somehow received word of her plan to use the marquis. That her effort to retain secrecy had failed terrified her.

Someone had overheard—a guard perhaps? It could be anyone. Perhaps a guard at the Amboise dungeon when she'd first confronted Fabien? Even a docteur. She turned her gaze slowly toward the door standing ajar. Yes, it could be anyone, even Fabien. How very Machiavellian if true!

"My enemies at court are many, and they lie," she hissed. "I wish the duc naught but bonne fortune. And you, Francis, you must not shed blood."

He bit his lip. "Mother, I am most miserable. I curse the day when Father died and I had to become king. I never wanted to be king. I would surrender the crown in a moment and go far away with Mary if I could— even to Scotland, oui, to be free of the cardinal and—"

Francis stopped, and his gaze swerved to hers as though he had not meant to say those words.

"And to be free of me, too, my son? You need not fear me, my poor sick Francis. I am going to help you be free of the cardinal. You and Mary both."

His eyes showed a sparkle. "You will help us, Madame Mother? If only we could go away—"

"Trust me, my son. Oh, you will soon be free of the Guises. I have a way to open your cage and let the petite birds fly away."

Footsteps entered too quietly behind her, and Catherine whispered, "Say nothing of what we discussed. Not even to Mary." She stood, smiling down at Francis. "And now you must rest, my son. We must not overtire you." She turned, and Mary stood with a cool glint in her eyes.

"Ma petite Reinette, do not look so grieved. Francis will be stronger soon, you will see. The new medicine the docteur has given to me will assuredly help him."

"Given to you, Madame? The royal physician has said nothing to me about a new medicine. This new docteur you brought today—"

"He did not wish to overburden you. You are so disturbed over your beloved Francis. Come now and sit beside him. Play on the lute for him and he will fall to sleep. We must not tire him."

"No, Madame, we must not. This new medicine you mention —"

"He has not yet sent it, ma petite, but he will deliver it soon. If you like, it shall be sent to *you* to give to Francis."

Mary looked relieved. She showed her smile. "Oui, Madame, I should like to take care of Francis myself."

"But of course you would, and you shall. Why not play the lute for him now? He so enjoys it. I shall leave you both in peace."

Catherine smiled at Francis, then at Mary.

You smug spy!

"Ah, adieu, my little lovebirds."

ANDELOT RECEIVED HIS DREADED summons from the cardinal to come to the king's chamber. He arrived tense and prayerful to find King Francis looking pale and stressed, sitting on the throne chair.

"I — I have also sent for Antoine, King of Navarre," he told Andelot.

"Yes, Your Majesty."

The king was studying his slender white hands, turning a jeweled ring round and round on his finger.

Andelot was aware that the marquis had gone to warn Prince Antoine. The Guises had secretly arrived, and Andelot could hear them moving about behind the curtain in the antechamber, talking in low voices with Maréchal de Saint Andre.

The time crept by. Andelot grew more confident when two of the Guise followers came with the message that Antoine was sick. Duc de Guise came through the curtain and spoke to Francis.

"Send the captain of the guard, sire. He is not ill. This smells of a ploy."

Andelot waited in prayer. At last he heard the captain of the guard coming with Antoine. The door opened and Andelot snatched a glimpse of Marquis Fabien and Gallaudet in the outer corridor flanking the prince, but when they attempted to follow him in, the guards stopped them.

Prince Antoine entered, his manner silent and cautious, and bowed low to the king.

At least he knows what to expect.

Antoine remained across the chamber, far removed from Francis. Andelot noticed that he wisely carried no weapon. He kept his hands folded at his chest, fingers interlaced. Andelot took careful note of all this should he need to testify of Antoine's actions.

The three of them were alone now. The fire sizzled and crackled in the hearth and, to Andelot, overheated the chamber, causing sweat to dampen his forehead. King Francis stood up suddenly from his chair and pointed a finger at Antoine. "You! You and Louis! You are traitors—both of you. Traitor! Fie! I should—I should have you executed—you, with Prince Louis. Speak! Confess you are a traitor. Have you nothing to say, you coward?"

Antoine moved even farther from Francis and said not a word.

Francis frowned, and a crimson stain stood out on his pale, boyish cheeks. He averted his eyes. He plucked at his hands. He began again: "Have you nothing to say for yourself?"

"I am innocent of any rebellion, my lord King. I was not involved in the Amboise rebellion. I knew nothing of it until it was over."

Francis looked about him as though wondering what to do next. Unexpectedly, he yelled out, "Help! Help! Assassin!"

But by this time, Antoine, warned by the marquis of what to do, had inched closer and closer to the door. As soon as Francis cried "Assassin!" Antoine ran out of the royal chamber to where the marquis and Gallaudet were waiting. Antoine was escaping before the three plotters could dart from the antechamber with daggers unsheathed to protect their king.

Andelot remained mute and as far away as he could from those in the royal chamber.

Duc de Guise held a dagger in hand. His eyes were hard, and his mouth slashed his disapproval across his white face.

Andelot, sickened, was sure he considered Francis a failure for not hurling enough venomous charges against Antoine to provoke him. The Cardinal de Lorraine also held a dagger, and his mouth was twisted with mockery as his voice dripped with scorn toward Francis.

"Behold the most lily-livered king that ever sat on the throne of France!"

Andelot felt the injustice of it all stir his heart. He clenched a fist behind his back. *And you Monsieur le Cardinal — a hypocrite! As if I would ever wish to follow your steps. I shall not stay at court. After my days with Scholar Thauvet are accomplished, I shall leave France.*

⁂

AT FONTAINEBLEAU IN EARLY DECEMBER, the execution of Prince Louis was days away. The rains darkened the afternoon, and candles burned in the Queen Mother's chamber. She walked to and fro, her feet treading soundlessly over the burgundy and gold carpet. She brooded over the narrowing course of action open to her.

She pressed her kerchief to her lips, biting on the cloth, her mind racing. She had hoped that as Francis grew older, he would begin to assert himself and come into his own rule, but he remained intimidated by the lecherous cardinal.

If only my Anjou had been born ahead of Francis. Anjou, third in line to kingship, would not permit himself to be controlled by the house of Guise. *Francis was never meant to be a king.* She sank into a chair with wearied resignation.

There was no way out of her trap except to wait — wait for her son, so tired and exhausted, so ill, poor petit Francis, to die.

Catherine rose and walked slowly about her chamber, head bent, pondering. Charles would become king, and Charles did not fear the cardinal — he hated him. *The house of Guise will not be able to control Charles. He will not submit his scepter to the Guises. It is I alone who control Mad Charles.*

Charles will not come into his maturity for years. If am voted the regent by the Estates General, it will mean that I will rule France for years — with Antoine de Bourbon.

And Mary? If Francis died would she remain at court? Yes! Yes! With the Guises scheming to marry her to Charles, who was besotted with her, though he was but a child. Even so, the Guises would seek to arrange a wedding between them for the future. Ah, she knew the Guises well.

Catherine hardened her mouth. *Ah, that spy will be sent back to Scotland.* Let her shrewd red-headed cousine, Queen Elizabeth in England, take care of the petite reinette in her own fashion.

She pushed her kerchief to her mouth to silence a gusty chuckle.

The days slipped by. King Francis complained of severe pain in his ear. He was in so much pain that all of the court physicians did not know the answer to His Majesty's ailment and suffering. Catherine insisted on helping her son with her own remedies of herbs and drugs.

"As I did when he was my enfant. My herbs and powders from Florence help lighten the pain," she said. "I cannot bear to see my son, my Francis, suffer so."

"But Madame," Mary cried, looking pale and red-eyed from crying. "The medicine you give Francis puts him into dumbness. He cannot move. He does not speak to me."

"My poor petite Reinette Mary, how your tender heart grieves, and I understand why."

If Francis dies, your days here are finished. You will be off to your wild and churlish Scotland, as you fear.

"Your sorrows are many. This is so hard on you, is it not? But what is most kind? To ease his pain in deep slumber, or allow him wakefulness to toss and turn in agony? You too must rest. Yes, you are driven by your anxiety."

"Oh, Madame, after all that has occurred — " Mary's eyes snapped — "First at Amboise, with the beheadings of so many Huguenots, and now with Prince Antoine — how can Francis and I not be overwrought?"

And who was it that wished the execution of so many Huguenots at Amboise and planned to murder Antoine? The Guises! Your oncles!

Catherine caught herself and replaced her inner snarl with a look of compassion.

"So true, so true. These have been dreadful days. That is why you must get some sleep and leave me to sit by his bedside for this night at least. Go, ma chère. Is not the royal physician also here to watch over him?"

"Yes ... yes ..." Mary put a hand to her forehead.

"Tomorrow," Catherine continued soothingly, "tomorrow? Who knows, ma petite? Perhaps God will hear the bonne cardinal's intercessions and Francis will awaken feeling much better!"

"Yes, you may be right. Mon oncle, the cardinal, is offering a Mass."

"Oh, well then! Francis will assuredly do better." Catherine smiled.

Catherine beckoned for Mary's ladies to come forward, and they took her away to her rest for the night.

Catherine dropped her smile. She walked briskly to the bedside and gazed down at her son. She remembered the happy moment when her first son had been placed in her arms. How Henry had been pleased!

She continued to stare down at him.

She sat down gently so as not to disturb his slumber.

During the long night, she thought, planned, and watched him.

If only you had permitted me to arrange a marriage for you instead of letting Henry's debauched mistress arrange it with Mary Stuart, matters would be different for you, for us. You would have been happier, my son, and there would be no house of Guise manipulating your throne.

My poor little son, the king.

Later, she sent the docteur away. "You also, Maître d'Fontaine, must take your sleep. Docteur Ambroise le Pare will soon be here — there is no need to wait for him. I shall keep vigil. Au revoir."

❧

ON THE FIFTH OF DECEMBER, King Francis died.

Catherine took refuge in her chambers where the walls were hung in black mourning drape. She locked her door, making plans to send Mary back to Scotland.

Poor petit Francis. She took another moment to remember his life and his illness of the blood disease since infancy. She dabbed her eyes with her kerchief. Now he was gone — but so was Mary.

Well, the docteur had always told her he could not be expected to live long.

After the death of his elder brother, the boy-prince Charles de Valois became King Charles IX, crowned in 1561 in the cathedral at Reims by the Cardinal de Lorraine. And Catherine, according to her plans, became regent of France, with Prince Antoine de Bourbon as her general. She had received the quiet support of the Huguenot Admiral Coligny, to whom she had promised the religious convention at Poissy. She had also promised to work for an end to the relentless persecution.

Nevertheless, Fabien believed she would throw them all to the lions if she thought it would prevent Spain from supporting the Guises with an army in order to replace her.

Fabien was in the council chamber, standing near the Queen Mother, when Duc de Guise entered. His sour gaze swept away from Catherine to fix on Fabien. Fabien gave him a measuring glance, refusing to yield.

The duc walked up and bowed stiffly to Catherine.

"Madame, what is this I hear of Prince Louis being released from the Amboise dungeon? And mere days before the axe was to fall? This smells of injustice and treachery. I believe you should have the new king look into this matter, lest the people come to think suspiciously of your reign."

Fabien reached to smooth the lapel on his velvet jacket and ended by drumming his fingers.

"Monsieur Duc, you forget yourself in my presence," she said.

"Madame, I could not forget myself in your presence. If I have seemed to you too blunt, I beg pardon, but my words spring from an injustice."

"An injustice?" Fabien asked.

His voice, equally blunt and aggressive, caused Duc de Guise to turn toward him, lifting his chin.

"Do you know something of injustice, Messire?" Fabien asked.

The duc blinked, his shock apparent. "You are suggesting, Marquis?"

"That Duc Jean-Louis de Bourbon, my father, was left to die on the battlefield near Calais. That too, was injustice. An injustice that as yet has not been satisfied."

The duc's left eye watered, and the scarred eyelid twitched.

Fabien could not see Catherine's face, but this was the tense environment she hoped for. So be it. It mattered not whether he was playing into her plan. These were the words he had long wanted to throw at the duc, and more.

The duc's small mouth came together in a thin line beneath his short ginger-colored beard.

"The death of Duc Jean-Louis de Bourbon was an honorable one,

Messire. I know nothing of any injustice; the day he took a sword thrust and was left on the battlefield, I was miles away in a battle of my own."

Fabien was on the verge of pressing home the attack when Duchesse Dushane, standing nearby, stepped toward them, her ebony walking stick clicking on the glossy floor. She had grown thin and pale from a detrimental change in her health.

"Madame," she said to Catherine, and inclined her silvery head with its glittering diamonds. Her smooth voice seemed to try to ease the matter by changing the subject back to Louis.

"Is it not true, Madame, that legally Prince Louis was imprisoned by the will of the late king?"

"Duc de Guise would know that, Duchesse, since it was he who insisted Francis send for the Bourbon princes to arrest them."

"And rightly so, Madame," Duc de Guise snapped, giving a hard look at Duchesse Dushane.

"Then," said the duchesse, "is it not a matter for the new king to either carry through on his brother's wish, or to release Prince Louis, which he has chosen to do?"

His lean face sullen, Guise remained in silent opposition.

"The new king has chosen to show mercy on his ascension to the throne, my lord Duc," the Queen Mother said.

"Was it His young Majesty King Charles who wished to show mercy to Prince Louis, Madame?" And with an abrupt bow, Guise turned on his heel and strode from the council chamber.

Catherine laughed and made as though the scene were nothing, but Fabien could see the cold venom in her eyes over Guise's affront in public.

Later, he received her summons to come to her chamber. The Queen Mother was alone when he entered, her arms folded across the bosom of her severe gown.

"The effrontery of the man," she spat. "I had hopes he would pick up the gauntlet you tossed to his feet. Ah that was clever, my lord Marquis. Most clever, but he is too cunning for that."

In truth, Fabien had not planned for the moment with Guise, but he permitted the Queen Mother to think so. In retrospect he considered the rash moment of anger detrimental to his true purpose, which was safeguarding Rachelle. It would have been wiser had he not drawn attention to his resentments over his father's death. He owed the smooth intervention of the duchesse for slipping out of his own trap.

The Queen Mother, of course, knew nothing of his true feelings. She turned and faced him.

"A duel may yet work, but keep in mind his son may also challenge you. Young Henry de Guise worships his father."

He wondered if she may not want the duc's son to turn on him since all blame for his death would be taken away from her.

Fabien continued to feed her fears of Spain so as to muzzle her raging appetite for the duc's quick death.

"Madame, my loathing of the man who murdered my father does not waver. Even so, with Louis released from the dungeon and the Guises embittered, I may have been unwise to alert the duc this night. They are more watchful than ever. I found one of the Spanish ambassador's spies loitering near my appartement."

She watched with her unblinking serpentine stare. "What do you mean to suggest?"

"You know better than I the many secret correspondences the ambassador sends to the escorial," he said of King Philip's court.

He saw her emotionally withdraw her claws. Caution now scribbled its fears across her face. He stepped closer, pressing in with his words.

"I would suggest, Madame, that until the gossip settles down, we keep a cautious distance from the Guises."

She drew her fingers tighter about the black lace at her throat. "Gossip? What gossip! Parisians are fools for Duc de Guise and his son."

Fabien lowered his voice. "Pardon my saying this, but I would keep nothing back that concerns Your Majesty."

"Yes?" she breathed, her skin pale and moist in the candlelight that flickered and weaved.

He continued to stir up her fears of Spain. "Suspicions run rampant in Catholic Paris, no doubt begun by Guise followers themselves, that the late king's death was not as it seems. If Spain hears of this — well, Madame, you can imagine the response."

He lifted a brow. He waited for what, he did not know. Her square jaw flexed, and he saw the muscle in her throat move as she swallowed.

"Gibberish. Forever my enemies hiss and snarl about poison! Lies, lies, and more lies."

Fabien pressed home the final attack. "The Parisians are already whispering that the 'Italian Woman' cannot be trusted with France."

She grimaced her anger.

"Ask yourself, Madame, is this the wisest hour for Guise's death?"

She drew her head back, her eyes studying him from beneath heavy lids.

"If Paris is led to believe by the duc's son and the cardinal, or the Spanish ambassador, that the throne had anything to do with an assassination of the duc, it could, coming so soon after the king's death, ignite a civil war against you and the young king."

He watched the look of anger turn into alarm and was satisfied with his tactic.

"Be assured, Marquis, of my caution when dealing with the enemies of the house of Valois."

"I am indeed aware of your vigilance in matters of state, Madame. And with the Guises now licking their wounds, a reprieve may be granted us for a time."

"And as you yourself know, they will regroup and do all they can to regain power. In my allowing the religious colloquy to be held at Poissy, I will be plagued with denunciations from Rome. Remember, I am depending on the Bourbon-Huguenot alliance to stand with me."

She took a sudden step toward him, surprising him, her finger tapping his chest for bold emphasis.

"They are in a weakened state. This is your opportunity to at long last avenge the murder of Duc Jean-Louis, just as you have dreamed and planned."

How crafty of her to throw the assassination of Guise back into my realm, as though it were my solitary ambition to avenge my father's murder.

Suddenly, it was not she who wanted the removal of Guise, but he alone. Whether intentional or not, this alerted him that if he failed to cover his tracks completely, he would find no quarter with her once he had accomplished the task — she would abandon him to the mob. Perhaps that had been her ambition all along.

At Court

RACHELLE FOUND HER NEW LIFE AT FONTAINEBLEAU WITH FABIEN both exciting and dangerous. She was constantly under watch by spies, so that whether she was walking in the garden with Nenette or in the corridors of Fontainebleau, she sensed the eyes of Madalenna watching her from the shadows, or perhaps a dwarf among the trees, or a guard outside the appartement.

Despite this fear, Fabien came home to her in the afternoon, and once again within his embrace, she felt secure. At last bride and groom were together and love was fulfilling, the unity of spirit and mind could be as wondrous as the physical passion of marriage.

They had not been living in the Fontainebleau appartement for many weeks when Fabien left a meeting with the king earlier than usual and came to inform her that the Queen Mother was sending him to Paris for a few days on court business.

"I'll take servants with me to retrieve your bolts of silk and sewing equipage from the Louvre. That will make you happy."

It did. She had gone so far as to write a lettre to the Queen Mother asking that her sewing equipage be sent to her here at Fontainebleau. Rachelle was surprised by the freedom the Queen Mother was granting Fabien.

"The Queen Mother is not concerned with my coming and going as long as you remain at court under the watchful eye of spies. She knows I will always come back to you. You, ma belle, are my greatest treasure. She knows I would not seek freedom without you."

Until Fabien assassinates Duc de Guise?

She could see his thoughts working as he tapped his chin, looking out the window to the courtyard below.

On more than one occasion since his release from the dungeon, they had quietly discussed the Queen Mother's unmentionable secret plan to rid herself of the Duc de Guise. Each time Fabien went away on business for the Queen Mother, Rachelle felt her concern quicken. Whenever she brought up the matter, Fabien managed to slip around the subject, lightly evading her questions.

"This journey has nothing to do with Duc de Guise?" she whispered. She spoke with caution even though he had already searched every corner of the appartement for listening tubes.

"Guise is not in Paris. He is here at Fontainebleau," he said, sidestepping the issue once more. "He is with the cardinal and an associate in the chapel forming a three-man holy league. They are taking Communion together and vowing to do all in their power to destroy the Reformation in France."

Rachelle shuddered. "You saw them in the chapel?"

"I came in through a curtain behind them," he said, no suggestion of apology for spying in his voice.

Rachelle sat down on the rose colored settee.

"That is why war is inevitable at this point," he said, frowning. "No matter the laws of toleration passed by King Charles and Catherine, the Guises and their following will ignore the laws and continue the persecution." He paced. "You may not have heard, but the cardinal has increased burnings all over France."

"Are they deliberately provoking?"

"So it would seem at times. Duc de Guise has the promise of soldiers and gold from Spain. If the Huguenot nobility decides to move to defend their serfdoms, they will need to financially sponsor the war and pay for added mercenaries. Guise can outnumber the soldiers with men from the Duc of Alva, and he will have plenty of gold from the treasure ships coming to Spain from the Americas."

Now she understood his silent frowns as he oft mused in silence. And how would this affect them and their longed-for escape? When would it come, if ever?

She thought of the coming arrival of her parents and Pasteur Bertrand. She looked up at him quickly.

"I wonder if it is wise for my parents and Pasteur Bertrand to come to the colloquy?"

"I doubt you could keep them away, chérie. They are so dedicated to the truth war. But you speak rightly. Even with permission from the king for French Bibles and debate, there may be those who will wish physical harm."

He ceased pacing and turned about to face her.

"What is it?" she asked, standing.

"Do you realize how many of the chief Huguenot Reformers will be gathered together in one place, coming from far and near, including Geneva and Navarre? Queen Jeanne and Prince Henry are attending as well," he said of his kinswoman and her son, the heir to the throne of Navarre.

Her eyes met his, searching to confirm the strange shiver that inched along her back. The church burning that took the life of her petite sister Avril flashed before her. She could hear the doors and windows being nailed shut by the enemy, hear the crackle of the fire as it spread.

"Do you think there could be some sort of attack planned by Duc de Guise and his soldiers?"

"It is possible. I'll speak of it to Prince Louis and Admiral Coligny." He took hold of her. "The truth is we must always be alert."

She bit back the words, *I could almost wish the duc were assassinated!*

What if Fabien thought she wanted him to do such a murderous deed, knowing she counted Guise responsible for the death of Avril and the violation of Idelette?

But would his lone death solve the persecution of the Huguenots throughout France? As the Reformation was stronger than one man or even a group of men like Calvin and Luther, so was the Counter-Reformation enacted by the Vatican. Ultimately the enemy was Satan himself, for we wrestle not against flesh and blood but principalities and powers.

"Oh, Fabien, if only we could escape now. I fear the Queen Mother will never release you. If we do not escape soon, it will be too late."

He drew her close, fingering her hair, stroking her back, and speaking confidently.

"We will gain our freedom. I do not have the answer yet as to how and when it will be managed, but I will not give up. There is not a day that goes by that my thoughts are not upon it. May the Lord open a door that only He can unlock."

These were Rachelle's thoughts and prayers as well. God could do anything. She knew that. But it seemed to her at times that the enemy was so strong and purposeful that they would be swallowed up. Aside from Duc de Guise, there were other enemies of concern at court. Nor was she the only one being watched. Fabien had many powerful enemies, including the Spanish Ambassador Chantonnay, who had not forgiven him for sinking the Duc of Alva's galleon.

"I do not like the ambassador," she said.

"Chantonnay," Fabien said dryly, "must spend most of his time before keyholes."

"Nor do I like the way he looks at me."

Fabien turned his gaze on her, alert. "I can see why he would look at you, ma belle, but what do you mean?"

She shook her head. "He does not look at me with masculine appreciation, but as though I were a heretic he might like to turn over to the inquisitors. I think he would abduct us both and send us to his master if he thought he might prevail."

Fabien's jaw set. "If he makes one step toward you, I shall use a few inquisitional tactics of my own. I will hang his gizzard out to dry and send it in a belle package to the morose Philip."

His remark made her smile. "A tactic you learned from Capitaine Nappier, no doubt?"

"No, a Hollander who hates papists, as he calls them."

"It sounds as if he has learned a few odious techniques himself."

"Oh, he has. He always leaves one or two of them alive to go back and tell the others what they saw."

She smoothed the already neat and spotless dark blue velvet of his jacket. She looked up at him and traced the line of his jaw with her finger.

"I think you caught buccaneering fever, and it is incurable. It will flare up now and then with great allurement to take you from me," she teased.

"Think so? I did come back to you. It was you alone who captured my heart from the lure of the sea."

She sighed. "The *Reprisal* . . . how fair it sounds now, even to me; and to think the ship waited within reach at Dieppe to take us to England."

"And then along came Maurice. Ah, I should have shown no pity but wrung his neck. By the way, where is he? I have not seen his bright plumage about court in weeks."

She laughed. "Nenette found out that he is nourishing his wounded pride at the Beauvilliers estate. The comtesse and Madame Trudeau went with him."

"To soothe and solace him? They may have feared he would drink hemlock. Ah, well, chérie. He will return one day, I am sure. Maybe he will come back a little wiser. But! Enough of Maurice."

"Yes, quite enough. Fabien, mon amour, do be extraordinarily cautious with the precious bolts of cloth and my equipage."

"For you? I will watch the servants load the wagons with a heinous scowl and a drawn sword. And because you have told me of the Spanish ambassador's unfriendly glances, I shall leave Gallaudet to guard you. I will feel better while in Paris knowing he is with you."

He drew her closer, kissing her long. "I loathe leaving you for even a day."

"As long as you come back."

"You can be certain of that." Then he swept her up into his arms and carried her off toward their bedchamber.

PART 2

In the Shadow of the Serpent

Gowns for a Princesse

IN JUNE, WITH PREPARATIONS FOR THE COLLOQUY PROCEEDING AT a feverish pace, Rachelle received an unexpected summons to join the Queen Mother in the Fontainebleau gardens. The call forecast ominous potential.

Rachelle entered the garden and saw her ahead in the trees, a forbidding figure, stately and somber, who always put her in a tense mood. Almost at once her heart began to beat faster.

Rachelle met her and dipped a curtsy. "Bonjour, Madame."

"Ah, you are looking most well, Marquise. Marriage must be to your favor. It is the marriage of my daughter, the princesse, I wish to speak with you about. Come, walk with me. I am sure by now you will have heard that my long-intended journey to Spain with Marguerite is delayed."

Rachelle was secretly pleased but kept her personal feelings concealed. Even before her marriage to Fabien, the worrisome thought of having to attend Marguerite and the Queen Mother on a journey to Spain with its darkly morose king had given her shudders.

The Queen Mother walked along, her gown floating darkly behind her heels. "Marquis Fabien may have mentioned to you that negotiations with his kinswoman Queen Jeanne over a marriage contract have once more begun in earnest."

"He did mention Princesse Marguerite and Prince Henry of Navarre, Madame."

"The marquis is pleased over a Huguenot marriage of the princesse?"

Trapped. What could she say? Fabien agreed with Queen Jeanne that her son should marry a princesse of his faith. Marguerite was untamable.

"The marquis thinks well of both the princesse and the prince," she said truthfully.

"It was the wish of my husband the king, when he was alive, that Marguerite should marry the son of Queen Jeanne and Prince Antoine de Bourbon."

"I did not know it was the late king's wish," Rachelle admitted. "The princesse, your daughter, assured me — " She stopped, forgetting herself.

"Assured you it was young Henry de Guise? Ah, but no, she will not marry the young duc."

The Queen Mother's voice took on a hard note, and Rachelle was sorry she had allowed her tongue to slip.

"Marguerite is excessively emotional," the Queen Mother went on abruptly. "She is willful. No doubt she will carry on like a silly fool over negotiations resuming with the Queen of Navarre, but my daughter must come to accept it. It is for the good of France. So it must be done."

I am blessed, Rachelle thought. *I have been given the man I love and respect to be my husband.*

"Queen Jeanne is skeptical of the serious mind of my daughter, so it is necessary for Marguerite to adorn herself in fashion that will not offend when Jeanne arrives at court to attend the colloquy later this summer. That is where your ability as a couturière is needed to create gowns of modest colors and cut. I am determined she dress modestly and dutifully at the various functions, you understand?"

"Assuredly, Madame. I deem it a great joy to once again put my hands to the cloth and needle."

"Your passion for silk and design will prove most beneficial. It is not every couturière who is chosen both by the Queen of England and the Queen Mother of France to design gowns that will be worn while history is made. I have heard of the special gown you made for the English queen. It may be that I shall not be outdone and request one of my own, not for the colloquy, but for Marguerite's marriage to Navarre."

Rachelle dipped a bow. "Should it be, I shall deem the opportunity an honor, Madame."

"The court will soon be leaving Fontainebleau for Paris. Marguerite will send for you to discuss the plans for her gowns. Do remember that I wish to see the designs before you commence work. It will be my approval and not my daughter's that will permit you to proceed. Understood?"

"Indeed, Madame," she murmured dutifully.

A few days later Rachelle heard from Fabien that they were expected to join members of the court who were moving to the royal château at Saint-Germain-en-Laye, located just outside of Paris.

"The Poissy Dominican monastery is within walking distance from there," he said, "and only a short drive by coach from Paris."

"Then the colloquy will be held at the monastery?"

"Yes, with the biblical debates and speeches conducted in the imposing dining chamber."

"I wonder if I shall be allowed to attend?"

"Do you wish to hear the doctrinal debates?"

She arched her brows. "But of course! The very safety of the Huguenots in France depends upon the outcome of this colloquy. Besides, I wish to see Monsieur John Calvin."

He smiled. "You never cease to amaze and amuse me."

She cuddled up beside him, her fingers smoothing the tendrils of his hair. "Why so?"

"Most women do not wish to see Calvin," he said. "And doctrinal issues bore them."

"How can you say that? To understand the great doctrines of Scripture safeguards us from error that will stunt our growth as Christians."

"Your father trained you well." He smiled, reached up, and drew her face down toward his and kissed her until she was breathless.

"Then my lady shall go to the colloquy! That is," he said wryly, "if I can gain permission from the Queen Mother."

❄

THE ROAD TO SAINT-GERMAIN-EN-LAYE lay westward from Paris through the village of Saint Cloud. Seated in the carriage with Nenette, Rachelle looked out the window and watched the road begin to climb through the hamlet of Marly, then to twist and turn through the wooded country which thickened into the forest of Laye.

The gray castle came into view, and within a short time the coach neared the gates and passed through into the courtyard. Hostlers came forward to convey the carriage to the stables, and Fabien, who had ridden on horseback with the guards and other courtiers coming from Fontainebleau, escorted her to what would be their chambers through the summer and fall.

While the chambers were comfortable and elegant, she thought only of her difficult position. She was held captive as it were until Fabien accomplished his dark deed. She sensed that Fabien, too, grew anxious and restless.

The designs for Marguerite's dresses took up her time and thoughts and brought her satisfying pleasure, as did the thrill of entering her atelier. Fabien had requested from the Queen Mother that Rachelle be granted one of the east-facing morning chambers to turn into her atelier. The chamber was next to their living quarters so that when she decided to remain up late with Nenette and work, she need not walk halfway across the castle to come and go.

The shelves and long cutting and sewing tables were now filled with bolts of Macquinet silks, satins, velvets, and various styles of lace and ribbons. Her spirits cheered at the sight of her familiar case in burgundy with her gold initials. She remembered how she had chosen the color burgundy because of her infatuation with the Marquis Fabien de Vendôme on the first instance she had seen him.

While she struggled to develop her designs for the gowns, he would ask to see her day's work and make comments.

"There is too much lace for Margo," he said. "She would look more élégante in a simple style that emphasizes color and movement."

"I have a notion she will balk at these gowns, lace or no," she said with a sigh, studying the modest lines.

"She is flamboyant to be sure. The Queen Mother's attempt at under-dressing will not deceive Jeanne or Henry of Navarre. Margo's reputation is established with her amorous affair with Henry de Guise."

"I can hardly imagine Marguerite married to a Huguenot."

"Henry may be a Huguenot, politically, but his faith is mere outward form, as is Margo's. She goes through one form, he goes through another. Neither of them truly believe."

"How can you say that! How do you know?"

"Look at the fruit of their lives. It tells where they've sunk their roots. It is in the world, not in Christ. Believe me, I have been examining my own heart to see if I am truly in the faith. Henry of Navarre is already engaged in numerous affairs. What does that tell you at his young age?"

Rachelle tossed her drawings aside and stood, distraught.

"The son of Queen Jeanne, that devout woman? How can that be?"

"Chérie, faith is an individual response to Christ, is it not?"

"Yes."

"And Jeanne could make sure he was well taught, but his heart, and its softness toward the Bible and the Savior is all his own responsibility. Having a godly mother like Jeanne does not guarantee the children will follow God. Look at the family of King David. And Scripture is full of examples. As Pasteur Bertrand likes to say, we are all one generation away from paganism."

"Paganism! Oh come. Did Bertrand tell you so?"

"He did," Fabien said gravely. "If one generation fails to pass on the truth to their children, the heart of those who follow will be bent to follow the wrong path. That is why Calvin has come up with a confession of faith to teach the children at home. The Lord told Israel to talk of his Word when they rise, when they sit down, when they walk, and when they lie down."

Rachelle threw her arms around him. "Mon amour, I can see, to my delighted surprise, that you will be an excellent father."

"Does that mean you will give me seven sons and three daughters like Job?"

"What if it were seven daughters and three sons?" she taunted.

"Well, we had better think this through with caution. With seven daughters who bear your beauty, I will need to keep my men-at-arms even in the Americas."

"Do you think Marguerite and Prince Henry will marry?"

"Not if Margo can thwart it. If there is a marriage, it will be political. Forced on her by the Queen Mother for dubious reasons of her own. No doubt they are dark reasons."

In late June, certain Huguenot ministers from Geneva were already beginning to arrive in and around Saint-Germain-en-Laye and Paris. Fabien told her of the Bible studies held in the private châteaus of Huguenot nobles disposed toward the Reformation.

While Rachelle anticipated seeing her parents and Cousin Bertrand, she was in the midst of a concerted effort to produce the gowns for Princesse Marguerite to wear during her meetings with Prince Henry of Navarre.

Rachelle sent the designs for Marguerite's gowns to the Queen Mother as ordered, and Madalenna returned them with authorization to proceed. Rachelle breathed easier. But convincing Marguerite herself was another matter. She met with the princesse in the atelier, laying out the bolts of silk and lace and other materials in various colors.

"I tell you, Rachelle, I will not wear them unless I do so for my only amour. There is but one Henry for me. I loathe Navarre, and I will not marry him."

"My Princessse, my sympathies are with you, I assure you. Even so, I beg you to understand I have no choice in this matter. If I do not make these belle gowns as ordered ..." She deliberately fell silent.

Marguerite raised her dark eyes toward the ceiling and heaved a sigh. "You need not explain. I know. I am well aware of your palais arrest and difficulties with the Queen Mother."

She knew? But she could not know about Duc de Guise. In loyalty to young Henry, she would alert him of the danger to his father, and that would put Fabien at risk.

"If I must meet with Navarre and go through this charade, then I shall do so most reluctantly. It will keep me from being whipped again, and you from her dreadful ire."

Rachelle smiled her relief. "I vow to do my best to make the gowns most belle."

In the days that followed, Rachelle took solace in the handling of her exquisite bolts of silk and familiar sewing utensils transported from Paris. So much had happened since that first day at Chambord, working on Princesse Marguerite's gowns with Grandmère and Idelette, which had brought about her first conversation with the marquis.

And here she was again with Princesse Marguerite, ankle deep in samples of silks and satins, velvets, brocades, and laces. Despite Marguerite's loathing of the cause for which she would wear her new gowns, she nonetheless adored the rich silks and lush colors.

Rachelle unrolled a bolt of pink silk from Lyon and Nenette unpacked the gold silk, followed by the snow-drift white that would become a wedding gown. There were also strips of the softest ermine, to be studded with diamonds and added to collar and farthingale.

"But, mon ami, I should like the bodice lower. It is too high as you have drawn it—it will make my chin itch." Marguerite raised a hand and scratched beneath her chin.

Rachelle sighed. "I have no choice in the matter, my Princesse. The Queen Mother has insisted I raise the décolleté. Also, the color cannot be crimson as you wished, but something softer. *More innocent*, was the meaning of the Queen Mother. Look at this lovely peach color, or what about the rosebud pink?"

"Non! I loathe pink. It makes me appear as if I am always blushing. "I know why Madame-Mère insists on a high neck and dull, frigid colors. It is because she wants me to deceive the old religious crow, Queen Jeanne, when I meet with her ill-smelling son. She loathes me as much as I do her."

"Oh, Princesse, surely not."

"I tell you it is so. And I will not have her son for all the gold in her Huguenot kingdom."

Rachelle attempted to defend Fabien's kinswoman, but Marguerite waved aside her protest. Marguerite, however, was not politically minded, nor was she a fanatic who desired the deaths of all Protestants. She, like Queen Jeanne, was well-educated, and had even studied medicine under the royal surgeon and physician, Ambrose le Pare. But from Marguerite's antics and her moral looseness, one would not have guessed that intellectually she was the finest of the Valois children. She was more tolerant than those in her family and was not antagonistic, despite her outbursts of anger. Rachelle was fond of her and oft enjoyed her company even when saddened with her behavior.

At last Marguerite accepted the peach color with a sullen face.

"It is not your fault, I know. Oh, why do I not simply wear crow's black and surrender to the funeral pyre?" She walked across the atelier out onto the balustrade while Rachelle rewound the bolt of silk.

Marguerite, rather plump and sensuous, with dark hair and eyes and an excessive passion for men, turned dramatically back toward Rachelle, her white hand with jewels placed against her heart. "Even so, all your belle work is in vain, mon ami. I am sad to say it is so, but I must. For I will not wear the gowns to meet that unwashed, prickly boar of the forest, Navarre. Nor will I marry him and sleep in the same bed with him. I swear it. I have vowed my everlasting amour to Henry de Guise, and so it will be, even though my neck is put to the chopping block by Charles and Madame-Mère."

Rachelle winced and rubbed her aching head.

Marguerite continued needlessly pacing up and down the stone floor of the balustrade, while now and then peering over into the courtyard below where the road to town could be seen. "You do not know how much I loathe Henry of Navarre."

"Oh, I do know, ma chère Princesse. You have told me every day for six weeks. He has dirty fingernails, he never takes a bath, and he laughs too much." *And is as loose with the women at court as you are with men!*

Marguerite scowled at her, then laughed. "You left out that he is a heretic. How can I marry a heretic?" she asked innocently, as though it truly mattered to her. "How can Charles and Madame-Mère even suggest I should?"

There were political reasons, as Fabien had said, and Marguerite knew them far better than did Rachelle.

Marguerite came back into the atelier and took her reluctant place on the stool again. Rachelle began to take measurements, for Marguerite looked to have put on a bit here and there since Amboise.

"Have you ever talked to the prince?" Rachelle asked. "Maybe the two of you could become friends even if you do not love passionately."

"La, la. I have met him once too often, I assure you. He was at the Louvre when we were children. Nor does he have the élégant manners of the true Parisian. He is from Berne and behaves as crudely. I vow he chews on garlic for sport. Nor does he wear handsome finery, but rough, woodsy garments."

Rachelle couldn't help but laugh, imagining the Prince of Navarre munching garlic cloves for sport. "And yet the tales of his prowess with belle women?" Rachelle asked warily, for it would not do for her to insult a future king even though Marguerite did so. She wondered how Queen Jeanne could not know of her son's escapades. "Many Parisian women have desired him, so I hear; the belle dames from court and even demoiselles from wealthy noble families. Are you most sure he is as uncouth as you remember him?"

Marguerite snapped her fingers dismissing him. "He is. Besides, for me it will be forever my amour Henry de Guise. So galant! So tall and fair!"

So every inch a king? Ah, what the Queen Mother would read into her daughter's last statement.

Marguerite walked over to the railing and looked below. "Come, Rachelle, look, did you ever see such a sight!"

Rachelle set her things aside and joined the princesse at the balustrade.

Along the outer street she saw a long procession of horses, mule-drawn wagons, and carts. Seated inside the wagons were men and women, even children, all garbed in modest dark apparel, with the men wearing wide-rimmed black hats. The Huguenots from Geneva! Rachelle's spirits revived in hope. These Christians were Monsieur John Calvin's small theological army, and they had traveled from Geneva to plead with the cardinals and bishops on the reasons for the Reformation.

"They look like a flock of crows landing on the city," Marguerite said with a touch of amused scorn.

"They are dedicated to Christ, my Princesse, and as such they are no enemy of yours, but wish you well and pray for you."

"I do not want to be converted." Marguerite tossed her head. "I am content to be as I am."

Rachelle looked at her, and in that moment possessed a great affection for her despite her weaknesses, knowing how many she had of her own — for which she had a great Savior.

"Are you truly content?" she asked gently, hoping the simple question would awaken a need in Marguerite's empty heart.

Marguerite's eyes flashed. "Do not be flippant. I love you, and you are mon amie, but though you are now a grand marquise, that in no way permits you to insult me."

"Oh, Marguerite, I thought you knew me better than to think such a thing."

"I do not want to discuss it. Religion bores me." She turned on her heel toward the atelier. "I have had enough for today, Rachelle. I am going to see Henry tonight—Guise—" she said with corrected emphasis. "Adieu," she tossed over her shoulder as she went out, calling for her ladies who waited in the next chamber to follow.

Rachelle looked back at the long train of arriving Calvinists and smiled. Despite the darkening clouds over France, she experienced a wave of joy in her soul.

On an impulse, she waved down at the godly caravan bringing ministers and Bibles in French. "Welcome, bonjour!"

Here they come, brave soldiers to bring the truth of God's Word despite the obstacles. They are willing to risk their reputations and lives to debate Cardinal de Lorraine and the bishops on the important doctrines of faith.

They did not wave back. She had not expected them to do so. Reserved, no doubt concerned with how they would represent the Lord and stand against the wiles of the devil, they must have thought her a silly court belle.

Her gaze moved on along the trail of horsemen and came across a man in black with a white beard. He was escorted safely through the street by the Bourbon Prince Louis de Condé and his men-at-arms.

That man with the white beard . . . Why, it is Minister Beza, Calvin's disciple. I am sure it is he. I have seen a painting of him.

If only Père Arnaut and Madame Clair were here now. They would be so thrilled to see this victory after so many prayers for the deliverance of France. And Cousin Bertrand too—

She straightened from the railing. On one of the horses near Minister Beza, there was another beloved and very familiar figure, a tall, severe-looking monsieur with a short white beard and slashing brows. He was all in black except for the stiff white ruffle of lace about his neck — it was Cousin Bertrand Macquinet.

"Oh — " Rachelle turned from the balustrade and ran across the atelier toward the door to the corridor. Nenette, who had come in just then with Philippe, stopped and looked at her with wide eyes.

"What is it, Mademoiselle?"

Rachelle laughed. "Cousin Bertrand Macquinet! He has arrived! Go to the balustrade and look. The Huguenots are coming!"

"The Huguenots are coming!" the boy Philippe cried, laughing.

"The Huguenots are here!" Nenette caught Philippe's arm playfully and danced him around the atelier, then out to the balustrade to see the parade.

❖

RACHELLE FOUND HER WAY THROUGH THE PRESS until she caught up with the front of the long train bearing Beza and his twelve ministers from Geneva toward the palais château gate. She saw Cousin Bertrand again and called to him, waving as he rode along on the big bay horse. He heard her, for his head turned sharply and she saw his gaze scanning the spectators following along.

"Cousin Bertrand," she called again, smiling. "Over here!"

He saw her and a smile cracked his otherwise sober face. He tried to break away and ride toward her, but the crowd was too dense.

"In the courtyard," she called, pointing toward a small entry that wound to the public side. He gestured that he understood.

Rachelle hurried ahead to wait for him. Did his arrival mean Père Arnaut and Madame Clair were in Paris?

She wondered where Fabien was. That morning he'd informed her the Geneva Bible teachers would arrive this week. Although the meetings did not officially begin until September, they had desired to spend more time beforehand with any and all who wished to discuss the Reformation or to attend private Bible studies. The Bible meetings were permitted during this period of time by the king as long as they were held out of sight within the private residences of the chief members of the nobility, such as Prince Louis, Admiral Coligny, and Queen Jeanne.

A few minutes later she saw Cousin Bertrand dismounting from the horse and turning it over to the hostler. Rachelle smiled. How relieved she was that he was here again.

He walked toward her, an élégant figure who might have passed for Calvin himself, except that Bertrand was heavier. She hurried toward him.

"Cousin Bertrand!"

"Ah, ma petite Rachelle! A married woman—a marquise and a Bourbon! Well, well."

She had worried about the moment when she would face him over her marriage. She had practiced just what she would say, but now the words fled like a flock of nervous finches.

He smiled and then laughed and drew her into a hug. "I am proud of you, little one. And you could have no better husband than the buccaneering Marquis de Vendôme."

She was startled by his response, then saw the twinkle in his eyes, and she too laughed. All was well; he approved of Fabien.

"I have so much to explain."

"Ah, yes, so you do. And Arnaut and Clair are on the way. I hope you have prepared yourself?"

"Yes, oh dear, when will they arrive, and where?"

"They have gone first to Lyon to see how matters move along at the Château de Silk. They will await the second group of Calvinists who are coming from Geneva across the border and down through Lyon. They will be here, God willing, in late August." His mouth turned into a smile. "So you have plenty of time to prepare."

"How have they taken the news of my marriage to the marquis?"

"No need for concern. At first they were upset, especially your mother. Then the lettre arrived from the marquis. Whatever he wrote to her has brought her great peace, and she is now as joyous as a spring robin."

Rachelle laughed with relief and pleasure. "I did not even know he had written her."

"Ah, he is most wise. He wrote them separately and won them both over. He even wrote to Idelette, and to me as well."

She found her respect for Fabien's wisdom deepening. He had picked up the mantle of responsibility as a husband and Huguenot leader with smooth efficiency. He always knew when she needed him. He could be understanding, tender, and amusing, or passionate and firm. She was not disappointed in marriage.

"Come, Bertrand, let me bring you to the appartement. We have a chamber all ready for you."

"I would not wish to be a burden, ma chère. I shall stay with Andelot."

"A burden?" She laughed, looping her arm firmly through his and walking with him across the courtyard. "I am in high spirits that you are back with us. You do not know how we have longed for this moment."

He put his arm around her shoulder and walked with her.

"We?"

"Fabien has been waiting for you. There is much on his mind. He looks forward to having many discussions with you. I think he must have enjoyed your presence aboard the *Reprisal*. He often quotes you."

"Does he! Well, well."

"Remember, he is a declared Huguenot now. Although he has his kinsmen, Louis and Antoine, he needs the support of one who is seasoned in the Scriptures."

His white brows came together. "I thought the trouble over his arrest had settled."

She lowered her voice as they entered through a side entrance into the château.

"The Duc of Alva has not yet ceased to be a threat. King Philip is persistent with his demands that the Queen Mother and Charles arrest Fabien for sinking the Spanish vessels. It is only her mantle that safeguards him. I, also, am held in palais arrest as a second incentive. If he will not comply with her demands for his service, she will be rid of us both." She glanced at him. "I think you know what she demands of him?"

His lean face turned grim. "I do. We discussed it in London before he returned here to France. So then, it is just as I feared."

They entered the appartement, a private world of solace amid a sea of intrigue and danger.

"Fabien's chosen to use delaying tactics until a way of escape develops." She glanced about the salle. Her eyes automatically went to a large chest of drawers. She went there and checked inside.

Bertrand's brow went up.

"Spies," she said briefly. "Some are the size of children. We always check."

He gave a nod of understanding and looked even grimmer.

Confident they were alone, she came back to him, speaking in a quiet voice.

"Fabien has plans for our escape, but he keeps them to himself and his loyals, like Gallaudet and Julot. I am the difficulty, you see. He is quite free to come and go. He was even sent to Paris on court affairs, but I cannot leave the castle grounds. I am watched day and night. By now they have reported that you are here with me."

"As long as she has you under rein, the marquis will always come back, is that it? Most clever of her. I see that we are in a dangerous trap set by a shrewd and cruel mind. A hasty decision will lead to disaster. Fabien must plan with careful expediency."

Bitter News

THE CHESTNUT STALLION AND THE GOLDEN BAY RACED ALONG NECK AND NECK down the level road with the forest trees rushing past. As the riders turned the corner, the golden bay inched ahead, Andelot bent low in the saddle. He laughed over his shoulder, and as the race came to a close he slowed to a canter and then eased to a stop near the trees.

The chestnut stallion slowed to a walk and stopped across from the bay. Fabien reached over to console his horse with a pat on the neck.

"Do not be unhappy, beau ami. We both know Andelot cheated."

Andelot threw back his head and laughed. "Now you sound like Comte Maurice. Are you certain, Marquis, that you do not want me to return the bay? I tell you, he is unbeatable."

Fabien grinned. "No, I gave him to you, he is yours. And now I owe you my sword and scabbard, though why you want them and what you will do with them is a mystery. You are as clumsy at fencing as a bear."

"So you think, Marquis. But just you wait. You have not watched me practice recently at the armory. I am becoming as light-footed as a deer. One day I shall equal you, and if need be, I shall be able to take Maurice on."

"You are going to attend Monsieur Calvin's theology school in Geneva, remember?"

Andelot dismounted. He dug a cloth out of his saddlebag and began to wipe down the bay.

The wind rushed through the pine trees. Fabien thought of his ship, the sea, and freedom.

"What makes you think I will leave for Geneva?" Andelot asked a moment later.

"Because it is the wisest decision you could make for your future. You should follow the steps of Pasteur Bertrand."

"What! Marquis! Go to Geneva to Monsieur Calvin and abandon my opportunity to go to the Guise Duchy of Lorraine? Why, I shall follow in the steps of my most honorable kinsman Cardinal de Lorraine."

Fabien scowled and was ready to cuff his ears until Andelot looked up and smiled ruefully. Fabien curved his mouth. So Andelot had a malicious sense of humor, did he?

"For a moment I believed you." He remembered how indignant Andelot had been at Amboise when Fabien had first informed him of how the cardinal kept mistresses and was a Christian in garb only.

Fabien took a moment to look around him at the sage green forest beneath a powder blue sky. Summer had fully arrived, yet he had no rest of spirit or mind. Tension was building, moving closer to conflict, to a decision.

He fingered the leather reins thoughtfully and looked down from his mount at Andelot. Fabien could see that he was troubled. Early that morning Andelot had sent a message and requested to speak with him alone. Fabien had bought a new stallion and was anxious to try him out, so he'd suggested they ride away from Saint-Germain-en-Laye to where there was no possibility of being overheard. On the way they had turned the leisurely ride into a contest.

The reason for being here now confronted him. Fabien swung down from the saddle and stood hands on hips.

"Well, mon ami?"

Andelot frowned. "I am not pleased with the news I bring you, Marquis."

"That is why we are here. Have you heard something in the chambers of the cardinal?"

He sighed. "I would hold naught back from you, Marquis. But it brings me to grief to be uncovering your kinsman's transgressions. And when so many of us held such high hopes after Prince Antoine became general of all France."

Fabien leveled a look at him. *So it is Antoine.* "Your reticence is appreciated, Andelot. Even so, in speaking of misdeeds, we do not sit in final judgment: that is for Christ alone. But Antoine's high position at court as a Bourbon holds him to scrutiny. He represents the Huguenot cause. As such, his testimony can affect the reputation of the Geneva church."

Andelot shook his head sadly. "That is what is so disturbing, Marquis — it will give the enemy opportunity to mock and cause the weaker Christians to stumble."

"Is it actually that dire? Then out with it, Andelot."

"I shall be most forward. I overheard Cardinal de Lorraine talking to Duc de Guise, and they were laughing in low voices that reeked with scorn and delight." He cleared his throat. "Prince Antoine has a mistress at court, Mademoiselle Rouet." He tossed up his hands, as if embarrassed. "And she is, well — enceinte."

Pregnant!

"The woman was deliberately sent to entrap him," Andelot hastened.

"And he fell for the trap."

"And worse, Marquis. His wife, Queen Jeanne, will be here at the colloquy in September. By then, Mademoiselle Rouet will be close to giving birth."

Fabien gritted his frustration and kicked a stone. "That fop! I can hardly believe his stupidity. With such a God-given opportunity as this was, he has thrown it away. How could he have been such a fool? I could wring his neck!"

Andelot loosened the band about his throat.

"This is just the kind of depraved trap that the Queen Mother would plan for him, for he is as weak as water. I feared something would happen to lure him away, but nothing as common as this." Fabien leaned his hand against the saddle and glared off at the forest. "But it makes no sense, Andelot. Why would she use Louise to ensnare him at this particular time? She needs the Huguenot alliance to stand against the Guises."

"Louise?" Andelot asked, wrinkling his forehead.

"La Belle Rouet," he said with a flick of his hand. "I know of her — who does not? As you say, a belle dame, a woman in the Queen Mother's *escadron volant*, but I can think of no reason why Catherine would arrange for Antoine's downfall now. It plays right into the hands of the Guises. Why would she do such a foolish thing?"

"Perhaps it was not the Queen Mother?"

"Then who would send Mademoiselle Rouet to entrap Antoine?"

He narrowed his gaze on Andelot. "They wish to weaken Jeanne, but aside from the obvious reasons, why now? The Queen Mother has plans to try to arrange a marriage contract between her son and Marguerite. One would think she would wish to appease and flatter Jeanne."

"But as you so often say, Marquis, her way of thinking is not our way."

"All paths lead to money and power, Andelot. In this case, it is power. Jeanne rules Navarre as a Huguenot. Spain has long wanted to join that region of Navarre in the south of France with what he calls 'Spanish' Navarre. If we could understand what is to be gained by the weakening of Jeanne, we may understand the reasoning behind plotting Antoine's downfall. At the moment I am at a loss to explain this. It makes no sense to me when the Queen Mother is wooing the Huguenots."

He walked about, angry and frustrated. This was a heavy blow to the Huguenot cause, not to mention the personal pain that would be heaped upon Jeanne.

"Adultery will destroy their marriage. And if Louise is having a child, that will seal its doom. I know Jeanne." He turned away again, taking out his frustration on the wooded road as he walked. "I see no hope for their relationship to be mended. Then what will this mean?" Fabien turned to look at his friend.

Andelot ran his fingers through his hair, scowling. "It will weaken Queen Jeanne of Navarre as you said. But it will also weaken the Bourbon-Huguenot alliance."

"Précisément! And the Queen Mother could not possibly want that result. This must be a Guise plot."

The wind whispered through the tall forest trees.

Andelot found a tall stump and sat down, chin in hand.

Fabien stood hands on hips staring off at the forest.

After a moment Andelot said, "The cardinal mentioned again just yesterday that I shall go to the Lorraine palais château immediately after the colloquy. Is that not odd? Why he wishes to wait until then, I cannot say. And why emphasize *immediately* afterward? It is most unusual that he wishes to send me at all." He looked at Fabien. "Do you not think so, Marquis?"

"There is something being planned in secret, Andelot — some course of action similar to the plot they conceived to murder Antoine, and if so, we need to learn what it is in time to stop it."

"I, too, discern trouble afoot. I keep alert when the cardinal calls for me, but so far there are only loose hints. It keeps me pondering till the late hours."

"I suspect they may want to use you again in some other nefarious deed."

Andelot scowled. "I will refuse. I will flee to Geneva as you suggested. If necessary, I will leave *before* the colloquy. With the golden bay I am at liberty to go whenever I wish — except that I would prefer that we might escape together with Mademoiselle Rachelle."

"If you had not been close to the cardinal and willing to alert me, Antoine may have been murdered." He walked over to where Andelot sat. "Now, again, you must play the spy. Discover what you can of what the Guises are planning. How often are you called in to serve the cardinal?"

"Now it is every day, which is also unusual. I saw him only this morning. It was then that he told me I would leave for the Guise estate in Lorraine as soon as the colloquy ended."

"They may have planned for something to occur during the colloquy. But what? Does it concern Jeanne and Antoine?"

"And whatever it is, if I am sent away immediately afterward, I will not be at court to speak of it."

"Exactement! Are you willing to stay on with Thauvet until the end of the colloquy, to keep alert, and play the spy?"

"I shall keep both the ears and the eyes open. I will convey any news to you posthaste."

Fabien glanced about. "You should also know that my plans to leave for London are even now developing with Nappier and the privateers. The details are not all in place yet, but our general plan is sound. We will escape sometime near the end or after the colloquy as the opportunity presents itself. Julot is my messenger with Nappier. For caution's sake the *Reprisal* weighed anchor and left Normandy after Maurice announced its whereabouts at Amboise."

"Ah, Marquis, I remember that terrible hour — I wanted to clout him!

I have heard he has left Fontainebleau for Beauvilliers. I am most surprised he seems to have surrendered his pride."

"The *Reprisal* will be anchoring at La Rochelle," Fabien told him. "If we separate for one reason or another, mon ami, you will know where to locate the ship. Unless you wish to go to Lyon and cross the border into Geneva? Pasteur Bertrand has told me he will depart after the colloquy for the Château de Silk with the Calvin ministers and then cross into Geneva. You may wish to travel with him and the ministers."

"Perhaps yes, Marquis, but you see, for several months now I have been corresponding with an acquaintance in the London area and would wish to visit for a time."

Fabien turned to look at him while Andelot avoided his gaze. Fabien thought he knew who that acquaintance might be.

They walked to their horses and mounted for the leisurely ride back to Saint-Germain-en-Laye.

IN THE DAYS FOLLOWING, as she and Nenette worked tirelessly on the last of the three gowns for Princesse Marguerite, and her meetings with Henry of Navarre drew closer, Rachelle waited in anticipation for her family's arrival from the Château de Silk in Lyon. In Madame Clair's most recent lettre from the château, she confirmed to Rachelle that they would be staying with the duchesse at the Dushane château in Saint-Germain-en-Laye.

She also wrote that Idelette had given birth to a healthy boy and was living in London with Madeleine and Comte Sebastien. "And your sister Madeleine's daughter, Joan, is healthy and growing. I thank God for my grandchildren. They are the most beau in all the world."

Rachelle smiled, but then her amusement faded and she bit her lip over a disquieting thought. She was not wishing for pregnancy at this dangerous time when she would need all good strength for flight, but as the planning of their escape drew on, she was beginning to wonder about her own health.

After nearly than a year of marriage, it seemed that she should have become enceinte by now. She tried to shrug off the tiny fear growing at the back of her mind. *What if I am barren?* The thought brought cold fear. *What if I never give the house of Bourbon a son through Fabien's line?*

Rachelle kept this emerging fear to herself and never spoke of it to Fabien, and though she rejoiced at the news of the healthy birth of Idelette's baby, she became tense and sometimes cross, blaming her ill mood on the many long hours of work demanded by Marguerite's gowns.

Unlike the gowns she had made Marguerite in the past, which had won praise, the princesse utterly hated these gowns. She took the peach silk and threw it on the floor. "I swear I will not wear such a drab and dull gown."

Rachelle, feeling a headache coming on, complained to Fabien as she came home to the appartement weary and hurt.

"She threw the gown on the floor. All of my painstaking efforts! Why then must I waste further time in sewing the third gown?"

Fabien took her in his arms. "You know Margo. She can behave like a child at times. This rejection has nothing to do with you or your talent, chérie. I suspect her dislike is because the Queen Mother insisted on the design and colors. She has no interest, as you know, in Navarre. As for you, your fame is known far and near. A hundred élégante ladies would give much to have la belle couturière Rachelle designing their fine gowns. Remember Queen Elizabeth?"

Rachelle brightened. Yes, the Queen of England had been delighted with the gown she and James Hudson had made for her. "Tell me again her reaction when you saw her take the gown."

"Ah, her sweet eyes brightened, and she broke into a tender smile." Fabien's tone exaggerated with passion. He squeezed Rachelle and kissed her lips. "Then she nearly swooned. Just as I nearly swoon each time your delectable lips touch mine."

"Tell me more." She smiled.

"About the English queen, or how your beauty turns me to melted wax?"

"About how my work with the needle thrills the Queen of England," she said, just as disingenuously.

"The queen even inquired of Hudson whether or not you would come to London and become her couturière."

Rachelle sighed as she laid her cheek against Fabien's chest and imagined the scene.

"I wish I could have been there to see it."

"So do I. I would not have needed to return to France to claim you. But you will yet be there one day. And you may yet attend the whims of the Queen of England and her wardrobe."

He grew serious and lifted her chin until their gazes met. "The plans of escape are all in play now. I have informed Bertrand. The final details, however, will await the last hour."

She held to him tightly. "May God grant that nothing goes wrong."

The day drew close when Rachelle could sit with her beloved mother and enjoy a long talk. Rachelle knew some of what had happened from the letters received since her parents had arrived at home at the Château de Silk. Both sisters had also written Rachelle after their safe arrival in England. However, only her mother had written that the silkworm experiment of Rachelle's father near London had failed. Rachelle knew few details, but Fabien had seemed to think the silkworms had died of a disease for which there was no known cure.

What all this would mean for Arnaut's wish to start a silk plantation in England, Rachelle did not know. She missed the sunny days in Lyon and wished for a visit home to the Château de Silk. Would she ever see it again?

As September neared, the hopes of the Huguenots were mounting that the regent Queen Mother and Charles would grant them a certain freedom to conduct Protestant worship services in various locations outside of the French towns and villages. Rachelle could not imagine Cardinal de Lorraine permitting this worship activity without ramifications, no matter how many petitions were accepted or edicts signed. She was sure the house of Guise, though quiet at the present, was busy planning traps for the Huguenot leaders, perhaps even their murder.

On a day not long after Marguarite had thrown the peach gown to the floor in disgust, Rachelle was in the atelier adding the finishing touch of embroidered silk rosebuds to the bodice of Marguerite's third gown using Grandmère's special needles, gold thimble, and chatelaine.

What would Grandmère think if she were here now, knowing the family couturières were leaving France for London to carry on the family work? Rachelle did not think she would be pleased at the loss. The Château de Silk should continue, and while there was no word from her parents that they expected to leave it any time soon and return to England, Rachelle worried over its future.

It will never be the same again. The four women of the Dushane-Macquinet calling were going their separate ways. She looked at Grandmère's needle and thimble. Will another generation of sons and daughters return to Lyon to the château and carry on? Or would this branch of the family merge with the English line? If so, what then?

As for her own future, Fabien had made no clear decision to remain in England even if they eventually took solace there for a time of safety. He had mentioned this to Bertrand when discussing Admiral Coligny's old plan for a Florida colony, which had been postponed indefinitely.

"Someday," Fabien had said, "I would like to see Florida and the Caribbean."

Now, as Rachelle tacked on the final rosebud on Marguerite's gown and mulled over these divergent thoughts, she wondered what the gracious Lord had planned for them all in the years ahead. Would they be together as a large family?

No matter what happens I must not fail to safeguard what Grandmère has entrusted to me.

She was blessed to be a recipient of old family trade secrets. The work they had such affection and passion for would continue as long as she and Idelette pursued it and passed on what they knew to the next generation of silk growers, weavers, designers, and grisettes.

She held the gold thimble in her hand as the bridge to the future.

I may have the honneur of being a member of the royal Bourbon family, but I am a Macquinet daughter of silk, and I will continue to be one wherever the Lord may take me.

Nenette came running in, her eyes bright and a flush of excitement on her cheeks. Her red curls appeared to quiver.

"Bonne news, Mademoiselle Rachelle! Pasteur Bertrand sent me to tell you the family has arrived. Monsieur and Madame Macquinet are here."

Rachelle was quickly on her feet, joy enlarging her heart.

She left the atelier and rushed into the salle. Her father and mother stood waiting with Bertrand.

"Daughter Rachelle," her parents echoed. They came to meet her as Rachelle uttered a cry of delight and laughter and tried to embrace them both at once.

"You are looking well, ma chère," Madame Clair said. "Marriage has done you well."

"I am most happy, Mother — it could not be otherwise being married to Fabien. Happy, that is, except for my invisible chains, a 'marriage gift' from the Queen Mother."

Madame Clair's expression changed, but she was always so self-possessed that even when she was worried or ill, she could mask it with a certain poise that made her seem to Rachelle a pillar of beauty and strength. She remembered her mother's courage during the tragic horrors of Avril's death and Idelette's trial. Her hand squeezed Rachelle's arm with tender motherly love. "Surely the Lord will come to our aid in due season if we continue in prayer and trust His grace. Your father has been making plans with the marquis."

"Is it safe to discuss such matters here?" Arnaut looked about the walls meaningfully.

"Fabien is assured."

"And where is our new son-in-law? The buccaneer?" Arnaut gave a wink at Rachelle.

"Arnaut." Clair shook her head forbearingly as Pasteur Bertrand gave a dry chuckle.

"I dare to wonder what my Geneva colleagues would think of me if they knew I had sailed as his chaplain to sink the Duke of Alva's galleon."

Arnaut threw back his head and laughed, and Madame Clair put a hand to her forehead and closed her eyes.

Rachelle said, "Fabien is in a council meeting with King Charles and the Queen Mother. He was given Sebastien's seat at the table."

"A position he finds distasteful," Bertrand added. "I have sent Philippe to let him know you both are here."

WHEN FABIEN ARRIVED, Rachelle grew composed when she saw how smoothly matters between him and her parents slipped into place. Fabien was his most élégant self, especially with Madame Clair. Rachelle's heart heaved a sigh of relief. She saw the pride in Arnaut's eyes as Fabien discussed the colloquy with him in knowledgeable terms, showing he understood spiritual truth and what was at risk for France and the Huguenots should the meetings fail.

Later, when Rachelle was alone with Madame Clair in the salle on the damask sofa, they talked of all that had happened since last they saw one another.

"Ma chère, I admit I was wrong about Fabien's character. Any man who would risk what he has in order to protect and keep you is most chivalrous. I feel at peace with you in his care. I know your father and Bertrand feel the same."

Rachelle kissed her cheek.

"And Idelette is adjusting to events and is much more at peace. She is happier now that Andelot Dangeau is corresponding with her so frequently. I do believe she may care very much for him. I must say I am surprised. I thought for a time that a strong relationship would develop between her and James Hudson.

"We must not leap to conclusions. I am sure their relationship has not progressed so far as to mention marriage. Bertrand has told Arnaut that Andelot wishes to go to Geneva to Monsieur Calvin's school."

"That will prove no stumbling block for Idelette," Rachelle said. "Idelette is so dedicated that she will surely rejoice and encourage him. Why, she may even go with him. By then the bébé will be old enough to journey."

"If that were to happen I would daily give thanks to God for his mercy. You may not know how I have agonized over your sister. After what happened it looked as though her life would be destroyed, or at least irreparably damaged. But see how our Savior not only redeems us, but can make crippling events in our lives a door to wider horizons of His grace. Even sin and Satan cannot destroy Christ's own sheep. 'Rejoice not against me, O mine enemy: when I fall, I shall arise,'" she said. "God can create blessing even when only ashes remain."

Rachelle rose from her seat and put her arms around her mother. And then they clasped hands and prayed that the Lord would bring His will for Idelette and Andelot.

When Madame Clair told her the details of how Sebastien and Madeleine, with Idelette, had escaped Paris, Rachelle's faith grew yet stronger.

"Sebastien was recognized soon after escaping and stopped near the Louvre gate. They thought it was the end. The guards knew him. One was well aware of his imprisonment in the Bastille. Sebastien begged them to arrest him if he must but to allow his wife and bébé Joan and Idelette to go on. As it turned out in God's Providence, the guard was a recent père himself, and seeing the two women with frightened faces and the bébé, he turned his back and told them to pass on quickly. They eventually arrived in Calais where the ship was waiting, all the while concerned the guard might change his mind and send soldiers to overtake them. Madeleine has said that while they were in the coach and Sebastien was pleading with the guards, she and Idelette were praying through Psalm 91."

I will say of the LORD, He is my refuge and my fortress: my God; in him will I trust. Surely he shall deliver thee from the snare of the fowler …

Rachelle poured tea for Madame Clair and offered the silver plate of éclairs.

"Fabien mentioned that the silkworms died …" Rachelle looked up at her, wondering how dismally her father was taking the loss.

"Such a tragedy. The cocoons that hatched were less than a quarter of what we brought on the ship. They were weak and listless and eventually died. We purchased another group of cocoons that hatched but the worms all had strange little spots on them and they too died. Arnaut believes it was some manner of disease rather than the climate. He remembers long ago that his grandpère mentioned something of this ailment. It destroyed an entire estate of silkworms. Even so, had the worms survived, we discovered the English weather is too chilly and damp to be beneficial, and the fog lasts for weeks at a time."

"So what will the family do?"

"We have decided to keep the raising of silkworms to the south of France. The weaving of silk, however, is another matter, so is dress making. Both can be done most favorably at Spitalfields, so we are opening warehouses with the Hudson family and shops for the haute monde in London under James and Idelette."

"But if Idelette and Andelot marry and journey to Geneva?"

"Madeleine has mentioned her interest in the ready-made dress shops, and we will be going to London at least once a year on business. And if you and the marquis go to London, then I am most sure the situation will be solved. James constantly asks whether you will come. He is training grisettes but desires some of our experience."

Rachelle thought of Nenette. She was anxious to sail with her and Fabien to England. She would be thrilled to work for Dushane-Macquinet-Hudson. It would not take Nenette long to become so proficient in the trade that she could be trained by James Hudson to teach or manage workers.

"The future is very uncertain, Mother."

Madame Clair took her daughter's hand. "It is. We know not what a day may bring. But we know the One who cares for us and plans our steps. It is enough for us to rest in that cradle of faith."

Oh, Beulah Land!

THE GUSTY WIND ON THAT SEPTEMBER NIGHT AGITATED THE GARDEN TREES below the chamber window. Andelot felt besieged by events surrounding him.

"Why am I being moved here?" he had asked Jaymin upon his arrival. His new chamber connected with Cardinal de Lorraine's private bungalow at Fontainebleau.

"Have you reason for complaint at receiving such a chamber? It is tenfold more luxurious than the bedchamber you had near Monsieur Thauvet's study."

"It is most merveilleux, Monseigneur. I merely wonder why I should be so ... blessed."

Andelot made a sweeping gesture toward the burgundy velvet drapes and rugs, the tapestries of gold and blue, the large bed with engraved headstand — and across the chamber toward a foreboding door that entered into the cardinal's receiving chamber and office. On the other side of his new chamber was a second door that entered into Père Jaymin's chambers.

"It was Cardinal de Lorraine's order. With the official opening of the colloquy next week, he thinks it wise to have you nearby. Moreover, you are now one of his official pages until you are sent on to the Duchy of Lorraine where, I understand, you will continue your studies. You are indeed favored."

"A privilege to be sure, Père Jaymin. Do you know when I will journey to Lorraine?"

"The day has not yet been decided. Until then, you will also attend Scholar Thauvet's daily lectures."

When Andelot had last seen Marquis Fabien, the day the golden bay won the race, little had he realized he would be handed the opportunity to spy on the cardinal.

And for the cardinal's staff to spy on me.

Here he was in the middle of the Guise web. Père Jaymin, the cardinal's chief secretary, kept him daily, if not hourly, in sight. How would he ever get word to the marquis should he need to?

On this gusty evening with the chill of fall in the air, Andelot was seated at his new desk with what must have been fifty lettres to answer from the various secretaries of lesser dignitaries.

Andelot saw Duc de Guise arrive at the cardinal's council chamber, followed some minutes later by the wily Spanish Ambassador Chantonnay. As they spoke, their voices were undistinguishable to Andelot. He was about to get up and go to a bookshelf nearer the open door, when Père Jaymin walked in with a satchel of papers. Andelot bent over his work as though fully occupied. He felt Jaymin's eyes watching him but behaved as though he didn't notice.

Andelot heard their low, conspiratorial voices in the next chamber, and then quite clearly — "the isle of Sardinia — "

Andelot glanced toward the cardinal's chambers and saw shadowy forms on the wall. The robed figure left no doubt who was moving about. Every crackle of pinewood burning in the hearth caused him distraction as it snuffed out his ability to catch another word.

Someone came to the doorway. "Monsieur Jaymin? The cardinal calls."

Andelot's nerves were prickling.

He heard their voices again. He got up from his desk and moved soundlessly toward the door only to meet Jaymin rushing back out with a paper in hand, his eyes eager. Or was he overwrought?

"There will be little sleep for you tonight, Andelot."

"There is trouble, Monseigneur?"

Jaymin's eyes reflected the candlelight, and he was smiling as he leaned across the desk and placed the paper on the lettres Andelot was working on.

"The cardinal and duc need a special map drawn up. All else must wait. Locate a map of the island of Sardinia and draw it anew according to these written instructions: You will be adding cities, bountiful mountains, and forests. You must have it ready for an urgent meeting tomorrow in the cardinal's chamber."

"Sardinia?"

"Yes. Make haste, Andelot. You will find old maps in the library."

Hours later, Andelot was seated at his desk, drawing the mysterious map of Sardinia. He must alert Marquis Fabien to this odd situation. He would wait until Jaymin retired to his bed, then slip out.

During the windy night, with all asleep in the chambers about him, Andelot's candles burned low. He worked doggedly on the new map from one old drawing he had found of Sardinia.

He grew more troubled over each new addition he made, knowing it was a sham map. According to the list of instructions written by Ambassador Chantonnay, Andelot added rich pastures, rivers, and farmland where only rocky areas existed. And yet, he was also curious. *This must be important. What will happen at tomorrow's meeting in the cardinal's chamber?*

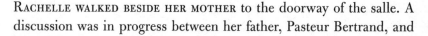

ANDELOT ARRIVED UNEXPECTEDLY and with stealth, and this alerted Fabien at once. He left the appartement unnoticed, minutes before the discussion about Antoine was to begin in the salle de sejour with Monsieur Arnaut and Pasteur Bertrand.

It was a chilly night for early September, with the winds gusting.

You have news?"

"Indeed, Marquis. Most suspicious. Can you walk with me in the garden while we talk?"

"It is best we talk where we cannot be heard. I will send Gallaudet for a coach."

RACHELLE WALKED BESIDE HER MOTHER to the doorway of the salle. A discussion was in progress between her father, Pasteur Bertrand, and several Huguenot seigneurs garbed in the characteristic dark and sober dress of the Geneva Calvinists. She did not see Fabien.

Madame Clair leaned toward Rachelle and whispered: "Let us not intrude." She sat down on the settee near the doorway, and Rachelle did the same.

"This news is grievous," her father was saying, disappointment surfacing in his voice. "Antoine now encumbers the cause of the Reformation in France by playing false with his own honneur."

"Why are they bereaved over Prince Antoine?" Madame Clair whispered.

Rachelle realized her mother must not have heard the sad news. She whispered, so as not to disturb the meeting, "Antoine has taken a mistress — that is failure enough, but she is a Catholic and holds great sway over his emotions. The news is bandied about court for all to snicker over. They mock what they call the 'self-righteous Calvinists' who have descended upon them to preach against their errors. And all this is being disclosed just before the colloquy."

Madame Clair shook her head with grief. "I feel deeply for Queen Jeanne. She will be arriving from Navarre within days, I am told."

Père Arnaut's voice drew them back to the discussion.

"I would not be surprised to discover the house of Guise is behind Antoine's fall. We know, do we not, that the duc is our worst foe? He is enraged against us with the contempt of Satan."

Pasteur Bertrand stood and walked to the hearth, his piercing eyes looking from one to the other. "Messieurs, regardless of Antoine, we cannot allow ourselves to be intimidated. We must be prepared to lay down our lives if called upon to do so. Let us go forward boldly, but not foolishly. We are the torchbearers for this generation, so that the generations to follow may recover the Scriptures. It is our duty, our honor, and our privilege to be about our true King's business. If the Reformation fails in France — then I fear all is lost for us as a great nation in Europe."

Rachelle was stirred. *For what is our life? It's duration is like the fading memory of a June morn. What we do for Jesus, we must do now, while it is yet day.*

Rachelle watched her father standing grimly, hands folded behind his back.

"For the Huguenots of France, for each of us here, so much depends on the outcome of this coming religious debate. In fairness to Prince Antoine, he believes that in compromising with the duc and cardinal, he is working for peace and tolerance."

Pasteur Bertrand shook his silver head. "But peace at what price? And what will be tolerated? The weakening of truth?"

Silence prevailed.

"I suggest we send word to Navarre to ask Queen Jeanne not to come to the colloquy," one of the Huguenot leaders said.

Pasteur Bertrand stroked his short, pointed beard. "There is not enough time. Word has come that she draws near the town."

"Messieurs," said another, "I beg you not to be too hasty in this matter. We all know how the Word warns against various whisperings that often murder a brother's reputation. We must stand firm with the prince. Surely he will come to see his transgression? As the first prince of the blood he can, by working with the Queen Mother, secure the Huguenot cause."

There was a pause, as though they all contemplated their consciences.

"I often worry," Pasteur Bertrand said at last, "that we do ourselves harm by looking to men for our betterment in France. We must not place our hope in the weakness of flesh. Although cloaked in the garb of princes and lords, the feet of all men are lame."

"It is true," Père Arnaut said. "Our final hope of deliverance in the land can only be established in our Lord, but we must have seigneurs, Cousin Bertrand. We must have our king."

"Must we, Arnaut? I wonder," Bertrand said in a thoughtful voice. "Oh, I agree we must have leaders. But it is one thing to have our Moses lead us through this wilderness with the staff of God — but quite another matter to be led by one whose very salvation we are uncertain of."

"But let us not rush to gather stones," said another. "Let us first and foremost pray for him."

There came a murmur of assent.

"Marquis Fabien told me a short while ago that he's learned how the Guises, supported by the Spanish Ambassador, are laboring to convince Antoine to join their three-man holy league and so break with the

Bourbon-Huguenot alliance," Pasteur Bertrand said. "The marquis is looking into the irksome news this very moment."

"If that is so," Père Arnaut said, "Antoine's moral fall poses a greater threat to the Reformation in France than we had thought."

There was a groan around the chamber.

"He is no match for such serpentine intriguers. Irresolute, he knows not with which side to align himself."

"With truth!" Pasteur Bertrand said. "I believe Marquis Fabien was right when he said the Guises knew Prince Antoine could be compromised if isolated from his strong allies. And his strongest support was his own wife, Queen Jeanne. So they attack when he is most vulnerable. How like Satan who prowls about seeking out the weakness of men, to trap and destroy."

"Be vigilant," Père Arnaut said with a thoughtful nod, "because your adversary the devil, as a roaring lion, walketh about seeking whom he may devour."

Then perhaps it is bonne news that Queen Jeanne is arriving, Rachelle thought. She was always one of Antoine's strong resources, so Fabien had said.

I want to be that manner of wife and woman — to do Fabien good and not evil all the days of our journey together.

Oh, Antoine, choose righteousness, choose your family, and make your royal stand for truth!

"Let us attend the colloquy with humble spirits, making our private petition to our Lord that we may find grace in the sight of the French throne. Messieurs, shall we end our discussion with prayer for God's intervention?"

They readily responded to Pasteur Bertrand's plea for prayer and humility.

As one by one they prayed, pleading for the Reformation to take root in the dry soil of their beloved France, Rachelle added her own petitions for a spiritual stirring throughout her country. *What of me? If there is to be revival, it can begin with me. Am I faithful, honest, and pure? Am I dedicated? Do I love the Savior with all my heart?*

"Jesus must be honored and glorified if blessing is to come to the people of France," Pasteur Bertrand had said on several occasions.

Make me in my daily doings what I am in Christ, O Father. Amen.

❧

LATE THAT EVENING WHEN FABIEN RETURNED, Rachelle was in the bedchamber preparing to retire. Her parents had departed to stay with the duchesse at the Dushane château where they would remain during the colloquy, and Cousin Bertrand had retired.

She noted at once his somber mood, though his calm remained.

He removed his handsome jacket with gold embroidery and armorial bearings in jewels and tossed it on a chair, then loosened the white shirt with Alençon lace.

"My apologies, chérie, for leaving earlier this evening. I will explain to your father why I had to leave when I did. Andelot brought disturbing news. We had to discuss something unusual about Sardinia."

"Sardines?" She wrinkled her nose.

He laughed. "Sardinia. There is a meeting in the morning between the Guises and the Spanish ambassador. It's likely to have far-reaching consequences." He walked up to her, and taking her into his arms, kissed her.

"About Andelot, what sort of disturbing message did he bring?"

He sobered and released her.

"You may read it yourself. He thought first to send it to me, but then brought it himself."

He took her arm and walked her toward the candlelight.

Rachelle took the message and read, pondering the odd words of Andelot's brief message.

> *"Marquis Fabien, I am now in a chamber between the cardinal and his secretary, Père Jaymin. It is most intimidating at times. I cannot come and go without being watched."*

Rachelle's frown deepened. She read on.

> *"A bizarre incident is in progress. They told me to make a false map of Sardinia. My instructions were to turn this rocky, desolate island that is like the Rock of Gibraltar into a mythical tropical*

paradise with great cities, farmlands, and fruit trees according to a list written by Ambassador Chantonnay. Tomorrow morning there will be a meeting between the three messieurs, the duc, cardinal, and ambassador, and my map must be ready for them. What think you of this?

I shall send another message after the meeting in the morning. I shall get little sleep this night."

Rachelle looked at Fabien, lifting her brow. "*Sardinia?* Whatever is Sardinia?"

"Not 'what' is it, chérie, but 'why' is it? Just what do the Guise brothers and that wily Spanish spy have in mind? Scholar Thauvet has suggested that Spain is involved in this, since Sardinia is under their flag. I am inclined to agree that it was Chantonnay who made the list of what Andelot was to include on the map."

She could see Fabien was apprehensive.

"A mythical map ... but why?"

"I have an idea, but I will wait until Andelot sends me a report on the meeting with Antoine in the morning. Whatever they plan, it is likely to mean danger for someone."

"Do you think Andelot will be safe staying so near the cardinal's watchful eye?"

"They need him. At least until they send him to Lorraine. That is not likely to happen until late November, after the colloquy. At the moment, he could not be better situated to spy."

"As long as he is not caught."

He scowled. "Yes, as long as Jaymin does not discover his spying, or that he's a Huguenot at heart. But Andelot is more astute than I think even you understand. He is no longer the amenable ami, but he has matured. If I thought he was gullible I'd never ask him to spy. Something dark is afoot, and we need to know what they are planning."

She watched as he burned the message with the candle flame.

"I too have some news about Andelot. Madame Clair says he and Idelette have been corresponding. Eventually there may be a marriage. I could not be more enthusiastic."

"I suspected it could be so. He mentioned that he wished to go to London for a time before going on to Geneva to study under Calvin."

"I am most sure Idelette would say yes if he asked her for her hand in marriage. She will be so supportive of his decision about Geneva."

He cocked a brow. "But first, we must escape France. That will be a feat in and of itself. What did Arnaut and Bertrand discuss with the Huguenot leaders tonight?"

She put a hand to her forehead. "Prince Antoine." She sighed. "And that which concerns his mistress, Mademoiselle Rouet. Is it true the Guises intend to use her to woo him into becoming a Catholic?"

"Be assured they will if they can, thereby endangering the Bourbon-Huguenot alliance at Court. If the colloquy fails to bring an end to persecution, there will be a civil war. As general of France, Antoine controls the army. His support is crucial."

She noted the sobriety in his violet-blue eyes.

"You would like to believe in his honneur, chérie, as would I. But in this situation, do not place your confidence in Antoine to work for the betterment of the Huguenots. That may have been his goal at first. But I fear he's lost his way. Greater horizons fill his vision. I know him too well."

That he would speak so bluntly about his kinsman surprised her. "But despite his fall, he is one of us, a Huguenot. Surely he will see his error and forsake it."

"He is not known for his steadfastness. I tell you, Rachelle my sweet, there is so much intrigue at work presently that one walks through a palais of vipers. They lie in wait at every turn, in every shadowy crevice, ready to sink their fangs into the gullible. Unfortunately, Antoine has never been a messire of discernment."

"If only there were something to be done to win the day!" She gazed longingly at the candle flame.

He stood, hands on hips, looking at her with a tender smile. "Chérie, you want so much for the golden trumpets of God to sound at this very moment and for angels to intervene. I too wish for it. However, this may be that hour when, like the Church of Smyrna, it is with much tribulation that we enter the kingdom of God."

He leaned over and blew out one of the candles. "It may be that we will never see what we long for: a wise sovereign on the throne. We may never see France embrace the truths of the Reformation as has Holland, England, and Germany."

There was a quiet thoughtfulness to his voice that frightened her.

"Fabien," she whispered, aghast, "how can you speak so? Why, it is what we are all praying and struggling to bring about. The colloquy begins next week!"

"It does. The truth will be taught, a victory in itself. Even so, the response depends upon the hearts of those who will hear. Arnaut, Bertrand, the Huguenot leaders — they should realize there will be a continued struggle in France, a long one. I have brooded over my conclusion for weeks now. I've decided we nobles have put too much hope in our ability to bring about the kind of change that only a love for the truth can establish in a nation. If the church, or a nation, loses that love, how great becomes the darkness. When that happens, stalwart men with swords can accomplish only so much."

She was convinced that he had agonized over this. Did it take more faith to believe in great victories, or to stand firm when it seemed the battle was being lost?

"Yes, we nobles can sink galleons," he was saying. "We can send mercenaries to aid the Dutch, but we cannot thwart a civil war here in our own France." He looked at her. "For the Reformation to win in France it must seize the hearts of the French people. We nobles have little to do with that. French serfs must be won a man at a time. France is at a crossroads. The question hounds me. What if a love for the truth does not take root?"

Perhaps for the first time, she could feel his anguish over the France he loved — and might lose. She went to him and threw her arms around him, her eyes wet with tears.

Fabien embraced her, holding her close.

❈

THE NEXT MORNING AT FONTAINEBLEAU, Andelot was called to the Cardinal de Lorraine's receiving chamber. He entered, rolled map in hand, not knowing what to expect. The cardinal, in his red and white robes, stood with polished sophistication beside the Duc de Guise. The duc looked to be in good spirits and was smiling, his hands folded behind him.

"Bonjour, mon petit Andelot. You have located the map we wanted from the library. We knew we could depend upon you," the cardinal said.

The prick to his conscience hurt. *I should not have made this, but what else could I do?*

Andelot held out the rolled parchment. "The map, Monseigneur."

"Come forward, Andelot," Duc de Guise said cheerfully. "Stretch it out on the desk here." He turned, saying, "Chantonnay, this is a young kinsman of ours, Andelot Dangeau."

"And a kinsman of Marquis de Vendôme, I hear."

"But a Guise," the cardinal said with emphasis. "Andelot has proven a great help to us. He will be going to our country estate in Lorraine after the colloquy."

Was the cardinal convincing Chantonnay that he was trustworthy?

"The marquis is also my kinsman," a pleasant voice spoke from behind Andelot.

"Ah, sire, come and behold the map," the cardinal said.

Sire? A *king*! Andelot turned quickly on his heel to face the pleasant voice and saw Prince Antoine de Bourbon, the King of Navarre. So, this ruse concerned Antoine?

Standing with Antoine, as though they were close comrades, was the shrewd Spanish Ambassador Chantonnay. A smile lighted Chantonnay's swarthy face. Andelot covered his surprise.

"Come, sire," Chantonnay again urged Prince Antoine. "You will not be disappointed at what you see. All that we told you is here before your eyes. Sardinia — the magic isle! I could wish to go there myself. But when you are king there, I am sure my master, the King of Spain, will visit you to enjoy the tropical air."

Andelot tightened his lips. *That serpent-toothed deceiver!* He stood near the wall trying to avoid attention now, hoping they would not dismiss him. The four gathered around the desk, murmuring in low voices, as they pointed out various amenities on the map. From the way they smiled, it would appear they were the finest of comrades with Prince Antoine. How this change had come about recently Andelot could not guess, but the Guises and Chantonnay were champion deceivers. What amazed him most was that Prince Antoine would trust them enough to gather alone with them. He knew they had tried to assassinate him only months ago. And yet, here they were discussing a phony map that he was accepting without question.

Was Chantonnay behind this trickery? Andelot had heard Chantonnay had been trained in the art of diplomacy since a small boy and was an expert in the ways of intrigue. Père Jaymin said that Chantonnay constantly spied on the Queen Mother and reported even what she had for her evening dinner to the King of Spain.

"Ah, sire, we all agree that a grand future awaits you, for we in Spain know how you are the Bourbon prince to best deal with the differences between my country and yours. The Queen Mother?" He pursed his lips and shook his head. "You should have been made Regent of France. My king believes she cannot be trusted. She is, if you will pardon me for saying so, too close to the Huguenot leaders she has brought to court."

"Sire," the duc said, "you have always been the level-headed prince. Come, Chantonnay, explain the majestic plan King Philip is offering him."

Prince Antoine looked from Duc de Guise back to Chantonnay. "What plan, Monsieur?"

Chantonnay began to talk of King Philip's wondrous plans for Antoine de Bourbon, if Antoine would cooperate with Spain. King Philip was prepared to sacrifice a rare and precious jewel in his far-flung empire to Prince Antoine for peace and friendship. This glittering jewel? The island of Sardinia. And what did he ask for? Little Navarre. Surely Prince Antoine understood that a section of that province in the south already belonged to Spain, won from the King of Navarre in war many years earlier. Why should such a small province be divided when Prince Antoine could rule the far greater kingdom of Sardinia? And Sardinia was merely the beginning of all that would become Antoine's with his cooperation with Spain.

"Monseigneur, look at the map. You will see an important and astonishing island! Look at its great cities, its excellent coastline, its fine natural harbor for ships to anchor from all the trading lanes of the world. And you alone, sire, will become its king. My sovereign fears to surrender such an important island to anyone else, except to you. Of course, it will prove necessary to become a Catholic, for King Philip can have no dealings with heretics."

"It is so, sire," Cardinal de Lorraine added. "The King of Spain has told me this in correspondence. He is concerned for your soul, as am I. Ah, sire, give up being leader of the serpent-headed Huguenot alliance at court. Give up the new opinions and receive so much more in return."

"A triple crown awaits you, sire," Duc de Guise said. "How can a wise man turn such a treasure trove down?"

"A triple crown?" Antoine asked. "Are you saying I could gain other crowns?"

"Indeed so, sire," Chantonnay said in a lowered tone. "If you become a Catholic. But you could not remain married to a heretic."

"Monsieur! Jeanne is my wife."

Andelot gave him a sharp glance. *It is good you finally remember that, sire.*

Chantonnay sighed with the suggestion of grief. He shook his head. "Ah, Monseigneur, the pope has said — sadly so — that you cannot have the triple crown while bound to a rebel. He has written my master, Philip, that if you would cooperate, he will authorize your divorce."

Prince Antoine frowned. "But — Jeanne — she would not want a divorce and neither do I."

"Sire," Cardinal de Lorraine added with a grave smile, "there will be no difficulty in divorcing the woman who has become a rebel and a heretic."

"If I were in your shoes, sire," Duc de Guise said, "I would not hesitate to seize my responsibilities to France. Claim the triple crown and save France from this onslaught of heretical slander that comes from Geneva's mouthpiece."

Antoine rubbed his chin, looking down at the map. "But I received the title of king only through marriage to Jeanne."

Chantonnay moved his hand as if cutting through mist. "It is nothing to worry us, nor should it worry you, sire. All can be handled. Jeanne will lose all her possessions anyway, including her kingdom. All heretics must surrender their possessions, so you would have the crown of the jewel island of Sardinia — and in addition, the crown of Scotland and the crown of England. The triple crown."

Andelot's head lifted. He glanced from the shrewd eyes of Chantonnay to Duc de Guise, who was smiling a tight little smile. Cardinal de Lorraine ran his long white fingers along his crimson robe and also smiled at Prince Antoine.

"Monsieurs, England — Scotland — I do not understand."

"It is simple," Chantonnay said in a whisper. "I will share a secret because my king has confidence in you. The heretic usurper of the English throne, Elizabeth Tudor, will not remain queen. Soon, she will be deposed through war with Spain. When she is removed, who should be the new queen?"

Prince Antoine's eyes began to show excitement.

Duc de Guise said, "It is our blood niece who will be Queen of England and Scotland, our belle Mary Stuart."

"Sire, now do you see what wondrous opportunities my sovereign offers for your future?" Chantonnay nodded. "If you divorce the heretical Jeanne, marriage with the Guise niece, Mary, Queen of Scots, is possible."

Antoine raised a hand to his forehead. "Yes ... yes, I understand now."

"How Mary continues to grieve for the loss of France," the cardinal said. "How she pleads with us to arrange for some marriage in order to return to the land she cares about. All of this, sire, is possible for you — and our Mary."

"How true. And all you need do is take this beautiful island of Sardinia, become a Catholic, and divorce Jeanne," Chantonnay explained.

"Bonne fortune smiles upon you," Cardinal de Lorraine said with a smile.

"I should say it does," the duc said.

"The triple crown is held out to you on a silver platter," Chantonnay persisted.

"And do not forget France," the cardinal said. "Glorious France. As a Bourbon of the royal blood, you are but small steps from assuming the throne. You and our belle niece, Mary,"

One look at Antoine, and the flush of excitement in his face told

Andelot they had him nearly convinced. Pity filled his heart. And it angered him to see these three serpentine liars luring him slowly, methodically, and heartlessly to the edge of the pit.

Cardinal de Lorraine laid a hand on Antoine's shoulder. "Do not think about it for too long, sire. We would not wish to see this glorious offer slip from your fingers."

"This is a great honneur you offer me, but it is such an important decision — I must discuss it with Jeanne."

Andelot's hopes revived. Prince Antoine was drawing back. Then he heard the words from the three men, coming like the thrust from a dagger.

"But, sire, you certainly will not be able to discuss it with Jeanne. She will wish to divorce you when she hears the news that you took la belle Rouet to be your mistress."

"Your wife will arrive here for the colloquy in just days," the duc said. "And your mistress will be unable to conceal the fact that she is carrying your child."

The Growing Menace

Princesse Marguerite had changed her mind about hating the style and colors, for once the gowns were nearly completed, she could see how belle they were. She had clapped her palms together, and in her teasing way pretended to swoon into the lap of Nenette. "Oh they are beautiful, so delicate, like summer butterflies. I adore them, Rachelle. I will wear the pink gown first. I no longer loathe the color. I am told to meet Navarre on the Saturday after the colloquy begins."

Rachelle saw an opportunity and leapt to take advantage. "Oh, if only I could see you in the gown meeting Prince Henry of Navarre."

"Then you shall, ma chère," she said, holding the gown against her and admiring the soft drape of the folds.

"But the Queen Mother does not permit me to leave the palais."

Marguerite gave her a sly glance. "So you wish for me to arrange your escape from the palais, do you?"

Rachelle snatched the moment. "Oh, could you?"

"How do you think I slip away to meet Henry de Guise? I can slip you out to go with me to the divertissement. You will need to look most élégante."

Rachelle held down her excitement. She could hardly wait to tell Fabien that an opportunity of escape could soon come. This would be her first night away from captivity in almost a year!

"I have the most perfect gown to wear, my princesse. Wait until you see. The gown is all lace netted over powder blue satin, with velvet cuffs."

"Wear it, mignon, but make certain you do not look more belle than I."

When Rachelle left the atelier late that afternoon, she anticipated Fabien's response to her news, but when she arrived she found a short note from him:

Chérie, an important meeting has come up. I will be late.

She was already aware of the upcoming meeting with Andelot about the map of Sardinia and anxiously awaited Fabien's return to hear what was discovered.

During the evening, while Cousin Bertrand was away with Minister Beza preparing for the opening day of the colloquy, she and Nenette worked on the finishing touches for the third and final gown. All was complete except the adornment of the frilled fan-style neck made of pleated ecru lace of palest eggshell over an underlining of pink silk. She had brought the gown and her sewing case to the appartement knowing she would be working late, for she wished to finish the project tonight and submit the gowns to the Queen Mother for approval. Fortunately, the Queen Mother had not requested a new gown, and except for their meeting in her chambers earlier in the summer, Rachelle had not been called back to report to her.

Rachelle and Nenette had pulled back some pieces of furniture in the salle de sejour, and with the carpet clean and swept, they laid the gown out carefully and began the final work.

Will this be my last gown as a couturière in the French court?

❧

FABIEN RODE THE CHESTNUT STALLION by starlight into the Fontainebleau Forest, away from the king's section, toward the cottage of the old pasteur, Claud Mornay, who was now his personal chaplain. With Mornay content to stay in the antechamber of Bertrand's bedchamber, he had offered to let Fabien hold covert meetings in the cottage with his men-at-arms under Julot Cazalet and Gallaudet. Fabien hoped to receive the latest news of Nappier and the *Reprisal*. The boy, Philippe, had brought him a message from Andelot saying that he would be able to attend because Jaymin had been sent to the Poissy monastery to prepare a study chamber for the cardinal, giving Andelot a breath of freedom.

When he and Gallaudet neared the cottage, they approached with caution.

"The candle is in the window," Gallaudet said, "a sign that all is well."

They secured their horses and approached the bungalow from different directions.

As planned, Gallaudet went to the back door while Fabien waited near the trees.

The September night was crisp and clear with a vivid canopy of stars showing above the tall forest trees. The moon had already set and a deep stillness had settled over the forest. A short time elapsed, and then the front door of the low-roofed cottage opened, and Gallaudet appeared on the porch and lifted a hand.

Fabien came up the porch step and entered the room. Andelot greeted him, but most of the others were not present.

"Where is Julot?" Fabien asked.

"The men-at-arms arrived last night from Vendôme," Gallaudet said. "Julot took them into the forest where their camp would not easily be discovered. But they are not far, Monseigneur, we can be there in a short ride."

"He left you this, Marquis Fabien." Andelot handed him a lettre.

Fabien and Julot had met on at least a dozen occasions in the past months to go over the plans of escape to La Rochelle, where, as the time drew near, Capitaine Nappier would come with the *Reprisal*. He looked forward to meeting with him again and hearing the news of all he had been doing recently in aiding the Dutch privateers against Spain.

At the last meeting with Julot, Fabien had looked over the list of possible men-at-arms who were anxious to attach themselves to the Marquis de Vendôme of the house of Bourbon. Fabien had studied the names of the chevaliers, and the brief recommendations by Julot, Gallaudet, and those who knew them. Fabien had chosen those he thought more advanced with weaponry, loyal to the Bourbon house, and unattached.

Fabien looked toward the wood fire in a hearth where a kettle simmered. He removed his hat and cloak.

"Is that tea?"

"I thought you would want some, Marquis," Andelot said.

A short time later, Gallaudet took his mug of brew and disappeared into the nearby pine trees to keep watch while Fabien stood warming himself. He could see by Andelot's countenance that the meeting in the cardinal's chamber had not gone well. So be it. Let it stew a few minutes more while he relished the hot drink and read Julot's report by the firelight.

When Fabien had finished reading Julot's report, he placed it on the flames. Andelot rose and put another piece of wood on the fire.

"Capitaine Nappier has arrived at La Rochelle," Fabien told him, satisfied. "He will be waiting with the *Reprisal* for us to manage our escape." He looked down at Andelot, feeling concern.

"I have been thinking, Andelot, that with the cardinal and Jaymin occupied with the colloquy, this is your best time to leave. The sooner you can reach La Rochelle and join Nappier, the better."

"You would have me flee now — and leave you and Mademoiselle Rachelle behind? I may be of some need to you, Marquis. The news I bring is not of bonne fortune."

"I am sure it is not," he said wryly. "It will be better for you to leave from here at dawn. When Jaymin or the cardinal notices, I can suggest that you may have gone with Scholar Thauvet to Paris for a short time to help him settle into his new chambers at the university."

Andelot frowned and resettled the wood in the hearth. "I would feel cowardly and ungrateful to ride off free now, Marquis, and leave my friends still in the thick of the trouble."

Fabien frowned back. "The opportunity is set for you to depart at dawn, and you are ready. You have the golden bay, and you can ride to La Rochelle and wait for us. Or if you so choose, you can ride toward Geneva."

"I cannot, Marquis — all of my possessions remain in my chamber."

"We will celebrate your new freedom by buying all new possessions. If you have personal items of sentiment, then I will see they are brought. Gallaudet can retrieve them."

"I would miss attending the colloquy if I ride out at dawn."

"You already know the truths Minister Beza will discuss, Andelot. The Lord has opened the door for you to ride free. Everything has come together for you at this time, even Thauvet's return to Paris. There is nothing here for you any longer, mon ami. It is time to begin a new phase of your life. Whether it is Geneva now, or London and Idelette first, only the decision to leave is important now."

"Why did you say Mademoiselle Idelette?"

Fabien smiled. "Madame Clair mentioned to Rachelle your frequent lettres. She is hoping, as is Rachelle, that this meeting of the minds will become a meeting of the hearts."

Andelot smiled. "Yes, I was thinking of asking for her hand in marriage."

"Well, you can think of it more freely on the golden bay come dawn. What say you, Andelot?"

Andelot played with the coals a minute longer. He sighed.

"I could leave at dawn. Yes, perhaps this is the time, as you say. But first, I must tell you what happened at the meeting. It may be you will change your mind and need me in some way. The news is dark, Marquis." He shook his head in discouragement, staring into the hearth.

"And what do the Guises have planned for the tropical paradise of Sardinia?"

"They plan, with Ambassador Chantonnay, to give it to your kinsman Prince Antoine in exchange for the province of Navarre. If he becomes a Catholic as they say he should, they will also arrange for his divorce from his heretic wife, Queen Jeanne. Then they will give him a triple crown if he marries their niece, Mary, Queen of Scots. Spain will depose Queen Elizabeth, and he will then have Sardinia, Scotland, and England. And — la belle Rouet is enceinte. She is so far along that she may give birth during the colloquy while Queen Jeanne is here."

The coals in the hearth popped, snapped, and sizzled.

"Anything else?"

"They also mentioned the possibility of him having the throne of France," Andelot said.

Fabien put both hands to the top of his head and groaned. He sank into the chair. *Antoine was being successfully bribed. And for reasons that made no sense, Antoine had trusted the Guises who had, not so long ago, tried to kill him!*

"Explain it to me," Fabien said, frustrated.

Andelot sat on the small rug before the fire, chin in hand. He shook his head. "Seeking to understand these things is like following footsteps fading off into the mist."

"Then finding out the foggy path brings you to a precipitous edge," Fabien added dryly. "I can think of one main purpose behind this Guise action. It seems like an assault upon Jeanne of Navarre and the Bourbon-Huguenot alliance to enhance the power of the Guises. If Antoine becomes a Catholic and there is a divorce sanctioned by the pope, Mary, Queen of Scots, and Antoine together would allow her oncles to seize power. The triple crown they tempted Antoine with—as much of it as might become reality—would be their crown, for they could manipulate him even as they did King Francis. Can you imagine the duc and cardinal overseeing not just the affairs of France but Protestant Scotland and England? Ah, I must present this fearful possibility to the Queen Mother!"

Andelot frowned. "Dark and cunning."

"Straight from the pit. I tell you, Andelot, I think it is all beginning to make sense, at least about Louise and Antoine. The Guises are pleased she is enceinte in order to bring about his divorce from Jeanne. They knew what her reaction would be, and rightly so, for Antoine has played the dog. But the consequences are far reaching. If there is a divorce, their son Henry will lose the right to rule the kingdom of Navarre.

"And that makes me wonder why the Queen Mother is trying to restart marriage discussions for Margo and Henry."

Andelot threw his hand up. "What good is it for Princesse Marguerite to marry Prince Henry of Navarre if Queen Jeanne loses all as a heretic?"

"Perhaps they will take Henry and try to make him a Catholic, as well."

"Yes, they would try that. And I have found out the chief papal legate is coming to the colloquy from Rome, and do you know who is coming with him? The head of the Jesuits."

Fabien stared at him. *The head of the Jesuits—the Inquisition leader.*

"This may be the most important, Andelot. Who told you this?"

"Père Jaymin. He seemed most intense. Do you think it could have something to do with your kinswoman?"

"It could. If she is branded a heretic, then Antoine will inherit all."

Fabien frowned, hands on hips, staring off. The suspicion troubling him for weeks was that the Guises and Ambassador Chantonnay had some devious plan in mind for the colloquy.

"What will happen to Queen Jeanne if their plan to use Prince Antoine is successful, if Prince Antoine divorces her . . . ?"

Andelot stopped as though the truth were also dawning on him.

Fabien said, "If she shows herself here at Poissy during the colloquy, Andelot, she could be arrested as a heretic. And if she refuses to change her religion, they could turn her over to the Inquisitors."

Andelot looked alarmed. "That could explain why the papal legate Cardinal Ferrara is coming with the head of the Jesuits. But would they dare arrest her during the colloquy?"

"Not easily—unless Duc de Guise secretly prepared a contingent of men-at-arms to attack unexpectedly. But afterward, if for some reason Jeanne lingered in Paris, all they would need is a royal summons. Remember the ploy they used to lure the princes here to Fontainebleau, promising them fair and generous treatment by the king?" Fabien shook his head. "They are certainly not troubled by lies."

"But what about Prince Antoine? Surely he would not agree for his wife to be arrested? I understand he stumbled and took a mistress, but—"

"I can hardly fathom him agreeing to her arrest, myself. As you say, he loved her once. He must still have feelings for her and his children by her, despite his folly with Louise. There is much about Antoine that is fair and decent. But he is weak and vacillating. We cannot depend on such a messire."

"A double-minded man is unstable in all in his ways."

"We cannot take even his good conscience for granted. The unquenchable thirst for power and glory can do strange and dangerous things. I always knew that, but now I have seen it in action. Antoine, even Maurice. If I had not swerved from him at the very last moment, his sword would have penetrated a few more inches to my heart. Though we were at cross purposes many times, I had not thought we could become enemies."

"Sometimes, Marquis, it is not a conscious decision to allow our sinful natures to direct our steps, but a little compromise here, then there."

"Précisément. And as insane as matters have been recently, who can say what my kinsman Antoine will do? I must talk to him — and the Queen Mother. I cannot think this plan to arrest Jeanne could take place without her knowing of it; she has too many spies crawling about."

"But what of the meetings between her daughter, the princesse, and Queen Jeanne's son? Does that not seem to lessen of the Queen Mother's chance of involvement?"

"It would seem so, Andelot, but the gowns and the arranged meetings may be a ruse to throw us off guard as to the real intentions. That is the way she maneuvers."

What Fabien did not want to discuss was the possible consequences of Jeanne being arrested and turned over to the inquisitors. The clouds of civil war were even now gathering in the sullen sky over France. Winds of persecution whipped feverishly. But burning Jeanne of Navarre at the stake would turn France into an open battlefield between Huguenots and Catholics.

Duc de Guise and Cardinal de Lorraine were likely to welcome such a war. The duc would receive Spanish troops and money from the pope, but the Queen Mother wished to avoid civil war, for it would weaken the Valois reign.

Presently, Catherine was siding with the Huguenots against the house of Guise, but Fabien knew she would not be guided by principles but by her desire to hold on to the throne and preserve it for her favorite son, Anjou. She would wait and watch. Fabien hoped she did not get impatient to see Guise dead, for it would put pressure on him to act sooner.

"The least I can do is warn Jeanne. The quandary facing us is that she has already left Navarre with Henry. Her retinue would be well on its journey by now; the colloquy begins in days."

"I think, Marquis, I should go back to Fontainebleau."

"Non, you will respect our friendship, Andelot, and ride out at dawn. Believe me, there is nothing you can do to help me in this matter of my kinswoman."

"Then — as you wish, I will go. If Gallaudet can pack my personal things and take them with him, I shall be very much grateful."

Fabien felt a well of relief. "Where will you go first?"

Andelot hesitated. "London, to see Idelette . . . and request her hand in marriage. Then, if she accepts me and is willing, to Geneva."

Fabien grinned. "We will attend your wedding at London—God willing, mon ami."

"God willing, Marquis Fabien."

❊

LATER THAT NIGHT, AFTER FABIEN RETURNED from his meeting with Andelot in Chaplain Mornay's cottage, he entered the Fontainebleau appartement by the back side entrance where royal guards greeted him. Fabien had spent long months trying to earn their loyalty, and with the aid of Gallaudet, was confident that he had done so. This camaraderie had been helped along with a few jewels and a promise of fine horses from Vendôme one day when they were in the region. Fabien now understood better what Sebastien must have suffered all those years as a reluctant member in the Queen Mother's council. One day in London he would sit down with his oncle by marriage and ask him how he had endured those turbulent years that included his arrest and incarceration in the torture chambers of the Bastille where the cardinal insisted he renounce his faith or lose Madeleine and his daughter. All this was a part of Sebastien's legacy.

Fabien was pleased to learn, through the Macquinets, that Sebastien and Madeleine were adjusting well. Sebastien was already beginning to move in some political circles in the London court of Queen Elizabeth due to a past friendship with Elizabeth's brilliant Protestant secretary of state, Sir William Cecil, her counselor and loyal friend.

Fabien had carefully made friendships in the royal guards and it would assist him during the important moment of getting Rachelle, Nenette, Bertrand, and Chaplain Mornay out the side door to waiting horses.

He went to the appartement and entered quietly to avoid awakening Rachelle, and though weary, he found that restful sleep evaded his troubled mind. He stepped out on the balustrade and leaned against the rail. A silent landscape greeted him with stars and planets in place above forested hills. The lake reflected the starlight like a mirror. So many thoughts raced through his mind: civil war, treachery, love, his future as a Bourbon noble, and soon now, if war did come, what it would mean for his kinsman Prince Louis de Condé and Admiral Coligny.

What would his own followers do without him? What of his marquisat? Though he had thought of these things before, the events at hand reopened old regrets and brought them anew to his mind and his heart. Departing France was something he had once told himself he would never do, for the sake of the honor of Duc Jean-Louis de Vendôme and of his mother, Duchesse Marie-Louise de Bourbon. Regardless of the necessity of leaving, doing so would be traumatic. He could not see himself living in England for the rest of his life when he was a Frenchman. Though he could communicate well in English, he spoke more fluently in Dutch.

War was coming, surely. Under normal circumstances, it would be his duty and honneur to gather an army of followers from Vendôme and lead them to join the head Bourbon, now Condé, since Antoine no doubt would side with Duc de Guise and the Catholic alliance.

Ah! If Duc de Guise *were* dead . . .

What would it mean for him? For Rachelle?

The Queen Mother would be satisfied. Her grip upon him would be broken.

But unfortunately, Guise looked healthy. Fabien knew he could be removed from the French scene by a quiet but firm thrust of a dagger. One clean thrust would bring him to his eternal destiny.

But I am no murderer. Nor will I be, not for all of France! He pushed the idea away and ceased to toy with it.

He deliberately turned his thoughts to the colloquy. As yet, though he had his personal family chaplain who was a Huguenot, he had not publicly taken Communion with the Protestant leaders from Geneva. When the colloquy began, he would do so, declaring himself with Minister Beza, the twelve theologians, and those with Condé and Coligny.

But many, like John Calvin, had been forced to leave, and why not him? And Andelot would ride away on the golden bay. That beloved horse! What would Andelot do with him? Maybe he could arrange to have him taken to the Château de Silk under the care of Messire Arnaut.

This is something! He laughed at himself. He could relinquish Vendôme but not a horse. *I cannot think of leaving France without worrying about a horse — non, two horses.* For already, the beau chestnut stallion was upon his heart.

Soft footsteps came up beside him. He turned, and Rachelle was there, his comfort and amour, as always. She slipped her arm through his and leaned with him against the balustrade, looking off at the dark forest under the gleaming stars.

"I heard you come in. I was unable to sleep for thinking about Sardinia. Tell me what happened. You did meet with Andelot?"

This would not be easy for him, but he respected her too much to keep the unpleasant truth concealed. She too must know what was at risk. He quietly told her everything that had occurred with Antoine, the Guises, and the Spanish Ambassador Chantonnay. He went into detail of what he believed the plans were to arrest his kinswoman Jeanne and the scheme to marry Mary, Queen of Scots, to Antoine and what such a union would mean, not only for France but England and Scotland. He finished by telling her Andelot was going to England to ask Idelette to marry him, whereupon they would journey to Geneva where he would train as a Huguenot pasteur or a teaching theologian at Calvin's school.

"So, ma chère, all is not dark. Happiness awaits your sister after all her grief, and Andelot will fulfill his spiritual gifts from God. He will be a tender shepherd for Christ, I am sure of it."

"Happiness awaits us too, mon amour Fabien. I am already happy in your arms and always will be — and I have a wondrous secret to tell you."

He studied her lovely face and wondered how he could have missed the sparkle of excitement showing in her eyes.

"A secret? It must have something to do with the belle gowns you have made Margo. What is it, chérie, perhaps you have been asked to create a gown for Queen Jeanne?"

Her smile deepened, and she slipped her arms around him and came closer, laying the side of her face against his chest. He held her close.

"All a reason for excitement, but not my cherished secret." She looked up at him.

He lifted a brow. "Then you have me baffled and most curious."

She drew in a breath. "I had feared being barren, but I now am enceinte with our first child. I could not be more excited and thankful to our God. I hope you will also find it so?"

For a moment he did not speak, and then he could not find the appropriate words.

His immediate response was to squeeze her tightly and bury his face in her fragrant hair. He kissed her earlobe, her throat, her lips, and tenderly communicated his delight and his abiding love.

The Dark Agreement

THE QUEEN MOTHER TOOK HER MORNING PETIT DÉJEUNER ALONE IN HER chamber. She was vexed. She pondered again the message from one of her spies in the Guise camp. With the opening ceremonies of the colloquy to begin the following day, events were moving too quickly away from her control.

So the Guises, with their chief collaborator Chantonnay, were inducing Antoine de Bourbon into becoming a Catholic, using bribes and flattery. Losing Antoine would weaken her. She must either draw closer to the Huguenot alliance under Admiral Coligny and his brothers, or reverse the direction she was going and show the Guises and Spain that she was truly their friend and working on their side.

Months ago when she had met with Antoine in the garden and whispered her plan to make him her general of France, it was with the idea of joining forces against the Guises, but she had not reckoned on the machinations of Ambassador Chantonnay, Philip's formidable spy.

She used her dagger to slice off a section of her sweet breakfast melon. She sealed her lips tightly and laid her knife and spoon down, mulling over Spain's offer to Antoine to exchange Sardinia for the Kingdom of Navarre. And that swayable fool Antoine was impressed by the prospect. A tropical island! That slab of rocky wasteland? Ah, if Jeanne knew her husband was willing to negotiate away her father's kingdom for Sardinia, how incensed she would be.

Catherine needed no spy at Navarre to tell her what Jeanne was thinking, for she had been reading the lettres sent between Antoine and Jeanne for the last year.

Antoine, so typical of him, held nothing back in his correspondence —
except all of the truth. He was carrying on an illicit relationship with
Louise de la Limaudière, la belle Rouet. Catherine was scornfully amused
by one of Antoine's exaggerated statements to Jeanne — "I promise that
neither the ladies of the court nor any others can ever have the slightest
power over me, unless it be the power to make me hate them."

Catherine chuckled. He undoubtedly had convinced his conscience it
was true, even so, such words were not likely to fool an intelligent woman
like Jeanne for long. She would decide Antoine sounded too defensive.
Jeanne understood how weak her husband's fidelity was. So too was his
signature. "Your very affectionate and *loyal* husband, Antoine," might
send an uneasy qualm through Jeanne. Was that promise of loyalty not
a little overstated?

Catherine called for her woman in the escadron volant and demanded
further news. Louise de la Limaudière reported that it was true, Antoine
was wavering in his commitment to the Huguenot cause and showing a
growing willingness to become a Catholic. He would then join Duc de
Guise and Cardinal de Lorraine in their holy league, meant to thwart
any movement at court that would tolerate the Huguenots in places of
power.

Holy league, she scoffed. Made up of murderers and adulterers to
defend their faith! What was holy about it? *At least*, she thought with a
tinge of self-righteousness, *I do not pretend to act for God, but for my own
ambitions!*

"And will you be given anything in return for turning the vacillating
Bourbon prince into a dedicated Catholic?" she asked wryly.

Louise ducked her blonde head. "I have been promised rewards,
Madame."

"Have you now? Well, is that not festive and mirthful." Catherine
looked at her coldly. "What manner of rewards, Mademoiselle de la
Limaudière?"

Catherine saw her swallow as if her throat were dry.

"Marriage to Antoine de Bourbon, Madame."

"Marriage! How celebratory. And do you have no qualms that your
Antoine might not take a mistress from my escadron volant?"

Louise drew her heavy maternity cloak about her as she knelt there on the carpet before Catherine's black skirts.

"I shall become his queen."

"You shall become his—" Her jesting voice caught and tightened as the words startled her.

Catherine stood rigid. *Queen!* Then she relaxed.

"Of Sardinia?" She laughed.

Louise licked her lips. "Non, Madame, of France."

Catherine's hands trembled with rage. Her breath came quickly as her heart thudded.

And the Valoises? What did Spain have in mind for the Valoises? What would become of Charles? And Anjou? And if Louise were fool enough to believe that they would make her queen of France, what would that make Antoine?

She leaned toward Louise, her skirt rustling, and the woman looked up with a white face and eyes that widened with alarm.

Catherine took a step toward her, but the woman, large with child, was unable to rise. She fell on her side and let out a shriek like a cat.

"Hush, you fool."

Catherine seized her own spiraling emotions back under control. She clenched her hand to keep from striking the woman's bent head.

Louise grew silent. A moment passed as the sound of their breathing closed around them.

Catherine leaned down toward her again, her voice a whisper.

"If you even hint to them that you have mentioned this to me, you will regret you have a tongue. Do you comprehend?"

"O-oui, Madame."

"Now go."

Louise tried to get up but could not. Catherine impatiently called for her ladies to help her up and take her away to her bed.

A coldness settled over her. It would not be long before Antoine would need to explain to Jeanne of Navarre about the illegitimate child that had somehow emerged during his *most loyal* absence.

It was likely, however, that Jeanne already knew about Antoine and Louise through the Huguenot women here at court who had tried to keep Antoine from slipping into the adulterous pit.

What Jeanne does not know is the plot to have her arrested. Ah, the sly cardinal and papal legate have put her in a position of weakness and great danger.

Later in the afternoon, Catherine was able to sneak away unseen to keep her clandestine meeting with the Duc of Alva in the forest. No one, not even the Guise faction, knew that Alva had returned to France briefly and was here to meet with her. He had departed for the Netherlands a year ago, after Marquis de Vendôme was put in the Amboise dungeon, but he was back again with an urgent message from King Philip, who was furious with her for the colloquy.

No wonder my indigestion is upsetting me again. I live among scorpions.

❈

THE QUEEN MOTHER WAITED in the trees far enough from the château not to be seen easily by anyone out strolling. She had covered herself from head to toe in black gown and head scarf.

The Duc of Alva arrived alone, also in austere black with a touch of red silk ribbon. The duc was a man of solemn countenance with a thin face and a short, well-groomed pointed beard. Behind those shrewd dark eyes lay a fanatical allegiance to his country and his generation's concept of the religion he served with a ruthless sword. She could admire his strength if he were not her opponent in statecraft. She would need to be shrewd to appease Philip of Spain by convincing Alva of her genuine faith. She was, of course, neither Catholic nor Protestant at heart. The occult, Nostradamus, and the Florence astrologers who made her zodiac charts stimulated her primary spiritual interests.

"Madame," he stated with a bow.

"My lord Duc." She tipped her head, feeling her dark coif sway gently with the hem of her long black gown.

"It is imperative we meet alone like this to touch upon certain religious matters of which my king, His Most Christian Majesty, is deeply burdened."

"That he is burdened troubles me, I promise you."

His bleak smile was in place on his lean, sallow face. "It is well that we meet here, Madame, not in the palais. The walls, I believe, have ears."

She ignored what she thought was an allusion to her spying and kept a serious face.

"Ah, but you would know about that better than I, my lord Duc."

He managed a semblance of a chuckle. "Perhaps, Madame."

The air was cool and crisp as they walked, the fallen leaves crunching beneath their feet.

"How unfortunate for us that you will depart so soon for your own country," she said with a friendly smile. *She could hardly wait for his entourage to make their exit.*

"My deepest regret, Madame," he said, matching her slippery tongue. "But my king is anxious to know your reply to his solemn concerns. So much so, Madame, that he wishes my immediate return. Much that is important in the ways of war and peace depends upon your cooperation."

The warning in his voice gave her a chill.

"Ah, so profound, monsieur. You bring worry to my already overburdened heart."

There was a cool warning in his eyes that alarmed her. Not even she could thwart Philip of Spain. He was in league with Rome and could not be easily turned aside from the wishes of the Holy See. Like the first Crusaders who went to war in the Holy Land against the invading Moslem Turks, Philip, too, believed Spain was blessed of the pope to use sword against another threat to Christendom: the spreading Reformation throughout Europe. The enemy now was Protestantism and certain realms in Europe breaking away from the pope's authority.

Catherine knew that France lacked a well-equipped army to withstand a large invasion force from Spain. She understood what the Duc of Alva was doing in Holland, and what he and King Philip were hoping to do to Protestant England and its heretical queen if she did not return to Rome.

And she knew what could befall her and France should the Duc of Alva hurl his seasoned army of soldiers and German mercenaries into France to bring down the Valois throne. She would then be replaced by the house of Guise. Any army that she and Charles could call together would not be sufficient. To attempt to stand against them, she would need the Bourbons, Admiral Coligny, Prince Condé, and others.

Catherine and the Duc of Alva made a twosome as bleak as the fall day. As they walked along, the wind moved in clouds that were masking the sun and making a low moan through the fir trees.

She resented the way in which he began at once to bring up the religious conflict in France. She tried to ignore this affront and instead carried the theme of conversation to her inquiry into the marriage of Marguerite to Philip's son, Don Carlos.

The Duc of Alva's chill smile refused to oblige her, nor was he intimidated by her as others were.

"Madame, I am here as spokesman for my lord, the great King of Spain. I was ordered by his direct command to set aside any discussion of marriage between the two royal families until he rests assured that you and your son, the young king, come to terms with the enemy, the Huguenot nobility."

"Ah, my lord Duc, is it so easy then to murder so many?" she asked coldly.

"Madame, you would know better than I. Other enemies have been removed, have they not?"

The audacity of this man!

"You speak as if France is responsible for the Reformation," she snapped. "I assure you that Luther the German was neither born at our courts nor bred by our royal line. This matter of disagreement between Catholics and Protestants over the interpretation of Scripture did not spring up from French soil."

"Madame, John Calvin and Geneva are the fruits of France."

"Messire John Calvin was chastened out of France by the king's grandfather, Francis I. It is in neutral Geneva that Calvin now abides."

"Geneva, the horned beast of heresy, yes. And this same Calvin is invited to your court to discuss his differences at the Poissy colloquy. My king is as grieved and outraged by this folly as is Rome."

"Poissy," she said with a wave of her hand, quickening her sturdy step along the wooded path beside him. "It is next to nothing, my lord Duc, a mere carnival, as it were, to appease the heretics in my kingdom so that their nobility might better serve my son the king. We are all true Catholics, I promise you."

"If you are loyal to Rome, Madame, then you must put a stop to this 'carnival,' as you call it. For neither Rome nor Spain is amused by such a profane entertainment. It is an offense."

Her anger leaped like a flame. "What offense is it for Frenchmen on both sides of this religious controversy to meet, to discuss, to come to an understanding that will save my country from a civil war? Perhaps it is we who should find offense, my lord Duc, with Spain's meddling."

"Then you will not call an end to this offensive religious carnival?"

"It is not for me to call an end to it. It is the king and the people who wish for peace," she said, knowing indeed that it was she who had promised Admiral Coligny that he could have the colloquy in order to gain Huguenot support for her regency. She could not admit this now, for Alva would wish to have her over a bonfire, but by the time he learned the truth he would be back in Spain.

"That, Madame, is not what Ambassador Chantonnay tells my lord the king in his correspondences."

Chantonnay, that vile spy!

"Ah, but our galant Ambassador Chantonnay has misunderstood matters as they truly are. On your return to Spain you must assure His most noble Majesty that I am a true Catholic and a loyal friend. Is not my daughter Elisabeth Queen of Spain?"

She looked at him evenly, using her daughter's marriage to Philip to set him back on his heels.

For the first time his eyelids fluttered. *Ah you viper! You would be the next to go the way of all flesh if I only dared!*

"Truly, Madame, your daughter is indeed the glorious Queen of Spain. But even she worries about her brother, the king of France, not ridding the land of her birth of its infestation of heretics."

"Does she? Well then, I shall write her at once and soothe her nerves. Perhaps I shall send her a box of my special herbs to ease her mind. My son is indeed the king. The Huguenots shall not undermine his rule."

"Let us pray not, Madame. But my king fears your friendship with those same Huguenots will be to your harm in the end."

Her harm? A veiled threat?

They had stopped beneath a cluster of fir trees with the clouds gathering overhead. He looked at her. "You are friends with Prince de Condé and the Huguenot Admiral Coligny, are you not?"

"Did I not imprison the Bourbon Prince Condé in the Amboise dungeon?" she asked coldly. "And this action was taken by me despite the pleas of his wife, Princesse Eleonore, that madame of leading Huguenot causes. And despite her sister-in-law, the Queen of Navarre!"

"Ah, the Queen of Navarre ... that you have brought her up is conducive to our discussion. She must be arrested and held prisoner before she returns to Navarre. She must become a Catholic like her husband Antoine or lose her kingdom. If she is allowed to persist, she will continue to embolden and support the heretics and turn France to the ways of Calvin. The admiral of France, Coligny, must also be removed. This, Madame, is not pleasant, to be sure, but it is the message of Rome. It is the message of Spain. If not, Spain will declare war."

"My lord Duc! And how am I to rid the land of such eminent nobility and royalty?"

His brittle smile infuriated her. "Madame, King Philip is confident you have both the authority and ability to do so. Now you must also have the will. For the good of France, for the longevity of the Valois throne, I am told to inform you that it must be done."

"Their followers number in the many thousands. They could raise an army of fifty thousand, I have no doubt of it."

"And Spain can offer you a hundred thousand soldiers to cleanse France of its heretics."

She paced beneath a tree, the newly fallen autumn leaves beneath her sturdy stride. She turned and met his eyes. "I cannot agree to plunge my country into civil war. Nor will my son, the king."

"War cannot be dismissed from our discussions, Madame. I was given one message from my king. If all else failed in our discussions and France refuses to destroy her heretics, then Spain will do it for her. Instead of fifty thousand Huguenots, you will see thrice that of Spanish soldiers — followed by a new king."

She knew Philip would invade if he thought it necessary and remove the Valois from the throne. Then, with Rome's blessing, Duc de Guise would be placed on the throne.

She must have gone pale, for his expression changed, and he removed his black coat and threw it on top of a tree stump.

"Madame, if you please, I assure you I am but the servant of King Philip, I take no pleasure in this."

Lies. He would rejoice to see Duc de Guise as king of France — or now, Antoine the new puppet. She made use of what he judged to be feminine weakness and sat down on the stump, pretending a headache and rubbing her forehead. The wind stirred the dying leaves.

"This is for our ears only. No one else need know — no one, you understand?" She smiled. "Not even King Philip."

He paced, his steps quickening.

"The goal of destroying the Huguenot leaders must be foremost in your actions, Madame. For I must bring a word of fruitful promise to my king that you and your son the king will join with Spain in ridding the human plague of heretics from France."

She stood, shoulders back, the wind blowing her black skirt. It was beginning to sprinkle, making a pattering noise on the crisp leaves.

"You may assure King Philip I am his friend and have no love for the Huguenots. I will cooperate to remove our shared enemies even as Rome also wishes. This must be done slowly and cautiously, however. We both know such a thing as we have in mind cannot be done in a hasty manner but must be well planned, my lord Duc. If the attempt should fail, or if suspicion is aroused . . ."

He nodded, walking beside her, for they had started back for the château.

"On one condition."

"And what is that?"

"Queen Jeanne of Navarre is not to return to Navarre. She will be arrested and incarcerated. Then turned over to the inquisitors."

"Queen Jeanne of Navarre and I are not allies." *And yet, her son must become Marguerite's husband; she must not be arrested until after the marriage contract has been signed.*

"Then Rome will take notice of you as a friend if you do not intervene to protect her when the hour of her capture strikes, Madame."

"You may carry the message of my cooperation to your king."

"He will rejoice that you at last have come to see the urgency facing France and all Europe."

"One thing more, my lord Duc, if you will. I should feel more confident in our game of statecraft if we keep our little secret about Admiral Coligny and the rest of the Huguenot leadership from my son the king, the cardinal, and Duc de Guise."

"This is our secret alone, Madame. You need have no fear."

Catherine felt relieved. She had connived her way out of a dilemma. Her ploy would demand a careful balance, like if she were standing upon two wild horses she must not turn loose of the reins. She was not ready to be rid of her Huguenots. She needed them to oppose the house of Guise, Spanish Ambassador Chantonnay, and the conniving papal legate.

"Our secret," she repeated in a hushed voice as they neared the château.

They stopped, for he would return by way of the same secret route that had brought him to the place.

Cold drops continued to fall from the gray sky.

"The results will benefit your beloved Spain—and my France."

The Duc of Alva smiled thinly. He bowed. "So be it, Madame. I now return to my king with your fair words of promise."

"Au revoir, my lord Duc. All we need is patience. Neither you nor King Philip will be disappointed in the end."

Truth War

Ye should earnestly contend for the faith which was once delivered unto the saints.

JUDE 3

O<small>N THE NINTH OF</small> S<small>EPTEMBER, THE OFFICIAL OPENING OF THE COLLOQUY</small> held at the Poissy monastery dawned with a mixture of anticipation and doubt.

The Huguenots were amassing in full force at Paris, Saint-Germain-en-Laye, and Poissy. Rachelle heard it said of those who assembled in support of the new opinions that they were equal in number to those who strongly opposed them. This greatly encouraged the Huguenot-Bourbon alliance and showed the king and the Queen Mother how many of their subjects were Huguenots and why freedom of worship should be permitted in France.

The news spread that Fabien's kinswoman, Jeanne of Navarre, had arrived and was staying in Paris. It was alarming, coming as it did on the sober heels of the quiet entry of the papal legate, Cardinal Ferrara.

"The Queen Mother has invited Jeanne to stay at the Louvre," Fabien told Rachelle, frowning and looking out the window to the busy courtyard below.

Rachelle, too, was gazing below uneasily, her hand on his arm.

Already a queue of coaches, smaller carriages, and saddled horses were lined up for the procession to Poissy.

"Jeanne is at the Louvre?"

"Non. She wisely preferred to stay with Louis and Eleonore at the Hotel-de-Condé," he said of Prince de Condé and his wife. "Jeanne has never fully trusted the Queen Mother, and surely not the house of Guise."

"Does she know about her husband?" Rachelle felt sympathy but certainly not pity. There was no reason to pity Queen Jeanne. Such an emotion might be reserved for Prince Antoine if she could look beyond his folly to what she believed was the true enemy.

"The news about Antoine has passed to Jeanne through her allies at Court," Fabien said. "La Duchesse Montpensier wrote Jeanne before she left Navarre."

"And Queen Jeanne knows the risk of her being arrested?"

He placed his hand on her back, but his attention was directed toward the courtyard. There was sobriety in his violet-blue gaze.

What was he watching or who was he waiting for to appear? She scanned the courtyard as well but could see nothing of interest.

"Louis was told of the grave danger that surrounds her," he said quietly. "I spoke with him in secret two nights ago. He will be straightforward with Jeanne. I only wish I could have stopped her from coming at all."

Fabien had secretly requested the duchesse to send Page Romier racing toward Navarre to warn Jeanne not to come to Paris, though the word was out that she was even then on her way. Romier had come upon Jeanne's entourage on the road as it journeyed toward Paris and the lettre from Fabien passed on to her, but she would not return to her palais at Nérac.

It was like Jeanne, he had told Rachelle later. Jeanne's personality was the opposite of Antoine. Where he vacillated, she was resolved. Early in their marriage, they had laughed about their differences.

If only they had been left alone at Navarre, Rachelle thought again, becoming angry with the Queen Mother. And now Catherine meddled in Rachelle's marriage, using her to keep a tether on Fabien.

Fabien must have sensed a change in her, for he turned his head and looked down at her.

"Is the Queen Mother attending the opening today?" she asked.

"Yes, King Charles is to give the opening address," he murmured absently.

"Who were you expecting in the courtyard?"

His jaw tensed. "The papal legate, Cardinal Ferrara. He was sent here from Rome with a plan to win over Jeanne of Navarre. If she does not recant and publicly attend Mass with Antoine, then the papal legate will resort to other means — and we know what that is."

She shuddered, taking hold of his arm. "How did you find out?"

"Do not forget the admiral's brother, Cardinal Odet, is a Huguenot at heart. He is well aware of what is going on.

"I am thinking, chérie, that Cardinal Ferrara may have plans to 'woo' me as well."

Her heart felt as if it sank to her stomach.

"You?" she repeated in a small whisper, connecting his fearful words with their plans for Queen Jeanne.

"But — why?"

He took her face between his palms. "Because it is not in their purpose to lose another noble to the Reformation. Word has reached him of one more heretic in the ranks of the Bourbons. Until recently, I was considered a Catholic. He is also interested in the belle Marquise Rachelle de Vendôme, whom he believes was used by the enemy to turn my head from Rome."

"But — *me*?" she said with a little squeak that brought a slight turn of his lips, in spite of the sobriety of the subject.

It surprised her to think the powerful papal legate even knew of her, let alone compared her to the conniving women of the escadron volant used to draw men away.

"They think I am responsible for your Protestant leanings?"

"Mind you, Rome is not yet sure what to believe about me. I have not yet come out publicly as a Huguenot. Perhaps I shall be offered something of value, or maybe they will take certain titles and lands and add them to what I have, granting me my father's title of duc, similar to Antoine — who, after all, will be given the triple crown, with France thrown in for flavor," he said dryly.

Fabien's mood altered quickly. "They know about you, ma chérie, and the Huguenot chaplain I took for our household. All of this is laid at your feet."

Her heart thudded.

He pulled her to him. "That is why the plan of escape is being employed earlier than I first intended. If they imagine they can arrest Jeanne as a heretic, they may as easily add others. We will take no chances. And believe me, Cardinal Ferrara will try to woo me back because I plan to publicly meet with Minister Beza and other Huguenots."

She was startled, feeling delight as well as fear. If anything happened to Fabien, it would mean her end as well. Without his protection, she would be swiftly arrested. Her only hope would be to try to escape the castle here at Saint-Germain-en-Laye to reach her parents at nearby Poissy with the duchesse.

"If you waited to take Communion until England ... ?"

He gently lifted her chin until their eyes met.

"I could, but this hour, at the opening of the colloquy, is meaningful to me. It is an honneur to associate myself with the courageous Huguenots, and with monsieurs like Beza who have risked so much to come from Geneva to stand for Christ and the Scriptures. These men stir me, Rachelle. I cannot but admire their courage, and I want to at least make my public stand for Christ here in France before I leave the land I love."

She looked at him, feeling gratitude to God for such a husband. She threw her arms around him, closing her eyes and holding him tightly.

※

RACHELLE STOOD WITH COUSIN BERTRAND on the balustrade watching wagon after wagon roll down the road past fir trees of the Laye Forest carrying Bibles and Scripture portions in the forbidden tongue, all printed in Geneva, to be passed out freely to all in attendance and to any on the street who wanted them.

"We could give out many thousands more if we had them," Bertrand said, pleased. "Everyone wants one — even some of the priests come back alone to ask for a copy, but they do not want the bishops and cardinals to know. And remember, Rachelle, it was money from the silk and the

Château de Silk that helped pay the expenses of some of these wagon-loads of Bibles. This is a day for you and Arnaut and Clair to experience joy."

She did experience joy and only wished that Idelette were here to see the scriptures handed out freely, for she had given money she had saved in a beaded jar.

We will tell her all about the success when we arrive in London.

Besides Bibles and Scripture portions there were crates of special writings.

"By the learned pasteurs and teachers in Geneva," Bertrand told her.

"I am still amazed the Queen Mother would allow this," she said, her eyes following the wagons. "Books written by Calvin?"

"She is desperate to stop a civil war. For this I highly commend her. From what Fabien tells me, she is daily harassed by the infuriated Spanish ambassador, and Duc de Guise is livid."

She'd heard that Calvin's writings would also be smuggled into the University of Paris to the curious students.

Fabien, after attending public Communion with the Huguenot assembly on the first day of the colloquy, received a special Bible printed in Geneva from Minister Beza.

Rachelle was thrilled with it. She ran her palm along the burgundy leather with his family name in gold.

"I anticipate writing the name of our firstborn child on the family birth page," she told him. But she blinked back a tear. She did not want Fabien to know she was saddened at not having been able to witness him publicly taking Communion for the first time as a Huguenot.

In special ceremony Bibles, the words, "with love from the Geneva church," were bestowed on King Charles de Valois IX and the Queen Mother.

"No doubt they were all wrapped in prayers," she said.

Rachelle was excited to hear how the Huguenot leadership was invited to stay in the châteaus of the nobles, while fine dinners and discourses by Minister Beza on doctrinal issues were open for all to attend if they could find a place to sit, stand, or climb up on.

"Even the stable workers wash their faces and scrape the mud and manure from their shoes long enough to listen near the windows or on the porches."

Bertrand added, "If France is won, it will be won by the common man. The most encouraging news we could hear is that the Geneva Psalter is being sung in the stables, in the cooking rooms of the châteaus, and by serving women as they scrub and polish floors."

Madame Clair wrote to Rachelle: "Even if we are not able to accomplish all we had hoped for in this conference, it will be a victory for the truth of Christ, for while the great nobles may reject our message, the maids, servants, stable boys, and blacksmiths hear the word gladly and turn to Him with open hearts. We may not win the royal palais, but we are winning the kitchens."

In those early days of the colloquy, Rachelle received the first reports from Cousin Bertrand, who discussed all that had happened with her and Fabien after dinner.

"Many of the nobles in the audience listening to Beza are the same people who watched the Huguenots die at Amboise. Now they are accepting Bibles and many of them are becoming Huguenots themselves. You see how the blood of the martyrs is not in vain?"

"I am missing everything," Rachelle said, fuming.

Fabien went out of his way to spend the evenings with her and Bertrand and included secret information that she would not have received even if she had been able to attend.

During those days came the prominent men and women that upheld the Protestant and Catholic interpretations of Christian teaching. They gathered each day in the Dominican monastery dining hall for moderated discussions and debates on subjects as far-reaching as the supremacy of the pope, whether or not the Mass was biblical, the spiritual meaning of the broken bread and cup, rituals, relics, and religious traditions. Beza insisted the Bible alone was the true foundation for judging all other religious traditions and teaching; Cardinal de Lorraine insisted that besides the Bible, the Mother Church itself decided what was truth.

"Minister Beza asked if a sinner was made perfectly righteous through Jesus Christ alone. Or were works necessary, such as baptism and others," Fabien relayed to Rachelle.

"What did the cardinal say to that?" she asked.

"What you would expect. That works were an essential part of salvation. The debate was still raging when I left. Some of the highest-ranking bishops grew so angry with Beza they shouted at him and walked out, shaking the dust off their feet against him."

The next day she learned that the bishops who had walked out returned.

"Primarily to spy — not on the Huguenots, but their own bishops," Fabien said.

"I'm surprised there are a number of bishops who desired to break away from Rome's control."

"They wish to form a national church of France," Cousin Bertrand said. "It would enable them to end the burnings, reach out to the Huguenots, and unify France."

"If only these Catholic bishops were in control instead of Cardinal de Lorraine and the papal legate," Rachelle said.

"The cardinal threatened the bishops with heresy if they pursued these ideas with the Huguenots."

"Which shows how meaningless heresy can become, when left to religious leaders like Cardinal de Lorraine," Fabien said.

"The cardinal uses the term just to silence those bishops who may oppose his ambitious agenda."

"Did you notice Duc de Guise walk out in a temper?" Bertrand asked. "The look on his face can keep one awake at night."

Rachelle listened, encouraged as Fabien told of a discussion between the ministers from Geneva and the cardinal and some of his bishops.

"At last the cardinal agreed to see for himself what the first five hundred years of the early Christian church did with the doctrines under discussion. The Huguenots came with manuscripts and ancient texts, but the cardinal didn't show up. The bishops that did come lacked even one authoritative church writing in which to appeal. Their only source of authority was what the popes had already declared."

"If only Protestant and Catholic alike would turn back to the Bible for the answer to all things," Bertrand said. "There is too much reliance on what men say, even men of faith. Let us go straight to the Word. Then revival will sweep in like a warm, refreshing wind of God."

THE QUEEN MOTHER ARRIVED in Paris from the Poissy Council with her youngest daughter, Princesse Marguerite, much later that evening than she had planned. She was in a foul mood with both her daughter Marguerite and the serpent-tongued Spanish ambassador. As the Queen Mother's grand coach came through the front gate into the courtyard of the Louvre palais, she ordered the guards to not make a stir over her arrival.

"I wish for no fanfare this night," she ordered.

"Just so, Your Majesty."

The coach moved on toward the palais. She and Marguerite were both exhausted from the long day of religious bickering. She would relish casting both Catholic and Huguenot out of France!

She curled her fingers on the lap of her dark skirts. Her spy inside the Spanish ambassador's own retinue had been sending her copies of Chantonnay's lettres to his master, King Philip, for some time, but they were becoming incriminating, fomenting fires of outrage in Philip's fanatical mind.

Catherine was vexed over the ambassador's latest lettre, in which he reported that she was permitting heretical prêches in the Huguenot's chambers at court.

> *While daily walking down the corridors or entering a salle,*
> *Huguenot voices are heard singing Psalms set to music. Imagine!*
> *Singing! They spend their time gathering into little conclaves*
> *and singing. When I registered a protest to the Queen Mother, she*
> *pretended she knew nothing about it, but she lies. To my face she*
> *swears she hates Admiral Coligny and the other Huguenot leaders*
> *and that she wishes they were dead. Even so, each night I see Admiral*
> *Coligny and his brothers enter her private chambers, where they sit*
> *with her and talk for an hour like close amis until she retires to her*
> *bedchamber. Then the admiral and his brothers go down to the lower*
> *salle and have friendly discussions with others of their mind-set. They*
> *toast the king, and then finally go off to their own bedchambers. It is*
> *all revolting, as Duc de Guise has said to me in private. Cardinal de*

Lorraine insists something will be done about them. I even saw King Charles and his puppyish amis sneaking off to Admiral Coligny's bedchamber at midnight to awaken him and tease him as though he were his père. The king pretended to arrest him and carry him off to his dragon's lair — and the admiral played along! Outrageous! That the king loves this Huguenot admiral is dangerous. As Duc de Guise assured me, something will be done to stop this friendship. If not, France will go the way of Germany and England.

Catherine narrowed her gaze as she stared out the coach window, hearing horse hooves clattering over stone. *That crafty jackal. Ah, what I would like to do with him.*

Then, uneasy in the company of those who plotted as she did, she wondered and worried. *And just what could Duc de Guise mean that "something will be done"?*

Philip had also lamented the Poissy Colloquy and demanded to know why she was embracing the vipers to her heart? He feared she was no longer a Catholic and this grieved him to sleeplessness. For if it was so, then her lapse put her regency at grave risk. Rome fully agreed with him and also lamented her unwise and questionable behavior. Why must there be so many Huguenots at court?

Yes, Catherine was alarmed.

Why must that somber admiral continue to urge war against Spain? His compassion for the Hollanders would be his own death. She could not sit by and have him meddling with the will of Charles. Coligny had actually talked Charles into agreeing to send soldiers to help the Protestants.

Coligny will continue to meddle, and if he does not listen to me and stop, he must be removed. Yes, the admiral is in danger. The colloquy is not proceeding as I had hoped it would.

Marguerite was sighing again and the whining prickled Catherine's fraught nerves. She turned her head sharply. Marguerite had displayed her stubborn streak all the way from the castle at Saint-Germain-en-Laye, pleading that she not meet the "barbarian Navarre." Marguerite complained of everything about the young prince, from his ill Gascon manners to his "unhealthy" odors. There would be a small divertissement to reacquaint her troublesome daughter to Jeanne of Navarre's son Prince Henry, and one would think the plague had struck.

"Cease! I will hear no more of this talk, my daughter. You will marry Navarre. I will not have Philip of Spain claiming Navarre on the southern border of France. Already Spain promises Antoine much for its surrender. But, my child, with Jeanne and Antoine's princely son married to you, the royal daughter of France — Spain will not dare interfere, for young Navarre would lead an army of many thousands of Protestants into the Netherlands. Ah, yes!" She gave a brief satisfied chuckle at gaining one up on Philip.

Catherine grew stern again. She reached across the plush seat and caught firm hold of her daughter's wrist until she saw Marguerite wince.

"And," Catherine snarled in a low whisper, "if I see you sneaking off with the 'other Henry,' that scheming son of Duc de Guise, I shall have you whipped again. You will not portray yourself a loose woman in front of the fanatical Huguenot Jeanne of Navarre. She already looks askance at you. And you will wear the modest gown Rachelle made you, just as I told you. The pink one." She reached her fingers beneath Marguerite's chin and pinched playfully. "You look so sweet and innocent in pink, ma petite."

Marguerite gave her a sly glance.

A brief time later Catherine left her daughter at her chambers and then entered her own appartement quietly, not wishing to be disturbed.

Madalenna curtsied as she entered, then went about lighting the candles, her hand shaking. Catherine watched her as she threw off her cloak and coif.

"Have you been stealing my bonbons?" Catherine mocked. "Why are you so nervous, my petite cat?"

Madalenna bowed again and licked her lips. "No, Madame, no bonbons, I swear it — "

"Do not be foolish. I was teasing you. Something is disturbing you. What is it? Or is it my unwanted return?"

"No, Madame, I am most pleased you have returned."

"Then speak."

"The holy league is meeting in the state council chamber, Madame."

"Ah?" Alert, growing tense herself now that she understood, she swished a hand at Madalenna. "No more candles. Very good. You have done your work well. You may go now. And Madalenna — "

The girl turned, her dark eyes wide. "Yes, Madame?"

"I may give you your bold request to go home to Florence to visit your relatives."

Madalenna stared at her. She twisted her fingers together. She curtsied again.

"We shall see — perhaps after the colloquy," Catherine said.

"Madame, I am most grateful."

"Then run along."

When she was gone, Catherine stood pondering.

So, the mighty holy league has become the "council of four." They were the scheming Guise brothers, Maréchal de Saint Andre, and the recent fourth — Prince Antoine de Bourbon. Once again they were meeting in secret.

Swiftly now, she took the key at her wrist and unlocked her door to her closet and entered, relocking it. She removed her end of the listening tube from concealment in the wall and held it to her ear. In the council chamber, the other end of the tube hung behind the arras where she'd had it installed years earlier by the Ruggerio brothers. It had served her well these years.

And what was she to learn now?

She listened intently. There were voices and the scraping of chairs across the floor as they settled themselves.

She came alert, all mockery disappearing as she listened. The Cardinal de Lorraine said in his laconic voice that somehow dripped with cynicism: "It is intolerable, messieurs. Her intervention in matters of religion threatens France. We must act. If we do not, Cardinal Ferrara informs me that Rome will have Spain act for us. If they cannot depend upon us, then they will find bolder, more dedicated leaders on whom they can depend. So what will it be?"

Duc de Guise's voice came, short and ill-tempered: "It is my suggestion, as it has been for some time, that we get rid of her. I have told her that if she is not loyal to the true religion, then I will not serve her regency."

Catherine's breath came quickly as she tried to catch every word. Surely they were not speaking of her?

"Then do so. Remove her from the regency," Antoine said.

"Now, messieurs, listen to me," Saint Andre said. "Why not rid ourselves of her by drowning her in the Seine? It could be easily accomplished without discovery, I assure you, for I believe there is no person in all of France who would take the trouble to investigate the Queen Mother's disappearance."

Catherine's mouth slipped open. She stared at the wall as the one candle flickered like the eye of a serpent.

There came the scraping sound of a chair again as though someone had jumped to his feet.

"I will have no part in that!" Antoine cried.

"Then let us discuss the other woman who is equally as dangerous. Monseigneur, it is your wife, Jeanne of Navarre," the duc said.

"Yes, I have given you the orders from the papal legate and Spain," the cardinal said. "This is most painful, Antoine. It grieves us as it does you. But she must be arrested as a state prisoner at the earliest possible moment."

"She is staying here in Paris for that debacle of heretics at Poissy," the duc said. "Now is the time we must move. She must not leave Paris."

Catherine's fingers tightened on the tube. *So, the Duc of Alva had told her the facts as he knew them. Jeanne was to be caught and trapped for the Inquisition.*

"It sometimes becomes compulsory, for the sake of true religion, to comport ourselves in a mode that is abhorrent to us," the cardinal said.

Catherine could not hear Antoine's answer, but the duc said: "Then every one of us consents to a warrant to be issued for the arrest of Jeanne of Navarre on a charge of heresy."

A moment later the silence was broken as the cardinal said, "This, Monseigneur Antoine, is an act worthy of you! May God give you a good and long life."

"So be it," Duc de Guise said.

The council ended.

Catherine stood holding the listening tube in silence, hearing herself breathing.

So they wish to throw me in the Seine, do they? And they intend to turn Jeanne over to the inquisitors — to suffer the rack and many other horrible tortures — ah, but knowing that stalwart Huguenot as she knew Jeanne, the Queen of Navarre would never recant.

Catherine concealed the listening tube and returned into her main chamber. She left only one candle burning as she paced slowly, methodically across the rug, her steps soundless. Outside her window Paris was dark, but the lamps burned in the courtyard and the torches sputtered in the wind.

She went over to her desk, sat down, and drew the golden inkwell toward her. She dipped the quill into the ink and addressed her message to Marquis Fabien de Vendôme at Saint-Germain-en-Laye.

Danger and Providence

THE BUSY SEPTEMBER DAYS SCURRIED BY. THE FROSTY NIGHTS AND SUNNY days touched the leaves in the Laye Forest with the tints of flame and gold. On one such evening when Fabien did not return from Poissy as usual, Rachelle paced the salle de sejour, her green silk skirts swishing about her ankles.

Rachelle rubbed her forehead as if removing the unanswered questions that were lodged there. Could Fabien have been detained?

"Oh, Mademoiselle Rachelle, the last I saw of the marquis, he was walking with Gallaudet toward their horses," Nenette said.

What if something has gone wrong? Just then the door opened and Fabien entered, handsome in the black velvet with gold. Rachelle hurried toward him, and Nenette gathered up the spool of lace she'd been winding and ducked out of the chamber.

"Is all well?" Rachelle asked quickly.

He held her close, kissing her thoroughly. "It is now," he said with a smile.

She reached up with both hands and removed his hat, tossing it aside on the chair.

"You are learning my lazy habits," he said, kissing her again tenderly. "How do you feel, chérie?"

"The same answer, mon amour; now that you are here I feel better."

"Seriously."

"I feel as if I am, well — enceinte," she said. "At least the sickness is as Madeleine always said it was, in the mornings. I feel stronger in the evenings."

He frowned. "I do not argue with destiny, but this is the wrong time for you to feel unwell. Tell me the truth; can you journey a long distance? It will of necessity be in haste and an ordeal."

She forced a smile and kissed his chin: The thought of travel on the rough roads made her queasy again. "You worry about me too much. Surely thousands of women have endured a long journey while in my happy condition."

"Thousands of women do not belong to me, but you do. You say you are happy about this pregnancy?"

"To carry your child?" she asked with arched brow. "Mon amour, how could I ask for anything more than to love and be loved by you and to have that love, with God's blessing, give us a child?"

He drew her head against his chest, his fingers playing softly with her hair. "I think it will be a girl. I shall have the most belle daughter in all of France."

She lifted her head and met his warm blue gaze.

He smiled. "I mean in England."

"In France! France! At Vendôme! If only — oh, to give birth in the bedchamber where Duchesse Marie-Louise de Bourbon bore you."

He hugged her tightly. "My sweet, any bed with you will be wondrous, even an English bed."

She laughed. She took his hand and pulled him toward the sofa. "Tell me all the news. Is something wrong?"

"There is always a circumstance or two that is very wrong, my pet. But, on the other hand, I have bonne news as well. First — " He glanced about as he loosened his shirt at the throat. "Is Bertrand here?"

"He has gone to the duchesse's château to speak with Père Arnaut."

"Then I must ride there later tonight."

She became more tense. "What has happened?"

"A change of plans. Sit down ... we will talk." He looked toward the antechamber where Nenette was working, and as if on second thought asked: "And the gowns for Margo? They are done, she has them?"

"Yes, the third one was delivered before the opening of the Poissy ceremonies. Why?" She wondered why he would ask again. Had he forgotten? But then, so much was beating upon his mind and heart recently.

"The gown is necessary for Margo. Her meeting with Navarre is being arranged sooner than expected in Paris." He lowered his voice. "Sit down. The Queen Mother sent me a message. Antoine has agreed to turn Jeanne over to the inquisitors. It is unbelievable to me that he would — or could — do so, for I know he loved her once. He may still love her in his selfish way. I can only think his mind is dazed by the indoctrination of the Guises. And when I say indoctrination, I mean the feeding of the lust for power and glory. He is with them constantly. Jeanne must either attend Mass with him publicly in Paris, or they will issue a warrant for her arrest on heresy charges."

Rachelle silenced her gasp before it escaped her lips. "It is horrible. From what I have heard of Queen Jeanne, she will never relent."

"You have heard rightly. The Queen Mother may have also sent a secret warning to her. Not because she cares anything for Jeanne, but she wants the marriage between Navarre and Margo for reasons of her own. Nor do I fully trust her. An innermost spy at court tells me she met secretly with the Duc of Alva. There is some agreement between them to rid the court of Admiral Coligny and other chief Huguenots. The secret agreement to kill them all may have included Jeanne, but evidently this present warrant against her has come too soon for her plans. She must not have expected it. Her message was terse. My own secret agreement with her where Duc de Guise is concerned must happen soon. For some reason she was most urgent about Guise, but she did not explain why. Maybe she knows something of Guise's plans that she has not shared with me. I am sure that is the case."

Rachelle felt dazed. She shook her head. "I shall only be relieved when I am no longer serving her and that I have not spent much time in her presence here."

"That was my doing, chérie. And the best days for us are ahead."

"Oh, Fabien, may it be. But you have more news? Continue."

"At least now we know why Guise left the colloquy in a temper yesterday and went to Paris. The cardinal must have ridden there last night after the meetings all ended, for he was there at the council chamber in the Louvre where the Queen Mother overheard their plans."

"Is there nothing to be done to save your kinswoman? Oh, Fabien, we must if there is any chance at all!"

"Without a doubt I will do all in my power. But she knows of their treachery. She has some men-at-arms with her but not as many as I could wish. Louis was also informed and will do what he can. But Paris! Paris belongs to the house of Guise. Jeanne is in jeopardy, there is no question of it. But there is an opportunity for her escape and ours. That is what I wish to discuss. What we do in this matter, we must do within the next few days."

A tide of desperation swept over Rachelle. It all appeared so monumental, so hopeless.

"Escape? But Fabien, how? I am not even permitted to walk the garden without the Queen Mother's guards watching me."

"Unexpectedly, a door of opportunity has opened to us, and without my prodding. I believe it is providential."

Her heart beat faster with excitement. She squeezed his hand.

"You truly believe it. There is a strong opportunity?"

"Catherine approves of your companionship with Margo. She has promised to do all the Queen Mother wants where Navarre is concerned but has pleaded for you to attend her this Saturday evening in Paris. It is a divertissement arranged for her and Navarre, and the Queen Mother has agreed. It may be that the hour of our escape is dawning."

The hour of escape is dawning. The delightful words rang like the bells of freedom. Then she thought of the Louvre with all of its gates and guards. Would it be any easier to slip away from there than here at the castle of Saint-Germain-en-Laye?

"But Paris? The Louvre?"

"We will take whatever opportunity provides itself. You will not be under guard at every possible moment, chérie — that is the difference. You are expected to be with Margo when she meets Navarre."

"Expected? Do you mean I will not?"

"Not if my plan works as I expect. I have a daring idea, and if Gallaudet and I are able to bring it to pass, we should be riding out of Paris before Margo and Navarre ever meet again."

Her heart began to pound.

"You remember, of course, the day Sebastien and Madeleine escaped from the Louvre, and how you saw the Queen Mother leave for the Ruggerio brothers shop on the quay?"

She stared at him. Slowly the truth of what he proposed to try made her draw in a breath. "Fabien, the secret passage!"

"Exactement. The secret passage Catherine uses to get in and out of the Louvre without being seen by guards. Well, ma chérie, I nearly grew up at the Louvre with the royal children. I spent much time exploring secret passageways."

She took hold of his arm, feeling the iron muscle beneath her fingers, too dazed at the thought of his proposal of escape to speak. If they escaped the Louvre late at night by way of the Queen Mother's secret passage, they could ride from Paris before the dawning of a new day. They could be long gone from the Queen Mother before she ever missed Rachelle.

"But how will you get in and find my chamber?"

"Leave that to me. Henry of Navarre is a Huguenot and on our side. If events fall into place, you will hear me tap on your chamber door well after everyone is asleep."

She was excited and afraid all at once. So many things could go wrong.

He scowled. "It is the horses that worry me. Riding is not safe in your condition."

"Mère rode a horse out of necessity, early in her pregnancy, and there was no harm done. We must go through with this and trust God."

"We will trust in God, chérie, and we will also use the wisdom He has given us. I will have a coach waiting somewhere on the road out of Paris. In fact, the idea of the coach may work even better than my first plan of traveling through the woods." He stood, hands on hips, staring at the fire as though the flames contained all the answers.

"What do you mean? Why would it be better not to go by way of the woods?"

He turned. She watched him tapping his chin.

"Do you remember when we met at Amboise at the masque the Queen Mother gave for Margo and the King of Portugal?"

"Yes, Marguerite slipped away and forced me to attend her ... She met her amour, Henry de Guise. We all wore masks."

"Yes, and a disguise may work again this time once we make it to the coach and turn our horses over to Gallaudet."

She thought she followed his ideas and her mind raced ahead. "The red wig that Princesse Marguerite wears at times—" She looked up at him. "I could borrow it—though I do not know how I could return it."

"Never mind that, she can have more made freely enough. Besides, she has always been an amie. I do not think she would mind helping me at this time. Bring another wig for me, one of her black ones. Do you know where to locate them?"

"Yes, a closet in her chambers is filled with such things. I think I can manage."

"If by fortuitous circumstance our departure is observed once we leave the courtyard, and the chase is on, I will have my men cut away from the road into the woods, as I first intended we all should. The guards—with any fair windfall blowing our way—will pursue my men on horseback into the woods ..."

"While we proceed on the road by way of the coach unsuspected," she said, standing.

"Exactement. With two occupants inside, one with red hair, the other with black. No one will suspect who rides in the coach making its way leisurely along the road. We will then make our way south toward La Rochelle and eventually rejoin my men—as I say, ma chérie, *if* bonne events blow our way."

"Oh, Fabien, they *will*, they *must*."

He went on to tell her of the plans he had already been devising with Gallaudet, Cousin Bertrand, and Julot Cazalet, to meet up with his replenished men-at-arms and Capitaine Nappier, who were even now somewhere in the Laye Forest.

"Our plan is to make our way to the Huguenot stronghold of La Rochelle. Capitaine Nappier will be somewhere near the coast with the *Reprisal*. Once at La Rochelle we will remain out of sight until the ship is sighted."

Then a longboat would be sent out late at night to alert Capitaine Nappier of their arrival. When the ship was anchored as close in as possible, she and Fabien and his men would row out to board the dark vessel on a moonless night.

"The plan does not make for an easy escape; even so, it is our best hope," he said when she slowly sat down on the blue-and-gold chair.

"The other plan — my first — was to reach Lyon and then cross the border and enter Geneva by land. If that plan is used, that route will also be challenging, since we will need to wait until late October when the colloquy ends."

"Why October?"

"In order to smuggle you out of Poissy in one of the wagons of the Huguenots returning to Geneva. I would join you later on the road. But October is too far away. Events are moving too rapidly and too dangerously to wait."

"What of my prized sewing possessions, the equipage of Grandmère?" she asked quickly.

For a moment he simply looked at her, then he smiled. She stood quickly and went to him, taking his hands. "I am serious. Fabien, I cannot even fathom the idea of leaving my sewing tools behind."

"Ma chérie, that is perfectly understandable. I cannot promise you the large trunk, not now, but pack the most precious items in your smaller case and have it ready. I will see that Gallaudet has it before we leave for Paris. The large trunk and the rest of the equipage can be taken to the duchesse. Messire Arnaut and Madame Clair will be staying with her throughout the colloquy."

Relief swept over her heart. Yes, of course, Mère would take her trunk home to the Château de Silk. Once she was in London they would have it shipped to her.

He held her as though what he was about to tell her would disappoint.

"What is it, Fabien?"

"Nenette. We will need to think of some reason to send her over to Madame Claire at Duchesse Dushane's château. Your grisette cannot come with you on the escape, Rachelle."

She had learned that whenever he used her name in discussion, the matter, from his viewpoint, was settled.

"Oh, but Fabien! My petite Nenette? I cannot leave her. I promised her she will come with me to London."

"And she will. We will send for her after we are in London. Snatching you out of Paris will be most difficult. Trying to get both of you away at the same time will lessen the chances."

"But — "

"Nenette will be in the way. She will be safer if she remains here at Saint-Germain with Madame Clair."

She sighed, for she understood that he was undoubtedly right, and the added burden placed upon him and Gallaudet might put the plan in jeopardy at the last minute. After all, it was not as if Nenette was in any immediate danger the way Andelot had been when Fabien counseled him to ride on to La Rochelle from the bungalow.

"Very well, I will not protest further. I rather agree she will be safer with Mère. I will need to console and convince her we will indeed send for her later when it is safe."

"Do not tell her here. She may cry and carry on. In fact, let me explain after I take her to Madame Clair."

"Then I will at least write her a lettre."

"I will give the lettre to Madame Clair. She can hand it to Nenette after you are safely out of Paris. I trust no one. The tongue slips so easily."

Rachelle was not worried about Nenette. She would be as well taken care of by the Macquinet family at the Château de Silk as she had been in the past. Père Arnaut had just recently made the decision to remain in France for the foreseeable future. Two evenings ago at the family dinner, he announced that the London experiment to establish an extension of the silk plantation was a task doomed to failure because of the weather. Silkworms must have a warmer climate. He had concluded by saying, "Fabien is telling me that Admiral Coligny has not given up his idea of another colony in Florida. There are other possibilities in the Americas, as well. Even the Caribbean. We shall see what the future holds for unlocking new doors. If the opportunity is not suitable for our generation, then it will be left to our grandchildren's generation."

"Perhaps Nenette can return to London with Bertrand," Rachelle said. "He told me last night that he is leaving with the Huguenots for Geneva after the colloquy. Even so, he plans to return to Spitalfields eventually, stopping first to visit Pere Arnaut at the Château de Silk. Nenette could be brought to me then."

"We will find a way. I do not want you worrying, chérie. The hours and days ahead will be difficult enough for you."

And for him. He carried her and so much more on his shoulders and in his heart.

Rachelle was content to put aside the concerns for the moment as they stood in one another's arms before the glowing embers, the sound of the autumn wind stirring about the battlements of the gray stone castle. In just a few days she would go to Paris to be with Marguerite. And then? Ah, then! The *Reprisal*, and London. A life all their own to pursue the way the Lord planned for them and for their child that she carried. A daughter as he said? A son? She wondered with anticipation. Their child would grow up with Idelette's bébé boy and Madeleine's daughter Joan. They would form a new generation for which the plans of Providence would make a way.

And who knew what those plans would be, or how different each of their children would be? Cousins ... And always, because Fabien was a royal Bourbon and a marquis, their own offspring would rank above Madeleine's and Idelette's children. But in the eyes of God, there was no respecter of persons.

As she dreamed of what their children would be like and what lay ahead, she waited with anticipation and faith.

We have come too far to lose it all now, to have happiness and purpose slip through our fingers like wind.

Au Revoir and Godspeed

In Paris at the Louvre, the deep night waited expectantly. Rachelle's nerves were on edge and her heart seemed to beat unevenly as she waited for Fabien's stealthy footsteps outside the chamber door. This was the night when he would come, when they would escape from beneath the watchful eyes of Madame Serpent.

She had arrived the day before under Fabien's escort, though he had to leave her at the palais and take a separate residence as the Queen Mother had said. Could she be wary that Fabien might attempt to leave with her? Rachelle believed the Queen Mother continued to watch her.

Earlier, when he left her in the chamber, he said he would stay with his Bourbon kinsmen at the Hotel de Condé, which was near the Louvre.

If the Queen Mother did not think Fabien could rid her of Duc de Guise, I think she would poison me while I am here. As long as she needs him, I should be safe.

The family is praying ceaselessly for us, she thought, comforted. Père Arnaut and Madame Clair had sent her a message before she left Saint-Germain-en-Laye, saying they would be up all night in vigil, and Cousin Bertrand had given her a portion from his favorite psalm, which said: *"If I take the wings of the morning, and dwell in the uttermost parts of the sea, even there shall thy hand lead me."* Then he had taken Nenette to the Dushane château to wait through for the remainder of the colloquy.

Rachelle worried again over Duchesse Dushane. Her frailty grew worse day by day, and Docteur d'Fontaine, whom Fabien had brought to see the duchess, could not discover what was ailing her. Rachelle was saddened, for she had wanted so much to see her before departing for London, and now that was not possible. She would fondly remember the older woman who had risked herself to help them and Andelot during the past two years. She had written a lettre to the duchesse and entrusted it to Nenette before she had departed, in which Rachelle had expressed her gratitude.

Nenette had suspected Rachelle might not come back from Paris, but surprisingly she had showed courage and managed to kiss her cheek.

"Do not forget me," she had whispered.

"Never, ma petite. Fabien will send for you."

Nenette smiled, her lips quivering, but she hid her emotions as she left the castle with Cousin Bertrand lest the Queen Mother's spies left at Saint-Germain noticed, grew suspicious, and contacted her.

Now, here in Paris alone, Rachelle could not shake the emotions of looming catastrophe that hung over her like a thundercloud.

I feel as if something dire is going to befall me . . . or Fabien!

She placed her palms against her womb and paced the floor, a prayer forming from her heart.

Let Your grace enfold us, deliver us, bring us to our safe harbor. And again she found herself returning to the same plea: *Protect Fabien, please do not let anything happen to the one you gave me to be my husband and the père of this bébé.*

Rachelle tried to rest on the comfortable bed, hoping to get a little sleep before the long wearisome journey to La Rochelle began. *If we escape*, she kept thinking. And each time the worries would tumble back in and she would become less sleepy and more tense.

The wind was blowing outside the palais. Each time she thought she heard his footsteps it proved to be a creak in the structure.

The last time she was here, Sebastien and her sisters had escaped, and Fabien had arrived after she returned from the quay and heard the Queen Mother asking the Ruggerio brothers for a poison to use on someone. Who might it have been? The duchesse perhaps. Non! No one important had died in the past year. It might have been Duc de Guise. Now the Queen Mother believed Fabien would do it for her.

Rachelle placed her palms against her temples and closed her eyes. *I am emotionally depleted, and I am enceinte. I must use reason, not just feelings.*

Fabien was staying with Prince Condé, Princesse Eleonore, and

Queen Jeanne, for the Hotel de Condé was not far from the Louvre; for that matter, neither was the Hotel de Bourbon where Prince Antoine was staying while Jeanne was in Paris. The thought that Fabien and a strong alliance were nearby encouraged her. Soon now, he would come — but what was taking him so long? What hour was it?

Rachelle, unable to rest, arose, fully garbed for travel, and moved about the chamber. *What was that sound?* She paused and looked toward the door. Outside the door she thought she heard footsteps, but could not be sure. She hurried, but stopped — wait, he said he would tap.

But no tapping came. Fabien had assured her he had amis among the guards who would arrange for certain guards to be on duty who would look the other way when he came. What if one of them betrayed him? If Prince Antoine could betray Jeanne, why couldn't a guard betray the Marquis de Vendôme?

Where is your faith? You will soon go mad worrying about every detail that can go wrong. All your brave talk these many months means little. When you need trust, you fail to lay hold of it, and fret.

Something appeared under the door. In the dim light of the candle, she saw a white piece of parchment. Her fear leapt into action. *Fabien will not be coming. He has been caught —*

She rushed to snatch it up and turn to the candle. The note shook as she read:

Madame Rachelle,

The life of the Queen of Navarre will be worth nothing when the sun rises tomorrow. The warrant for her arrest on heresy charges is being drawn up at dawn. The house of Guise will not allow her to leave Paris. They have talked Prince Antoine into putting soldiers around Paris to stop her from leaving. If she does not leave tonight, they will catch her. They will turn her over to her worst enemies. I tell you this because the Huguenot queen is a kind woman, not like my mistress. You too have been kind to me. I will leave the door of the secret passage of the Queen Mother open for the marquis as he asked me. Burn this lettre unless you wish to see me murdered. I hope you will be at peace.

Madalenna

Madalenna! Rachelle reread the message, her throat dry. So the Florentine demoiselle had been part of Fabien's plans all along. Her compassion reached out to her again. Madalenna had shown much courage in risking herself like this. Rachelle prayed for her, then Queen Jeanne, then held the message to the flame and watched it burn and turn to ash.

Tonight! How could Jeanne escape so quickly? She must be sound asleep at this hour with no thought in her mind of an arrest come the morning. Unless Madalenna had slipped out and found her way to the Hotel de Condé? But no, the demoiselle could not manage that, and that was the reason she had given her the warning instead, so she could tell Fabien — when he arrived! Where was he? And now it was all the more urgent that he come quickly.

Rachelle paced, hand at her forehead. Fabien would bring Jeanne word of her danger. He would never leave Paris now without his Huguenot kinswoman. This complicated their escape, making it more dangerous ... and more likely to fail. And yet how could she even think of that now when the trap was being set to surround her.

Antoine — how could he do this?

Rachelle had made sympathetic excuses for him, blaming his failure on being left alone with the Guises and the Spanish ambassador at the palais without strong upright fellowship. Yes, how true the apostle Paul's words in 1 Corinthians 15:33: "Evil communications corrupt good manners." Antoine had joined the league, and soon the Guise influence led him down their own path. "Blessed is the man that walketh not in the counsel of the ungodly," she murmured.

The first psalm could be Antoine de Bourbon's epitaph. What is mine?

She turned swiftly, hearing a whisper of footsteps in the outer corridor. She held her breath, waiting, then came the signal — the light tap, tap.

In a moment she was there, sliding back the bolt, and Fabien entered, closed the door quietly, and wrapped his arms around her. He kissed her as though they had been separated for a year.

"All is ready. I see you are rightly dressed. Come, make no sound."

She pulled at his sleeve. "Wait, I must tell you news."

After he had heard Madalenna's message, he scowled. "Arrest her by dawn? Saints! She must leave at once. It is essential I return to the Hotel de Condé, but not before I turn you over to the captain of my guard. Quick, chérie."

He looked into the corridor to make certain no one was there, then, with her hand securely clasped in his, they were rushing through the corridors, across a salle, down some stairs, and along a back passage to the little-known door left unlocked by Madalenna. In a few moments, they were inside the passageway, and a lone candle he must have lit earlier guttered. The air became dank and stale. The sound of their feet echoed, and as they neared the outer door facing the quay she could hear the drip of water and smell foul odors. Fabien held to her tightly and guided her along. Then they were out the door into the dark night, facing a gust of wind that made her shiver with relief. She looked at his smile. With his arm around her they rushed forward toward the river Seine.

The night closed about them. They had not dashed far before Gallaudet appeared. The three of them disappeared into the garden trees. Gallaudet watched for anyone who might be following while Fabien strode ahead, his hand firmly clasped on his scabbard. He was ready for any trouble. She would tremble to be a guard who stood in his way at this moment. It was all she could do to keep up without running.

"Not far now," he whispered as if he could read her mind.

She recognized the landscape as the route to the quay. This was the way she had taken on that morning that had brought such fear into her life. What if once again they were being deceived by the Queen Mother? What if she knew they were planning to escape? What if soldiers were waiting, and once again Fabien was attacked and torn from her, this time to be sent to the Bastille? Oh forbid! Let it not be. Not this time —

Her heart thudded. Her hands were clammy, and her throat felt cramped and dry. The water lapped against the wooden pilings, and small boats creaked and looked like silhouettes of dragons looming up in the Seine. Did they come to aid their escape or war against them? The smell of river was unpleasant; the wind was biting, its cold making her eyes water. Her teeth chattered from fear. She was not chilled, but perspiring. *Hurry!*

A little way farther, to horses that waited with a dozen of his men-at-arms. A little way and then freedom waited, England waited — *if only* —

She saw the men ahead; two hurried to meet them. She pushed forward, her mind screaming the one worry that pulsated through every heartbeat: *hurry, hurry*—

Fabien swept her up in his arms when she moved too slowly for him and made a hasty move toward the horses. The men fanned out, watching the way from which they had come, hands on their scabbards. Nothing moved, nothing stirred but the wind.

A moment later Fabien swung up into the saddle and rode up beside her.

"Fear not, he smiled, his dark eyes flashing. "Away, mon belle amour!"

Rachelle held the reins and started her mare trotting behind him. She looked back over her shoulder for one last glimpse of Paris.

The sprightly mare dashed ahead after Fabien's stallion, and soon they were galloping away, away from the quay with its dark memories, away from the Louvre palais silhouetted against the dark Parisian background, forward to the road, to the coach, toward La Rochelle—and England. A few tears wet her cheeks, as the wind, caressed them.

Adieu my beloved France! Au revoir!

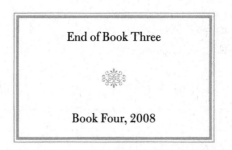

End of Book Three

Book Four, 2008

Catch Up on the First Two Books in the Silk House Series!

DAUGHTER OF SILK, BOOK ONE

Pursuing the family name as the finest silk producer in Lyon, France, Huguenot Rachelle Dushane-Macquinet is thrilled to accompany her famous couturière grandmere to Paris to create a silk trousseau for the Royal Princesse Marguerite Valois.

The court is magnificent; the Queen Mother, Catherine de Medici, deceptively charming ... and the circumstances, darker and more dangerous than Rachelle could possibly imagine. At a time in history when the tortures of the Bastille and the fiery stake are an almost casual occurrence in France, a scourge of recrimination is moving fast and furious against the Huguenots — and as the Queen Mother's political intrigues weave a web of deception around her, Rachelle finds herself in imminent danger.

Hope rests in warning the handsome Marquis Fabien de Vendome of the wicked plot against his Bourbon kinsmen, the royal princes. But to do so, Rachelle must follow a perilous course that puts her at risk — but she finds that her heart, too, is in danger of being captured by Marquis Fabien.

WRITTEN ON SILK, BOOK TWO

Rachelle Dushane-Macquinet, a couturière from one of France's foremost silk-making families, has been commissioned to make a magnificent gown for the Queen of England. But Rachelle is uneasy. She occupies a precarious position in the court of the Queen Mother, Catherine de Medici, who has not officially sanctioned her stay at the Château de Silk.

As Rachelle works on the gown, persecution rages against the French

Huguenots. When the rampant slaughter of the Protestants brings tragedy to her sisters Avril and Idelette, Rachelle needs the love of her life, Marquis Fabien, more than ever. But Fabien has his own way in warring against the persecutors — he has left on a privateering venture to strike a blow against the Spanish supply lines of the persecution. Rachelle must fend for herself.

When she receives a summons to return to Catherine de Medici's court, she welcomes the chance to spy on the Queen Mother known as "Madame le Serpent," believed to use poison on her enemies.

When Catherine decides to lure Marquis Fabien back to Paris in order get him to assassinate one of her enemies, she threatens to give Rachelle in marriage to Fabien's cousin, Comte Maurice. Will Marquis Fabien return to claim Rachelle for his own and risk being captured and sent to Spain?

Glossary of French Words

à bientôt — so long, see you later

adieu — bye

affaire d'honneur — duel

ah ça non — definitely not

ami — (m) friend, pal

amie — (f) friend

amour — love

appartement — apartment

atelier — shop, workshop

au contraire — on the contrary

au revoir — good-bye

beau — (m) good looking, fine looking, beautiful

bébé — baby, very young child

bien sûr — of course

belle amie — (f) my lovely, sweetheart

belle dame — painted lady (unflattering)

belle des belles — the most beautiful

bon — (adj, n, m) good

bonjour — hello, good day

bonne — (adj, n, f) good

ça alors! — good grief! (exclamation)

capitaine — captain, sea captain, skipper

cercle — group of close associates, often the Queen's

c'est bien compris? — is that clear?

charmante — (adj, f) charming

chatelaine — a hooklike clasp worn at the waist for suspending implements

cher — (n, m) dear, darling, cherished

chère — (n, f) dear, darling, cherished

chéri — (n, m) dear, darling

chérie — (n, f) sweetheart, honey

chevalier — the lowest title or rank in the old French nobility, also *cavalier* or *chivaler*, i.e., a "chivalrous" man

closet — a small room, for sleeping, dressing, writing letters, reading, etc.

coif — stiff ruffle around the neck (period clothing)

comte — nobleman, count

comtesse — countess

coup d'état — decisive overthrow of government, usually by a small group

Corps des Pages — School for Pages

courtier — a person expected at court by royalty

cousine — (n, f) cousin

couturièr — (n, m) designer, expert in sewing

couturière — (n, f) designer, expert in sewing

dame — lady (woman), madam, ma'am

demoiselle — young lady, damsel

dîner — evening meal

divertissement — diversion, amusement, recreation

docteur — doctor

duc — duke, highest ranking noble except a prince of the blood

duchesse — duchess

duchy — the territory ruled by a duc or duchesse

élégant — (adj, m) elegant

élégante — (adj, f) elegant

enceinte — expecting, pregnant

enfant — child

escadron volant de la reine — Catherine de Medici's ladies-in-waiting and maids-of-honor; forty immoral woman of beauty who served her political intrigues

exactement — exactly, right, precisely

fanfaronnade — fanfare

faux pas — false step

fiat accompli — accomplished fact

fleur-de-lys — lily flower

galant — chivalrous man, suitor

grande dame — great lady

grandes pasteurs — greatest pastors

grandmère — grandmother

grisette — (n, f) a seamstress specializing in dressmaking, embroidery, design; usually still under training

haute monde — upper class, fashion

honneur — (n) honor

honoré — (adj) honored

Huguenot — French Protestant, of Calvinistic doctrine

joie de vivre — joy of life

la — (f) the

la gloire de la france — the honor of France

le — (m) the

lettre — letter

ma — (f) my

ma belle — my lovely

madame — missus, madam

mademoiselle — miss, damsel

magnifique — magnificent, wonderful

maître — form of address for a doctor, schoolmaster, professional

maman — momma, mommy

ma petite — (f) my little one

marquis — highest ranking nobleman next to a duke

marquise — feminine form of marquis

marquisat — the territory ruled by a marquis, including land estates, wealth, future title of Duc

merci — thanks

merci mille fois — thank you a thousandfold

mère — mother

messire — mister, an honorable man

messieurs — plural of mister

merveilleux — marvelous, terrific

mignon — cute

mille diables — thousand devils (slang)

mille fois — a thousandfold

mon — (m) my

monseigneur — lord, addressing someone of high rank or respected office

monsieur — mister, sir

mûreraies — a grove of mulberry trees for feeding the leaves to silkworms

neveu — nephew

noblesse oblige — nobility obligates

non — no

oncle — uncle

ordinairs — commoners, ordinary citizens

oui — yes

palais, palais-château — palace, palace-castle

par exemple — for example

pasteur — Bible pastor, teacher

père, mon père — father, my father

petit — (m) little, small, young, humble

petite — (f) little, small, young, humble

petit déjeuner — breakfast

petit noir — coffee

prêche — Bible study

précisément — precisely, exactly

princesse — princess

reinette — young girl-queen

salle — hall, large room

salle de garde — room for guards

salle de sejour — living room

seigneur — master

s'il vous plaît — please, if you please

tenez ferme — stand firm (as in Eph. 6:14)

tout de suite — at once, immediately

très amusant — very amusing

Macquinet/Dushane/Dangeau/Beauvilliers Family Tree

(Fictional Characters)

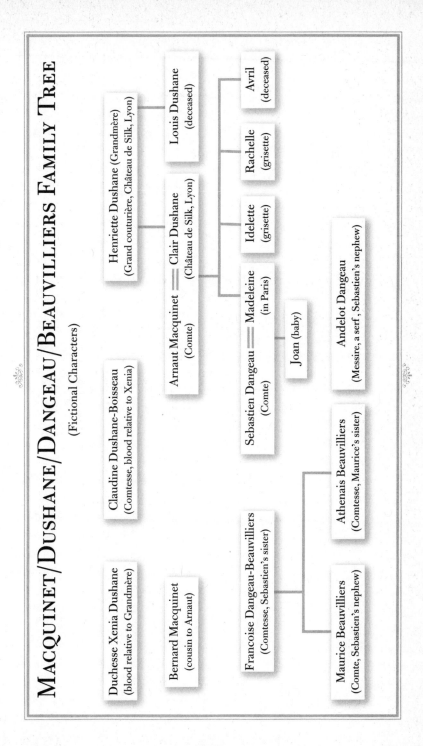

Duchesse Xenia Dushane
(blood relative to Grandmère)

Claudine Dushane-Boisseau
(Comtesse, blood relative to Xenia)

Henriette Dushane (Grandmère)
(Grand couturière, Château de Silk, Lyon)

Louis Dushane
(deceased)

Bernard Macquinet
(cousin to Arnaut)

Arnaut Macquinet ══ Clair Dushane
(Comte)   (Château de Silk, Lyon)

Idelette
(grisette)

Rachelle
(grisette)

Avril
(deceased)

Sebastien Dangeau ══ Madeleine
(Comte)   (in Paris)

Joan (baby)

Andelot Dangeau
(Messire, a serf, Sebastien's nephew)

Francoise Dangeau-Beauvilliers
(Comtesse, Sebastien's sister)

Athenais Beauvilliers
(Comtesse, Maurice's sister)

Maurice Beauvilliers
(Comte, Sebastien's nephew)

The Royal Valois Family Tree

(Historical)

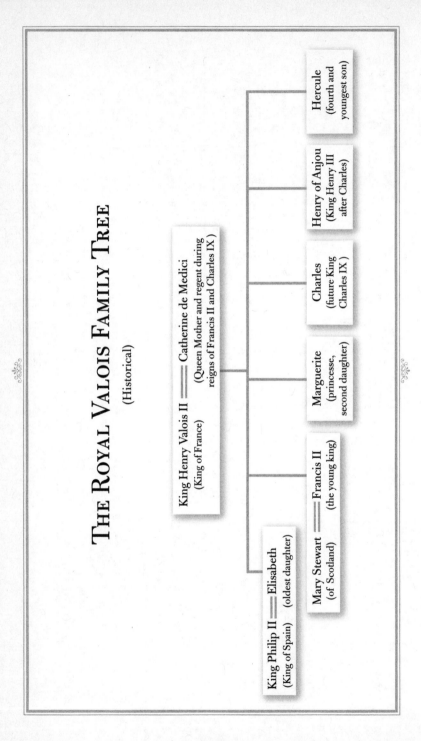

King Henry Valois II
(King of France)
═══
Catherine de Medici
(Queen Mother and regent during reigns of Francis II and Charles IX)

King Philip II
(King of Spain)
═══
Elisabeth
(oldest daughter)

Mary Stewart
(of Scotland)
═══
Francis II
(the young king)

Marguerite
(princesse, second daughter)

Charles
(future King Charles IX)

Henry of Anjou
(King Henry III after Charles)

Hercule
(fourth and youngest son)

The House of Guise Family Tree

(Historical)

Anne d'Este ═══ Duc de Guise (Francis)
(Marshal of France,
persecutor of Huguenots,
blood uncle to
Mary of Scotland)

Cardinal de Lorraine (Charles)
(younger brother of Duc de Guise
and a leader of the French inquisition
against Huguenots, blood uncle
to Mary of Scotland)

Henry de Guise
(the love of Princesse
Marguerite Valois)

Daughter of Silk

Linda Lee Chaikin, Bestselling Author

Pursuing the family name as the finest silk producer in Lyon, the young Huguenot Rachelle Dushane-Macquinet is thrilled to accompany her famous couturière grandmère to Paris, there to create a silk trousseau for the Royal Princesse Marguerite Valois.

The Court is magnificent; its regent, Catherine de Medici, deceptively charming ... and the circumstances, darker than Rachelle could possibly imagine. At a time in history when the tortures of the Bastille and the fiery stake are an almost casual consequence in France, a scourge of recrimination is moving fast and furious against the Huguenots — and as the Queen Mother's political intrigues weave a web of deception around her, Rachelle finds herself in imminent danger.

Hope rests in warning the handsome Marquis Fabien de Vendôme of the wicked plot against his kin. But to do so, Rachelle must follow a perilous course.

Softcover: 0-310-26300-X

Pick up a copy today at your favorite bookstore!

Written on Silk

Linda Lee Chaikin, Bestselling Author

A royal wedding masks the unfolding of Catherine de Medici's murderous plot against the Huguenots. Will any of the Huguenot princes survive? Life and death rest with two people ...

Rachelle Dushane-Macquinet, couturiére from a celebrated silk-making family, has come back to the Louvre Palais to create the royal wedding gown. Recruited into the evil Queen Mother's ring of women spies, she must use her wits to preserve her honor—and the lives of her fellow Huguenots.

Marquis Fabien de Vendome has also returned from a buccaneering venture against Spain. The Queen Mother plans to implicate him in an assassination. But Fabien has designs of his own.

A man and a woman caught up in history's deadly swirl and love's uncertainties seek to escape the venom of Madame le Serpent. Faith in Christ must uphold them, and all who stand alone, in a city gone diabolically mad.

Softcover: 0-310-26301-8

Pick up a copy today at your favorite bookstore!